Eva Woods grew up in Ireland and lives in London, where she writes and teaches creative writing. She likes wine, pop music and holidays. And she thinks that online dating is like the worst board game ever invented. This is her first romantic comedy.

THE
Thirty
LIST

Eva Woods

MILLS & BOON

This edition published in Great Britain 2015
by Mills & Boon, an imprint of Harlequin (UK) Limited,
Eton House, 18-24 Paradise Road, Richmond, Surrey, TW9 1SR

© 2015 Claire McGowan

ISBN: 978-0-263-91533-4

097-0615

Harlequin (UK) Limited's policy is to use papers that are natural, renewable and recyclable products and made from wood grown in sustainable forests. The logging and manufacturing processes conform to the legal environmental regulations of the country of origin.

Printed and bound by
CPI Group (UK) Ltd, Croydon, CR0 4YY

To Alexandra Turner,
my favourite primary-school teacher

Prologue

If you believe the films, there should be a moment in life when it all comes together. When you've got everything you ever wanted, and your happy ending is here. The music is swelling. Everyone's smiling at you.

Well, this was mine. This was my happy ending. And I was more terrified than I'd ever been in my life.

Beside me in the portico of the church, Dad was nervously tying and retying his cravat, ready for the short walk we were about to undertake. It was only thirty seconds, tops. But once it was over, nothing would be the same again. I'd be married to Dan. I'd be someone's wife.

'All right, Muffin?'

'Just a bit...you know.'

'Nervous?' In fact, I was frozen in terror, unable to move my vintage-style Mary Janes a single step forward. 'I don't blame you. All those eyes looking at you.' He shuddered. 'It's just like my recurring nightmare about being on *Countdown* and only able to make three-letter words.'

'Yes, it's *exactly* like that.'

'Except I've got my clothes on in this one.'

'Thanks, Dad.' Inside the door of the church, the organ was already playing. I hadn't wanted it—we weren't religious, but it meant a lot to Dan's family. I could see his mum, her enormous hat dominating the front row, and his dad looking frail, leaning on a walking stick. He'd had a stroke the month before and was still wobbly. I'd suggested we postpone the wedding, but Dan wouldn't hear of it.

I clutched my posy of freesias, which was leaking water onto my ballet-length lace dress. My veil was snarled around my face, making me breathless. 'Dad?'

'Yes, Muffin?'

'How do you know? I mean, how can you be sure? About the person you marry?'

'Eh…' He looked deeply uncomfortable, and not just because his tie was cutting into his neck. 'You just meet someone, and you like them, and you make it work somehow. It isn't hard. Not like *Countdown*.'

'But at least *Countdown* has rules.'

'You are…fond of Dan?'

'Of course! Of course. We're very happy.' Eight years with barely a row, sliding easily into dating, cohabitation and now marriage. Of course we were happy. We'd even bought a house, in Surrey. After the wedding we'd be packing up and leaving Hackney with the police sirens and falafel joints and shop downstairs that still sold Panini stickers from the 2002 World Cup. Dan had casually suggested it a few months ago, right in the middle of wedding planning. There'd be more space, less crime, a garden. All those things you were supposed to want. I'd already given notice at my job in the cool little design agency above a tattoo parlour in Shoreditch.

'Muffin,' said Dad, growing alarmed at my failure to move. 'We have to go in. Everyone's waiting. Unless you...'

'I'm fine! Fine! I'm just nervous!' Through the crack in the doors, I could see eyes begin to turn, murmurs going up. Looking for me. At the front of the church, my sister, Jess, and my best friends, Emma and Cynthia, were already waiting in their lavender prom dresses. Jess as usual looked stunning. The vicar, a friend of Dan's family, was in place. This was it, my moment. Just waiting for me to move forward.

Gently, Dad took my arm. 'Come on, Muffy. You don't want to go back, do you, call it all off? Because if you do...'

'No!' I loved Dan. We had a whole life together. I remembered what he'd said to me yesterday, before he went to sleep at his parents: 'I'll never leave you, Rachel. I promise we'll always be together.' He'd even stroked my face, although it was encrusted in an avocado skin mask.

'Even if I look like this?'

He'd smiled. 'You always look good to me.'

Dad patted my hand. 'Well, if you can't go back, you have to go forward. Your time's up, Muffy.' He began to hum the *Countdown* theme tune. 'Do do-do do-do...'

'OK, OK. I'm ready.'

'You know what marriage is, Muffy?'

'A nine-letter word?'

'It's *eight* letters, Muffs. Honestly, Maths never was your strong point. Anyway, it's not a word. It's a sentence.'

'Um, that's not helpful.'

'What I mean is, it's a beginning. It's not an end.'

Far down at the end of the aisle, I could see the back of Dan's head, his ears slightly red with the pressure of eyes watching him, his arms crossed in front of his dove-grey morning suit. I thought of our life together, our new house, our friends, our families. This was right. This was what you were supposed to do. I took a deep breath. 'OK, Dad. Let's do it.'

'Excellent. Consonant, please, Carol!'

The music changed. The doors opened. I started to move forward.

Chapter One

Two years later

Things that suck about divorce, number three: at the exact moment your life has hit rock bottom, and all you need is a particular inspiring tune to lift your spirits and provide guidance and cheer, you can't find the CD you want because your ex-husband, your soon-to-be ex-husband, has moved it and you can't ask him where it is, because, you know, you're getting divorced and it probably isn't very high up his list of concerns.

I was lying on the floor on my stomach, feeling under the shelving unit we use—*used*—to keep CDs in. Where the bloody hell was it? Why would he take the KT Tunstall CD? KT Bumstall, he called her.

When my friends came back into the room, staggering under boxes, they found me still on the floor, weeping and trying to hum my own jaunty backing track in a voice

Eva Woods

choked with tears, dust and the two-bottles-of-Chardonnay hangover I was nursing from the night before.

'Rach! What is it now? Did you find another one of his socks? Did you listen to your wedding first-dance song?' Emma rushed over, dropping her box into Cynthia's awkward embrace.

'Careful, Em! That's the Le Creuset in there! You could have crippled me.'

I was babbling. 'KT... Can't find it... Need the song!'

'What song?'

'That one!' In the depths of my grief, I couldn't remember the name of it. 'The makeover montage song. From *The Devil Wears Prada*. You know, the one that goes—do do do-do do-do-do. I need it! So I can walk along in great shoes and get a dream job and nice clothes, even if my boss is mean to me, and everything will be OK!'

Emma and Cynthia exchanged a look, then Cynthia took out her iPhone and pressed some buttons. 'Do you mean this one?' 'Suddenly I See' began to play out of the phone, slightly tinny.

I was still crying. 'This is rock bottom! I need to listen to this song and then feel better and walk along in my heels. You see?'

'You aren't wearing heels, darling,' said Cynthia kindly. 'You think they're tools of patriarchal oppression, remember?'

On my feet were mud-encrusted purple welly boots, which I had donned for uprooting some of the plants I'd grown in the garden, thinking I might pack them in a box and take them with me, before realising this was crazy, as I had nowhere to live, let alone a garden. That's what you do when you're getting divorced. You go crazy. I started crying again. 'I know! I don't even have any heels! Everything is awful!'

Emma and Cynthia had a quick muttered eye-rolling chat, and then Emma called out to me in a 'talking to a mad person' voice: 'Look! We're walking for you, love!' They were marching up and down my soon-to-be-ex living room on the exposed wooden floor, Emma in sensible walking shoes and Cynthia in expensive brown knee boots.

We had noticed several subtle changes in Emma's character since she became a primary school teacher: one, an exponential increase in bossiness; two, a habit of asking did we want to go to the toilet before we went anywhere; and three, the total loss of any physical shame. Now she was prancing about the floor, accompanied by an eye-rolling Cynthia, who gamely waved her long limbs about, then broke off as the song stopped and her phone rang. 'Cynthia Eagleton. No, for Christ's sake, I said send them out already. Listen, Barry, this is a serious question—what do you mean that's not your name? Never mind, I'm going to call you Barry. Can you not do anything for yourself? How do you manage to get out of bed in the morning? Just get it done.' She hung up, sighing. 'I swear it's a miracle he can even blow his own nose, that boy.'

'Was it hard for you to get a day off?' I mumbled dustily.

'Only about as hard as it was for Richard Attenborough and his mates to get out of that prison camp. But don't worry, darling. I'm here to help. Barry, or whatever his name is, will just have to learn to tie his own shoelaces.' Cynthia's had a lot to contend with in life. Not just the fact her mum saw fit to call her Cynthia—there was some great-aunt's will involved—but also the fact she was ten years older than her siblings, and the only one to be fathered by her mum's first love, who'd been deported back to Jamaica before Cynthia was even born. Still, she'd clawed her way up to a top legal job, she strikes terror into the hearts of her colleagues and she does have *really* nice hair.

Emma looked down at me kindly. 'It's good you want to listen to this song, you know. You're done with all that R.E.M., then? Sixteen renditions of "Everybody Hurts" in a row?'

'Not sure,' I mumbled into the floor.

'Well, you'll have to be, because I've buried the CD in the garden and I'm not telling you where.'

'Oh.'

'Do you want to get up now?'

'Not really.'

'Come on, love. I'll give you a sticker.'

So this was me, Rachel Kenny, aged thirty, imminently to be divorced, having to be prised away from my hard-wood floors, my back-garden hydrangea and my wind chimes and exposed-brick chimney piece. All those things I barely looked at but saw every day, and which were mine. I had floor dust down my front and was wearing an old college sweatshirt, partly because everything was packed, and partly because I had owned it before I met Dan, and I wanted to try to reset to that person.

This was the kind of crazy logic I was operating on at this moment in time. Things that suck about divorce, number seven: you go completely and totally out of your tree.

Finally, after two emergency trips back for things I'd forgotten that seemed really important at the time (hairbrush, muffin tray, mop), we were in the van Emma had hired me.

'Ready?' Cynthia asked me, settling into the wide front seat.

'I don't know. It's... My whole life was there. I don't know what I'm going to do now.'

She squeezed my arm with her manicured hand. 'I know, darling. But what's that thing your dad always says?'

'Um...*Countdown*'s never been the same since Carol left?'

'No, I mean that other thing. If you can't go back, you have to go forward.'

I stared back at the house. Dan would be coming back later. I didn't even know where he'd been staying while I moved my things out. This was what we'd come to. 'Do you think I should leave him a note? I mean, I can't just...*go*. That can't be the last conversation we ever have. We were together for ten years!'

They exchanged another look. 'We've talked about this, Rach,' said Emma gently. 'I know it's hard, but this is just how it has to be.'

We drove off. The house receded in the mirror to the size of a Lego cottage, till I almost felt I could pick it up and pop it into the pocket of my hoody, and then I couldn't see any more anyway because of the tears filling my eyes, spilling out and running down onto my dust-stained front. Cynthia passed me a flowery tissue and Emma patted my hand as she cut up school-run mums in massive Jeeps. I closed my eyes.

Things that suck about divorce, number nine: moving out of the home you spent years creating, with nowhere else to go. And remembering halfway up the M3 that you left the KT Tunstall CD in the car, which was no longer yours, along with all the rest of your life.

List of things you find when you move house

1. Random box of electrical leads, none of which seem to fit the items you actually have in the house.

2. Small pot full of screws, none of which seem to belong to any items of your furniture, which leads to worries about your table collapsing one day right in the middle of a sophisticated middle-class brunch.

3. One lone flip-flop.

4. A copy of the Yellow Pages, which has never been taken out of its plastic wrap, but which you keep 'just in case' (presumably in case a nuclear war knocks out all telecommunications, but you still need to order a pizza).

5. Dust. Lots and lots of dust.

I cried four times on the journey from Surrey to London. One was in the forecourt of a garage while Emma filled up (Cynthia refused to get petrol on her green leather driving gloves). Dan and I had done a lot of driving when we first got married and bought our car, a fourteen-year-old Mini. When we still had things to say to each other. We'd get the worst compilation CD we could find in the garage—*Seventy Valentine's Day Rockers! Fifty Smooth Driving Tunes!*—and sing along, eating crisps, our hands touching in the greasy packet. I wondered if I'd now be sad every time I went to a garage for the rest of my life. It would make popping out for a Twix quite problematic.

One good thing about crying is it's quite a useful way to pass the time, if you don't mind chronic dehydration and people staring at you, so the journey went by for me in a blur of motorways, hiccuping sobs and love songs on Mellow

Magic FM, and soon we were at Cynthia's Chiswick-based palace. She has three storeys and even a garden you could swing several cats in.

We had stopped. The girls were looking at me, worried. I wiped my face, feeling like one of those criminals who needed to be bundled out of court in a blanket. *You messed up your marriage, Rachel Kenny! Even though you had three Le Creuset pans and a fixed-rate mortgage! This court finds you guilty of being an idiot!*

'Come on, darling,' said Cynthia. 'Let's get you down for the night.'

'I'm not a baby, you know.'

'Funny,' Emma said, 'because with all the crying and dribbling, it is actually quite like being with a baby.'

I gulped. 'At least I still have bladder control. Unlike you that time with the Red Bull shots.'

Emma smiled and patted me on the hand. 'That's my girl. Don't let the bastards grind you down.'

Cynthia actually had a spare room, with a bed and soft white sheets and a carafe of water on the bedside table, plus arcane things like armoires and runners that I'd only ever seen in design magazines. Once I was settled into bed for the night—completely shattered, all my stuff in archive boxes, with no idea where my toothbrush might be—my phone bleeped with a text. Dan? My heart did a sort of funny swoop and fall, guilt and sadness and something else all in one. But no, of course it wasn't Dan. I doubted he would ever text me again. It was Emma, asking if I was OK. I didn't know how to answer that, so instead I composed imaginary texts to Dan, supposing he were actually talking to me and might listen to what I had to say.

I'm sorry. I'm so, so sorry. Please let me come home.

I miss you.

I can't do this on my own.

I didn't send them, and for the rest of the night my phone stayed as dark and silent as the R.E.M. CD that was now buried somewhere under my bedding plants, ex–bedding plants, in a garden I'd probably never see again. I thought of him saying two years before: *I'll never leave you, Rachel.*

Yeah, right. But then, neither of us had exactly kept the promises we made that day.

Chapter Two

When I woke up in Cynthia's white-cotton-and-distressed-wood (why would it be distressed? It's in a lovely house in Chiswick. I've never understood that phrase) spare room, I'd no idea where I was for a moment. Had I fallen asleep in a branch of the White Company? Then it all came back and I felt the first tears of the day push against my eyelids. None of that. Today I had to find somewhere to live. I got ready in the en suite, with its rainfall shower and roll-top bath (if I was very quiet, maybe I could just stay here forever) and dressed in jeans and Converse. I brushed my hair, as I had to appear like a normal functioning member of society today, and that was hard for me at the best of times.

Cynthia was at the scrubbed wood table with *The Sunday Telegraph*—she married a Tory; I know, but it can happen to your dearest friends sometimes—croissants and fresh coffee. Unlike how I'd have been on a Sunday in my own kitchen—toothpaste-encrusted jammies and butter in my hair—she was dressed in a grey wool dress and different, equally expensive knee boots. 'There you are. Ready for the first day of the rest of your life?'

'I thought that was yesterday.'

'No, that was the last day of…a different bit of your life.'

'Catchy.'

'Croissant? Bagel? Scrambled eggs? Toast?' Cynthia was one of those people who would hostess you to death if you let them.

'Croissants would be lovely, thanks. Do you have any tea?' It was tragically uncool, but I'd never learned to like coffee.

Cynthia found some PG Tips hidden shamefully in a cupboard, holding them away from her as if they were toxic waste, or a shopping bag from Lidl. 'They must be the cleaner's.'

Of course they had a cleaner.

She furnished me with tea, croissants, jam and bits of the paper. 'What do you want to be depressed by? The stagnant house market, the rising price of ski holidays or the dangers of uncontrolled immigration?'

'I'll take immigration. I need a laugh. You know, you should get them to interview you. Young Tory lawyer who had a black immigrant dad. They'd choke on their crumpets.'

Oh dear. Maybe I shouldn't have mentioned her dad. But she only said, 'I'm not a Tory. I just married one. It could happen to anyone.'

'Where is Rich, by the way?' It was easy to forget someone else lived in this palace of white and sisal; he was so seldom there.

'Went into the office.'

'On a Sunday?' Of course he did. I shouldn't have asked. I might have been a lot poorer than most of my friends—

if we were the UN, I'd be Yemen—but at least I could lie in bed and mope whenever I wanted to. You couldn't put a price on that.

I was reading an article on house prices and feeling gloom settle over me. 'I'll never get on the property ladder again. There's a cardboard box here for sale for a hundred grand. Apparently, it's "bijou" and "compact" and made of "environmentally friendly materials".'

'You're not *off* the ladder. You've just stepped away for a while, is all.'

'Fell off, more like.'

'Frank fell off a ladder once. Broke his leg in three places.'

That was me, I reflected gloomily. Fallen back to earth with a crash, while up above me everyone else just kept on climbing that damn ladder. It was like doing gymnastics in PE all over again. 'How are your mum and Frank?'

'Fine. Talking about joining the Caravan Club, so that'll be nice and embarrassing for Rich's parents when we have them over at Christmas. They think caravans are for stable hands and New Age travellers.'

I wondered again how Cynthia felt about the fact her dad had never tried to contact her. I'd known her as long as Emma, the three of us meeting in the first term at Bristol Uni, huddling together in a refuge against the posh girls with long blonde hair, ski outfits and double-barrelled names, but sometimes I still had no idea what she thought about things.

'So you're house-hunting today?' she said.

'Urgh. Yes. Nightmare.'

'You can stay here as long as you like, you know that?'

'Thank you. But I think me and my existential crisis need a room of our own.'

Cynthia dropped me off at the station in her BMW, pointing out helpfully where I had croissant flakes in my hair, and I began the first of my viewings.

Two years ago, when we were still congratulating ourselves on our good life decisions—getting married, eating five portions of fruit and veg a day, opening pensions—Dan and I had bought a semi in suburbia, which wasn't much but had two bedrooms, a bathroom that wasn't incubating new species of mould, and a small scrappy patch of grass where we sentimentally thought our children would play, and before that our border collie, or golden retriever; we hadn't got that far yet. Remembering some of the places I'd lived before this, I dreaded flat-hunting.

Now, I like to think I'm a fairly positive person.

I mean, I'm not, not at all, but I like to *think* it, and I try to give what my Buddhist friend Sunita calls 'a cosmic yes to the universe'. Spending the day flat-hunting in London is enough to make you give a giant no, no, no, and hell no to the universe, and crawl back into bed with the duvet over your head, reflecting on how you can't really afford a bed, or even a duvet. My day went something like this:

The 'sunny studio' in Sydenham turned out to be one room with a single bed in a house share of five other people, one of whom showed me the room wearing just a pair of Y-fronts and a jokey rape-themed T-shirt. 'You're OK with parties, right? One house rule though is everyone, like, has their own stash. It's just cooler that way.' No.

The 'quiet garret room' in Blackheath was a single bed in an alcove off the living room of a nervy older lady.

'There's no door?' I said, edging to the window. The

place was where light came to die and there was a strong smell of cat pee.

'Oh, no. The little ones don't like to be shut out.' She said this cooing at one of the three cats I had spotted so far, a black tom with a scar over one eye and a malevolent glare out of the other.

The bedcover was chintz, approximately forty years old, and as she showed me it, a different, ginger cat jumped off the wardrobe and raked its claws over my neck. 'Oh, he likes you!'

No.

The 'lovely room in modern flat with friendly city gent' in Docklands turned out to be a nice place, if a bit 'chrome and leather are the only decorative materials that exist, aren't they' for my taste, but I was followed round at a distance of three centimetres by Mike, the owner, who told me at least five times he didn't need the money, like, he earned a packet in the City, but he wanted a bit of 'feminine companionship' round the place. No.

The 'delightful double in house with fun girl' turned out to be the living room, turned into a bedroom, in the flat of Mary from Camden, who handed me a list of her 'house rules' when I stepped in. First was, always take off your shoes when entering and put on special slippers, which were embroidered with cat faces.

No, no, no, hell no.

List of things that suck about house-hunting

1. The expense: finding out you have to pay £300 in fees for things like being shown into your own home, on top of the fortune in rent you're shelling out every month for a damp room in zone four.

2. The lies: in estate-agent speak, 'charming' means 'one step up from the gutter', 'simple' means 'not much more than a cardboard box' and 'neat' means 'you can touch both the opposite walls at the same time'. And half the time the flats were already let, and no one turned up once you'd trekked across London in the rain with your shoes falling to bits.

3. The nosiness: they'll ask you why you need to move, if it's just yourself renting (yes, thanks for rubbing it in, Mr Foxtons), and what you do for a living. On paper I wasn't the best prospect—unemployed and getting divorced. I basically needed a note from my mum to say I was well behaved and wouldn't make all the furniture into a giant nest like those people on *Britain's Biggest Hoarders*.

4. Wondering if the odd smells/stains in the flats you've been viewing mean you're only being shown the scenes of gangland shoot-outs, or if they've all been built on top of ancient Indian burial grounds.

5. Much like with online dating, feeling the slow lowering of your own hopes and dreams. 'Well, I suppose I could live in zone five…in a shed…and I suppose it IS really handy being able to reach the fridge from the bed…'.

The only thing that made house-hunting vaguely bearable was to imagine I was researching locations for a new gritty TV show where people got murdered in the dingiest possible flats. *CSI: Croydon*. I put in my headphones as I trudged about and asked myself what Beyoncé would do, as I often pondered in moments of stress. Well, probably she'd charter her private helicopter and get airlifted to one of her mansions, so that was no use. I repaired to a café in Kentish Town, trying to cheer myself up with tea and a Florentine. Then the bill came to £4.50 and I realised I might not be able to afford cafés at all after this. I'd have to be one of those people who knitted jumpers and always took their own sandwiches wrapped in tinfoil, just like at school. This wasn't what I'd grown up for. It was depressing indeed to realise you were no further up the pecking order than you were at seven.

I was on my phone, scanning the property websites for anything under £700 that didn't look likely to have fleas/mould/sleazy landlords. Could I live in Catford? Was that even in London? Would I be able to stomach a large flat share, given I currently worked from home? Alternatively, could I live and work in a studio flat where you couldn't open the fridge without moving the bed? Could I possibly get my freelance work going again to the point where I'd actually make some money?

I began scrawling figures on a napkin, but it was too scary, so I ordered another Florentine instead and then worried about money and calories and being single again at thirty. Not even single. Divorced.

I was getting back into some very bad thoughts—*you should ring Dan, beg him to take you back, you can't afford this, you can't manage alone*—when my phone rang. Emma. 'Are you busy?'

'No. Just contemplating the ruins of my life.'

'Oh dear, is it not going well?'

'Put it this way, the only person with less luck than me at choosing where to live is Snow White. I've seen most of the seven dwarves today—Grumpy, Horny, Druggy...'

'Remind me again why you had to move out. It was your house too, and he was the one who wanted—'

'I couldn't afford the mortgage on my own. And you

know it's better to be in London for work.' Work that I didn't have yet. I wasn't going to think about that.

'Well, check your emails. I just sent you something.'

'OK, let me find my phone.'

A pause. 'You're on your phone now, Rach.'

'Oh, right. What did you send?'

'An amazing flat share. It's in Hampstead, lovely garden and house, but, best of all, it's free!'

'What? How is that possible?' I was thinking of Mike, the 'city gent'.

'There's some house-sitting and pet-sitting involved.'

'Pets?' I said warily, thinking of the cat house—ironically, not in Catford.

'A dog.'

'Oh my God!'

'I know. So call them now! When I get off the phone, I mean.'

Sometimes I wondered if my friends thought I was a complete idiot. 'Thanks. You're sure it's not a sex trafficking thing though?'

'You can never be totally sure.'

'Oh.'

'I've got the address just in case.'

'Thanks.'

'I can craft the orders of service for your funeral. I just got a new glue gun.'

'I'm going now! Bye!'

I hung up and waited for the email to download.

A flip of excitement in my stomach—when you reached thirty, property websites gave you the same feeling that dating websites did in your twenties. Not that I'd ever dated. The house was beautiful—three storeys of red brick, set among trees, and there was even a turret! Oh my God. I read on. Underfloor heating, en suite room, massive kitchen with dishwasher—some of the places I'd looked at didn't even have washing machines. What was the catch? As I'd learned from my property search, there was always a catch. Under price, it said 'N/A'. Could there really be no charge? I looked at the number listed and on impulse dialled it. I was only ten minutes from Hampstead, after all.

It went to voicemail. A man's voice, deep and clipped. Slightly posh. 'This is Patrick Gillan. Please leave a message.'

Voicemails are my nemesis. Cynthia still talks about the time I rang her at work to tell her I'd seen cheap flights to America, and ended up singing 'Hotel California' down the line while her entire office listened on speakerphone.

'Erm…hi. I saw your ad. I'd like somewhere to live. I don't have much money at the moment—' Oh no, I shouldn't have said that. Like with jobs and dating, the only way to get a room you really needed was to pretend you didn't need it at all. 'Erm…I mean, I'm looking to relocate and I am most interested in your room. I should like to view it at the earliest convenience. Erm…I'm down the road right now. Call me. Oh…it's Rachel.'

I hung up. Classic rubbish voicemail, I'd managed to sound mad, posh and needy all at once. I paid for my biscuit and went out into the drizzle. Approaching me was a shiny red bus, slick with rain and the word 'Hampstead' on the front.

I've heard people say that they sometimes have moments when they feel as if Fate is tapping them on the shoulder and saying, 'This way, please,' like one of those tour guides with the little flags being followed around by Chinese tourists in matching raincoats.

I've never had this happen. Even if I did, I'd get stuck
on the Northern Line and Fate would have left for another
appointment. But that day I thought, sod it, I'm getting divorced, I have nothing to do and the bus is right there. So I
got on. And, ten minutes later, I found myself ringing the
bell at the house of Patrick Gillan.

Chapter Three

As I stood on the doorstep of a house on a tree-lined street in Hampstead, a dog started barking inside. I smiled. There really was one. I caught sight of myself in the shiny door knocker and sighed. My hair was frizzy with rain and I wore a fraying mac, jeans and holey Converse. When I worked in an office, tights were the bane of my life, like having cling film applied to your most delicate areas, always wrinkling round your ankles or laddering if anyone breathed in a ten-mile radius. So since going freelance—this was how I was choosing to describe my current circumstances to myself—I mostly worked in jeans…OK, pyjamas. The door had panels of stained glass, and I saw someone approach, turned different colours by the light. I stuck on my best 'not a crazy person' smile. The man who opened the door was holding a phone in one hand, and with the other had a barking Westie by the collar. 'Shut up, Max!' He, the man, not the dog, wore jeans and a soft blue-grey jumper. He had greying curly hair and a cross expression. 'What is it? I don't plan to vote in the council elections. Not until you do something about the disgraceful state of your recycling policy.'

'No— It's— I saw your ad. The room. I was in the area and…'

He stared at me for a few moments while the dog tried to climb up me.

'I'm not mad,' I said quickly.

'That's good to know.'

'I suppose a mad person might say that.' I laughed nervously.

He looked me up and down. Sighed. 'You better come in.'

Sometimes, when you walk into a place, you know you were meant to be there. It just smells right or something. Dan hated this method I had of choosing houses. *What do you mean it didn't feel right? It's got outdoor decking and a dedicated parking space!*

'It's amazing,' I said. The inner doors all had stained-glass panels, filling the hallway with a kaleidoscope of colour. The floor was old-fashioned parquet, a little scuffed, and the place smelled of coffee and daffodils, of which there was a large handful crammed into a jam jar. I could tell instantly it was a middle-class home because:

List of things you find in a middle-class house

1. Posh scented candles

2. Some kind of cork board or whiteboard detailing the activities of the family

3. Abel and Cole veg box

4. No family photos, only arty prints and black-and-white blurred shots, the kind of which my mother wouldn't

dream of hanging up because 'you can't see what it is, can you?'

5. Wine fridge

6. Coffee machine that looks like it was designed by NASA for use on the International Space Station

7. Recycling. Lots of recycling

The man still looked cross. 'Come into the kitchen. I'm in the middle of something, so I wish you'd waited, but never mind.'

'You're sure?'

'I said so, didn't I? Do you want coffee?'

'Oh, thank you, I don't drink it.' I may as well have said I didn't believe in changing my socks.

'You don't?'

'I don't like the taste. I like the smell and I love coffee cake and those sweets you get in Roses. Isn't that weird? I mean, hardly anyone likes those.'

He studied me. The phone in his hand chirped and he looked at it, frowned. 'Tea, then?'

'Yes, please.'

'How do you take it?'

'Milk, quite strong, but sort of milky if that makes sense.'

Once I sat down, the dog scampered across the kitchen and hurled himself onto my knee, where he crouched with his chin on my shoulder, panting. 'Oof! Hello.'

'He goes mad for new people. Sorry.'

'It's OK. I wish I had that effect on men.' *Oh, shut up, shut up, Rachel.* Another side effect of working alone—you forget that there are supposed to be 'inside head' thoughts as well as 'outside head' sayings.

Patrick peered at the kettle. 'So, Rachel—that's you, I assume? What made you want the room?'

'Honestly? I need somewhere to live at short notice. I also work from home at the moment, so I can't really be in a big flat share.' Or the sex slave of a rich city banker, come to think of it. All the sex-slaving would probably cut right into my freelancing time.

He was still frowning. 'And where have you been living?'

'Out in Surrey. I owned a place.'

'Don't you want to buy again, then?'

Things that suck about divorce, number fifteen: having to explain it to strangers. 'My husband and I are splitting up. He's keeping the house for now, so I have to move out.' I cuddled the dog. 'I'm in bit of a bind. But—'

'You're not mad.'

'No.'

'You're getting divorced.'

'Yes.'

He leaned against the counter and I saw he had no wedding ring on. 'Join the club.'

'Oh.'

'Not much fun, is it?'

'It sucks. In fact, I'm keeping a list. Things that suck about divorce.'

'How many things are on it?'

'Several hundred and counting.'

'How about this one?' The kettle had boiled, but he kept staring out the window. The phone beeped again, but he ignored it. 'Having to find a lodger so they can dog-sit and look after the house, because you spend too much time at your job, and that's why your wife left you in the first place, because with all the time she was on her own she had to find new hobbies, like, for example, having an affair with the next-door neighbour?'

I followed his gaze to the house just visible over the fence and nodded slowly. 'I'll put that one in after having to move out of the house you bought in the suburbs because your husband doesn't want you there any more, but not being able to rent anywhere in London because you're broke, so your only option is to move into massive house shares, or live with mad cat ladies or sex pests, or…answer weird ads that don't list any rent.' I paused. There were posh Waitrose biscuits on the table, so I crammed one into my mouth to shut myself up.

Patrick Gillan was watching me curiously. 'Look, I have a demanding job, so I need someone here during the day, to be with the dog and take deliveries and maybe do some light au pairing, but I can't afford a full-time housekeeper. I was just…thinking outside the box. I thought someone might do it in exchange for free rent. It was sort of a mad late-night idea, to be honest. I'm kind of at my wit's end here.'

Free rent. FREE RENT. Suddenly, I was ripping up the calculations I'd done on the napkin and feeling a large weight lift from my chest. I wouldn't be totally broke. I wouldn't have to bring my own sandwiches when we went to Pizza Express and divide up the cost of each dough ball. He was still looking at me. 'Why are you here, Rachel? I mean really?'

I was a little high on all this unexpected honesty, among the lies you get told when looking for a place to live, about south-facing lawns and nearness to transport and exactly how many cats there are in a given household. 'Really? When I got married, we moved to Surrey and my husband, I mean, my ex—' it was hard to say the word '—got me a

Eva Woods

job at the local council where he worked. Graphic design. But then he asked me to move out, and coincidentally, the next day, I was made redundant.'

He was still looking at me. 'Kettle's boiled,' I pointed out. The biscuit was lodged in my dry mouth.

He shook himself and got a cup. 'So you're at home all day?'

'Most days.' I held my breath. This had been a problem with many of the rooms I'd looked at, landlords muttering about extra bills and so on. 'I'm going to look for a job, obviously, but also try to build up my freelance work. I used to do a bit on the side.'

'And you like dogs?'

'Love them.' I stroked Max's head. 'I was about to get one, but then—well. Everything happened.'

'And would you mind sort of housekeeping a little, answering the phone, getting parcels, maybe sticking dinner on?'

'Of course. I love cooking. And I don't smoke and I'm… *fairly* tidy. You mean you literally wouldn't charge me any rent?' I looked at him suspiciously. 'What's the catch?'

He laughed, and instantly he looked ten years younger, happy, even a little wicked. 'I was wondering the same about you. I suppose I should ask for references.'

'Well. My previous landlord is my ex-husband, and my current boss is myself. Can you prove you're not a mad killer?'

'It's hard to prove a negative.'

'Hmm.'

'Phone a friend, tell them where you are.'

'But I would be dead by the time they found me.'

'True, but at least you'd have a nice funeral.'

I was still thinking when there was a noise and the back door opened, and in trudged a small child in red wellies, clutching a big muddy bunch of daffodils. He was gorgeous— dark glossy curls, brown eyes. Maybe four or five. 'I got some more, Dad.'

'That's good, mate. Give them here.' Patrick looked at me over the child's head. 'I may as well explain—this is the catch.'

'Cynth!' I hissed.

'Hello? Who is this? I'm not interested in PPI claims, thanks. Unlike some, I wasn't stupid enough to buy it in the first place.'

'It's me. Rachel.'

'Ohh! You're still alive, then.' I had emailed her to tell her about the possible flat share, figuring the more people who knew the better for retrieving my murdered corpse.

'I took the room. God, the place is gorgeous.' The room I was sitting in had more stained glass in the window, which looked out over Hampstead Heath. It was on the third floor, filled with light. I could put a drawing table in the window. There was an old wooden bed, a thick cream carpet and an en suite with a deep claw-foot bath. On the bedside table was a jar with more daffodils.

'Alex,' Patrick had said when he'd shown me up. 'He won't stop picking them.'

Ah yes. Alex.

'So is it really OK? How on earth can he be offering it free?'

'Well, there's a kid.'

'Ugh,' she said. Cynthia felt about children the way most people felt about mould spores—some unfortunates had to live with them, but careful vigilance could prevent them from ever taking hold in the first place.

'The dad, he's getting divorced, so he has the kid.'

'Where's the mother?'

'I'm not sure. Gone overseas to work for a while, I think.'

'I see. He wants a free nanny.'

'Well, Alex will be at school during the day. I think Patrick just wants someone to be here. Answer the phone, put the washing machine on.' He'd described it as 'Maybe I can help you, and you can help me'. I understood, I thought.

Cynthia was talking. 'Make sure it's not a de facto employee post, sweetie. You know how people are. Since you're there could you just make the dinner, and do the shopping, and re-grout that bathroom... Working from home still means working.'

'I know. But where else can I go? This is a million times nicer than anything I could afford.'

'Well, OK. If you're happy.'

I realised I'd talked myself into staying here, and before I knew it I was arranging to collect my things and move in that very night. Me, my ten thousand sketchbooks, my fifteen pairs of trainers and Bob the dog-substitute bear were going to make our home here.

Alex, apparently the world's most biddable child, had presumably gone to bed when I came back with the van, and Patrick was in the kitchen with an iPad and glass of wine. There was a smell of stew in the air and a Le Creuset dish soaking in the sink. It felt weird. Like coming home, but to a home that wasn't mine. He jumped when I let myself in, and I wondered if he'd forgotten he'd given me a key or, worse, forgotten me entirely. 'Hello,' I said.

'Hi. You've got…things?'

'Yes.'

'I better help you.'

We hauled my meagre goods up the stairs. 'What's in here, rocks?' Patrick asked, and I'd had to admit that yes, there were rocks in some of the boxes; I collected them for drawing practice. Dan had kept all the Ikea/Argos chipboard that furnished our marital home, so there wasn't much. 'Do you want a glass of wine?' Patrick said, when the room was a mess of boxes and cheap Ikea blue bags.

I did, but I felt odd about sitting with him, and I was worried I'd been drinking too much as my marriage fell apart. 'I'm OK, thanks. I'm very tired.'

'I'll leave you to it, then.'

I liked to think I was fairly spontaneous and fun. The kind of girl who'd jump on a train to Madrid with only the clothes on her back and not even book a return flight in advance. The kind of girl who bought train tickets at the station instead of getting them online for up to a third less. Who didn't know what they were doing three weekends hence but was fairly sure it would involve a music festival and a twenty-four-hour drugathon with dubious men in goatees, and not a trip to Ikea for a new magazine rack.

I wasn't spontaneous. Plus, I hated goatees. Things that suck about divorce, number twenty-two: nothing is where it should be. If you wanted to make your famous lemon risotto, the recipe books were still in the house, and you didn't manage to get custody of the food processor. If you wanted to go hiking, your boots were in the car your husband/ex-husband was still driving to work every day. You wanted to wear a blue dress and realised it was at the dry cleaner's, the ticket

God knows where, and you weren't making the thirty-mile trip for a frock from New Look anyway.

Nothing is where it should be. Not you. Not your heart. Not your life.

Finally, I'd unpacked nothing but my toothbrush and pyjamas, but I was in bed and was listening to the unfamiliar house around me. The trickle of old plumbing. The creak of the attic. I took out my phone—my screen saver was still a picture from two years ago, Dan and I doing a selfie at our wedding. He was planting a kiss on my cheek and I was smiling widely, as if I couldn't even imagine a time when we wouldn't be that happy. I thought about texting him to tell him I'd found somewhere, but I knew he wouldn't care. That was another thing that sucked about divorce. You were hurting and lost and alone, and the only person you could think to tell about any of it was the one who no longer wanted to talk to you at all.

Chapter Four

When I woke up, it was the day after the first day of the rest of my life. No one ever talked about that. That's the day when you have to live with your momentous decision, start redirecting post, unpacking boxes. My overwhelming wish was to lie in bed, sorrowfully dwelling on the terrible mess I'd made of my life. When you're freelance, you see, you have those luxuries. But I didn't get the chance, because I was woken at six by a tapping on the door. Mice? Ghosts? I cleared my throat. 'Hello?' Indistinct mumbling. A shy ghost? 'You can come in!'

There was a fumbling and the door creaked open. In flew twenty pounds of overexcited dog. Max leapt up on the bed, where he rolled over with his feet in the air, indicating I could do as I wished with him. Sadly, it was only dogs who reacted this way to me in bed.

In the doorway stood Alex, holding yet more dripping daffodils. He wore one red welly, the other foot clad in a

stripy sock, and a pretty on-trend onesie with Thomas the
Tank Engine's face on front. 'Hello,' I said.

''Lo.' He stared at me out of his dark eyes.

'Those are nice flowers.'

'Flarrs for you,' he muttered, darting in and crushing
them onto my bedside table, where they left green smears.

'For me? Thank you, Alex.'

'Mummy likes flowers.'

Awk-ward. 'I'm sure she does. And how is Max today?'

'He's not allowed on the bed.'

'Is he not? He's naughty, then, isn't he?'

'Yes. Can I come in the bed?'

'OK. The more the merrier.' Alex needed my help to get
up, and I suggested he leave the remaining welly behind.
He sat cross-legged, looking at me.

'What's your name?'

'Rachel.'

I pitched around for four-year-old conversational topics.
I liked kids but was still having conflicted feelings over
whether I wanted them or not. Dan and I hadn't even been
able to manage a dog. I could feel the panic reach up in
me from the pit—the one of 'I'm broke and thirty and I'll
be alone forever'—so I focused on Alex. It's hard to have
existential horror when you're with a four-year-old. They
barely understand the concept of 'tomorrow' let alone 'the
rest of my miserable life'.

'So who's that on your onesie?'

''S Thomas.'

'Oh yeah? Who's your favourite person in *Thomas*?'

Alex and I were having a little chat about animated
trains—I bluffed my way through, my sister has kids—
when I heard footsteps coming up the stairs and Patrick

burst in. He too wore a onesie in a fashionable nautical stripe, a thick grey jumper on top. 'Alex! I told you to leave Rachel alone. She was sleeping.'

'No, she wasn't,' said Alex, with impeccable logic. 'Brought her flarrs.'

'Yes, we've talked about this, mate. We have to leave some of the flowers in the garden or there won't be any more. Come on, get down. You too, Max.' Child and dog slid off the bed. Max waddled out, wagging his little tail and wheezing. Alex clung to his dad's hand. Patrick took a look at me, in my alluring sleepwear—Bruce Springsteen T-shirt, fleece pyjamas with sheep on. 'I'm sorry about them.'

'It's OK. It's a nice way to wake up.' Then I worried he'd think I meant him in his onesie, so I quickly said, 'Max and Alex, I mean—I've always wanted a dog.'

'That's fortunate, because Max is very hard to shake off. I found him inside my coat the other day. I'll try to keep them both out of here.' He looked round at the mess of boxes and bags, paintbrushes rolling on the desk, reams of paper stacked about the place. 'You're an artist, are you? I didn't quite catch what it was you did.'

'I'm a graphic designer really, but I used to also be a sort of freelance cartoonist. I do caricatures of people, for weddings and birthdays and that, and sometimes a bit for magazines.' As I said it, I realised this sounded like the world's flakiest career, like 'vajazzalist', or 'toenail consultant'. I also realised the room was an absolute tip.

'I'm not finished unpacking,' I said hurriedly. I was not tidy. I liked to pretend it was something to do with my artistic temperament, but really I was just a slob and quite forgetful. I'd put down bits of toast and then wonder what happened to them and make some more. It used to drive Dan crazy. That's how it goes, isn't it? When you start out, when you're in love, it seems as if these things could never matter, as if they're just crumbs in the bed of your love. Then as time goes by, all you can feel is the crumbs. They're itchy. They keep you awake. I suppose all those little crumbs become a big loaf in the end, rising between you, keeping you apart.

That wasn't the best metaphor I'd ever come up with. Moving on…

Once I was up, showered in my lovely en suite, and had pushed some of the mess into the fitted cupboards, I stuck on Destiny's Child's 'Survivor' on a loop, looking for inspiration, and sat on the bed with a notebook to make a list. A list for the rest of my life.

I liked lists. They were my way of trying to put some order on the desperate mess of my life. In fact, I even had a list of my favourite lists, ones I'd been keeping for years:

List of my favourite lists

1. Things to do before I'm dead. Was originally things to do before I was thirty, which when I started it seemed pretty much the same as being dead: you were stiff and no one wanted to see you naked.

2. Things I do not like in a man. This list spanned many diverse areas, including footwear (no coloured and/or pointy shoes); grammar (no smiley faces, and must know the difference between 'your' and 'you're'); and musical taste (no metal, no electronic, no wearing massive headphones, absolutely no folk-that one was underlined several times).

3. Things my sister has done to slight me-this one wasn't actually written down anywhere, but I was keeping it all right. I imagined she kept one on me too. All families do.

4. And, finally, my masterwork—the list of things that suck about divorce. I couldn't see myself completing that one any time soon.

I opened my notebook—a pretty one with a pink silk cover, my lists deserved the best—and chewed on my pen.

I'd thought my life was going to be all Volvos and trips to Sainsbury's, dogs and mortgages and maybe babies in a few years. My friend from yoga suggested I think positively about all the things I could achieve now I was 'on a different life path'—Buddhists are always saying things like this. For example, I'd always wanted to try lots of hobbies. Languages, maybe. Kick-boxing. That looked like fun and would come in handy with all the awful men I'd probably have to date now I was single. Oh God. Dating.

The thought was so depressing I crawled back under the covers, in my jeans and jumper, and lay there panicking about being alone forever.

After a while of this, the phone rang. It was Emma. 'Hello! Are you lying in bed panicking about being alone forever?'

'No. Well, yes, but least I got dressed.'

'Good girl. Now, can you come over tonight? Cynthia has promised she'll leave work by seven, and Ian will cook.'

'Will you help me with my list?'

'Which list is this?'

'The list of what to do with the rest of my life.'

'Of course. I love a good list.' It was true. It was one of the main reasons we were friends.

I agreed to come over and settled down for a good long worry about life.

List of things I was worried about

1. Being alone forever. Being a crazy cat lady (even though did not like cats)/mad aunt to Jess's kids, with dyed red hair, booming voice and electronic cigarette. Possibly take up wearing turbans.

2. Having to date. Being killed by one of those predatory online murderers as featured in *Chat* magazine and having to appear in articles where my friends looked sad and held up pictures of me as a warning to others not to meet up with Barry from Walsall in a branch of Nando's.

3. Never having any money. Having to move in with my parents and watch back-to-back episodes of *Midsomer Murders*. When they died, getting them stuffed and carrying on having conversations with them in the living room.

4. All my friends falling out with me because I was so boring all I could talk about was my divorce and how worried I was I'd end up alone.

I must practise some conversation topics for tonight, I thought. House prices might be a good one.

Chapter Five

Emma and Ian lived in Acton, clinging on to the very edge of London under the flight path of whooshing aeroplanes. The flat smelled of curry and oil—Ian was seriously into bikes, both motor and road, and when you went for a wee it was quite normal to see bits of inner tubes in the bath. Emma opened the door in what looked like pyjamas.

For a moment I was confused. 'Did I get the wrong day?' I'd like to say this had never happened before, but...

'No.' Emma looked puzzled, taking my bottle of corner-shop wine, the £4.99 sticker clearly visible. 'Oh, you mean the onesie. Isn't it cool? Come out here, Snugglepuss.'

Ian appeared with a pan in one hand and a spatula in the other. He too had donned a onesie shaped like a dog, with little ears on the hood. Emma's was purple with stars on. 'Aren't they great?' She beamed. 'They're so cosy, you wouldn't believe. We've saved a fortune on our heating bills.'

'That's nice,' I said weakly. Onesies? Did everyone

except me get the memo about this trend? I remembered when Emma was famed for streaking our graduation ceremony in a protest at the uni's continued stocking of Nestlé-made Kit Kats. Her boobs had been on the front of the local paper—it was pixelated out, but you could tell it was her by the Danger Mouse pants. Now it was all onesies and pukey pet names.

In the background, an episode of *University Challenge* was playing, which they were watching so they could keep score on the whiteboard they used every week. On one side it said 'overprivileged students' and on the other 'Emsie and Ian'. They were also hosting me to death. 'Drink?' asked Ian, going back to the kitchen. 'Beer? Wine? Vodka? Meths?'

'Or water first?' Emma frowned at the TV screen and shouted: 'Swim bladder!'

'Bread? Crisps? This will be ready soon. Potassium chlorate!'

I felt it should be me in the onesie, with them as my helicopter parents. 'Beer, please. Who else is coming?'

'I asked Ros, but of course she never leaves her own postcode. The dissolution of the monasteries! She says she'd love to see you soon and lend an ear though.'

Get all the juicy details, more like, while revelling in her own two kids and semi in Hendon. I was becoming very bitter with all the solicitous, coupled-up friends who wanted to mother me. 'Any sign of Cynth?'

'Isiser? No, it's not the eighties.' Ian laughed to himself. 'Henry the Fifth! Oh, come on, that was an easy one.'

Emma rolled her eyes. 'Snugs, that was dreadful, even by your standards. She said she'd leave at seven. Burkina Faso!'

'Reckon she'll come?' Often she didn't leave work at all, just stayed up all night and sent out to La Perla in the morning for clean knickers. This was called 'living the dream', apparently.

However, I'd barely eaten my way through five hundred poppadoms when she turned up, dispensing kisses and clinking carrier bags. 'Hello, darling.' Immediately, I felt bad that I had brought only one bottle. But then, I was broke and she could afford to chuck away La Perla knickers, so perhaps everything was relative. I was sure there was a Bible story just like this, except without the undies—Jesus being strictly an M&S guy, I feel.

'They let you out for good behaviour?' In the kitchen I could see Cynthia saying hi to Ian.

'Bad behaviour. Apparently, it's worth more by the hour. Mmm, smells yummy. I think the last time I cooked we still thought fringes looked good.'

'Taste.' He held up a spoon for her to try and she closed her eyes for a second.

'The Kelvin scale!' shouted Emma.

'Mmm. I can really taste the…whatever random ingredient you used that we're supposed to be able to detect.'

'Galangal.'

'Yep. I can definitely taste that, whatever it is.'

'Björn Borg!' shouted Ian. 'God, this lot are really thick this week.'

'Is it nearly done, Snugs? Fermat's Last Theorem!' called Emma.

'Just about. Honeybunch, don't use those plates. They don't match.'

'We don't own four that match, Snugs. You broke one last week doing air guitar to "Sweet Child O' Mine". The Appalachians!'

'Oh yeah. They've got some on sale at Sainsbury's. Should I pick some up?'

'OK, and get some more cleaning wipes. We're out. Samuel Pepys!'

List of things Emma and Ian were insanely
competitive at

1. *University Challenge*

2. Quiz machines in pubs

3. Cooking

4. The Post-it name game

5. Jenga

6. Being the happiest couple in the history of the world

I tried not to catch Cynthia's eye during this, partly because I still couldn't believe this was our rebellious Emma, who'd once refused to shop in supermarkets for an entire year until they started charging for plastic bags. But also because I missed having this with someone, passing words back and forth like dishes, barely listening to what you were saying. Reminding someone to buy milk. All that.

Ian, like many men, required you to make a whole performance of admiring his food whenever he cooked. You had to look at it, smell it, guess what spices he might have used, and only then were you allowed to dig in. Dan and I had given up cooking when things got bad. We were on first-name terms with the Papa John's delivery man—I'd even given him a Christmas card, to my shame.

'So,' said Emma, as soon as she'd finished wiping her plate with naan. 'It's Rach's first night with us alone.'

'Not really,' Ian pointed out. 'She hadn't brought him out with her for at least the past year.'

'He was always so busy with work,' I said defensively. 'I brought him. Sometimes.'

Things that suck about divorce, number thirty-four: finding out that none of your friends or family really liked your spouse in the first place; they just didn't say so at the time when you could actually have done something about it. We'd all been at university together, so my friends had had a good ten years to get to know Dan. It was sad to think he was going to slip out of their lives too, without a backward glance.

'It's her first night properly alone,' Emma repeated.

'Do you have to keep saying "alone"?' I was still working on my third curry helping and most likely only seconds from an Ian pun about passing out in a korma. Unlike those pale tragic women in books, misery made me eat everything in sight.

Cynthia rubbed my arm. 'You're not alone, darling. You're independent and fabulous.'

Easy for her to say when she was going home to Richy Rich and their mansion with a cleaner and once-a-month gardener.

'Anyway.' Emma was doing her 'could the class come to attention' voice. 'Rach, I know you're feeling a bit wobbly at present.'

'You could say that,' I mumbled through curry. 'Is anyone eating that?'

Ian passed over more naan. 'Your naan,' he said. 'Geddit? Like your mum.'

'Could you listen, please?' Emma was waiting. 'I think

what you need is a project. All the books say the first few months post-split are the hardest.'

'You read books about it?'

'Of course. I wanted to support you.'

'It's a bit worrying seeing a book called *Steps Through Divorce* beside the bed,' Ian said, chewing.

'You have to be married to get divorced,' Emma said, with a slight edge in her voice, which made me hurriedly swallow my curry.

'So you've got a project for me?'

'Better.' She smiled triumphantly and pulled out a small notebook. 'I've got a project *plan*.'

We all groaned. Cynthia said, 'Not again, Em. I thought we'd talked about this scrapbooking issue.'

'It's nothing! Just some glue-gunning, and a bit of découpage and sketching…you know.'

'Don't make us do another intervention. Remember my wedding invites.'

I winced. 'I thought we'd agreed, we do not talk about the wedding invites.'

Emma was huffing. 'I don't see what the fuss was about. They looked lovely. Everyone said.'

Cynthia ticked it off on her fingers. 'They cost five hundred pounds in materials! I could have got them at the Queen's stationer for that! They put indelible pink stains on everyone's hands!'

'Hand-dyed paper! It was a lovely touch.'

'Touch was exactly what they couldn't do.'

Ian met my eyes, pleading, as he gathered up our plates. 'Can I see the plan?' I said. I was the peacemaker in the group, which meant, like many peacekeepers, I was often riddled with metaphorical crossfire bullets. 'Thank you, Em. It's pretty.'

Emma was an excellent primary school teacher. She was authoritative, briskly kind, organised and on top of this a dab hand at cutting and gluing things. Unfortunately, she couldn't curtail this, and so was prone to a vice you might call 'scrapbooking gone mad'. Every page was decorated in sparkly gold pen, with glued-in photos and drawings. 'So what's the—'

'Well,' she jumped in, 'I read in this book that the best way through a big life change is to have a list. A to-do list.'

That didn't sound so bad. Lists were my comfort zone— I'd had interventions about this too. I turned the leaf. Page one said—*do stand-up comedy*. It was accompanied by a picture of me rather drunk, in a party hat, in the middle of saying something that was clearly very important. I looked up at them. 'What is this?'

'It's a bucket list,' said Cynthia gently. 'Except you're not dying, of course. Sort of an embracing-life list. All the things you said you wanted to do for years, then never did because you were living in the suburbs with Dan.'

'I never said I wanted to—what's this—eat something weird? Ew, is that a *snail* in the picture?'

'We sort of…extrapolated for some of them.'

'You extrapolated that I wanted to…sleep with a stranger? Nice abs on that dude though.' I tilted the book for a better look at the picture.

'You could do both of those last ones together,' called Ian from the kitchen. 'I mean, if you slept with a stranger, you probably would eat something weird. Two birds, one stone, etc.'

'Go away, Ian,' said Emma and Cynthia in unison.

I was leafing through the lovely rough handmade paper pages, with their crazy gold-penned instructions. 'Guys, what is this about? I didn't say I wanted to...do yoga properly. What?'

Emma leaned across the table to me earnestly. 'Rach. What's happened is you've had a disastropiphany.'

'A what?'

'A terrible thing has happened to you, but you can use it to make changes in your life, and generally become much happier.'

'Like in *Eat Pray Love*,' Cynthia chipped in.

There was a problem with that—no one was going to pay me to go round the world shagging Javier Bardem and eating ice cream. Julia Roberts would definitely not play me in the film of this. Maybe Kathy Burke. There was no way I could pull off prayer beads as a look. 'Oh,' I said. 'You must really think I've messed things up.'

In the silence that followed Ian pushed a large vegetable through the kitchen door. 'What do you think, eh? It's what Prince was singing about. "Little Red Courgette"? Eh? Eh?'

'Courgettes are green,' said Emma stonily. 'And get on with the dessert, will you?'

'Yes, sir!' In the kitchen we could hear him singing over the noise of the blender. 'She made some raspberry puree... the kind you find in a fruit and veg store...' Emma rolled her eyes affectionately. At least I hoped it was affectionately.

She lowered her voice. 'To be honest, Rach, when you and Dan split up, it made me think—is this all there is, working all day and every evening, falling asleep in front of box sets, saving for a deposit on an even smaller flat somewhere further out?' There was a silence from the kitchen. She went on. 'You've been so brave, Rach. You changed your life. Hardly anyone ever does. They just put up with it.'

I swallowed hard and look at Cynthia. 'You too?'

She squirmed. 'I'm all right, but, you know, Rich is away so much. I don't see him at all some weeks—it's like we have a timeshare on the house. I think what happened to you was a wake-up call, that maybe we all needed to try to have more fun.'

I pushed away the book. 'Guys—I know you're trying to help, and I appreciate that, really I do, but I don't suppose it occurred to you that I can't afford this stuff. I'm living in the box room of a stranger who is possibly a serial killer.' I was exaggerating here for effect. It was hardly a box room, and Patrick seemed nice enough, if a bit grumpy.

'We thought of that,' said Emma calmly. She didn't respond to passive-aggressive guilt trips—something to do with being told fifteen times a day that small children hated her and she wasn't their real mum. 'I'm going to organise it all, as an outlet for my madness—I'll be Official List Arbiter—and Cyn...'

'I'm going to pay,' she said. 'No, no, not in a patronising way. I'm going to do some of the tasks too, and I need you to make sure I actually go and don't stay in to work all night. You're going to be my social assistant.'

I glowered at them. 'Funny, because that sounds *totally patronising*.'

She sighed. 'Rach. Do you know how many pairs of pants I had to buy last month because I slept at the office? Twelve. I don't even go to La Perla now. I go to...Primark. I get them in *packs*. So you see, Rach. I need your help.'

Emma nodded solemnly. 'Her gusset is depending on you.'

Eva Woods

* * *

When I left that night, slightly tipsy and falling over my biker boots, I'd agreed to follow Emma and Cynthia's ten-step plan for the post-split, pre-divorce lady of a certain age (thirty). I must have dozed off on the tube from Acton, because I woke up at Tottenham Court Road in a panic—when was my last train? Did I miss it?—then I remembered I lived here now. In the city, not the sleepy suburbs. Back at the house, I struggled to get my newly cut key in the lock and, to my embarrassment, Patrick was still up in the kitchen. He had a bottle of red wine and the paper spread out on the table, classical music on the stereo. He was wearing dark-rimmed glasses and a red jumper. I felt myself relax as I stepped in. It was warm, and it smelled like flowers and beeswax polish.

'Sorry I'm late,' I said to Patrick automatically.

He looked puzzled. 'You can come and go as you like, Rachel. I didn't mean to suggest otherwise.'

'Oh. OK.' I realised I'd taken my shoes off, and it made me sad suddenly, all the nights I'd had to sneak back in beside Dan, cold and tired, and pretend I hadn't enjoyed myself. Waiting to hear the inevitable accusing voice. *You're late. I take it you had a good time.* Praying he'd be asleep already. 'First night out,' I explained. 'Since…you know.'

'I don't think I've been out since. Alex was so… I wanted to make sure he was OK.' He looked up. 'Would you like a glass of wine? I haven't talked to anyone in a while, at least not about more than Lego or walkies.'

At the magic word 'walkies', a little head popped up from a basket by the door. Max was awake. 'Woof!'

'Not now, silly dog.'

I sat down and Patrick got me a glass, patting the dog as he did. 'Thank you.' I was keen to hold on to the fragile, slightly drunk air of intimacy from the evening, so I took a big swallow. 'Can I ask—when did she go?'

'Michelle? A month ago.' He said the rest quickly. 'A month and three days.'

'Not seven hours and fifteen days?'

'Longer than that.'

'No, it's a song… Never mind.'

He smiled thinly. 'She just left. There was some big job in New York—she's from there, you see, and before Alex she was high up in banking—and we were fighting a lot, because I'd just found out about her and Alan from next door, and that was it. Sometimes it takes forever. Sometimes it all falls apart in what feels like days. Supposedly it's just for a few months, the job, but I don't know what will happen with us.'

'We were the opposite.' I was rubbing my finger where my wedding ring used to be. 'It feels like it was on life support for years—just dying day by day.'

'Sounds awful.'

'Yeah. But even with that, there's only one last time, you know? Like the last time he makes you a cup of tea or you watch *Mad Men*.'

'Like the start of a relationship, but in reverse.'

'Just like that.'

We lapsed into a sad silence.

He said, 'You had fun tonight?' And he actually meant it. Not like Dan's 'I can see you had fun without me' version of the question.

'I did. I saw my friends, and we had a curry.'

'What are they like?'

'Oh, insanely bossy. One's a lawyer, one's a teacher, and her boyfriend's a social worker. They sort of manage me.'

'Can't you manage yourself?'

'They think not. Look.' I fished the book out of my bag. 'Can you believe this? They've actually made me a list of things I'm supposed to do to get me through the post-split slump. They've even already booked one—supposedly we're doing a tango class next week.'

He peered over. Unfortunately, it had opened on the page that said 'sleep with a stranger'. 'Um...that one's just a joke.' I turned over hurriedly to 'do stand-up comedy'.

'Is that something you'd like to do?'

'I don't know. I used to rant about it, when we were at uni. How the comedians in clubs were always racist and sexist. And with my cartoons—I try to be funny with them. But I'd never have the guts to get on stage and be heckled.'

Patrick was looking thoughtful. 'I think this is a really good idea, you know. I used to do lots of things, before I met Michelle. She was so organised, really had her life planned out, so there wasn't time for hobbies. Then before I knew it I was married, and she was having Alex, and we were buying this place. I feel like I haven't done anything fun for about five years.'

'It's lovely though. The house.'

His face softened. 'You know I remodelled it myself? I don't know if I said, but that's what I do. I'm an architect. When we bought it, ivy was growing through the windows— the previous owner had been in a nursing home for years, no family to keep it up. So it was a wreck. Michelle wanted to gut it, put in beige carpets and take the walls down. But I wouldn't. Only time I managed to stand up to her. It took months, but it was like…finding hidden treasure. Those windows—I found them by scraping off the dirt. And the garden—there were all these roses among the weeds.' He stopped, as if realising he'd said a lot more than he meant to.

'Well, it's lovely,' I repeated. 'You should be proud.' Silence fell again, and I racked my brains for something to say. 'So what would be on your post-divorce list, if you had one?'

He frowned and got up to wash his glass. 'Oh, who knows. Don't get divorced, I suppose.'

'It doesn't work that way. If you can't go back, you have to go forward.'

'Is that a quote?' He dried his hands on the tea towel, then straightened it neatly over the oven door.

'Mmm…dunno. A quote from my dad, maybe.'

'I like it.'

'So what kind of things did you used to do?'

He was thinking. 'I used to be quite into extreme sports— skiing, climbing, that sort of thing.'

I was trying to suppress a shudder. 'You can do that again. Easy.'

'I haven't since Alex.'

'He could go skiing, couldn't he? All those French kids do. I went once. I felt like I should be on a Zimmer frame.' Dan had taken me—he was into snowboarding, or he had been before he stopped being into anything but TV and pizza. I'd fallen over on the first slope and spent the rest of the trip mainlining mulled wine while being jumped over by disdainful European tots on skis.

'He can't go skiing.' Patrick was surprisingly firm.

'Oh. OK.' Silence fell between us again. The wine was gone, and I felt the loneliness settle on my shoulders again, like a cat that had been lurking on a wardrobe all day (bad

memories). 'You could come to some of it,' I heard myself
say. 'When we do the dancing and the comedy and all that.
Not the sleeping with strangers part...er, that's a joke, but
the rest. I mean, if you want to.'

He turned from the sink, leaning on it for a moment,
and I thought how sad he looked, how tired. I wondered if
I looked the same, after years of trying and failing, trying
again, failing differently.

'Maybe,' he said at last. 'It's a long time since I did things
like that. And there's Alex.'

'Does he have a regular babysitter?'

Again, Patrick looked annoyed. 'There are a few people, but...I don't like to leave him. It's... Well, it's a little
complicated.'

I knew enough about dodgy emotional situations to recognise that 'it's complicated' meant 'please stop asking
about that, you nosy cow'. I stood up. 'Right, better go to
bed. I'll be working here tomorrow if you need me to do
anything. Housework, that sort of thing.'

He started out of whatever he'd been brooding about.
'You could hang out some washing, if you don't mind. Alex
will be at school, and then after-school club. I pick him up
at six.'

That seemed a very long day for a four-year-old, but it
was none of my business. 'Should I walk Max?'

'Would you?'

'Of course. I love dogs. You know those crazy women
who hang around outside shops and nick babies from prams?'

'Ye-es.'

'Dan—my husband, my ex-husband—he used to say I
was like that with dogs. He was afraid he'd come home one
day and there'd be hundreds, like in *Dr Doolittle*. So yes,

I'd love to walk Max.' Sometimes, I found if I ended the speech on the right note, it left people with the impression I'd said something vaguely sensible.

'That would be great. I've been trying to cut back on work, but they keep really insane hours at the partnership. I'll put out his lead and things. Just keep him on it, he's a bit overexcitable.' Max peeked over the basket again at this, as if he understood he was being slandered.

'Why'd you get a dog?' I asked. It was late and I was so tired and drunk I felt I could ask anything. 'I mean with you working so much.'

'I thought it would make us more of a family, I suppose. We were both so busy at work, and trying to look after Alex. She'd cut her hours way back at the bank, but she wasn't coping well. It was supposed to be a compromise, but of course that just means no one is happy. She hated Max. Didn't like his mucky paws and hair all over her beige furniture. But I wouldn't get rid of him—I think once you take something home, you're responsible for it.'

I wondered if he would feel the same about me. 'Have you never had a nanny or au pair or anything?'

He clammed up slightly. 'No. We never left him with anyone. It... We just decided not to.'

'Oh.'

He hesitated. 'Can I ask, what happened with you and... what was his name?'

'Dan. What happened?' God, not this question. 'I...'

I paused for too long, and he began to talk over me. 'Sorry, sorry, none of my business.'

'It's OK. It's just that I...'

'No, no, I shouldn't have asked. I'll let you get to bed.'

'OK. Goodnight. Thanks for the wine.'

'Goodnight, Rachel.' The use of my name was jarring, after we'd talked so frankly. It felt almost as if he was trying to remind me I wasn't his wife, and he wasn't my husband. We were just strangers, sharing the same space. I went to bed, taking out the list book again to read in the pool of lamplight.

Rachel's List of things to do to avoid the post-split, pre-divorce slump

1. Do stand-up comedy

2. Learn to dance

3. Travel somewhere on a whim

4. Do yoga properly

5. Sleep with a stranger

6. Eat something weird

7. Go to a festival

8. Get a tattoo

9. Go horse riding

10. Try an extreme sport

It seemed a paltry lot of things when set against the list of things I'd just lost—job, house, probably the chance of ever having a baby or dog, car, Jamie Oliver Flavour Shaker… I put it aside and turned off the light. In the night I woke up, lost, somewhere halfway down the big bed. *'Dan,'* I whispered, to the empty dark. I'd been looking for his warm back, snoring away, but it wasn't there, and it never would be again.

Things that suck about divorce, number thirty-eight:

there's no one there. Not to tell you off for being late, not to cuddle you close and warm your cold feet, not to snore and keep you awake. There's just you, alone again. Naturally.

Chapter Six

The next day I woke up alone in Patrick's house. Because I had to think of it that way, even if I lived here too. It was very definitely not my house. There were traces of other people all over the place—the old brass clock someone had placed in the bathroom, the candles clustered on the living room fireplace—Diptyque! If I ever had a Diptyque candle, I wouldn't even take it out of its packaging. They're about £1 a whiff. In the hall was a wedding photo, Patrick looking stiff and formal in a top hat and tails. Since he was already a head taller than anyone else in the bridal party, the hat just made him look ridiculous. He was frowning into the camera, as if the light was in his eyes. On his arm was a tiny, beautiful woman—she couldn't have been more than five feet tall. Patrick had mentioned that Michelle's mother was Chinese, and it meant her daughter had been blessed with poker-straight dark glossy hair and a pretty, heart-shaped face. Her wedding dress had been an enormous meringue of lace and tulle, almost but not quite hiding her slender arms and neck. This, then, was Michelle, whose house I was living in, whose dog I was walking, whose husband I was chatting to at night.

The rest of the house was beautifully decorated—arty photos in shabby-chic frames, expensive patterned wallpaper in the bathroom, polished wooden floors, a beige sofa that seemed a startlingly impractical choice with a small child and a dog in the family. There was an astonishing lack of clutter, no dishes left out in the kitchen, no toys on the stairs, no crumbs on the table. I began to feel guilty about the explosion of clothes and books I'd left in my third-floor turret. Even Alex's room was perfectly neat, his toys put away in blue boxes, his Thomas bedspread pulled straight. Patrick had already given me a list of 'house rules', mostly about what went in which recycling bin and how to sort the laundry correctly.

Luckily, Max was just as messy as me. I found him sprawled in his basket, with several chewed socks in there for company. He peered back at me, giving out a vague whiff of damp, ageing dog. Bless him.

I trailed around the kitchen, opening cupboards and trying to orientate myself. It was so strange being alone in someone else's house. Like having a good poke about inside their heads. They never kept anything in a logical place—the tea beside the kettle, surely? The vegetables in the salad drawer? Patrick—and Michelle, the ghost in the house—had a bread bin shaped like a cat. I wondered how Max felt about this. He seemed to be staring at it sadly, as if to say, *Oh, stationary cat, why do you taunt me with your stillness?*

There was a whole cupboard of herbal teas, and that's how I knew Michelle and I would never get on. I liked my tea the colour of brick and with a biscuit dunked in. I suspected she was the type of woman who considered 'celery with a dab of almond butter' to be an acceptable snack. I wasn't even sure what almond butter was. Marzipan?

I felt a presence and realised Max had got out of his basket and was so close he was breathing on my leg. 'Just having a look,' I told him defensively. 'I do live here now.' Even so, I felt like a burglar. I'd ascertained which cupboards held the cleaning stuff, the biscuits, the canned goods—there weren't many of them; this being very much an organic quinoa sort of house. There seemed to be one small cupboard on the end that was closed with a padlock. 'What's in there, Maxxy?' I frowned at it. Murder supplies? The heads of Patrick's previous lodgers? I wondered what my new landlord wasn't telling me. I could hardly protest, given everything I wasn't telling him.

'This is an awful idea.'

'Oh, come on. It'll be fun! Remember we're embracing life and making the most of it!' I wasn't sure I liked this new Pollyanna-style Cynthia. She'd actually arrived on time, changing in the loos of the bar from her terrifying work suit to a flowery dress with high strappy heels. I was wearing jeans and Converse, of course, but she had a cunning plan to get me out of them. 'Ta-da!'

A shoebox with similar heels to hers—black patent Mary Janes. 'But I can't...'

'Of course you can, darling, they were on sale. I practically made money.'

I glared at her. 'You have to stop this. I feel like a charity case.'

'Well, just borrow them, then, if it upsets your communist sensibilities. But you can't dance in Converse.'

I gave in, because she was right, and also because I was amazed she was there—albeit tapping constantly at her phone. 'How's work?' I asked. 'Where are we right now on *The Great Escape* scale of awfulness?'

'We're dropping soil out of our trousers in the exercise yard.'

'So, making progress?'

'Making progress. What about you?'

'We-ell, I'm not having much luck getting interviews. A few possibilities.' I'd applied for every single vaguely art- or design-related job I could find in London, but my inbox was deafeningly empty. When I thought about it, I got a gnawing fear in the pit of my stomach, so I tried to push it away as Emma ran in several minutes later in her work clothes, sensible trousers and a blouse, with paint on her hands and a foul expression. 'God, whose idea was it to meet in town on a school night?'

'Yours.'

'Hmph. Well, I suppose we better do it.' Cynthia gave her a look. Emma forced a smile. 'I mean, it'll be great. Yay! Dancing! My favourite thing! Embracing life!'

Emma had certain physical skills—I'm told at school she was the terror of the netball court, bearing down with murder in her eyes on hapless Goal Defences. She could lift up small children who were having hissy fits over the allocation of the class pencils and carry them right into the 'timeout corner'. She could make a working model of the London Eye using only drinking straws and toilet roll tubes. But one thing she couldn't do was dance. In fact, at uni we had a little dance routine we called 'the Emma', which involved stepping from foot to foot and waving your hands as if trying to dry nail polish. Cheered by the thought that someone might hate this more than me, I pulled on my shiny new shoes and stood nervously on the dance floor.

We were in a bar near St Paul's, all dark lighting and wooden floors. The tables had been pushed back to create an empty space, and around it were gathered twenty or so students, all wearing the same 'going to the guillotine' look of British people who are going to be called upon to dance in public without the aid of alcohol.

List of things British people hate doing in public

1. Dancing

2. Arguing

3. Looking at maps

4. Kissing or PDAs of any kind

5. Expressing any form of disapproval to a figure of authority

6. Nudity

'Hiya, everyone!' The teacher was a dancer. I mean, of course she was. But she was *really* a dancer. Slender, graceful, wearing leg warmers over her dancing shoes and a pink leotard. All the men in the room visibly straightened their spines. 'I'm Nikki, yeah.' She spoiled the graceful impression somewhat with a hard-as-nails Cockney accent. 'If everyone's here, then—'

There was a noise at the back of the room and someone bumbled in, a blur of expensive suit. I saw to my surprise it was Rich. 'He's here?' I said to Cynthia. 'He actually left work?'

She tossed her hair vaguely. 'I thought we'd better try new things—you know what I said about us both working all the time.' He was coming over. Her face morphed into a smile. 'Darling. You made it!'

Rich was frowning and stabbing at his BlackBerry. 'Had to cut the damn meeting short. The partners are *not* happy.'

'Well, you're here now. There's Rachel.'

'Hi, Rich,' I said, making a vague forward movement to hug him, which wasn't reciprocated, so I turned it into a pre-dance stretch instead.

'Hi,' he said briefly. He didn't ask how I was, though this was the first time he'd seen me since the split.

We were all amazed when Cynthia turned up with Rich on her arm. It was Emma's birthday, her twenty-sixth, I think, and we were at a World War II–themed dance. Emma had on red lipstick and a tea dress, and Ian was in a shroud—his idea of humour. I had on a pair of overalls and my hair in a victory roll, which fell out after half an hour. Dan, who didn't really do fancy dress, had reluctantly worn combats and carried a plastic gun. Rich, however, rolled up in a full Navy uniform, which it turned out had actually belonged to his grandfather Admiral Lord Richard Eagleton. At uni, Cynthia had joined us in mocking the public-school boys who banged on about rugger and tuck. Now she'd fallen for one. Granted, back then Rich had been tall, fair and strapping, though now corporate lunching and long hours were leaving him with a distinct brick-like appearance—red, square and hard.

Cynthia stood close to him, snuggling into his arms, and I was left with scowling Emma, who was limbering up as if going into the boxing ring. 'Right. At least I can dance with you if I have to…'

'Male-female partners only, yeah,' called Nikki. 'This

is tango, innit. The dance of love. Maybe you will fall in love *tonight*.'

She made us pair up. Cynthia clung to Rich and I got the feeling that if forced to move she'd draw up some kind of contract to show that her rights of dance partnership were clearly asserted. Emma, still sulking, had somehow been paired with a slightly geeky but cute man in glasses. And me, of course, I got Mr Groper. The only man in the room who was over fifty. He had awful breath and insisted on squeezing me tight. 'It's how you do it,' he said in that man-splaining way of men doing any activity. 'It's a dance of submission. I lead. You follow where I say.'

'We're not doing that,' I heard Emma say to her partner. 'It's 2014, for God's sake. I've read *The Female Eunuch*.'

'Um…me too,' stuttered Sexy Geek Man—I upgraded him on the basis of the Germaine Greer reading.

Nikki had us learn a sliding step—we had to get up close to the other person and then sort of slide our feet round theirs. I kept hearing Emma say sorry as she stepped on Sexy Geek Man's toes. 'Look, it's really better if you just let me lead.'

'It is,' called Cynthia, as she glided past in Rich's arms. Although she was naturally tall and gangly, she'd trained herself out of it with dance lessons before her wedding. Rich had learned at public school, and I'd remembered watching with a sort of mounting fear while he hurled her about the floor during their first dance, in a series of pre-learned moves to the strains of 'You're Beautiful'.

Dan had refused to get lessons for our wedding, pronouncing it 'totally naff'. So it was just us plopping about aimlessly to 'Dancing in the Dark', to totally different rhythms. Sort of a metaphor for our whole marriage, really.

'Not like that. Here, let me show you.' Mr Groper put his hand on my lower back. My very, very lower back.

I'd had enough. 'THANK YOU. I get it.'

Thank God Nikki then told us to change partners. I was hoping for Sexy Geek Man, but he got snapped up by an aggressive-looking girl in spandex, and Emma was on to someone on the far side of the room. Cynthia had Mr Groper, God help her, and I saw Rich had ended up dancing with the teacher, who seemed to be laughing at something he was saying—maybe she found corporate tax really funny. I'd wound up with Adrian. He was very nervous—his palms felt wet against mine and he had sweat stains under the arms of his beige shirt. He was nice, but after a few minutes being manhandled by him, coated in sweat and constantly apologised to, I was a bit fed up. How was this supposed to help me get over my disastropiphany and find a more joyful and fulfilling life? It wasn't fair. *Eat Pray Love* woman got to go to Italy and Bali, and I got to dance with sweaty men in East London.

Things that suck about divorce, number fifty-seven: other women thinking you're suddenly after their short, ugly, balding menfolk. I could catch the suspicious looks when I took a man's hands for the dance, as if I was just dying to seduce Derek, who worked in Accounts and had the remains of his lunch down his tie. I was starting to realise why people talked about their 'other half'. There were some things you just needed another person for. Dancing was one. So was Scrabble.

Another was, well, sex. I remembered that this was on the list too. Did that mean I'd also have to sleep with short men who had sweat issues? I tried to think of things I could do on my own. I could dine in restaurants, smiling mysteriously when asked if it was just for one. I could play solitaire and cook gourmet meals, then eat them by myself with a single candle burning. Oh God. It sounded even worse than sex with a Derek.

'Time for the circle dance, innit,' called Nikki. 'Change partners, yeah.'

I looked around, blinking, to see if my knight in shining armour would appear, dishevelled and gorgeous, having been tempted along to the dance class by his supportive wise-cracking friend, in order to get past the traumatic break-up/bereavement/death of his cat he'd just suffered. He'd see me there in my new shoes and the socks underneath that had pigs on them and think, yes, this is the girl for me...

'Lady needs a partner!' Nikki was yelling behind me. 'Single lady here! Needs a partner! Here you go, handsome gent for you, darlin'.'

I turned hopefully, looked up...then looked down. 'Hi,' said a voice from somewhere near my ribcage. 'I'm Keith.'

As I reluctantly smiled down—way down—I heard an agonised cry from the other side of the room. Emma seemed to have broken Adrian's foot.

I headed home after another day in the post-divorce world—or the post-split, pre-divorce world—tired, a little tipsy, with blisters on my feet from the new shoes. I wondered if this would be my life now. When we were at uni, I used to have a theory I called shoeology—studying Art History leaves you with a lot of time on your hands. The theory was this: relationships are like shoes. There are pretty ones you can't bear to leave in the shop, though you know they will hurt you and ruin your bank balance. You walk tall in those, feeling sexy and strong—until the blisters start. Then there are comfy ones, which let you run and walk easily, until they start to lose their shape. You don't want to wear them out of the house any more. You slump in those shoes, instead of walking tall. And with repeated wear they will simply fall apart.

There are relationships that are like slippers—nice for indoors, but you don't want anyone to see you wearing them. There are situation-specific relationships, like flip-flops or snorkelling flippers—fine for holidays, for example, but with no place in your real life. A key point of shoeology was that nearly every pair hurt at first—like my new dance shoes had chafed. Perhaps the first time I went on a date with someone it would be the same—leaving me with cuts and blisters until I broke them in. And who even was there? Sexy Geek Man had, it turned out, come with his fiancée, a dumpy blonde with a ponytail who commandeered him for the cha-cha.

As I turned my key in the door and went in through the living room, I saw Patrick was putting something into the cupboard on the end—the locked one. 'It's me!' I called needlessly. As I rounded into the kitchen, I saw him click the lock back on and wondered again what was in there— was it possible he shut away his valuables, that he didn't trust me? That was a little depressing, though I supposed we hardly knew each other.

'Oh, hello. I was just going to open some wine.' I wondered if he drank a bottle every night. Dan and I used to do that, when things were very bad and we couldn't talk about it, but I'd cut back since Cynthia had given me a booklet called 'Are you an early-stage addict?' after the night when I had to go and make myself sick in the toilets at All Bar One. I decided I'd just have a few sips. He did pick the best wines, rich and bursting on the tongue. I suspected he did not buy the ones with orange stickers on from the Londis round the corner.

'Good night?'

'Mmm. I'm not sure.' I told him about the Keiths and Adrians, the sweating and the difficulties of correctly crossing in the tango. 'I used to think I was a fairly good dancer, but seriously, I couldn't even do it right once.'

He stood up, holding his hands out to me after wiping them on his cords. 'Come here a second.'

Startled, I did. He was very close suddenly, and the wool of his jumper tickled my face. He smelled of lemons and fabric softener. 'Is it like this?' And he'd twisted me into a perfect cross.

'Yes! Why couldn't I get it before?'

'The man is supposed to lead. If it's not working, then it's his fault.' He dropped my hands quickly, sat down again. 'We had lessons. You know, for the wedding and that. Me and…my ex-wife. Wife. Whatever.' He seemed unable to say her name. 'She wanted this whole routine, to wow people. I'd always hated dancing, but I suppose I sort of enjoyed it. She didn't like letting me lead though.'

'Yeah, it is a bit sexist.' Oops, half the delicious wine was gone already. 'How's Alex feeling about the whole thing?'

His face changed. 'He's fine. They keep in touch, and there's Skype and stuff…you know. I've been trying not to let him hear anything about her affair. It's always assumed men are the ones who do it, but when you find out your wife cheated, well, it hurts.'

The topic was making me squirm. I didn't want to talk about this, or think about it. He misread my reaction. 'Rachel. I'm sorry. I'm completely oversharing and we barely know each other.'

'No, I don't mind. It's…'

'I'm sorry. I should let you get to bed. I tend to ramble on, I know.' Suddenly, we'd gone back to landlord and tenant, not what I wanted. He was washing the dishes, putting the bottle in the correct recycling bin, so I went up the three flights of stairs with my new shoes in hand. My blisters throbbed as I slipped my feet under the covers. I used to think Dan was a one-in-a-million shoe—those sexy heels you can dance in all night and still run in to catch the bus, that would shield me from the broken glass and chewing gum of life's pavements, and would never leave me with blisters. Then they started to chafe and bind, so some days I felt as if I might leave bloody footprints on the ground.

There's a lesson there—it's hard to wear one pair of shoes for the rest of your life. That and always keep the receipt.

Rachel's List of things to do to avoid the
post-split, pre-divorce slump

1. Do stand-up comedy

2. ~~Learn to dance~~

3. Travel somewhere on a whim

4. Do yoga properly

5. Sleep with a stranger

6. Eat something weird

7. Go to a festival

8. Get a tattoo

9. Go horse riding

10. Try an extreme sport

Chapter Seven

Outside the door was the sound of squishing. *Blop blop blop.* I put down the box I was reluctantly unpacking and listened. 'Alex?'

There was quiet for a moment. Then a small voice said, 'It's not me.'

I got up from my table and opened the door. 'Hey, look, it *is* you.'

His face creased in existential uncertainty. He was wearing his yellow mac and red wellies, and on his head his train driver's cap flattened his gorgeous dark fuzz. 'What's in there today?' I indicated his wellies. Patrick encouraged him to wear them for some reason, both out of the house and in.

He stepped carefully from one foot to the other. 'Guess.'

Something dry. 'Crisps?' I guessed. He nodded. 'What type?'

'Orange ones.'

'Wotsits? You've got Wotsits in your wellies?'

He nodded solemnly.

In the time I'd spent in this house so far, I had picked up
that Alex had a weird habit of putting things in his wellies.
Mostly food—Angel Delight, avocado, biscuits—but also
gravel, marbles and once his friend Zoltan's hamster. Luckily, Harry was rescued before any feet went into the boots,
and Alex received a lecture about not putting living things
in the wellies—and yes, frogspawn counted.

'Why does he do it?' I'd asked Patrick, over what had
become our nightly glass of wine.

'I think it's something to do with safety—he puts in
things he likes. To keep them there, maybe.'

I didn't want to ask why Alex would be afraid of losing
the things he loved, and for a moment, I felt stunned by
gratitude that Dan and I hadn't managed to have a baby. I
couldn't imagine bringing a child into the middle of everything that was going on.

'What are you doing?' Alex was watching me setting out
my art supplies on my new desk. 'Are you colouring in?'

'Sort of.' I showed him some of my old drawings, drafts
of wedding caricatures and funny sketches for magazines.
'People ask me to do pictures for their birthdays, or weddings. Cartoons.'

He looked puzzled. 'Cartoons like on TV?'

'Well, yes, those start off as pictures too.'

'They're on *TV*.' Alex was sceptical.

I gave up trying to explain animation, largely because I
couldn't understand it myself. Alex fixed me with his dark
eyes. 'Will you do a funny picture for me, Rachel?'

I looked at my things, my Japanese paper inset with silk,
my fine ink pens, my paintbrushes and easel. It would be
the simplest thing in the world to pick them up and draw.
After all, I used to make money from it. I knew I could do

it. And yet I hadn't lifted a pen or a brush since the Incident. 'I don't know, Alex. I...'

'Oh, please! Max really wants one. He told me he did.'

I sighed. I had to start sometime, and no one else had to see it except a small child and a dog, after all. I selected a fresh sheet of card and lifted my favourite drawing pen, feeling it snug between my fingers. I took a deep breath. 'What would you like a picture of?'

'Max,' he said immediately. On cue, the little dog emerged from round the door and took a leap onto my lap, putting his head on the table. Two pairs of dark eyes watched me. I've never really wanted to draw 'straight'—which is why I didn't go to art school and failed Art A-level—but I could do funny things, doodles and caricatures, and people seemed to like them. Or at least they had before the Incident. I quickly drew Max, a sad-faced dog, all droopy ears and big eyes. 'There you go.' In a thought bubble was a picture of some biscuits surrounded by hearts.

Alex's laugh went right to my heart, the purest sound I thought I'd ever heard.

I held out my hand to him. 'Come on, let's go and have a biscuit ourselves. But you can't eat it with your boots on.'

'Why not?' His hand was warm and sticky.

'Um...it's a very old rule. Bad manners.'

With this combination of bribery and lies, I persuaded him to let me rinse the Wotsits off his feet. Then I followed him downstairs, plucking up washing and toys as I did. I'd fallen into this routine in the two weeks I'd spent in the house, and it was a peaceful, ordered existence. When the kid was in bed, Patrick and I talked, getting to know each other, gently skirting around the topics of Michelle and Dan. It was so nice to have someone to cook for—for the past year or so Dan had rarely stopped working for dinner, or ate with his BlackBerry in his lap. Patrick was a real foodie, and when he cooked it was all seared scallops and marinated venison. My parents would have choked—Monday night was Dolmio and pasta for them.

'Rachel!' came an impatient voice up the stairs. 'You said I could have a biscuit!'

'Coming,' I called, scooping up the disembodied face of James the Red Engine on my way downstairs.

Today was going to suck anyway, because I had to see Dan's mum. Jane was everything I wasn't—elegant, controlled, decorous. I had never once seen her without heels on, even round the house. She'd been a nice mother-in-law, I supposed—all thoughtful little gifts and cards in the post when I had an interview, or an anniversary, or it was the pot plant's birthday, that sort of thing. But often I'd wished Dan had a gaggle of siblings milling about, so I wouldn't have to go to that beautiful empty house and answer questions in strained silence as the clock ticked.

It was Saturday, so Patrick was at the kitchen table as I tried to leave, watching me flap about trying to find my shoes while he drank coffee from his posh silver machine. I was scared of that thing. It had more buttons than a NASA launch pad. 'What is it today?'

'Mother-in-law,' I said miserably, lacing up my Converse with one foot on the stairs.

'Ah.' He winced. 'Luckily, my in-laws are in New York. I had to ask Michelle's father, the congressman, for permission to marry her.'

'Isn't that a bit medieval?' Dan had suggested the same, and once I had stopped laughing I'd told him not to be daft.

I hadn't asked Dad for permission for anything since I was seven, and unless it was about Airfix models or *Countdown*, he wasn't going to have an opinion.

'She insisted. I keep wondering if I'm supposed to sign her back in again like a hire car.' Look at him, making jokes about divorce while he ate those little teeth-shattering biscuits he liked. He had come on.

Finally, I was ready. A bit of dishevelment would probably help my case anyway. 'I better go,' I said reluctantly.

'Good luck,' Patrick crunched.

'Thanks. I need it.'

Things that suck about divorce, number fifty-nine: having to prise yourself away from your in-laws.

Jane was early. She was always early for everything and, as I was always ten minutes late, this stressed me out. I could see her through the window of the café, her hair perfect, her suit pressed, looking anxiously at her watch. For a moment I was tempted to run away, never have to see her again in my life—wasn't that what divorce was for?—but I remembered what I had to do, took a deep breath and jiggled open the door.

She put on a strained smile. 'Rachel, darling.'

'Hello.'

There was an insanely awkward moment where she reached to hug me and I backed off, so her Chanel lipstick smudged on my cheek. 'Sorry I'm late.'

'Oh, you're not—'

'Well, I am—'

'Well, that's all right. Would you like coffee?' A slip-up, rare for Jane. She must have been nervous. I don't drink coffee and never have, and she'd been pointedly remembering this since I first came to her house aged twenty, in my muddy red Converse that I'd drawn on with fabric pen.

'Tea, please,' I told the waiter.

List of things you get in posh coffee shops

1. Jam jars made into cups

2. Electronic timers, because letting your tea brew for three seconds too long or too little will tear a hole in the space-time continuum

3. Civet-poo coffee from Bali

4. Piles of old luggage instead of tables

5. Cakes made without egg, dairy, wheat or sugar (I mean, what is the point?)

6. More than one Apple device per customer

7. Awkward meetings with your soon-to-be ex-mother-in-law (that's a lot of hyphens)

Jane and I looked at each other. 'I—' I reached into my bag and took out the lump of cotton wool. 'Before I forget.'

She coloured. 'Oh, thank you. You didn't have—'

But I did. When someone gave you a family heirloom for an engagement ring, you couldn't keep it when they decided they no longer wanted to be married to you.

She unwrapped it—why, I wasn't sure, to check it was there, or more likely just for something to do—and the wink of diamond and sapphire filled my eyes. I couldn't believe it when Dan presented me with this rock and I was supposed to put it on my nail-bitten, ink-smeared left hand. Jane stowed it in her expensive bag and I said a brief farewell to the ring that had weighed me down for three years.

'So. Are you all right, dear?'

I shrugged. 'It's been hard. It wasn't easy to find a place, but I'm settling in now. It's been tough trying to find a new job, but I have a few interviews lined up and...'

Jane's face had tightened. Like many people who didn't lack for money, she hated talking about it.

'How's Dan?' I asked carefully.

'He's— I'm not sure. Won't talk, but he's working a lot and eating junk food. I worry. It just seems such a shame,' she said. I stiffened. 'You seemed so happy. I was looking at your wedding photos this morning. It was such a nice day. And of course, Michael was so happy...' Her eyes filled with tears and I felt my own nose sting. Dan's father had died six months after we got married, another sudden stroke carrying him away for good. It had been a lot to take so early on in our marriage.

Our drinks arrived, and I stared at the poncey infuser that came with my tea. I'd been doing my best to block out our wedding, how much I'd loved my dress, how the sun shone even though it was only April, how my mum got drunk for the first time in her life and danced on stage to 'Tiger Feet'.

I could feel it rising up in me, that wave of dark that drowned out even tears. I gasped for breath and said with difficulty, 'We were happy then. But we changed.'

'People don't change, darling. He's still the same Dan he was. I know his silly job has eaten him up, but maybe a holiday...'

'We had a holiday.' A few months before, we'd gone to Antigua on a last-ditch 'making the effort' trip. It was a disaster. I could almost hear the pounds cascading out of our bank account with every suck and hum of the air conditioner.

We were miles from anywhere in a package hotel full of Russians in thongs—and that was just the men. The drinks were watered down and the evening buffet gave Dan raging food poisoning. He stayed in the room for days, groaning, and I walked listlessly between the bar and the pool, trying to avert my eyes from Vladimir's hairy nether regions. I don't think I've ever been as unhappy in my life as I was on that 'luxury' holiday.

'What about couples counselling?'

We'd actually tried that too, for two sessions, which ended when Dan had stormed out kicking the door and calling me a particularly horrible name. I know he was…upset about what happened, but still.

Jane was speaking very carefully. My heart began to thud. 'You know, people can forgive a lot. I'm sure this thing now, with the girl…it won't last. He's just upset. I know him.'

I kept my face very still. What girl? *What girl?*

'So maybe if you both could get past…everything that went on, give it another try…'

I had to get out of there. My voice came from my stomach, weary and desperate. 'No, Jane. People don't get past it. I tried. He kicked me out. So no. I'm sorry. He said there was no chance.'

She dabbed at her lips, leaving a red stain on the napkin, like a tiny ruined heart. We jostled awkwardly over the bill, and then I abruptly left. I could see her through the steamed-up café window, the woman I'd thought I'd know for the rest of my life. Now I'd probably never see her again. Things that suck about divorce, number sixty-seven:

wondering whether you're pleased about that, or hurt, or somewhere in between, and what that says about you.

I walked back to the house past the shops of Hampstead, the dinky baby boutiques and upmarket clothes shops. Everywhere were yummy mummies with Boden tops and knee boots, crunching biscotti while adorable toddlers ran about in yellow macs. I was alone, adrift. I walked and walked to try to stay ahead of that wave inside me. I knew what it was like when it hit—the black water filled with rocks and debris, the suffocating slap of it. I walked until I was almost running, panting, not sure of what it was I was trying to get away from. What was I even running to? I had nowhere to go.

I was trying not to think about what Jane had said, wrapping the words in cotton wool like the ring I'd given back. Dan had a girl. Who was she? *Who was she?* In my mind I rifled through his Facebook friends. Someone from work? Most likely, he practically lived there. So who?

I couldn't believe he was ready to see someone else. I was nowhere near it. I was like an emotional octopus—legs everywhere, suckers desperately trying to attach onto anyone I could find. Just trying not to get swept away. He was moving on, swimming happily in the ocean of single life, and I was belly-flopping on the beach. I needed to work on that metaphor too.

Patrick was still in the kitchen. Damnit. I wanted to eat a thousand Jaffa Cakes and curl up to cry. 'You're back early.'

I tried to keep my voice steady. 'I thought I might walk Max.' Anything to keep moving.

'I walked him earlier.' He saw my face. 'Was it rough?'

I could only nod, and then the wave hit and my voice was

drowned in thick, choking tears. Patrick did what any man would do when a woman started crying in front of him—looked awkward. 'Oh. Let me get some tissues.' I managed to get a hold of myself while he was searching for the lavender-scented, balm-infused tissues Michelle bought—no Kleenex for that lady—so when he came back I was just staring at my hands, callused and bare, and snivelling a bit. He made me tea and found biscuits, until finally there was no more displacement activity and he had to talk to me. 'Did you fight?'

'No—she's very kind. Always has been. That's what makes it hard, especially when I don't de-de-deserve it.' I blotted my leaking eyes. I tried to think how I could explain. It's hard to tell your worst, darkest secrets to a stranger. 'During the end of the marriage, there were…things…things that made it worse…you know…and now she says he's seeing someone, already, and I guess it's my fault…'

He was standing behind me and, for a moment, I felt his hand on my shoulder. 'You mustn't beat yourself up. A failing marriage is like a war, Rachel—you'll both do terrible things, and neither of you will win. Even if your ex is seeing someone, it'll be a rebound thing, a disaster. You know that.'

'Hmm.' I stared at my hands, thinking—he wouldn't say that, if he knew.

'I know,' he said brightly, 'why don't you plan something off your list? I'll get it.' He took his hand away and I got a whiff of his sharp citrus smell, and it flashed into my head—number five: *sleep with a stranger.*

'Sounds good,' I said shakily, making a mental note to avoid that page. 'But which one?'

He was leafing through the book, which I kept on top of the fridge. 'How about stand-up comedy?'

I smiled. 'Yes, I'm hilarious right now. Would you suggest

the routine where I cry hysterically, or the one where I blow my nose loudly?'

'I think you're very funny. You always make me laugh when you're talking to Max.'

'Thanks. But I really can't. Look at me, I'm not fit for anything right now.'

Patrick looked at me helplessly, like a gadget that he didn't know how to fix. 'Is there anything I can do?'

I blew my nose. 'You've let me live here. That's a massive thing. I know I'm not much fun, moping around listening to Magic FM, songs for saddos, eating all the biscuits...'

'I've got an idea.' He leapt up. 'You sit here a minute.' He went into the living room and I heard him scrabbling around. 'Have you seen my iPad?'

'It's on the dock there.'

'Great. Now wait a second.' I heard more fiddling. 'Oh, what's wrong with this bloody thing? "Device cannot sync at this time". What does that even mean?'

I sniffed. 'You know, they said that about the *Titanic* too and look how that turned out.'

'Hey, that's good! See, you are funny. OK, it's working. Wait there a minute.'

I waited in the kitchen. My eyes felt red and sore and I was starting to be embarrassed about weeping in front of him.

'Hey, Rachel, what video is this?' Patrick was standing in the doorway. He wore a black polo-neck jumper, and on top of his head was a pale-coloured swimming cap, making him look bald if you squinted. Music began to play from the dock. He opened his eyes up really wide and started to sing along. 'It's been some-thing hours and I don't know how many dayyyys...since you took your love awa-a-ay.'

It was the video for 'Nothing Compares 2 U', which I'd
been playing on a loop since I moved in. I smiled. 'All right,
I take your point.'

'I'd just like to know though, what doctor is this she's
been going to? She's already said she goes out all night and
sleeps all day, and he's advising "girl, you better have fun no
matter what you do"? Fun is the last thing she needs. I'd like
to know who this doctor is, so I can have him struck off.'

'Yes, yes, very good. I'll write it down for my comedy
routine.'

'OK, well, how about this? Up the tempo a bit.'

He fiddled with the dock, then took off the swimming
cap, fluffed up his hair and pouted, dancing around by himself. 'What are the words again? Something about working
in a cocktail bar? Duh-duh duh-duh baby! Duh-duh duh-
duh wo-oh-oh-oooh!'

'Actually, we prefer the term "mixologist" these days.
"Waitress" is kind of demeaning. I'm waiting on a callback
about a part in *EastEnders* anyway.'

The swimming cap had left a red line around his forehead. 'Are you cheered up at all?'

I thought about it. 'A little bit.'

'Good!'

'Will you put the swimming hat on again though?'

'I knew it. Latex—works every time with the laydeez.'

'This explains a lot to me about why you're single.'

'Ha ha. So listen, will you think about the stand-up
comedy? It must be on the list for a reason, and it's a good
place to start.'

I heard myself say, 'I'll do it if you do.'

Chapter Eight

'Now, I'm recently single, so if you have any nice available friends…or brothers…or dads…granddads…I'm not too fussy. Seen all that stuff about *Fifty Shades of Grey*, eh? The trouble is, they don't make erotica for bookish ladies like me. My idea fantasy would be this—I'm a librarian. A man comes in wearing braces and glasses. Hey, got a copy of Sylvia Plath's *Ariel*? Which version? The one her damn husband didn't butcher, of course. Then we roll around in the stacks discussing gender politics.'

I crossed all that out with a big X and wrote a little note to myself: THIS IS RUBBISH.

'So, I'm recently single and I listen to a lot of Sad, I mean, Magic FM. You know in the song "Nothing Compares 2 U"? How great is Sinead O'Connor's doctor, advising her to have fun no matter what she does? All mine ever says is, "Really, are you sure it's just two to three units a week?" and "Come back in a week if it's still itching." Although I can't help wondering if in her emotional state

Sinead is confusing "doctor" with "low-rate pimp".' That
was better. Maybe I could do a whole riff on how when
you have a break-up you spend all your time listening to
maudlin pop songs, and overanalysing the lyrics of them.

I think it was the promise of Patrick on stage that had
made me say yes to the comedy. His uptight English manner making jokes and performing—I couldn't picture it.
So now I was neurotically writing down 'comedy'. What
was funny? I was getting divorced and effectively homeless and had no money—hilarious stuff! I'd have my own
sitcom by the weekend.

Things that suck about divorce, number one hundred and
forty-eight: there's no one who knows you better than you
know yourself, to tell you when, actually, you really can't
do something and should just stay at home and watch TV.

Patrick, with his annoying Type A personality, had already booked us into a weekend course by tapping two
buttons on his iPad. He was as bad as Cynthia for actually making things happen. By lunchtime, all I had was
a page of crossed-out phrases like 'loose women—tight
women, more like' and stupid lists like 'things you leave
behind when you move out of your house after divorce (KT
Tunstall CD, lemon juicer)'. I decided to go downstairs for
lunch. All my cartoon work was sitting undone, it was past
Doctors time and I hadn't even started on any of the moving admin I still had to do (change address, file for divorce,
buy laundry basket).

Patrick was at the kitchen table, his drawing board sitting
unused beside him. He'd decided to 'work from home' that
day—i.e. sit about obsessing about jokes. He was staring
at a piece of paper and muttering to himself. I recognised
a fellow comedy casualty. 'Struggling?'

'Is it just me, or is nothing funny any more? Literally nothing?'

'I doubt I would even laugh at a video of a cat running into a wall right now. That's how bad things are.'

'Why are we doing this, Rachel?'

I spooned Darjeeling into the tea infuser. 'Because if you can't go back, you have to go forward.'

He seemed to find this cheering. 'That's good. And I can't go back, can I? Neither can you. But do we actually have to go so *far* forward? I mean, we'll be on stage. The last time I did that I was nineteen and rocking out with my band, The Corduroy Underground, at my university summer ball. We were awful.'

'What did you play?'

'Bass. I sang too. It was sort of my band.'

'Do you play now?'

'Oh, no. Michelle made me put the guitars in the attic. They were cluttering up the place, she said, and Alex might fall over them.'

I thought about this as my tea brewed—I believe that was why it was invented, in fact. To let your thoughts infuse slowly as the leaves did. 'Patrick? Have you thought any more about doing your own list? They say divorce is the time to do things—you know, experiment. Take back all the parts of yourself you put away for the person you were with.' As I said it, I imagined bits of him locked in an attic—music, a sense of fun maybe, his laugh, which I hadn't heard since I moved in. 'So what would be on yours? You said extreme sports before.'

'Oh, I don't have time for a list.'

'You've got time to watch all five series of *Breaking Bad*,' I pointed out.

'Hmm. You have a point.'

'Go on, write it down. It'll free you for comedy at least. Get the brain moving, that sort of thing. Tell me one thing you wish you'd done in the past five years.'

'Get drunk,' he said right away. 'That sounds bad, I know. I just used to really enjoy going to the pub, chatting about nothing, getting into stupid rows about who was the best Batman, that sort of thing. Since Alex I've been too scared, in case he needs me.'

'Couldn't someone babysit?'

'I don't know who I'd trust.' I wondered why he was so reluctant to leave Alex with anyone—had he and Michelle just been really overprotective? 'I'll think of a way, I promise. No divorced person should have to do it without the aid of alcohol.'

'Glad to have you in my corner.'

'What else?'

'Skydiving is a definite. I've always wanted to try it.'

'OK. We have getting drunk and skydiving. Maybe not at the same time. More?'

He was on a roll now. 'I'd like to go to a festival. Michelle never would—she hates camping, and she's not much of a music fan.'

'A festival is on my list, so you can't have it, but you could certainly go. Alex could go to that,' I said, scribbling it down.

'Hmm, yes, he probably could. Max too.' I was getting another mental image—the little dog at Glastonbury, watching a field full of posh hippies dance about with no clothes on.

Patrick's suggestions were coming fast now. He also wanted to buy a really nice car, take Alex overseas for the first time, learn to fillet fish—I know, of all the things you can do in the world he wanted to handle fish innards; I guess the gut wants what the gut wants—take up climbing and enter Max in a dog show. These were getting more outlandish now. I could more easily imagine Max skydiving than obeying dog commands.

'You should put that you want to play in a band again,' I said. 'That was the first thing you mentioned, remember?'

'Oh, I don't know about that. I've sort of lost touch with most of my mates. Been so busy with work and Alex, you know.'

'True friends don't mind if you don't see them for a while.'

'I'd be rubbish now. I haven't played in years.'

'You think I was any good at dancing? The idea is to be slightly terrified at all times.' I rapped the list with my knuckles. 'If I can offer my opinion as a professional listmaker, these are too safe.'

'Skydiving? Climbing?'

'Yeah, but you're not scared of those, are you? I mean, no more than a normal person who isn't mad. You don't mind heights?'

'Not really.'

'Then it's too safe. So what's your idea of hell? Like the most terrifying thing you could do of an evening? Nothing with sharks though, please,' I said quickly.

'Why not?'

'I am really, really afraid of sharks.'

'You know they only cause about ten deaths worldwide per year? More people die from bee stings. Are you afraid of bees?'

'Bees don't come up from underneath you and bite you in half.'

'Or lightning, that's pretty dangerous. Are you scared of that?'

'Again, not likely to chomp me.'

'Tigers? They can be pretty chompy.'

'I'd see them in time to run away.'

'I see. So it's the element of surprise that frightens you?'

'A bit. Mostly though, it's the chomping. Now, pick something scary, that isn't about sharks.'

'I suppose…go on a date sometime.' He said this last very suddenly. Almost shyly. 'I mean, I don't want…you know. Your number five.'

He was referring to 'sleep with a stranger'. 'Er, neither do I.'

'OK. Dating does scare me, so it definitely counts, but I'd just like a bit of female company. Someone who didn't want to talk about Thomas the Tank Engine, or whose turn it was to clean the loo, or—'

'—whether you need to go to the garden centre to buy some trellising, or who was going to call the chimney sweep—'

'—or the kid, when he sleeps, when he poops, whether his nursery is "pushing" him enough, or—'

'—if it's time to change the car and whether you should upgrade to the new Ford Focus this winter.'

He smiled. 'I guess it's a while since either of us flirted over cocktails.'

'Yeah.' As he went to make coffee, I wondered if he would ever consider me female company. Clearly not.

Patrick's List of things to do to avoid the
post-split, pre-divorce slump

1. Climbing

2. Skydiving

3. Play on stage again

4. Get drunk

5. Go on a date

6. Learn to fillet fish

7. Enter Max into a dog show

8. Buy a nice car

9. Take Alex overseas

'You're still missing one,' I said, tapping the pen. 'That's only nine.'

'Who says it has to be ten?'

'Everyone knows lists have to be in tens.'

'What are you, some kind of list fascist?'

'It's just more…pleasing that way. Anything else you want to do—learn a language, hike the Grand Canyon?'

'I've done that.'

'Show-off.'

'It was OK. Hot.'

'So there's no number ten?'

'Put this down for now—number ten equals, find a number ten.'

'All right. Though just so you know, I disapprove of this meta-list-making approach.'

'Noted.'

'So.'

In front of me, the darkened room could have held any number of people—hundreds, even. Part of my brain knew it contained only fifty or so, but the rest of me was trying to run away and hide behind my own back.

I smiled. Always smile, that was lesson one. Don't seem nervous. Even if you're afraid to open your mouth in case you're sick all over the front row.

'Hello!' Always say something then wait for an answer. It engages the audience. Lesson two.

'Hello!' came back the lusty cry, reinforcing the impression that there really were hundreds of them. I blinked in the spotlight.

'My name's Rachel and...' Oh bugger, I hadn't done the microphone. You always had to 'do the microphone' first. That was actually lesson one. Somehow I found the idea of taking the mike from its holder, in front of all those people, more terrifying than anything else. I wasn't sure my hands could remember how to perform even the simplest action.

It was a Sunday night, and we were in the back room of a pub somewhere near Camden. Alex was staying with a school friend, which Patrick was apparently OK with. This was the moment I had somehow believed would never take place, even when we'd been on the intensive course for the past two days, even when the event had started and I was waiting in line for my turn to perform.

I had gone on fifth, after Adam, Jonny, 'Big Dave' and Asok from our course. I was wearing jeans and a T-shirt that said 'Devon knows how they make it so creamy'—the West Country featured heavily in my comedy shtick.

I had been silent for maybe three seconds, but every moment felt at least ten times longer on stage. I took a deep breath and tried to remember my own name.

'I'm Rachel, and I'm from Devon, as you can maybe tell. I recently became single after a long time.' I paused. 'You could have "awwed" there, but I suppose we don't know each other that well... That's OK. Anyway, I'm so out of the loop with London dating I feel like a foreigner. I went on a date recently and it was as if we were speaking different languages. He was very into computer games and we don't really have these in Devon. It took us a while to figure out the iPad 2s we'd been sold were actually just really expensive Etch A Sketches.'

A laugh! Someone had laughed! I knew the gang were here, but I couldn't see them with the lights, and Patrick was waiting his own turn backstage somewhere, so I couldn't be sure who it was, but it was for definite a laugh! Either that or someone choking to death on the suspect beer the place served.

'In order to help me through this trying time, I've been listening to a lot of music…' I did my Sinead O'Connor stuff. There was a mixture of chuckles and groans—I could see the faces of the front row, contorted with laughter. A rocket-shot of adrenaline went up from the soles of my Converse. This was going to be OK. 'My real favourite though is Beyoncé—I like to think of her as kind of my spirit guide. But I do find it interesting that her name is clearly the past tense of a French verb. I wonder what "to beyonce" actually means. To be totally fabulous? To look great in hot pants? To call your child a really stupid name?'

I took a deep breath. Halfway through.

'I'm from Devon originally, but my mother is Irish. So if I miss my family when I'm in London, I can always be reminded by going on Facebook, because it's basically a giant nosy Irish mum. All those questions:

'Do you know this person outside Facebook? Where were you born? What do you do for work? Have you a boyfriend? Do you know these people? Did you go to the toilet before we went out? Take your coat off or you won't feel the benefit.' Here I adopted a sort of cod Irish/West Country accent, which sounded nothing like my actual mother. I prayed she would never find out about any of this.

'Or else it's always showing you pictures of people who're just doing better at life than you. I sometimes think Facebook is like playing popular nineties board game The Game of Life, like you did when you were a kid. You get ten points for an engagement, extra if the question's popped up Kilimanjaro while you're in the middle of a charity trek for blind dogs. Twenty points for smug baby pics. If you're losing at the game of Facebook, it's even worse than losing at The Game of Life. Turns out, the friends who are super-smug now, with their holidays and babies and charity runs, are the same ones back then who'd boast about having to upgrade their plastic car so they could fit in all their little plastic peg children.'

The end of my routine had arrived suddenly, like the end of an escalator. Oh. I stopped. Smiled. 'I've been Rachel Kenny, thank you very much.'

And I was done, just like that. It was over. I took my seat, hearing actual applause and chuckles. As I did, I caught sight of Patrick, who was on after Gary—the guy off the course who told lots of dodgy Rohypnol jokes. I hurried to my seat so I'd have time to sit down and tut passive-aggressively. Patrick was too busy staring at the floor, mouthing his routine, to catch my eye.

List of popular topics in stand-up comedy

1. Dating

2. Public transport

3. Being stoned

4. Sexual assault—in a totally jokey, not offensive way, 'kay?

5. Hilarious observations on everyday activities, like doing the shopping and getting unexpected items in the bagging area

6. Stand-up comedy (meta)

I was pretty sure where Emma was after the end of Gary's piece, as I could hear her sighing loudly every time he made an off-colour joke about car boots, duct tape, Rohypnol cocktails and many other topics that were about as funny as a colonoscopy. It was this in itself that made me glad I'd tried it—otherwise I and every other woman in the world would spend eternity sitting in the audience listening to men tell jokes to other men about assaulting us. The world was our bad comedy show. At the very least we deserved to get in a few one-liners about penis size and tampons.

Then, thank God, Gary was off, to lacklustre applause and a clear 'SEXIST RUBBISH' heckle, I suspected from Emma, and Patrick was shambling on stage in his cords and curls, looking for all the world like a posh TV expert on antiques or civil war battlefields. I almost felt more nervous than I had for myself.

He 'did' the microphone with a quick flick and rooted himself at the front of the space. Rule number four—don't move about the stage too much. 'Hello, London Borough of Lambeth!' Some laughs. 'I'm Patrick, and I recently found myself becoming a single parent.'

Some real 'awws' from the audience this time. Whatever.

'Thank you. When I want to really impress women, I pretend my wife died in a tragic threshing accident on our farm and I have to raise little Billy all alone, but there aren't that many threshers in North London, so in reality she's fine. Just not fine with me. Apparently, she thinks I'm not stylish enough.' Another laugh, as he indicated his brown cords and fisherman's jumper. 'She says I'm the only man she knows who thinks the eighties were a genuinely good decade for fashion choice.' He shifted slightly. 'I'm getting used to being a single dad. I used to work in a very busy office, and now I do the school run, but you know, I've noticed a lot of similarities. For a start, in my office, if people don't get want they want, they also sometimes lie on the floor and have a tantrum, or pee in the managing director's shoes. But the CEO didn't take it too kindly when I offered him nap time and a snack of Dairylea Cheese Slices.'

Laughing. People were laughing. I could see why. He was very natural and appealing on stage, smiling, eyes open, gesturing to people in the front row and addressing them directly. It was all going to be fine. I let out a big sigh of relief.

'You were amazing! Hilarious! Much better than all those rubbish misogynists. In fact, who do I complain to about that?'

Cynthia bustled past a ranting Emma to hug me. 'You were great, darling. One of the best, easily.'

'Thank you!'

'I just wish Rich had come… We had such fun at the tango class, but since then he's been working non-stop.'

I wasn't sure Rich would like it much here. Even though to me, in the grip of a serious adrenaline rush, the grotty pub looked sublime. The flat beer tasted like Dom Perignon, the sticky floor looked glorious and I had never loved my friends more, even if Cynthia had her BlackBerry glued to her hand as usual, and Emma was scowling around her and wearing a T-shirt that said 'A WOMAN NEEDS A MAN LIKE A FISH NEEDS A BICYCLE', and Ian was looking decidedly hangdog with jealousy.

'You know, I think I should give it a go. This.' He waved his arms around.

'Comedy? Or opening a smelly pub?'

'Comedy. Most of those guys were *rubbish*.' He was just as loud as Emma. 'I could do way better than that. I mean, you were OK, I suppose, but the others...'

'Well, do it, then. It's not that bad.' I had conveniently suppressed the entire weekend of gnawing terror beforehand and the fact I hadn't slept in two days. 'That's the whole point, isn't it? The rest of you are meant to do things with me?'

'I reckon I could make it on the scene.'

'We call it the circuit, in the business,' I said, to annoy him.

'Hmph. Your landlord was good too. Natural.'

'He's not really my—' I stopped, because I didn't know what to call him. My employer? My friend? Nothing was right. He was coming over, a warm glow bathing his face and his curls dishevelled. To my surprise, he enveloped me in a hug. We'd never done that before. I breathed him in for a second, his aftershave and the faint tang of excited sweat, and felt his jumper against my face, because he was so much taller than me. I disengaged, a little breathless.

He was grinning. 'We did it!'

'You were great!'

'No, you were great!'

'Oh, do you think so? I sort of messed up that bit about Facebook, and—'

'No, you were great. I nearly forgot my set-up punch near the end and…'

I realised Emma, Ian and Cynthia were all staring at us as we jabbered, sweaty and wild-eyed with joy. 'These are my friends,' I said. How was I going to describe him? 'And, everyone, this is…Patrick.'

Rachel's List of things to do to avoid the post-split, pre-divorce slump

1. ~~Do stand-up comedy~~

2. ~~Learn to dance~~

3. Travel somewhere on a whim

4. Do yoga properly

5. Sleep with a stranger

6. Eat something weird

7. Go to a festival

8. Get a tattoo

9. Go horse riding

10. Try an extreme sport

Chapter Nine

'Hi! I'm Rachel. I'm a confident self-starter, I love touching base with people…er, not in a sexy way…' Oh God. This was going to be a disaster. Dan had coached me heavily for my last job interview, for a low-ranking comms job in the same council where he'd just taken up the exalted post of Head of Waste Services. In other words, he dealt with bins and recycling and shouted at people for fly-tipping. I suppose it was sort of related to his degree in Environmental Politics—though I'd always pictured him making impassioned speeches in the House of Commons, or chaining himself to whaling ships. 'But recycling is really important,' he would tell me earnestly. 'Household waste is responsible for millions of tons of emissions!'

And as for my job in Surrey, I suppose moving coloured text-boxes around was kind of related to design, and it was my own fault for not going to art school, having been thoroughly intimidated by my A-level teacher, who didn't consider illustration to be a valid art form, much preferring the moody wire coat hanger sculptures by Fiona Martin, with titles like *Hunger* and *Pain*.

I was rooting through my wardrobe of jeans and shabby New Look skirts, trying to find something that might say professional, yet creative, yet reliable, yet a totally fun gal. With no Dan to put me through my paces, shouting in 'Where do you see yourself in five years?' as I shampooed my hair—my answer being, probably in the shower again—I was petrified. My hair had frizzed out, and my serum had gone missing from my en suite. I suspected a certain curly-haired landlord and sure enough, in the main bathroom, I found the tube sitting empty on the side. 'Patrick!' I shouted in frustration. I'd have to go looking like Barry from *Brookside*. Soon I was out, hoicking up unfamiliar tights and trying to get the buttons of my shirt done up over newly discovered boobs. Misery eating had some unexpected side effects, especially with Patrick and I taking it in turns to make dinner each night.

I took the tube to Highgate, where I'd answered an ad for an 'artist's assistant'. It didn't pay much, but I thought it might be OK—cleaning brushes, nodding intelligently as they explained the finer points of Fauvism, answering the phone: 'I'm sorry, he's terribly busy—*The Times*, you say? You can always talk to me instead. Rachel Kenny. That's K-E-N—'

My pleasant daydream was interrupted by the tube stopping. I traipsed up the hill to a large redbrick house with roses round the door. This looked promising. It was answered by a tiny old lady, eyes blinking behind glasses. There was a strong smell of damp, and something else I couldn't put my finger on but which made me immediately uneasy. 'Yeess?'

'Hello, I'm here to see Sebastian.'

'He's in the basement. Darling. Darling!'

She directed me to a dark doorway at the bottom of some dusty steps. The house was piled with junk, old storage boxes, patchwork quilts, unpaired shoes, umbrella stands. From the gloom emerged the sound of plodding feet and panting as a large bearded man came up the steps. He wore an artist's smock and had a smear of paint on his fat hands. 'What is it, Mummy? I'm busy.' He spotted me, and his eyes swept over my blouse and black shirt and too-high cheap heels. I'd gone for the 'waitress at a silver service dinner' look in the end.

'Rachel.' I swear he licked his lips. 'Can you leave us, Mummy?'

She quavered, 'Would the young lady like tea, darling?'

'No,' said Sebastian rudely. 'Tea's so square, Ma.'

'I love tea,' I said nervously. She tottered off, holding on to the furniture.

'So, Rachel,' he said chummily, leaning on an old dresser. 'Sorry about the 'rents.'

'Rents! He was forty-five if he was a day.

'I'm looking for someone to help in my studio, cleaning up the paint—I'm, like, totally into a Jackson Pollock vibe now—admin and, of course, modelling...'

'What?' I'd been nodding along but stopped short at that. 'You mean...?'

'I'm moving into a major nude period. No biggie. You'd be great.' His eyes were fixed firmly on the second button of my blouse and I fought the urge to do it up to my neck.

'Um, I don't think...' I stopped again as a pair of malevolent green eyes emerged from the gloom of the stairs, followed by another. 'Are there...cats?'

'Oh yes, my little girls.' He scooped up one, a fat grey, and laid it over his shoulder like a living, evil-eyed stole. The other, pure white, sat at his feet and began washing its face in a threatening way. 'These are Betsy and Barbara—my muses.'

I was backing towards the door. 'Um, I can't, sorry, massively allergic, better go, byeeee—say sorry to your mum…'

'But I haven't even shown you the costumes you'd be wearing!'

I fled, wishing I could get into a bleach shower and remove all traces of damp, cat and sleazy middle-aged man.

The next interview was in Soho in a large fashionable advertising firm. I could tell as I sat in the egg-shaped chair, sipping a free bottle of oxygen-infused water, that they'd want someone more on-trend than me. Everyone else was in chic deconstructed dresses, or shiny suits and ties, with asymmetric hair. They were also all about eight years younger than me.

List of things you find in trendy offices

1. Vegan kitchens

2. Extensive collection of herbal teas. Nothing with caffeine in

3. Humidifiers

4. Meeting rooms with uncomfortable low chairs that when you sit in them threaten to reveal your knickers

5. Committees to organise going to the pub/organic brewery

6. Rice cakes. Lots and lots of rice cakes

After a while I was called in by the disdainful art director, Rowena. She had cropped platinum hair and huge earrings like Death Stars and wore what looked like hemp dungarees. 'Hi, eh…' She checked her clipboard. 'Rachel. I'm gonna ask you some questions, yeah, and then we'll do a little test. Cool?'

'Yes. Er, cool.' I pulled my skirt over my legs, noticing that a large ladder was traversing its way from my knee to my ankle.

'So, eh, Rachel. If you were a Pantone colour, like, what would you be?'

I laughed. She stared at me. 'Eh, OK. You were serious. Um, um, I guess I'd be…lime green, because I'm zesty and…fresh.'

'What number shade?' Her pen hovered.

'I don't know. I could look it up.'

She gave a little sigh, as if to suggest any moron could simply *look it up*. 'What do you think's been the most successful viral of recent years?'

My mind went blank. 'You mean like…ebola?'

She stared. 'I mean like viral online clips. Memes.'

'Oh. I liked that one of the cat running into a wall.'

'Which?'

'Um, all of them?'

Another sigh and mark on the clipboard. 'If you could take three things to a desert island, what would they be?'

My first thought was Dan. I'd take Dan. He'd know how to build shelter and purify water and find help. But he wouldn't be on my island, or anywhere else that I was from now on. For a moment, loss made me speechless. Things that suck about divorce, number one hundred and seventy-nine: the moments when you occasionally let yourself forget it. And then remember again. 'I guess, pen and paper—tea?

I suppose I'd need something to boil water with. Matches? Or maybe a spoon, if it's a dessert island, ha ha.'

She was still staring. I rearranged my face into a suitably 'cool yet eager' expression. 'So we're asking everyone to do an illustration before they go. It's for a new brand of pet food...'

Oh no.

'...so we'd like you to draw us some cats, yeah?'

This was it. The final interview, and my final chance. I'd applied for dozens more jobs and not even been shortlisted. I was out of options. I felt much happier in this office, a small and scrappy agency in a freezing building near Archway. I had to step over piles of paper to get into the manager's office, which was just a corner of the room walled off with boxes of printer ink. 'Sorry about the mess,' Louisa said, not sounding sorry. 'We find it sort of creative.'

'Oh, me too.' I liked her on sight—she was short and curvy, with a pencil holding up her dark hair, and Converse on her small feet. 'So, Rachel, I'll be honest with you. We're currently doing a lot of advertising stuff. It's not as cool as the funny virals or political blogs, but it pays the bills and keeps me in Reese's Peanut Butter Cups. But what I need is someone who can do Photoshop and, ideally, animation. It doesn't say on your CV that you've ever done that.'

'Um, it was mostly print stuff at the council. And they wouldn't pay for Creative Suite.'

'What did you use for design?'

'Eh...Word.'

She winced. I knew then I wouldn't get it. IT wasn't my thing—hand-drawing, paper and ink, that was my thing.

That was what could transport me for hours, make me forget all about Dan and everything that had happened.

Louisa said, 'Look, do you mind if we don't do the whole interview thing? It's just so tedious. I had you in because I liked your drawings. They're really funny and cute, especially the dog one. Reminded me of my parents' Pekinese. But I need someone to do the grind work too.'

'I understand.'

She leaned over the table to me. 'If you don't mind me saying so, I could read through the lines of your covering letter that you're having something of a hard time at the moment.'

I stared at the dusty carpet. 'You could say that. You could say I'm having something of a disastropiphany.'

She laughed. 'Disastropiphany? That's good. If you want my advice—and feel free not to—go back to the freelancing. You're good. You don't want to be stuck in some poky office.'

'But I still have bills.'

'I know. But I think you can make it. Send me more of your stuff, if you have it. I might be able to use it for a blog or something. Especially the dog.'

I shook her hand, sorry that I wouldn't get to work with her, but knowing that deep down she was right. Now, how could I magic up a whole salary out of scrappy bits of cartoons?

Eventually, I was home again, laden down with groceries. Since I wasn't going to be able to afford anywhere else to live for a while, I'd better make sure I wowed Patrick and Alex with my cooking. I mixed up some fresh pizza bases, pounding the dough together with my hands, enjoying the homey yeast smell and the elastic pull of it under my fingers.

A song came on the radio and I began to sing along. 'And I knead you now tonight, and I knead you more than ever... Once upon a time I was falling in loaf...'

I heard the door shut behind me and turned to find Patrick in the hallway, holding Alex by the hand and wearing his sheepskin jacket. 'Er, hi, guys.'

'What a mess!' Alex blinked around at the kitchen, which did indeed resemble an explosion in a bakery. There was dough stuck to every surface and everything I'd touched while kneading it, flour everywhere, pans and bowls and ingredients sitting out. I could see Patrick staring. 'Sorry about the mess. I'll clear it up.'

'Oh, it's OK. It's just...I don't think I've ever seen the kitchen like this.'

'I'm sorry.' I started to panic a bit. 'I didn't think...'

'Don't be sorry.' He walked over to the open bag of flour, scooped out a handful. 'Hey, Al, you said you hoped it would snow this winter, didn't you, mate?'

'It doesn't snow inside, Daddy.'

'Sometimes it does.' Patrick tossed the flour up in the air so it sprinkled on his dark hair, powdering it with white. He started to laugh.

Alex gaped at me. I shook my head—I didn't know what had come over Patrick either.

'I'm sorry about your jobs.'

'It's OK. Something will come up, I'm sure...maybe.'

We were washing the dishes after dinner, Patrick passing them to me to dry. Music was on the iPad dock—Marvin Gaye. The air smelled of the expensive fig candles he burned—I assumed Michelle had bought them, as I'd never yet met a man who saw the point of candles—same with cushions. Alex was in the front room watching a DVD of *Ratatouille*, which he loved—I didn't, as I was frankly uncomfortable with the idea of rodents being culinary experts—and Max slept in his basket, letting out a contented snuffling snore. Domestic bliss. Only problem— this wasn't my domesticity. It wasn't my child, my dog, my fig candles at £38 a pop, and it certainly was not my man, hair greying over his temples, softly singing to the radio. It all belonged to a woman called Michelle, a tiny beautiful woman who managed to wear lime green without looking like a Chewit, and who was currently off in New York somewhere being fabulous and making millions. And who could put me out on the street any time she chose to return.

'Alex showed me the cartoon you did,' said Patrick, interrupting my unfocused worrying. 'Those plates go in the high cupboard there.'

'Oh…right. Which cartoon?'

'The one of Max with the little thought bubble.' He smiled. 'I found it under his pillow and it made me laugh. Very sweet.'

'Thanks. I usually do people. But maybe I could branch into pet caricatures too. Make a nice sideline.' I was thinking I should add this to my website, try to get some freelance commissions again, but then I remembered Dan did all my IT and I was rubbish at it, and that sent me off into realising I'd left all my tax receipts at the house and I'd have to somehow get them back before year end, unless I wanted to pay all my meagre earnings into the large child-catching sack of HMRC.

'I was thinking more than that,' Patrick was saying. 'I have some friends who work in journalism. Broadsheets, mostly, but some magazines. Have you ever tried to get a comic-strip commission?'

I laughed heartily. 'Oh, you're serious? Well, no, seeing as I know none of those kind of people and have zero contacts. It's insanely competitive.'

'But someone does those jobs.'

'Someone who isn't me.'

'Could I at least show them your stuff?'

'You'd have to ask Alex. It's his cartoon. And Max, if he minds his image being used, I suppose.'

'And if they agree?' Patrick was dogged. Which was ironic, as Max was never dogged at all, unless sausages were involved.

'If you really want to,' I said, busying myself with the cutlery. 'But could you do me a favour, and not tell me when they say no? It's just I'm not good with rejection.'

'A freelancer who hates rejection. How did you get into it?' He was folding the tea towel neatly over the oven door. I had an urge to rip it off, untidy the kitchen, scatter biscuits over the clean floor. Nowhere with a child and dog should be this tidy.

'I did it for a friend, for a wedding,' I told him. 'Cynthia, actually. She and her husband as caricatures.' Though I'd had to tone Rich's down—with his ruddy face and rugger-bugger manner he satirised himself more effectively than I ever could. 'Anyway, they have a lot of rich friends, and like eighty per cent of them were also getting married that year. So I got more commissions. Then I started a website and did all that Google search wotsits. Birthdays, weddings, that sort of thing. Or sometimes people want an illustration for a blog, or a magazine. I used to do it as a sideline, but I gave up when we moved to Surrey. I'm like those annoying people you see on the street doing cartoons, except I'm not on the street.'

'Do you use that as a slogan? Because it might need work.'

'Um…no.' I was squirming. If a man was starting to fix your life for you, it was usually a sure sign he cared. Except Patrick barely knew me. He was just my landlord. We just happened to need things from each other at the moment.

'It just seems that if the job search isn't going so well, maybe you can expand your freelance side of things. Go to wedding fairs, that sort of thing. After all, now is the time to try new things, stretch your wings, and other clichés of that kind. You could also do some training in that software they mentioned.'

I threw the tea towel at him. 'Stop trying to fix me! Anyway, what about you, are you going to do any of your list items?'

'Oh, that. I don't know if I really have time, to be honest. But I did get in touch with some of my old bandmates, like you said. Turns out they're still playing. They have a gig next week if you fancied going.'

'Great! Can you get a sitter for Alex?'

'Oh, no, I won't go. I meant you and your friends. Seizing life, etc.'

'But don't you want to see the band? I can babysit, if you like.'

'No,' he said quickly.

'But honestly, I don't mind…'

'No. Thank you, but we don't leave Alex with many people. It's just…a hard and fast rule.'

We. Shutting me out. Did Patrick not even trust me to

look after his son, although we shared a house? Maybe he really did see me as just a lodger. My face fell.

'You OK?' He was looking at me curiously.

'Yeah. Think I'll have an early night.' I shut the cupboard door on the last dish, spotting a dirty jar on the counter, which had been full of sun-dried tomatoes. It was so oily I chucked it in the bin without thinking. 'Well, good—'

Patrick was staring at me. 'You threw the jar in the bin!'

'Oh—yeah, I thought it was just so dirty…' Oh God, Dan would have killed me for doing something like that. I opened the bin lid frantically. 'Sorry, sorry, I'll take it out. We can still recycle…'

I felt Patrick's hand on my wrist. 'It's just one jar, Rachel. You don't need to go through the bin.'

'But the recycling!'

'I won't tell if you don't.' He smiled. 'After all, does it really matter if there's sometimes flour on the floor or recycling in the normal bin?'

'Um, I thought you thought it did matter?'

'Maybe I'm changing.'

His hand was still on my wrist, his fingers brushing mine. I suddenly couldn't breathe with him there, filling up everything, his height and the breadth of his chest and his smell of lemons. He frowned. 'Rachel? What's wrong?'

'N-nothing. Right… OK. Well, goodnight.' I fled.

Up in my tower room, I tried to drift off and not worry about my lack of employment and my strange behaviour in the kitchen. I hadn't slept well since Dan asked me to leave. Or really for the past two years. Lying awake at night, I would do Panic Maths—you know the sort of thing. If I absolutely have to have a baby by age X—thirty-six, say—that means I have to meet a man by X minus one—thirty-five, at the latest. However, it would probably kill a new relationship if I said, *Hello, I'm a Leo with GSOH, and, by the way, could you get me pregnant in the next week or so? Let me just go and stick a thermometer up my lady bits.* So that meant, allowing for error and the severe lack of decent men out there, I'd have to be looking…now, really. And thirty-six was maybe a bit late. According to the magazines I scared myself by reading, I ought to be pregnant now—exactly when I was splitting up with my husband and moving out with my socks and pans in cardboard boxes.

You're so brave, people kept telling me. I didn't want to hear that. If I was brave, it meant what I'd done was genuinely terrifying, and I might be alone forever, dying, being eaten by cats, wearing turbans, etc. I wanted to be told it was a walk in the park.

Panic Maths—the one time you wish you'd actually failed your GCSE at school.

Chapter Ten

As the doors of the Northern line slid shut, I checked again I had all my supplies. Baby wipes—check. Clean T-shirt—check. Phone charged up in case I needed to stage a dramatic escape attempt akin to digging massive tunnel in *The Great Escape*—check. I was as ready as I'd ever be.

At university, Ros had hung about with me, Emma and Cynthia. She was studying History with Emma and often joined us to sprawl, hungover, on our beds, watching Disney videos and moaning about boys. After university she did a Masters, then a PhD. She was a friend I always looked forward to seeing, lively, a drinker, lurching from one romantic crisis to another while simultaneously giving papers on the subject of 'The role of telegrams in Nazi Germany' and 'Hitler's bunions—did they change the course of history?'

Then she met Paul.

I was actually there when it happened. It was Ros's twenty-fifth birthday, and she was, of course, drunk. In fact, I think she'd already been sick and then carried on drinking. Someone from uni turned up with Paul in tow—a friend from the Civil Service. He was quite junior, short-ish and already losing his hair at twenty-six. He was also clearly agog at Ros, with her short spangly dress and vo-ciferous drunken requests for the DJ to play Girls Aloud. I remember thinking, *Pah, he has no chance*, as I downed a tequila slammer. Cynthia got off with a male model that night, then texted us all pictures of his beauty cabinet. Dan and I woke up in bed with an inflatable guitar and massive fake sunglasses. Good times.

But Ros did give him a chance. A year later, they were getting married in a pretty church in Sussex, and she was promising to obey him while dressed all in white and being given away by her father, sitting silent and giggling while all the men in the wedding party made speeches, then a year later giving up her job as she was pregnant and wanted to 'really be there for her kids'. Poppy was now three and Ethan was eighteen months. When Poppy was one, they'd moved out of Ros's really cool loft apartment in Shoreditch and bought a two-bed semi in Hendon. At the wedding, turning our noses up at the little bags of sugared almonds and her dad's half-hour speech about the swimming medals young Ros had won, I remembered Emma turning to us, te-quila shot in hand, and slurring, 'Les never do this. Bloody OBEY. 'S not bloody Victorian times. Bloody marriage.'

And we had clinked glasses on it. But then I was mar-ried two years later and Cynthia in another one after that. Only Emma seemed to be holding out against the bourgeois shackles of matrimony. Of course, I soon wouldn't be mar-ried any more.

As the tube progressed up London, I reflected on the past few weeks. I was finding out various things about my landlord. He was thirty-eight—I'd discovered some birthday cards in a drawer—and he'd been married to Michelle for six years. He'd gone to Durham University, and he sometimes wore cords. I put those two facts together to conclude he was fairly posh—that and the fact he had a card that said 'with love from Mummy and Dadda'. He liked cheese—there were never fewer than four kinds in the fridge. He drank red wine, or whisky, or sometimes gin and tonic, and he liked fresh coffee and reading newspapers and books about war or science or architecture, and he kept the radio tuned to Radio 4 or old soul stations. When he turned it on and I had it set to Magic FM, music for saddos, he would get a look of great pain on his face. He was sometimes grouchy and liked everything very tidy and would rehang the washing if I didn't pair up the socks or leave everything perfectly straight. That was all I knew so far.

I'd learned a lot more about Alex, who was very forthcoming. He was more than four and a half but less than four and three quarters. His favourite toy was Roger the one-eyed bear, and his favourite TV show was *Thomas the Tank Engine*. His best friend at school was Zoltan, and sometimes Emily, because you could be friends with girls too, did I know that? His favourite food was chocolate biscuits, his least favourite celery. He had no opinion on carrot sticks.

What I didn't know about either of them was if they were OK, or how much they missed Michelle. She was never mentioned, save for Alex to once formally explain, when showing me around, that Mummy used to sleep in Daddy's room, but now she was 'over the seas'. I never answered the phone in case it was her ringing, but I knew the time difference made it hard for her to speak to Alex, who was usually either at school or after-school club or in bed. A few times I'd overheard chatter from Alex's room, which I think was him talking to her via Skype on Patrick's iPad. I didn't know if Patrick spoke to her himself. In the mornings, when he drank his coffee, I'd sometimes see him chuck the grounds over the fence into Michelle's boyfriend's house, then kick the fence for good measure. It was empty, of course—apparently, 'Alan' also had some kind of penthouse in New York. I was basically imagining Michelle's life now as *Sex and the City* crossed with *Big.*

As the train burst from the bowels of London into the light, we slowly left all the interesting places behind. I had a mild sense of rising panic, similar to when Dan had first brought me to our house in Surrey—a gasping for the nearest Starbucks, an anguished scrabble to find the closest tube. Ros had given vague directions that it was 'about twenty minutes to walk, I think... We're always in the car these days' and suggested I get a taxi. I'd imagined a row of nice black cabs with their friendly yellow lights, but I had to trek to a minicab office and wait among the smell of chips while they summoned one. Oh dear—after years of trying to convince friends it wasn't that far to visit me in Surrey, had I already turned into an urban snob?

Ros and Paul's place was a small terrace in a narrow street, each house with scooters and trampolines in the front gardens. Posters for the Neighbourhood Watch. Ocado delivery vans. Just like where I used to live. I rang the bell and listened to what sounded like a massacre inside.

'Shut up, Poppy! No, put your pants back on! We don't do a poo when we have guests!'

I suppressed a shudder and put on my brightest fake smile.

Eva Woods

List of things people like to talk about once
they've moved to the suburbs

1. Train schedules

2. The Neighbourhood Watch

3. School catchment areas

4. Garden centres

5. Decking

6. Parking regulations

7. Farmers' markets

'And there's the buddleia. We put that in last spring. It's come up beautifully.'

'Lovely.'

'And we bought that garden seat in Homebase. Reduced from £200 to £145.'

'Amazing.'

'Paul put up that shed there all by himself. It's great for storing the lawnmower.'

I seized on this as an escape from admiring every plant and item of furniture they possessed. 'How is Paul anyway? Still at the Department of Education?'

'He got a promotion. Working hard, so…sometimes he gets home late. Or not at all.'

'Oh?'

'But it's fine!' she said brightly. 'I mean, the kids see him on weekends.'

'And you—do you miss work at all?'

Ros blinked, as if this concept had never occurred to her. 'Well, I wouldn't trade this for anything. Being here when they're small—it won't come back again. It's just such a magical time.'

On cue, Poppy came out of the house waddling and holding the crotch of her tights. 'Mummy! I think I did a poo in my pants!'

'Oh! Well, never mind. It happens.'

It did indeed happen. I sat on the bench, reduced from £200, and soaked up the watery sunshine. Ros had offered me tea but then forgotten to make it as there was some crisis with Ethan trying to put Lego up his nose. It was a nice garden, but they were trying to pretend it was a country oasis, when in fact the neighbour's house was so close I could clearly hear the noise of the lunchtime TV they were watching (*Loose Women*). Every so often the bench shook as a lorry passed on the road, or a plane went overhead from Heathrow. Was this what lay on the other end of the ladder—poo, and getting bargains in Homebase, and saving up to fix the damp in the kids' room? They were sharing, as the house had only two bedrooms, but at some point the family would need to move even further out to get more space—maybe to the Home Counties. And then you might as well give up and start spending all your weekends in garden centres staring at displays of Yankee Candles.

'Here.' Ros burst out, holding a sticky Ethan. 'Could you hold him for a moment? I need to put Poppy in the bath and he keeps eating the pot plants.'

I took him, surprised as always by the weight of babies, lightness and solidness all at once. 'Hello,' I said to him. Ethan had something sticky round his mouth so I pulled out the wipes I'd brought and cleaned him up a bit. He let me dab at his face and hands, regarding me solemnly. His head smelled of milk and baby powder and I felt my arms ache a little even though he was in them, in a way that could only be soothed by a baby of my own. But was that really what I wanted? I began to spiral back into worry, so to stave it off I carried Ethan round the garden, pointing out the plants to him.

Ros reappeared ten minutes later. 'Sorry. She was potty-trained ages ago, but she seems to be going backwards.'

'Is she OK?'

'Embarrassed.'

'You could tell her about the time Emma wet herself after we drank all that Red Bull in Minty's that night. Make her feel better.'

Ros smiled, a glimpse of her old self, one who wasn't frazzled and looking ten years older and smelling of puréed vegetables. She made an attempt to smooth down her hair, in the process putting cotton wool in it. 'How are you, Rachel? Sorry it's constant madness round here.'

'Oh! I'm...you know. It's been a strange year.'

Things that suck about divorce, number one hundred and eighty-nine: having to tell friends and family. It was like announcing an engagement or pregnancy, but in reverse.

She looked concerned. 'I was so surprised. You and Dan always seemed really happy. Just the other day I was looking at some pictures on Facebook. You remember when we all went to Dorset for New Year? That was such a laugh. What happened?'

'Yeah, it was.' I couldn't tell her what had happened. I couldn't tell anyone.

'And you'd bought a house and everything. You seemed so...settled.'

I looked at the paving stones, the weeds poking up between

them. 'Well, I think that was maybe the problem. You can settle too much, you know?'

I could see from her face she didn't. Because what could be more settled than a house and two kids? You couldn't undo them by signing a form. 'Anyway, it's OK. We're doing this list thing, me and Em and Cyn.'

'Oh yes, Emma mentioned that. Some kind of bucket list?'

'A "non-dying, embracing life and having more fun" list. You should do it with us!' I looked around at the mess of her house, toys and nappies and dishes everywhere, and realised I shouldn't have made the offer so flippantly.

'Oh!' Ros paused. 'Well, maybe sometime. I don't get out much now.'

'No, I suppose not.'

'You're doing OK though—you've got somewhere to live?' She looked at me anxiously. I found that often, instead of really talking, people just wanted me to reassure them I was OK, so they didn't have to worry about me.

'I'm lodging with someone while I look for a job. There's a little boy too. He's four.' I fished out my phone, screening it first for any 'are you still alive or have you drowned in custard' texts from Cynthia. 'There he is!' It was a picture I'd taken of Alex with Max on the Heath, poking a stick into a pond and smiling angelically, in his yellow raincoat and red welly boots.

Ros was gratifyingly gushing. 'What a cutie! Isn't he gorgeous? How do you find it, living with a kid?'

'Not too bad. He gets up early, but he's pretty quiet and well behaved.'

'Hmm.' She cocked an ear to the sound of smashing from inside. 'They do say it's the first four years that are the worst, having to watch them every second, the crying, the tantrums—'

Ethan began to splutter and cough, and then sicked up something pink onto my top.

'—the lack of sleep, the bodily fluids, the total death of your sex life—'

Poppy began to wail from inside. 'Muuuuuummy! I did another poooooo! IN YOUR BEDROOM!'

'—never getting a second to yourself, not even to have a wee—'

There was the sound of something splintering from the upstairs window.

'—You know, I just really have to hope they're right.'

I took my phone back again as she hurried Ethan inside, grateful that Alex at least had control of his bodily functions.

The landline was ringing inside the house when I got back. I was on the doorstep, groping through my pockets and bag for the key. Why couldn't I just keep it in the same place? Bugger... Oh, there it was. It wouldn't be Michelle at this time of day, surely, so I could risk answering

I sprinted in and grabbed the phone, slightly breathless. 'Hello?'

A woman's voice, efficient. 'Can I speak with Mr Gillan, please?'

'He's at work, I'm afraid. I'm his...' God, I didn't even know what I was. 'Can I help?'

'I'm calling from Alexander's school. We were hoping Mr Gillan could come and collect him. It's a matter of some urgency.'

'Oh dear, what's the matter?'

'I'm afraid he's had a small bump in the playground.'

'Oh, well, I could come. I'm only up the road.' Alex's school was a posh private one near the Heath, the kind where the kids were expected to wear hats and blazers even though some of them could barely go to the loo by themselves.

'I'm afraid we aren't authorised to release him to anyone other than Mr or Mrs Gillan.'

She made Alex sound like a prisoner, the electric doors buzzing back as he held all his possessions in front of him in a cardboard box. I imagined Max's head poking out.

'What if his dad said it was OK?'

'That might be acceptable. If you could arrange for Mr Gillan to telephone us at the earliest opportunity, please.' What was it about posh people that made them speak as if it were 1920 and the Dowager Countess had just gone down to tiffin? I hung up and dialled Patrick's work number, which was inked in his strong hand on the kitchen whiteboard.

'Rachel?' He sounded harassed.

'Um, sorry, but Alex's school just rang. He needs collecting, they said.'

'Did they say why?'

'Something about a small bump. Is that normal, that they send them home for falling over these days? Cos—'

'Did they say he'd fallen over?' he interrupted.

'No, but—'

'Rachel, please think. What did they say?'

'What I told you. A small bump.' Why was he so tense? It sounded like a minor injury. My nephew Justin was also four and always running into things, or falling down them, or tripping over his own feet. 'Anyway, rather than drag you back I thought I could pop down for him, if you like—'

'No.'

'Oh, but it's no—'

'It has to be me, OK? If they call again, tell them I'm on my way.'

I bit my lip, replacing the receiver. Did Patrick not even trust me to pick up his son and walk three streets with him? I'd thought we were getting closer, becoming friends, but if he didn't trust me even with this, perhaps I was wrong.

I mooched about in my tower room, working on a cartoon for a new food blog—talking sandwiches, pretty fun—thinking I really understood how those captive medieval princesses must have felt. No fun, no suitors, just a pile of manuscripts to illuminate—or was that monks? I was like that, isolated from the world. Except without the nice hair and sense of entitlement. Sighing, I fired up Facebook on my laptop and had a good snoop among Dan's profile pictures. He'd unfriended me when I moved out, but I could still see some things. I clicked through his friends list again, looking for anyone new who might be the mysterious girl Jane had mentioned, but there was nothing. I heard the door slam far below—Alex and Patrick must be home. Still sulking, I decided to stay up in my room and make some more lists.

List of things I still had, despite the loss of husband, house, job, Flavour Shaker, etc., etc.

1. Drawing—a few bits of freelance money were starting to trickle in. It wasn't enough to live off, but I loved drawing so much, feeling the world and all its problems fall away as I gripped my pencil in my hand. At least I hadn't lost that, despite the Incident.

2. Friends—not everyone had friends who would force them to get over their divorce by jumping out of planes and

getting tattoos and sleeping with strangers and... Yes, I was truly blessed to have them. Probably.

3. Family-Mum and Dad were still young, healthy enough to interfere in my life. Jess was...a good sister (it wasn't her fault her life was perfect). My nephews were cute...

4. Health. I was still alive. I had all my limbs, reasonable eyesight, all my own teeth...

I stopped, hearing a yell from downstairs. What was going on? I pounded down the stairs, hearing Patrick's and Alex's voices in the kitchen.

'I'm sorry, mate.' Patrick's voice.

'Mummy does it softer.'

'I know. Her hands are littler. You're a brave boy.'

Silence. 'You have to make sure it all goes in, Dad.'

'I know.'

'You have to see the blood first in the tube.'

'I know. Is that right?'

I was coming through the living room into the kitchen. Alex was at the table with his arm bared. The table was spread with paper and needles. Into his arm went a needle and a long tube, which was attached to a bottle of clear liquid. Bloodstained cotton wool lay on the table and Patrick, wearing gloves, was prodding the needle into the child's arm.

'You have to slap the vein, Daddy,' said Alex patiently.

'I know. It's just wiggling away from me like a little worm...'

I saw their faces turn to me and then, oddly, the hardwood floor coming up to meet me as I fainted dead away. How embarrassing.

* * *

When I came round from my faint, I was propped up by the sofa. Alex was patting my face. He had a plaster in the crook of his elbow but seemed otherwise fine.

'How's the head?' Patrick was offering me a glass of water.

'Ouch. It's OK.'

'Alex, mate, why don't you go up to bed and rest? I'll come and tuck you in.'

He went, dishing out medical advice. 'You have to put a cloth on her head.'

'I know.'

'She can have Roger if she wants,' he called reluctantly from the stairs. 'I mean, if she's *really* bad.'

'Thanks, Alex,' I said weakly. 'I'm sorry. I'm really bad with needles. You keep Roger though. I might upset him with my silliness.'

'Trypanophobia,' Patrick said, as I took the water.

'Hmm?'

'It's not a fear of needles exactly that you have. It's of things breaking the skin, is that right?'

'Yes,' I said, startled. I could never stand watching surgery or people getting stabbed on TV—it wasn't the blood; it was the piercing.

'A lot of kids like Alex get it. He's OK so far, thankfully. He's got a sort of morbid fascination with it.'

I waited for him to tell me what 'kids like Alex' meant.

'He's got haemophilia,' said Patrick reluctantly. 'You know what that is?'

'Um…the royals had it? Your blood doesn't clot? Contributed to the Russian Revolution?' It was as if I was on

Just a Minute and had to give every fact about it in ten seconds. 'Is that right?'

'More or less. It's not as dangerous as people think—he's fine with small cuts, but the real danger is if he bleeds into his joints, or his brain, even. That's why I had to get him from school—they won't give him the treatment, they don't know how.'

'Is that why you didn't want me...'

'Yes. Sorry. It just has to be me. He can't do many sports either—that sort of explains the wellies. It stops him running too fast round the house, so I encourage him to keep them on.'

'Wow. He's so little. You know, to cope with all that.'

Patrick stared at his hands, his voice rough. 'He's very brave.'

'How long have you known?'

'Since birth. His cord wouldn't stop bleeding. It was a big shock. Michelle thought she'd have this perfect baby and you know, or maybe you don't, it's always carried by the mother. She found it very hard. At first she wouldn't let anyone else touch or hold him. Even me. She missed a lot of work and lost out on a big promotion. Michelle is very...driven. She couldn't handle something in her life going so wrong.'

I didn't know what to say. 'I'm sorry.'

I was surprised by his anger. 'God, why is everyone always sorry? There's no need to pity him. He has a medical condition, but otherwise he's a perfectly normal little boy.'

'Of course he is. But is there anything I need to know?'

'I should have told you, really. It's just... I don't know. People treat him differently when they find out. And you've been so sweet and natural with him.'

'But what if he'd hurt himself when I was here?'

'You've not been on your own with him. I'm sorry. I thought perhaps you'd reject him. Reject us.'

'I would not!'

'Rachel, you just passed out at the sight of a little butterfly needle.'

He had me there. 'I can learn the symptoms though...find out what I need to do in what situations.' Without thinking, I'd reached for the notebook and pen that lay on the table beside the paraphernalia.

Patrick gave me a little half smile. 'You're about to do a list, aren't you?'

'I find it helps in almost every situation, yes.' A thought occurred to me. 'All this medical stuff—is that what was in the locked cupboard?'

'Yes. I didn't want him poking about in it. Why, what did you think it was?'

'Oh, I don't know. Definitely not murder equipment or anything like that.'

'If I were going to kill you, I'd have done it by now. Think of all the good wine you've drunk in the meantime. I mean, that's just a waste.'

'You could just be a really incompetent murderer.'

Patrick laughed as he cleared up the equipment, and I felt a great relief settle over me. 'Hey, Rachel,' he said. 'You've got getting a tattoo on your list, right?'

'Yeah, why?'

'Nothing. I'm sure you'll be fine. Maybe they can get fairies to paint yours on.'

Chapter Eleven

It had been a while since I'd been out and about on the London scene. Trends had moved on. Times had changed. The top fashions I'd so far spotted in twenty minutes in the bar in Camden were:

List of fashion you see in trendy London bars

1. Visible whole-arm tattoos–for girls, mostly

2. Oversize, baggy jumpers, such as those knitted by your grandmother when you were three, often embroidered with a penguin or some other whimsical animal

3. Large bushy beards, such as those sported by redneck hillbillies who've just approached to help you out with your canoe in the Appalachians

4. Messy, backcombed beehives worn with bright red lipstick and corpse-shade foundation

5. Hipster glasses

I felt about a hundred and fifty years old. My friends were not helping. 'What kind of white wines do you have?' Cynthia was yelling at the tattooed barmaid.

'House.'

'No, I mean, is it Sauvignon? Sancerre? I *suppose* I'd take a Pinot Greege if that's all you've got.'

'It's house.'

Cynthia did her 'talking to the little people' voice. 'And what type of wine is the house?'

The girl peered under the counter. 'White.'

It didn't get any better than that. After Patrick's offer to see his friends play, I'd coerced everyone into coming out, stressing the need to seize life, embrace the day and so on. I took it as a good sign that Emma and Cynthia had agreed to a social event with less than a month's notice. But now we were here, the mood wasn't great. Emma turned up late, in a huff and refusing to talk as she 'had a cold coming' and 'needed to rest her voice'. By contrast Ian was on time and in an odd buzzy mood, ordering whiskies at the bar and whooping loudly at the bizarre support act, a man with a banjo and a girl—tattooed, natch—with a washboard. I think they were called Banjo's Ghost and, after ten minutes, they were equally unwelcome at the feast.

Ian also kept grilling me about stand-up comedy. 'Be honest, yeah, do you think I could make it on the scene, I mean, the circuit?'

'I don't know. They did say you're unlikely to earn any money for years, and most of the gigs are in places like Luton, and you don't even get travel fees.'

'*Luton.*' He repeated this as if I'd said 'the cratered surface of the moon', which I suppose wasn't far from the truth. 'Hmm.'

'See?' said Emma. She was drinking Diet Coke with a sour face and a red nose. 'We can't afford for you to be messing about with something unpaid. We need to save for a deposit on a flat.'

'But I'm funny! Everyone says so.'

'You're funny in certain social situations, Snugs. You couldn't get up on stage and make jokes.'

'Why not?'

'Come on, Snuggles. We're thirty now. We just have to accept this is our life. You're a great social worker.'

'Hang on,' said Cynthia, butting in. 'Isn't the whole reason we're doing all this—the dancing, and Rachel's comedy, and stuff—so we *don't* just accept this is our life? Commuting and working till we drop? That was the whole idea behind the plan, Em. Seizing life!'

Emma narrowed her eyes. 'Why are you taking his side?'

'There's no side. I just think it's good if Ian wants to embrace new things, that's all.'

'And who's going to pay for his expensive, non-earning hobby?'

'I am *here*,' said Ian crossly. 'Don't talk about me like I'm not here.'

Cynthia was squirming; she hated discussing money. 'Erm...maybe we could all...'

'The answer isn't always throwing money at things, Cyn.'

'I'm not suggesting that! I can just see Ian really wants to do this. And we said we'd all try new things, get out of our slump.'

Emma stared between them and abruptly drained her drink. 'Look, I'm going to go. I'm just not feeling up to being out.'

Cynthia rolled her eyes. 'Oh, come on, don't go into a mood.'

'I'm not. I already said I wasn't feeling well. Sorry, Rachel. You stay, Snuggles.' It was amazing how menacing you could make the name 'Snuggles' sound if you tried.

I escaped to the loos, gagging at the smell and wondering what the point of all this was. With Emma's departure Cynthia and Ian were both determinedly on it, each drinking with the grim-faced focus of Wild West gunslingers. I found the toilets quite stressful in these trendy bars—first, it was clearly too naff to call them male or female, so it was all wacky letters or names like 'Sandra' and 'Pete'— sometimes I genuinely didn't know which door to go in. Then there was the 'ironic' crumbling walls and the 'cool' lack of hygiene and the overheard conversations about recreational drugs. As I didn't go stronger than a three-bag pot of tea, I felt old and depressed. Was this going to be my life now, hanging out in bars where the music was too loud and my feet stuck to the floor? I went out, wiping my hands dry on the old band T-shirt I'd thought was quite cool back in my Hampstead tower but which now looked about as trendy as a nylon shell suit.

The next band were soundchecking, a wall of feedback. I wandered over to Ian and Cynthia, who were looking at me oddly.

'You never told us,' she said accusingly.

'Eh?'

'I almost didn't come. If you'd said, I wouldn't have dithered so much.'

'I didn't even know he played.' Ian was getting a look of fanboy adoration on his face. 'That's a *Fender*.'

'Guys, I have no idea what you're on about.'

'Look at the bassist.' Ian pointed.

I squinted. The man was tall, a little older than me, but cute in a beat-up way, his curly hair grey at the temples. *Oh my God!* The bassist was Patrick.

The lead singer was a short guy with a beard—not full-on redneck, more college boy gone to seed. He took the microphone. 'Hi, everyone—we're Solomon the Wise. I'd like to mention a special guest on bass tonight, filling in for Ed, who's got tennis elbow again. Please give a special welcome to Patrick!' Patrick smiled, ducking his head bashfully into the long neck of the bass.

'You didn't know?' Cynthia saw my face.

'No. But you see what he's doing? It's his list.'

'What?' she shouted over the music as they began to play.

'His list! It's one of the things—play in a band again. He's doing his list too!'

'Patrick has a list?' She looked confused, and then I couldn't explain because the guitars kicked in and we were drowned in a wall of sad, sweet sound, and I closed my eyes and smiled and swayed along.

He was doing his list. He'd listened to me. We'd do them together and it would be fun and— Oh, crap. I'd just realised this might mean I'd have to go skydiving.

'That was amazing.' Patrick and I were walking back from Hampstead tube station. The pavements were slick with rain, the lights of the cafés and bars glowing, and my ears ringing pleasantly with their rocking beats. 'I mean it, you were really great.'

'Hardly. It was just the backing to some dodgy Pixies covers. A child could have done it.'

'But you went out! You seized life!'

'I wouldn't say I seized it. I grabbed it limply, perhaps.'

'It's a start. So how did you get a babysitter for Alex?'

'There's a nurse at his special clinic who sometimes looks after kids. So I thought just this once...' Things had been more relaxed since my dramatic fainting fit, and I wondered if it was partly the pressure of keeping Alex's condition a secret from me that had made them strained at times. Alex himself was totally cool with it and had shown me, while I tried not to pass out, how he could put the needle in himself to get the 'medness' in his 'runny blood'—he was four! It was amazing.

'That's great. So what's next?'

He dug his hands into the pocket of his leather jacket, the sheepskin collar flipped up against his neck. 'Oh, I don't know. What about one of yours?'

'I've done dancing and stand-up. We should do another one of yours next. Come on, it'll be fun. I'll get the girls involved too.'

'Where was Emma tonight?'

'Oh, she left in a strop. She does that quite a lot. She'll have calmed down by tomorrow.'

'Ed does that too, when they don't have any craft cider behind the bar.'

'See, our friends have *loads* in common.'

We were almost home—or his home, my temporary lodging—and a light burned in the kitchen. He had his hand on the gate. 'Come on, let's have some decent wine. The stuff in that bar could have doubled for cleaning the toilets.'

'Patrick, don't be such a snob. I'm surprised at you.'

'But I didn't...'

'Cleaning the toilets? They don't *clean* them. I mean, what kind of bourgeois idea is that?'

Patrick's List of things to do to avoid the
post-split, pre-divorce slump

1. Climbing

2. Skydiving

3. ~~Play on stage again~~

4. Get drunk

5. Go on a date

6. Learn to fillet fish

7. Enter Max into a dog show

8. Buy a nice car

9. Take Alex overseas

10. ??

Chapter Twelve

'This is a terrible idea,' said Cynthia, regarding the pile of fish guts in front of her.

'It was yours,' chorused Emma and Ian.

Emma was already sharpening her knife in a frankly terrifying way, like a ninja in a blue striped apron. 'Anyway, that's the point,' she said in her primary-school voice. 'We all have to do things that scare us. I had to dance, Rachel had to do comedy—'

'—and *everything else*, let's not forget.'

'And you have to...'

'Cook,' said Cynthia bleakly. I'd been pleased when Emma emailed to say we were all booked into a cookery course, Patrick too, as it seemed as if she'd recovered from her grumpiness of the week before and got back into the spirit of seizing life, etc., etc. But I'd forgotten how the idea of any form of food preparation beyond making a sandwich threw Cynthia into a panic.

'You'll be OK,' said Ian in surprise. 'You always serve

up those gourmet meals when we're all round at yours. Venison and that.'

There was an awkward pause. Emma muttered something that sounded like 'caterers'. Ian looked crestfallen. 'Oh. Well, I think this'll be great. I've been wanting to sharpen up my blade skills for ages. Ha ha, sharpen.'

'It's chopping up fish, not fencing,' said Emma sniffily.

'That's where you're wrong. There's a skill in it. I wonder if he'll let us do *fugu*. You know, Japanese blowfish? If you leave any trace at all of its guts, you swell up and die.'

'Sure you didn't already eat some?'

'Ha ha ha HA.'

The bickering couple behind us, Cynthia and I were paired up. But what about Patrick? This was from his list, after all, and the rest of us were just along for the ride in the spirit of seizing life, etc., etc.

'He's not here, is he?' I looked around the room—there were about fifteen of us, definitely not including Patrick. He'd been making grumbly noises earlier about having a lot of work on, but he wouldn't pull out, surely? We began drifting to our workstations, putting on our aprons. I was counting to see who might not be paired up, when the door opened and Patrick came in, shaking out a great big middle-aged umbrella. Relief went through me.

'Sorry I'm late,' he said. 'There was some kind of crisis with a supporting wall.'

'That must have been a hard load to bear.' God, I sounded like Ian.

'Am I all alone?'

'You can cook with me,' said a sultry voice from behind. 'Hi! I'm Arwen.' It was a goddess in red and thigh boots, her dress covered in an apron and her shiny caramel hair up in a ponytail. She was American by the sounds of her. He liked Americans—he'd married one, after all.

I winced at him. 'Sorry.'

He seemed quite happy with his lot though, shaking hands with Miss America and getting into his apron. Well, that was good, I supposed. Maybe he could even take her out on a date, and get drunk at the same time, thus accomplishing his other goals.

List of people you meet at evening classes

1. The one who's already an expert, and presumably just trolling the class to feel better about themselves.

2. The one who's using it as free therapy and will take up all of Introduction to Spanish telling you about their failed marriages, bankruptcy issues and recent colonoscopy. Hola!

3. The one who's deeply talented but lacks all confidence and so will be completely overshadowed by no.1 as they're always too scared to speak up or raise their hand.

4. The devastatingly handsome yet sorrowful man who's taking Woodwork 101 as a means to re-enter the world after the tragic yet convenient death of his wife... Well, here's hoping anyway.

The teacher for this course was Phil, a vaguely threatening old-school chef, who slapped the food about as if it had personally grassed him up to the filth. 'Filleting is a delicate skill, innit,' he growled, leaning on his butcher's block at the front of the class, which was ironically taking place in his restaurant—CLASS. 'You need to put the knife in exactly the right place and whip it out dead quick. It's all in the wrists.'

'Like so much,' I heard Ian snigger.

Emma sighed. '*Listen*, will you?'

'Practise with me.' Phil had us wiggle our knives out in front and I fought the urge to cover my vital organs. 'You're not chopping it. You're filleting. Delicate, but deadly.'

'It is dead, isn't it?' Emma looked suspiciously at the fish on her slab. I wondered if this class would bring back her latent vegetarianism. She'd been one in college, but that was easy, because we couldn't afford meat anyway, and 'pasta and sauce' translated quite easily into being veggie— I hadn't the heart to tell her Parmesan wasn't vegetarian. Anyway, she'd cracked one day and eaten a whole packet of Bernard Matthews turkey ham, and Ian sometimes said he would leave her if she didn't let him keep Peperami in the house, so that was that.

I wondered how Patrick was getting on, but a deep peal of laughter from behind me seemed to be the answer. I could hear Miss America too, a gentle girlie giggle. I wasn't sure how I felt about that. I'd thought we were both too battle-scarred to even think about dating, but maybe it was only me. Things that suck about divorce, number one hundred and ninety-four: feeling as if you're failing in the 'who can win at being divorced' race.

'So how's work?' I asked Cynthia, who was stabbing at her fish like someone trying to unblock a sink.

'You know that scene in *The Great Escape*, where Steve McQueen gets put in the cooler all alone and plays with his baseball and mitt?'

'Uh-huh.'

'Like that, but without the mitt.'

'You could always quit, you know. If it's that awful.'

'I have a mortgage to pay.'

'All right, but couldn't Rich…'

She plunged her knife into the poor fish. 'Rach, we can barely afford that place on two salaries as it is. I can't give up work. Anyway, everyone's job is like this. You've just forgotten because you work at home in your pyjamas.'

I wanted to say they could move, that no one needed four bedrooms when it was just the two of them, but I knew it was hopeless. Cynthia did need all that, the house, the money, the security. She'd grown up poor and could never stop working until she felt totally safe. I didn't understand it, but no doubt she didn't understand why I needed solitude, paper and good light more than an actual home of my own.

'How's Rich anyway?' I was wiggling my knife through my fish, catching on bits of ligament in a fairly gruesome manner.

'Oh, he's…' She sighed. 'If I knew, I would tell you. I've hardly seen him at all for the past month. Not since the dance class, really.'

'Oh? Work's busy?'

'That goes without saying. He's practically living at the office.'

'He doesn't come home at night?' That rang alarm bells for me, but for all I knew it was perfectly normal to sleep under your desk and wash in the executive loos. Ros's husband, Paul, seemed to do the same thing a lot.

'They have rooms there, and he's travelling so much. He's been to America four times this month already. They have some big case on.'

'That must be hard.'

She blinked down at her fish, which just stared back. 'It's fine! This is how it works. I'd just like to see him sometimes.'

'Maybe you could organise a nice weekend away. A

country hotel, swimming pool, drinking champagne in the bath… He likes golf, doesn't he?'

She paused, as if she wanted to say something else, then answered kindly, 'Yeah. That's a good idea. I might.'

Behind us, I could hear Ian saying, 'Hey, Honeybunch. Look. Look!'

'I'm trying to focus!' Emma snapped.

He was silent for a moment. 'Hey, Rachel. Rachel!'

I turned. He was holding up a fish eye in his palm. 'I've got my eye on you… Ha ha. Get it?'

'Yes. Very good. Remember to wash your hands.'

'Hey, Rachel. Rachel!'

I turned again. Ian was holding bits of fish skin in front of his face. 'Look, the scales have fallen from my eyes! Ha ha!'

I looked at Emma, whose face was contorted into barely suppressed rage. 'I swear to God, if he doesn't…'

I gave her a sympathetic look. Ian certainly seemed to be upping the jokes since my stand-up comedy exercise had inspired him.

'Right, everyone,' growled Phil from the front of the class. 'Need a volunteer for this next bit.'

I didn't even need to look to know Ian's hand had shot right up.

Phil and his lovely assistant—who insisted on showing the whole class the eye-scales joke, which didn't go down so well—chopped the filleted fish up into little pieces and then assembled the bits of sushi. Ian held the mat while Phil reverentially laid out the crinkly seaweed, then spooned out the rice and popped the fish in. 'California roll,' he growled. ('You've gotta roll with it,' Ian said. We all ignored him.) 'Pukka, innit. Now you try.'

We did it in pairs. Cynthia was concentrating so hard

beads of sweat were springing out from under her one hundred per cent earthquake- and bomb-proof £200-a-bottle foundation. On our first go we ripped the seaweed sheet right down the middle. 'Come on,' she chided me. 'Let's get in the game! Let's do this! Give it one hundred and ten per cent, Kenny!' I stretched the seaweed out and she clamped it down with her fingers. 'Now the rice. Put it in! Just put it in!'

'Jeez, I hope you don't talk to Rich like this.'

The look she gave me made me envy the fish, whose entrails and eyes were currently staring up from the bin beside us.

By the end of the class, we'd made a plate of wobbly sushi, the rice bursting out and the seaweed torn. Emma's were perfect little circles that Phil described as 'pukka', making her preen. That must be all the cutting-out skill she'd developed in primary school. But the best sushi in the class was deemed to be that of Patrick and Arwen, who'd decorated their plate with cut-out carrots in the shape of flowers.

'Presentation, innit,' Phil growled. 'Give your guests a right proper treat. That's luvverly.'

'I, like, did a sugarcraft course last year,' Arwen said modestly. 'I guess these things kinda translate.' And as the class applauded, she actually threw her arms around Patrick and hugged him. The hussy! They'd only just met!

Emma was grumbling. 'Technically, she's cheating, if she's done it before. So really, we won.'

'There aren't any rules, Honeybunch,' said Ian. 'It's not a competition.'

'Well, thank God there wasn't one for worst fish-related joke, Snugs.'

'I had a better one. I just didn't have the guts to make it.'

I was still watching as Arwen laughed and accepted Phil's praise, tossing her hair. I hoped she'd get fish scales in it. I saw Cynthia watching me.

'So will you take some of this home to Rich?' I said hurriedly.

'Oh, he won't eat it. He thinks even French mustard is dangerously foreign.'

Sum total of this experiment—task six for Patrick, done. Task six for me, eat something weird, done—I'd tried raw sea urchin. Surely that was weird enough, though it was actually delicious. Cynthia and Emma seemed to both be on the verge of relationship strife. And Patrick was well on his way to completing another task—he had Arwen's phone number, and a plan to ask her out on a date.

> Patrick's List of things to do to avoid the
> post-split, pre-divorce slump
>
> 1. Climbing
>
> 2. Skydiving
>
> 3. ~~Play on stage again~~
>
> 4. Get drunk
>
> 5. Go on a date
>
> 6. ~~Learn to fillet fish~~
>
> 7. Enter Max into a dog show
>
> 8. Buy a nice car
>
> 9. Take Alex overseas
>
> 10. ??

Rachel's List of things to do to avoid the
post-split, pre-divorce slump

1. ~~Do stand-up comedy~~

2. ~~Learn to dance~~

3. Travel somewhere on a whim

4. Do yoga properly

5. Sleep with a stranger

6. ~~Eat something weird~~

7. Go to a festival

8. Get a tattoo

9. Go horse riding

10. Try an extreme sport

Chapter Thirteen

'This is a terrible idea.'

For once, Patrick did not try to change my mind or remind me it was all my plan in the first place. He too looked dubiously up at the tattoo parlour—Original Skin. It was decorated with pictures of lithe women and buff men, inked to within inches of their lives. Neither of which Patrick or I much resembled.

'They say it hurts,' he muttered. 'And with your needle phobia…'

'It's not needles so much as piercing,' I said, trying to convince myself. 'They don't actually pierce you, do they? They just sort of…draw on you.'

'With needles.'

'Um.'

He took a deep breath. 'This is on your list for a reason, Rachel. I'm not going to let you wimp out. I'd expect you to do the same for me.'

Emma and Cynthia had declined to come along for this

task, making vague mutterings about marking and having to wait in for a sofa delivery. Typical, just joining in on the fun ones, while I had to go through hell. In my next life, I vowed, I was going to have friends who understood the value of sitting on the sofa in your pyjamas watching *The X Factor*. But it was too late for that now. Patrick was propelling me through the door.

We'd spent a long time choosing designs. For me, it was going to be a paintbrush, which would possibly, depending on pain levels, be dripping ink in the shape of stars. Patrick was going to have a musical stave that represented a piece he'd written himself when he was twenty. 'Woo,' I'd said. 'I think that wins you double-triple pretension points all round. Maybe you could surround it with a picture of organic quinoa or the Boden logo.'

'What do you have against Boden? They make nice stuff.'

'It represents a consumerist ideal, which I as an artist reject. People don't need to be branded.'

'Like with Converse, you mean?'

'That's totally different.'

List of popular tattoo designs
(because if you're going to make a statement of individuality, you want to be as clichéd as possible)

1. Stars, flowers, hearts-basically anything you would have doodled on your folder at school during double Physics.

2. Chinese characters that you don't understand and probably mean 'gullible Westerner'.

3. The name of your significant other, with whom you will inevitably break up before it's even finished scabbing over.

4. The faces of your loved ones, for that real 'I killed them all and now I'm on Death Row' aesthetic.

The girl behind the counter was so cool she barely opened her mouth. 'Hi-I'm-Katya welcome-to-Original-Skin.' She had dyed black hair and her face looked as if the contents of a desk tray had exploded and peppered her with paper-clip shrapnel. Patrick showed her our tattoo designs, which I'd sketched out, while I looked around, petrified. It reminded me of the shop in my home town that sold tins with marijuana leaves on it and Magic Eye posters and troll dolls. I'd been peer-pressured into going once by Lucy Coleman, the bad girl at school—she wore eyeliner and subscribed to *Mizz* magazine. She persuaded me to try a legal high and I panicked and screamed that I could see a bunch of kittens coming out of the wall, until it was pointed out to me that this was in fact a Magic Eye poster I'd finally managed to solve. The next day our head did a special assembly on girls 'disgracing the uniform by being seen frequenting insalubrious establishments'. Thus ended my brief flirtation with drugs culture.

Katya was saying in her monotone, 'You will find your body art to be a beautiful expression of self-worth and individuality. That'll be eighty-five pounds each.'

Wow—a beautiful expression of self-worth and individuality didn't come cheap.

I looked at Patrick in panic. 'We'll sort it later,' he said soothingly.

'You'll be with me.' She nodded to Patrick. 'And your... eh—' She waved a hand at me. 'You'll have Wolf. He's our top artist.'

I could see why he was so named when he poked his head out from the back of the shop. Every bit of his body not covered in hair was tattooed, sorry, body-arted. He was so hard core he'd even tattooed his face. 'Hiya,' he said in an incongruously lilting Welsh accent. 'In here with me, you are, love.'

I suddenly panicked again. What if I was being sold into sex trafficking? 'Patrick?'

'I'll be right next door,' he said, keying in his PIN to pay for this torture. 'See you on the other side, when we'll be magically cool and more hip.'

Oh God. I'd somehow imagined he'd be in there holding my hand and cooling my brow. Perhaps I had confused tattooing with childbirth—I was imagining the pain to be about the same.

I lay down on the table and pulled up my jumper to reveal my lower back. I'd decided to get it there, so there was a good chance my mum might never find out. Patrick's was going round his upper arm.

'Better undo this too.' Wolf unpinned my bra with a quick professional gesture. Oh God. I really was being sold into sex trafficking. Things that suck about divorce, number two hundred and two: realising no one has touched you in so long that going to the doctor or hairdresser or, say, tattoo parlour starts to feel like a particularly hot date.

'Now, here we go, brace yourself, my love.' Then the most hideous noise started—like a dentist's drill crossed with an angry dog. I looked up to see Wolf brandishing a whirring needle. And that's when I realised that, hey, my phobia really was about needles, because I passed out.

I woke up a few minutes later with Wolf patting my face. 'I'm sorry,' I said groggily. 'I'm not good with needles.'

'You want me to stop, petal?'

'No, it's…' I thought of the damn list, and how Patrick had marched in so bravely to get his, and took a deep breath. 'Just…let me know when.'

The whirring got nearer and nearer. 'Now,' he whispered, and I felt the needle go in.

Dear God. I smothered a little scream, gripping on to the table so tightly my hands went white. I counted to ten in my head. One—two-three-four-five…siiiix… All the while the needle was burrowing right through my skin. I was sure I could smell burning. Behind me, Wolf was actually whistling. It sounded like 'Disco Inferno'. That did it. At least you were knocked out cold when surgeons chatted merrily over your comatose body.

The pain seemed to have stopped momentarily. 'That's the first ink drop done,' he said cheerfully.

'Can I— I think I need a break,' I said weakly.

'But there's still loads to do, petal!'

'I just need to see my friend.' I snatched up my top.

'But you can't cover it yet. It's not sterile, lover!'

I clutched my T-shirt to my front and leapt off the table. 'Just a second.' Patrick would remind me why I was doing this. I pushed open the bead curtains into the next cubicle. The lighting was red and low, and Katya in her tiny vest top was bent over Patrick's naked torso. His naked, quite buff torso, it had to be said. For a moment I just stared at the curve of his stomach muscles, the width of his shoulders, the smattering of hair across his chest. He shifted position. 'Rachel?'

'I—' My gaze fell on the needle she was holding. It was eating into his skin. And that was me out again.

When I came to this time, I really did have a cloth on my

brow, and I was lying on my stomach on the table. I could feel some kind of dressing on the tiny area of my back that bore a tattoo. The cloth was being yielded by Katya and was dripping water in my eyes. 'Everyone thinks they can hack it.' She sighed. 'But then they, like, *can't* hack it.'

'Sorry,' I groaned. 'I have a needle phobia.'

'How did you think the tattoo went on?' She looked at me as if I was insane.

'Er...drawing?'

Patrick was dressed again, cling film covering the tattoo and sticking out from under the arm of his polo shirt.

'Sorry,' I said weakly.

'Well, you still got a tattoo,' he said kindly.

'One that's about the size of a penny.'

'You can say it's a drop of ink that symbolises the vast potential of the imagination.'

'That's lovely,' whispered Katya.

'That's crap,' I said. 'I just wussed out.'

We were walking to the tube when another horrible thought struck me. 'Patrick? When I fainted, did I drop my top?' He said nothing. 'Patrick!' The tips of his ears were going red. 'Oh great, you saw me half-naked.'

'Well, you saw me half-naked too,' he pointed out. 'Now, let's get some cake. I'm pretty sure we need it to compensate for blood loss. And you know, a tiny tattoo is still a tattoo. You can tick that one off your list.'

'Thanks. That does make me feel better.'

He held open the café door for me. 'It's just a shame you didn't have a list item that said flash your landlord and two total strangers. Because you would have totally just ticked that one off too.'

Rachel's List of things to do to avoid the
post-split, pre-divorce slump

1. ~~Do stand-up comedy~~

2. ~~Learn to dance~~

3. Travel somewhere on a whim

4. Do yoga properly

5. Sleep with a stranger

6. ~~Eat something weird~~

7. Go to a festival

8. ~~Get a tattoo~~

9. Go horse riding

10. Try an extreme sport

Chapter Fourteen

Usually at this point in a task, I or someone else would remark on what a bad idea this was, and why had we ever got ourselves into it. This time I didn't. Even if I could get my mouth open without puking on my shoes, the noise of the aeroplane was so loud Patrick would never have heard me.

Skydiving. Otherwise known as hurling yourself out of the sky with only a bit of material to save you from certain death inside a you-shaped crater on the earth. I could barely even work out what was going on behind me. There was some kind of massive pack and an arrangement of strings and harnesses. It could almost have been kinky if it weren't so terrifying I could feel my skin shrivelling and trying to retreat back through every pore.

When you went diving under the water, you used hand symbols to communicate, since you couldn't hear each other. That was probably the last time I'd been this scared. Dan and I had tried it on our honeymoon in the Caribbean, and I could still remember the horrible weight of the tank pulling me under, seeing the surface way too far above me and promptly panicking and forgetting everything I'd been taught. It was stupid anyway. Who thought it was a good idea to use the thumbs-up, universal symbol for 'I'm OK', to mean 'go up', or in other words 'I'm not OK, get me the HELL OUT OF HERE'? At least I was so busy worrying that I couldn't breathe or see I momentarily forgot to panic about sharks.

Thank God Patrick's list hadn't included diving in water. But it had included this… Oh God. OH GOD, WE WERE IN THE SKY. The only thing louder than the plane was the sound of my panicked breathing.

Patrick was getting attached to his instructor. I would hardly have recognised him in that bulky suit and goggles. He gave me an enthusiastic thumbs-up with both hands. What did that mean? Go up? 'WE'RE ALREADY UP!' I screamed.

He looked confused, then shook his head and changed it to the diving OK symbol. I shook my head frantically. How could I be OK? I wasn't insane. We were thousands of feet up in the sky and about to jump out of the only thing keeping us aloft. If that was OK, I didn't want to be it.

Behind me, I could feel the instructor, a spiky-haired cheery kid called Chris, buckling me up. I felt like that goat they feed to the velociraptors in *Jurassic Park*. I could only manage a little bleat—no one would have heard me even if I tried to back out now. People did this all the time…right? No one died. Well, not many. Chris had cheerfully told us he'd done 'like, three hundred hops or something'. He called them hops, presumably to indicate it was no more to him than taking the stairs two at a time. Oh God.

They had opened the plane door. A harsh stripping wind rushed in, flattening me against Chris. He was moving forward inexorably, me held in front of him like a middle-class child in a BabyBjörn sling. Oh God.

I had to go first, apparently, because I was lighter, and Patrick would fall more quickly than me. I gave an anguished look back at him. He was giving me the OK symbol with both hands. I shook my head. I would never be OK again.

The door was open, the earth yawning below us, the fields like tiny patches, toy houses. All my life was down there, my friends, my mistakes, my lack of home and job and husband. It was all so very far. I took a deep breath. Remembered the mantra—if I couldn't go back, I had to go forward. And in this case, forward meant down. A long way down.

So I jumped. Well, OK, Chris jumped, because to him it was as boring as getting off a bus, and I had to go with him, because we were strapped together, even if I did try to clutch on to the sides of the plane at the last minute, feeling the cold metal through my gloves as it fell away.

Everything fell away. The plane, the worry, the fear. Me. For a few seconds, we were falling fast, screeching through the air, and my face was melting. I was all skin and sensation, the air knocked from my lungs. I could barely feel Chris behind me with all the suit and layers. It seemed like it was just me, falling alone into a massive void. Then Patrick fell past me, looking as if he might vomit, and for a moment he caught my hand in mid-air. I could feel it through the gloves, solid and warm. Then I jerked up and we began to float, our parachutes open. Thank God! We weren't going to die! Well, unless we hit power lines or an angry sheep or something.

It was over very quickly after that. The ground was

coming up to meet us, getting bigger and bigger, and then my legs crumpled onto it, leaving me sprawled beneath Chris and the parachute like a sex game gone very wrong. I let out a noise like *uh*...

'Rachel! Are you OK?' I could hear Patrick standing over me. He was obviously alive. We were both alive. And I would celebrate that once my bones stopped being liquid.

'Speak to me! How are you?'

Weakly, I raised my thumb aloft, unable to speak, but OK.

'You want to go up *again*? I know it was good, but I'm not sure that's allowed...'

As we traipsed back to the skydiving centre, I felt like the Apollo 13 astronauts getting out of that tin can in the sea, or Tom Cruise and Iceman landing at the end of *Top Gun*. Patrick was hopping with adrenaline. 'Wasn't that amazing? Such a rush! I felt so alive!'

Nearly dying will do that to you, I thought. I was just concentrating on making my legs move one in front of the other.

'Are you OK?'

'I'm just...' I pointed to my feet. 'Can't really...remember how to...you know, walk.'

'Oh, Rachel! Were you terrified?'

I thought about this. 'If you gave me the choice between doing that again and jumping into a tank of sharks?'

'Yes?'

'I'd be putting collars on those big bad fish and giving them pet names.'

List of things I would rather do than go skydiving again

1. Make friends with a load of great white sharks

2. Let a tarantula walk over my face

3. Snog David Cameron

4. Do a stand-up comedy gig every night for the rest of my life

5. Let Wolf tattoo 'I love Jedward' on my forehead

Suddenly, all the breath was knocked out of me again as Patrick grabbed me in a huge hug. 'You were that scared and you still did it for me? Oh, Rachel. THANK YOU. You can be my wingman any time!'

'You can…be…mine.' I waved my hands around pathetically, crushed against his protective suit. He was tall, and strong, and very solid. He could probably have lifted me right up without breaking a sweat. 'Patrick, are you having post-near-death-experience euphoria?'

'I don't know! I feel amazing! Look, there's my kid!' Alex was trotting over to us, holding on to Emma's hand. She'd come along to watch him while we jumped, and also as Official List Arbiter, to make sure I went through with it. I think she thought she was a latter-day Norris McWhirter off *The Guinness Book of Records*. Patrick was still wittering and waving. 'Hi, Al! God, I love him. And I love Emma, even though I've only met her twice.' Another crushing hug. 'And I love you, Rachel. I love you.'

Suddenly, I was seized with the same symptoms I'd had up in the sky—breathlessness, heart pounding, stomach churning. I felt dizzy and out of control. But this time it was nothing to do with falling. At least not out of a plane.

That evening, I realised I still felt uneasy. It was a feeling rising up from my ribcage, as if a little man sat inside playing on my ribs like a xylophone. I'd had a weird conversation with Emma when we got back to earth.

'Well done, love,' she said, thumping me kindly on the arm. 'Another one to cross off—that's definitely an extreme sport. You're doing so well.'

'Did you not want to do it too?'

'Oh! Well, it's expensive, isn't it?'

'But I thought the idea was…you, Cynthia…'

Emma's face changed. 'And do you actually see her here?'

'No, but…'

'That's the thing—it's easy to throw money at problems, when you've got loads of it, but actually understanding people's lives can be a bit trickier.'

I thought back to the night of Patrick's gig, when Emma had left in a huff after Cynthia took Ian's side over the comedy. 'Em, are you OK?'

'Me?' Patrick and Alex were coming over, Patrick still grinning like a madman. Both had ice cream smeared round their mouths. 'I'm just fine. This was all for you, really. We just wanted to get you out of your slump, see. Is it working?'

'Um…' Mentally, I prodded myself for areas of hurt—Dan, my lack of job, my lack of home, my lack of money…

'Rachel!' Alex hurled himself at my legs. 'I got you an ice cream. The pink one is your favourite, I told Daddy.'

'Thanks, dude.'

I'd looked back up to find Emma watching me, a strange expression on her face. 'You know what, Rach—I think you're getting there. The list is working. You just need to carry on.'

'Do you think so?'

She patted my shoulder. 'I know so. You'll be fine, love. We all will.'

'Will you make up with Cyn?'

'I haven't fallen out with her. I just think sometimes she

doesn't get we don't have as much money as her. But if it stops you asking why Mummy and Daddy fight sometimes, I'll call her.'

'Thanks, Mum.'

'I'm Mum? Why am I Mum?'

'Um, let's get some more ice cream.'

'You'll ruin your dinner, mark my words.'

'That was great,' said Patrick, pushing his plate away. 'Best burger I've ever had.'

It was my turn to cook that night, so I'd done home-made burgers, hand-cut chips, hand-mushed peas and hand-sprinkled salt—to be honest, I wasn't sure why doing something badly by hand was now considered a culinary plus point.

'You're just on a post-near-death high still. What did you think, Alex?'

He scrunched up his eyes carefully, like Gregg Wallace on *Masterchef.* He was wearing his train driver's hat on top of his dark curls and had ketchup on his cheek. 'It was nice, Rachel, but I like a Happy Meal better.'

'There you go. He pulls no punches.'

'And when did you ever have a Happy Meal, mister?' Patrick asked, taking his plate.

'I had one with Mummy once.'

Oh dear. I busied myself lifting condiments from the table.

Patrick said carefully, 'Did you now? That doesn't sound like Mummy.'

'She said she was "at the end of a tether". What does that mean, Daddy?'

'Er, just that she was probably letting you have it once, for a treat.'

'Can I talk to Mummy soon?'

'Of course, mate. I'll get her to Skype you.'

I leaned over the dishwasher, trying to hide my face. Oh God. It broke my heart.

When Patrick came back in from putting Alex to bed, he was whistling, as if the conversation about Michelle had never taken place. I hung the tea towel over the oven door, as he liked. 'I'm going up to finish some work.'

'You don't want wine?' He was surprised. Already he was expecting things from me, relying on me. It was my fault. I should have made it very clear I couldn't be relied on for anything just now. I could hang up his washing and feed his dog, but leaning on me right now was like standing on quicksand. You'd be lost.

'Did you not enjoy today?'

'No, I did—well, I enjoyed the fact that we did it and I'll never have to again.'

'So what's wrong?'

'Nothing. Nothing. I'm just tired.'

In bed I did my best not to think about that moment on the tarmac earlier, feeling his arms around me, the rush of air past my ears that was nothing to do with jumping. As I fell asleep, I kept dreaming I was falling out of the sky, starting awake to find myself in bed in Hampstead. I wasn't sure how much safer I was there, after all.

Rachel's List of things to do to avoid the post-split, pre-divorce slump

1. Do stand-up comedy

2. Learn to dance

3. Travel somewhere on a whim

4. Do yoga properly

5. Sleep with a stranger

6. ~~Eat something weird~~

7. Go to a festival

8. ~~Get a tattoo~~

9. Go horse riding

10. ~~Try an extreme sport~~

Patrick's List of things to do to avoid the post-split, pre-divorce slump

1. Climbing

2. ~~Skydiving~~

3. ~~Play on stage again~~

4. Get drunk

5. Go on a date

6. ~~Learn to fillet fish~~

7. Enter Max into a dog show

8. Buy a nice car

9. Take Alex overseas

10. ??

Chapter Fifteen

I tried to put my unease behind me, giving myself a stern talking-to. Patrick and I were love casualties, gasping on the battlefields of disastrous marriages. We weren't ready to date, not even close. If I sometimes caught my breath when he was near, or sniffed his jumpers before putting them in the wash, that was just because I was lonely and he was kind. He was my friend. That was all. As the days turned colder and it was dark by four o'clock, I had started to walk down to Alex's school in the afternoons, dragging Max along behind me on his little legs. After I picked Alex up, we often went for a walk on the Heath, poking about in the ponds, letting Max run with other dogs and sometimes even dropping into the café for a biscuit or cake. It was nice. I was getting a lot of work done too—in the peace and light of the tower room, I was secretly amassing a whole stack of drawings of Max doing silly things. I'd done the skydive one and one where he tried cooking—hey, if the rat in *Ratatouille* could do it... My cartoon work usually picked up around Christmas too, as desperate men—it was nearly always men—turned to me for present ideas. I'd also taken Patrick's advice and started advertising my services on wedding blogs and forums, which was bringing in a nice stream of commissions. I had time to do them all now as well, thanks to the convenient lack of employment I found myself in.

Patrick. He was busy at work but seemed cheerful. He kept saying I was doing too much round the house, but I was happy, and he still wouldn't let me pay a penny towards rent or food or bills. It seemed to be working.

One day in November, Alex and I had hurried home in the dank gloom of an early dark. He was full of chat about the Christmas, sorry, end-of-year play, as I dashed about putting the shopping away and making him a snack of crumpet and jam. 'Now, don't drop that on the sofa. So what role are you getting, do you think?'

'I might be the rabbi, but I think Joshua is doing that. Or one of the three wise Arabs. Maybe I'll be the dog.'

'There was a dog in the stable?' In the manger, presumably.

'What stable?' Alex looked blank. I didn't even want to ask what kind of multicultural lessons his progressive school would be shoehorning into the nativity.

'Take off your socks. They'll be wet.' I sounded like his mum. But I wasn't. I had to remember that.

He reappeared, trailing bits of clothing, his hair sticking up. 'Can we play Snakes and Ladders again?'

'You don't want to play Ludo instead? Scrabble? Hungry Hungry Hippos?'

'I'll let you win if you want,' he said kindly. It was true I hadn't been enjoying much luck with Snakes and Ladders of late. Every time I thought I was going to win, I slid right down the smiling faces of one of those lurking reptiles. Remember that big one that sat on square ninety-nine, so just when you thought you were winning it gobbled you all the way down to the last row again? That snake was my life now. Which was either an excellent metaphor or a sign I'd been spending too much time losing to a four-year-old at board games.

List of my least favourite kind of ladders

1. Snakes and Ladders

2. Ladders in my tights

3. The property ladder

4. *Property Ladder*, the TV show with Sarah Beeny (Kirstie and Phil all the way for me)

Alex had run off again, leaving his wet socks on the floor. 'Alex, where… Oh, hang on.' The doorbell had gone. Maybe a late delivery… I wrenched the door open.

A woman was at the door. Dark curly hair, tall, dressed in a quilted jacket and riding boots.

'Um, can I help you?'

She looked me over in my paint-stained jeans, messy hair with a pencil stuck in it and bare feet with unpainted toenails, holding Alex's sodden socks in my hand. 'Oh. I suppose he got someone, after all.'

'Um, what?'

She barged past me, taking off her jacket and passing it to me. I held it, slightly stunned. 'Is he here?'

'Patrick? He's at work.'

'Oh.' She looked at me, scowling. 'Where's Alex?'

'He's, um…'

Alex was standing in the doorway. With spectacular bad timing, he'd spilled strawberry jam all down his school shirt and some of it was even in his curls. 'I'm a bit jammy, Rachel,' he said, which was something of an understatement.

'Well, climb up and wash your hands,' I said nervously.

'I might have *maybe* touched my hand on the sofa already.'

'That's OK. We can clean it off. You better take that shirt off too.'

'Alex,' said the woman impatiently. 'Aren't you going to say hello?'

He looked confused. 'Hello, Auntie Sophie! Um, do you want a hug?'

'Let's get a clean top first,' I said hastily, looking at her expensive cashmere jumper. As I helped him out of his shirt, I was acutely aware of her watching. Was she Patrick's sister? She couldn't be Michelle's, surely. She was clearly British.

'So you've got a nanny, Alex.' She spoke to him, ignoring me.

He looked at me as if to say 'what's she on?' I nearly laughed. 'Rachel isn't my nanny, Auntie Sophie. She's my friend. Daddy's friend.'

'Um...' I hastily tried to explain. 'I'm sort of the lodger.'

'"Sort of the lodger"?'

'I live here, and I sort of help out. But I'm not the nanny. Or the au pair.' What was I? It had been easy not to answer that question when it was just Patrick and Alex and me. I realised I had no idea. Things that suck about divorce, number two hundred and forty-five: not knowing how to describe yourself any more. You're not someone's wife, you're not single—what are you?

She put her hands on her hips. 'Would it be too much for someone to have told me about all this?'

I clasped Alex's hand, jammy as it was, and spoke bravely. 'Well, it would be, yes. Seeing as I live here and I don't have the faintest idea who you are. And it's usual to be invited in before you enter a house.' I spoiled this rousing speech by muttering, 'Sorry,' and darting forward to put Alex's shirt in the washing machine.

'Perhaps Alex should explain,' she said, after a difficult pause. 'Since he knows who we both are, evidently.'

Alex was very calm in the face of all this hostility, letting Max lick the remnants of jam off his hands. 'Auntie Sophie is my auntie. Rachel is Daddy's friend and my friend. She lives here.'

'But not his…you know…' I tailed off lamely. 'Like, he's sort of my landlord.'

She gave me a searching gaze, then stuck out a hand. 'Sophie Gillan. He's sort of my brother.'

'Um, Rachel. I live here.'

'So I gathered. I'm sorry to barge in. It's just I haven't heard from my brother since he said Michelle was going—' she lowered her voice, but Alex was oblivious anyway, trundling in bare-chested to watch TV '—and I haven't seen my nephew in two months. I thought something was wrong.'

'He's fine. Well, as fine as he can be. We're…managing.' I cast about. 'Would you like a cup of coffee?'

'Yes, please. In the meantime, I'll take a certain person to get the jam out of their hair, shall I?'

'Um…' I regarded the coffee machine with terror. 'I don't really use this thing.'

'I'll do it,' she said. 'You do the jam removal. I'm sure you know where his things are.'

Upstairs, I tried to pump Alex for information. 'Where does Auntie Sophie live?'

'In a house,' he said helpfully, as I doused his curls in baby shampoo.

'Well, yes, I mean, where?'

'I don't know. Near Grandma and Granddad. I think.'

'Does she have any children, any little boys or girls?'

'No.' He shook his head so water flew everywhere. 'Grandma says she's a spin-ster. Does that mean she goes spinning?'

'Er. Sort of. And do you see her a lot?'

'Don't know.' He shrugged. His concept of time was limited to 'right now' and 'not right now', which was a situation of equal impossibility whether it was a year or a minute away. 'She has horsies,' he supplied. 'Lots of nice horsies, and she rides them, but Daddy won't let me. Because of my runny blood. Maybe when I get older, I can go on them and my blood won't be so bad.'

I tried not to hug him tight. It was hard to explain that, no, his blood would never get any better. 'Will we go and get Auntie Sophie some biscuits?'

I got him dressed and brushed down and we went downstairs, where Sophie had the machine going and was peering round the kitchen. 'I must say I thought it might be…tidier. I mean, Michelle was such a stickler. They didn't come to visit much because of the horses, all the hair and so on.' She bit into one of Patrick's biscotti and winced. 'Good Lord! I don't think I can afford to eat these. It's a filling per bite.'

'You can have some of my Jaffa Cakes,' said Alex kindly. Then: 'Some, I mean. Not all of them. Sorry.'

Sophie dusted off her hands. 'Come here, little fellow.'

He went for a cuddle, and she pulled him up onto her knee. 'I've missed you.'

'Can we go and ride your horsies, Auntie Sophie?'

'I think that might just be arranged.'

I was hovering. 'Do you want me to call Patrick? He should be home about six.'

'Oh, no need.' She smiled, and I saw she wasn't scary at all, just posh and annoyed at not seeing her nephew in ages. I wondered why that might be. 'Why don't you sit and tell me about yourself?'

'Rachel draws pictures,' said Alex, sneaking a Jaffa Cake. 'And she's *quite* good at Snakes and Ladders, sometimes.'

Sophie smiled. 'Do you know what, I would love a game of Snakes and Ladders.'

By the time Patrick came home, I was losing horribly to the hustling combination of Gillan family members.

He blinked, keys in hand, jacket still on and wet with drizzle. 'Er, what's going on?'

'I'm being crushed,' I said mournfully. 'It's like the reptile house at the zoo here. The cages are open. The snakes are everywhere.'

'Hello, brother,' said Sophie in that booming voice posh people use to barrel through awkward situations. 'Thought I'd drop by. Was down to see old Biffo, you remember him? My accountant.'

'Yes.' His eyes flicked to Alex, who had chocolate round his mouth and was happily running his finger along a snake, making a hissing noise. I gave a 'what could I do?' shrug.

Sophie got up. 'I must be off anyway. Just been meeting lovely Rachel here. You must all come down for a ride soon. No arguments. Ring me.' She gave him a kiss on the cheek and then was gone as she'd came, waving at Alex and me.

'Sorry,' I said. 'She just came in. Thought I was the nanny or something.' Actually, I was pretty sure she'd thought I was Patrick's bit of stuff at first, but I didn't mention this.

'That's my sister.' He sighed. 'Storm the beaches first, ask questions later.'

'I like her.'

'Yes. That's part of the problem.'

I wondered if he would tell me why he'd fallen out with her in the first place—clearly, something had happened—but I was getting used to Patrick's secrecy by now. I wouldn't ask.

'Daddy!' Alex said brightly. 'We're going to ride Auntie Sophie's horsies!'

Patrick met my eyes, and once again I shrugged. 'It's my inborn peasant mentality. Someone with RP says I'm doing something and I do it. I'm like a serf, really.' Which reminded me of the day's biggest revelation. 'You're posh!' I burst out.

'I'm not posh.'

'You so are. It all makes sense now. The cheese. The cords. The fact you call it "supper". I can't believe I've been living with a posho and not even realised.'

'Oh, stop it and go do your colouring in.'

I tugged on an imaginary forelock. 'Yes, sir. Whatever you say, sir.'

Chapter Sixteen

'Do help yourselves... There's quails' egg salad, seared pork belly with red cabbage and, for afters, salted caramel tart with ginger and pear ice cream.'

All this would have sounded more impressive had Cynthia not been reading it off the note that came with her delivery from the posh catering company she used when we dined *chez* her.

Ian was scowling. 'It's just not the same now I know. I thought you made it all yourself.'

Cynthia tossed her hair at him. 'When exactly would I do that, in between shutting down a high-net-worth company and keeping a Bahraini businessman out of jail?'

'Hmph.' He popped a tiny egg in his mouth. 'I do like these though. It's like being a giant egg-eating snake, isn't it?'

Emma rolled her eyes. 'So, Rach, how's it going with the list? What are we on now?' She was keeping a tally of what I'd got up to, never one to miss a chance to boss people around.

'Well, I've done stand-up comedy, dancing, and got a tattoo—OK, a really small one, but I think I have a medical exemption, and I technically ate something weird at the fish gut thing.'

'Being a wuss isn't a medical condition,' Ian said, but we ignored him, as his mouth was full of egg.

List of Ian's favourite kind of eggs

1. Scotch eggs

2. Crème eggs

3. Mini eggs

4. The kind of liquid egg you can buy in a bottle if you're really, really lazy

5. Pickled eggs

6. Egg McMuffins

'And Patrick has done cooking, skydiving, playing on stage… Oh, the skydiving counts as my extreme sport. So that just leaves travel somewhere random, yoga, festival and horse riding on my list, and, for him, dating and drinking, the dog show, going overseas and buying a car. Which is a rubbish one, I think.'

'Going overseas sounds good,' said Cynthia, forking up rocket. 'I'm desperate for a holiday and Rich doesn't seem to get time off any more. We could all go, what do you say?'

Emma sniffed. 'We definitely can't afford a holiday right now. Anyway, it's term time still.'

I said, 'We're booked in for riding next week. Do none of you want to come to that? It'll be fun. Patrick's terrified.'

Cynthia muttered something about 'end of year' and Emma said, 'I hate the countryside.'

'But wasn't the idea that we'd all do these things together? So we could all have fun and embrace life?'

'I'm just really busy right now,' said Emma, examining the cutlery.

Cynthia said, 'The thing about embracing life is it takes up a lot of time.'

'And money,' said Emma, in what seemed like a pointed manner.

'Well. OK. Maybe another time. We're also doing climbing soon, off Patrick's, if anyone's about...'

'We.' Emma muttered this while examining the napkins Cynthia had put out.

'Hmm?'

'Nothing. It's just you're doing a lot of things with Patrick these days.'

'Well, yeah, I do live with him,' I said, confused. Were they annoyed that I hadn't seen them as much? I'd invited them to all the tasks.

Cynthia turned to Ian. 'So how's it going with the comedy plans, Frankie Boyle?'

Emma sighed. 'Oh, don't encourage him. Spending every night in smelly pubs telling bad jokes to three drunks, for no money—why would anyone want to do that?'

'I'm sure Ian has a reason.'

Ian nodded eggily. 'S'hard to explain. It's just something I've always wanted to try.'

'Exactly. Seizing life, embracing new things—'

'—coming home stinking of cheap beer,' said Emma.

'Maybe that can be Patrick's number ten,' I joked, trying and failing to lighten the mood.

Emma was still pleating her napkin. 'Are these your wedding napkins, Cyn?'

Cynthia gave them a disinterested look. 'Yep. Four-hundred-thread-count Egyptian cotton. Rich's mum thought we absolutely had to have them, for some reason.'

'Hmm.' Emma folded hers and pushed it away.

There was a short silence. I said, 'You OK, Cyn? Work stressful?'

She gave a short laugh, picking at her salad. 'It's always stressful. Stress is a given. If you don't have a nervous breakdown by forty, then you aren't doing it right, they say.'

'How is Martin?' Martin was her boss at the law firm—five feet of pure evil and with halitosis like the fiery breath of Hades.

'Evil incarnate. Probably be leaving us soon to take up the CEO post in Hell.'

'That's a hot job,' said Ian feebly.

A vague malaise had settled over us. Cynthia was clearly hating work, Emma was exhausted from weeks of marking and teaching, and Ian was embroiled in some child protection case he couldn't tell us about. I was in the rare position of being the most upbeat.

I kept trying to lob cheer-grenades into the conversation. 'So what did you think of Patrick's band? Not bad, eh?'

Emma was staring viciously at her knife. 'This is the silver from the wedding list too?'

'Yes.' Cynthia glanced at it apathetically.

'How much was each piece again?'

'Um, let me see. I think the forks were £50, and the knives were a bit more than that—'

'Seventy pounds,' Emma said abruptly. 'Hard to forget that.'

'I guess they were, if you say so.'

'And it was a hundred-piece set?'

'The idea is you can sort of entertain ten people, I think... You know, fish knives, steak knives, soup spoons...'

'Have you ever had cause to use a fish knife?'

Cynthia looked at the packaging discarded on the table. 'Eh, tuna's a fish, isn't it?'

Emma was gripping the knife in a slightly disturbing manner. 'How much did we spend on our last canteen of cutlery, Snugglebum?'

Ian looked startled. 'Eh, fiver, I think. From the pound shop. They shouldn't really sell it there though, should they, cos it's not actually a pound? I prefer the "everything's a pound" ones. You know where you are there. 'Course, you get people asking all the same.'

'This better not be part of the comedy routine you're supposedly working on.'

'Patrick's band was great,' said Cynthia brightly to me. 'It's a shame he was so far back though. I mean, he's easily the best looking.'

'Do you think so?' I felt absurdly pleased on his behalf.

'Oh yeah. I do like a chiselled jaw.'

Ian piped up. 'Am I chiselled?'

Cynthia looked at him sideways. 'Only in the sense of "chiselled by a blind-drunk carpenter in the dark".'

'Thanks.'

'Geppetto on speed, that sort of thing.'

Ian sulked. Cynthia smiled. 'But Patrick is definitely chiselled. Don't you think so, Rach?'

'He's old,' Emma scolded.

'Old can be good. George Clooney. Sean Connery.'

'Patrick's only thirty-eight!' I protested. 'Sean Connery's about seventy, isn't he?'

'Rach hasn't answered the question,' Ian pointed out, spraying food in my direction.

I squirmed. 'I don't know.' He was handsome, no doubt about that, but there was something about him—he'd been so badly hurt and he had to look after his son and fight for him and I thought it was…disappointment. He seemed as if life had disappointed him. 'I suppose he is good-looking, yeah.'

Emma and Cynthia did that annoying glance of theirs for when I'd said something silly or meaningful. The two, it's fair to say, don't always get on—sometimes it's like having two territorial cats in the house—but they tended to be united when it came to advising me on how I'd gone wrong. It seemed whatever I'd just said was enough to bypass the weird cutlery-related spat they were having.

'What?' I said, irritated.

'I was afraid this might happen,' said Emma, her lofty position somewhat spoiled by the three quails' eggs she'd shoved in her mouth at once.

'What are you on about?'

'You've transferred,' said Cynthia. 'You're like a little orphan bird without Dan—you had your nest with him and now you've fallen out—'

'—trying to fly,' Emma said sadly.

'Yes, trying to spread your wings, but it was too soon and now you've imprinted on the first half-nice man you've seen. Classic rebound.'

'It's not like that!' I was indignant suddenly. I'd have considered storming out in a huff, but there were still two courses to go. 'We're just both a bit battered. I need somewhere to live and he needs helps. That's all.'

'What do you think of the ex-wife?' asked Emma innocently.

'Oh, she sounds awful. Hasn't seen Alex in months, and she had all these rules about food in the living room...' I trailed off, realising I'd played right into their annoying psychology-book-reading hands. 'Look, it's not like that. We're just friends. We help each other.'

'Did he say anything about Dan?'

'Um...he said he sounded like a cold workaholic and too staid for me.'

'Right.' They looked at each other again. Suddenly, it was too much for me. Caramel salted tart be damned. 'Look, it's OK for you two, with your perfect marriage and house, Cyn, and you and him, Em—' I pointed at Ian '—in your love nest watching *Pointless* marathons and making up songs about your toes. It's not like that for most people. You struggle, you have money worries, you don't get pregnant or you do get pregnant, and you have to fix the car and mow the lawn, and nothing's ever quite right, but you keep on working at it, then one day you wake up and there's a total stranger next to you.'

'But that's good,' said Ian, trying to lighten the mood. 'Sleep with a stranger, that's number five.'

'Shut up, Ian,' said Emma, with uncharacteristic rage. 'Look, Rach, you don't have an exclusive monopoly on money problems, you know? I work my arse off every day and every night—Ian does too—and it's hard work, mopping up messes, looking after kids when their own parents are too selfish or irresponsible to take care of them, and we get paid bugger all. Do you think we could afford to spend seventy quid on a fish knife? We don't all have it as good as Cynthia. We can't all take time out of life to do expensive hobbies, list or no list.'

Cynthia looked at her hands, with their manicured nails and glittering rings. 'I'm sorry you feel that way, both of you. I don't think anything is ever as perfect as you imagine.'

'Isn't this?' Emma indicated the stylish room, lit with expensive candles, the food in bright ceramic serving dishes.

'Money isn't everything.'

'Easy to say when you have it.'

'I guess it helps when you don't have anything else.' I saw Cynthia's hands were shaking. I also saw how empty the house was, when you looked past the beautiful furniture and tasteful art. There were no books, no papers, no one's shoes kicked off, no glasses laid by for reading, no cups of tea half drunk. No sign that anyone lived here, let alone of Cynthia's husband.

I was on my feet. 'I'm sorry. I just… It's been really difficult, all of this…' I could feel anger rise up in me, just as quickly to be drowned in tears. This was why I never won at arguments. 'OK, I'm sorry. I think I'm just going to go home. I'm sorry, Cynthia.'

Emma blinked down at her food. 'Rach, I'm sorry. I didn't mean to have a go. It's just been a really tough few weeks—there's lots going on, and—'

'Never mind. I just need to go.'

I tripped down the stairs, leaving Emma and Ian staring at their dinners. 'I'll see you out.' Cynthia got up.

'I'm sorry,' I said again. Cynthia held the door for me as I struggled into my coat. 'I just… It's hard. This is all so hard. Unless you've been through it…'

'I might have some idea.'

'What's going, Cyn?'

She stared at the door knocker—Italian, antique. 'Oh, just the usual. Work and stress and Emma's off on one about money. Ian's salary got frozen again, and he got a big parking fine that he forgot to pay, and she thinks they can't get married because they can't afford it—not that he's even actually asked her, which is another issue—but it's not my fault I'm doing OK, you know? I grew up in a council house, sharing a bed with my sister, doing my homework on the stairs. I've worked bloody hard for all this. And anyway it's not everything.'

I hadn't known any of this. 'And Rich?'

She wouldn't meet my eyes. 'Rich. I don't know. If I ever saw him, I might have some idea.'

'Cyn...'

'It's fine. Everything's fine. Just a busy week.'

Was nothing good and true? 'Look, I'll call you soon. Sorry.'

Her hug was brief and cold, as if we couldn't reach out to each other. I could hardly see my way to the tube from the tears in my eyes.

Chapter Seventeen

The date got off to a bad start when he was fifteen minutes late. As someone who was always late for everything, this annoyed me. So he was unpunctual. Damnit, I was unpunctual. If I could get myself there on time, then so could he.

Yes, I was, against all better judgement, on a date with a member of the opposite sex. Dating was a first for me. I'd met Dan aged twenty in the student union at Bristol, while I was hanging up a poster for the Art History course ball, and he was putting up one about five-a-side football. There was only one space left, and we'd got into a discussion about the various types of balls and their relative merits, and the rest, as they said, was history.

But then again, most of history is just people being viciously murdered or dying of the plague in a mud pit somewhere, so perhaps this wasn't so bad.

It was Patrick who convinced me to try online dating. He was still trying to find a date to 'touch base' with Arwen the glam American, who had an 'insane schedule'.

'She really called it touching base? I bet that's not all she wants to touch.'

'Yes, yes, get your mind out of the gutter. Now, what are you going to put?' He'd fired his laptop up and was trying to construct a profile for me on FriendsPlus, the dating site for over-thirties. May as well just call it the Last Chance Saloon and be done with it. 'Everyone else puts that they're easy-going.'

'But I'm not. Put histrionic, highly strung, scared of everything.'

'I'll put dynamic and creative. Now, would you say you like spending time with family and friends and going out?'

'No. I'm an agoraphobic orphan with no friends.'

'Come on, Rachel. Do you want to meet someone or not?'

That was a good question. I still looked at Dan's Facebook profile every night, obsessively searching for details of who his new girl might be. I was pretty sure I wasn't ready to date. So why couldn't I face up to a happily single future, wearing turbans, smoking with cigarette holders, taking Jess's kids to risqué plays once they hit their teens? Hope, maybe, that was the thing I was missing. Hope that this wouldn't be it for the rest of my life, living in people's spare rooms, wearing kids' pyjamas, going nowhere. And so I agreed to a date.

Ten minutes later, I was on the point of giving up on Barry, my date for tonight—and not without relief. I could go home, put on my jammies, watch *Nashville* online… Then he appeared, toting a huge bag. What was inside, the dismembered body of his last date? He was much hairier than I'd imagined, a thick gingery pelt extending over his hands, ears and neck, everywhere except for his head. What

I was finding a shock was how many men in their thirties were almost totally bald. I'd been spoiled with Dan, who'd retained his brown colour and the same hairline he'd had when we met.

As Barry walked towards me, I realised I wasn't ready for this. No way, no how. I had been with Dan for ten years and I'd never had an actual date, as opposed to WKD-fuelled embraces in student pubs. I couldn't do this. But there was no way out, because he was ambling over, relaxed, as if he weren't twenty minutes late.

'Hello!' I pasted on a polite smile and hoped my eyes didn't say, *My God, you're hairy, aren't you?* I didn't mind ginger—I fancied that guy off *Homeland*, after all—but, but…

He leaned in for a kiss on the cheek, and there was the second problem—he reeked of garlic. How hard would it be to pop a mint? I'd eaten about five on the tube, paranoid that I might smell. After all, Dan wouldn't have noticed if I had bad breath—he hadn't kissed me properly in about a year.

I'm afraid I recoiled a little, then tried to cover it up. 'Hi, hi, nice to meet you. Weather turned out OK in the end!'

Seeing I already had a drink, he went to the bar and came back with a lime and soda, the cheapest drink there was after tap water. 'I don't drink,' he explained, arranging his change into a little pile.

'Oh?'

'It's just not good for society.' He eyed my half pint and I cradled it protectively. I could already tell I'd need alcohol to get through this.

'Why do you say that?'

'People in this country just can't manage to drink in

moderation. Women especially—falling out of nightclubs, getting into unlicensed cabs in short skirts—well, is it any wonder so many are attacked?' He looked again at my drink. 'So yeah, I'm afraid immoderate drinking is something of a deal-breaker for me.' He peered at me suspiciously.

I downed my beer in one large gulp. I could maybe compromise on hairiness or garlic breath, but definitely not on victim-blaming. My inner Germaine Greer sat up, snarling. 'So, Barry,' I said, 'you don't think it's the fault of the men who actually do the attacking? It's definitely the short skirts and half pints of four per cent beer that are causing it?'

He gave a small patronising smile. 'I have a PhD in Sociology. Women give out signals, and men just act on them. It's what we're programmed to do, after all.'

'Well, I have a vagina, and I can tell you there is no unconscious signal for "please come inside and look around". But there is one for "please stay the hell away from me, you creep".'

He sat back, looking as if he'd choked on a garlic bulb. 'Oh dear. You aren't one of those feminists, are you? Isn't that a bit seventies?'

'There was plenty about the seventies that was bad, Barry. The oil crisis. Watergate. Flares. But some parts of it were so good they've lasted to the present day, feminism being one of them. Shame your hairline wasn't.'

'Dyke,' he muttered after me as I left.

'I'd rather be one than go anywhere near you!'

I was pleased enough with my snappy wit on this exit, but I then spoiled it all by bursting into tears as soon as I got outside. I wondered where in London I could find a shop that sold turbans and cigarette holders.

Of course Patrick was up when I arrived home, dejected and crestfallen and downhearted and lots of other adjectives implying doom and gloom. I was starting to feel we were in a sitcom, where he stayed on stage sipping his wine and doing ironic looks to the camera, and I walked in every day with a new problem or calamity. For example, 'I'm thirty and I just put my shoes on the wrong feet!' 'A man on the tube licked my elbow!'

'My date was a sexist bald ginger man!' I declared, on this occasion.

He took a swallow of whisky. 'Which is the worst bit of that?'

'The sexism, for definite. I don't mind ginger so much.'

'That's good. I'm half Scottish, you know. My beard is pretty ginger in the right light.'

'Oh God.' I flopped down in the chair. 'I'm going to be alone forever.'

He poured a tot of whisky into a small glass and slid it down to me like a bartender in a Wild West saloon. 'So, you were on a date?'

'Huh. Define "date".'

'As in, a prearranged romantic meetup in a place of mutual convenience?'

'Yes. Although it wasn't mutually convenient, it was in Fulham to suit him. Bloody District line. From now on I'm making "favourite tube line" a criteria.'

'Bakerloo,' he said instantly. 'Old-fashioned, cool name, goes to good places, named after Sherlock Holmes, essentially. Oh, and it's "criterion".'

'DLR,' I countered. 'You can pretend you're in the future, and you get phone reception. Oh, and you're a pain.'

'It won't always be this way. Look, there's a guy at my accountant's who's your age, single. Really nice bloke. I could set you up.'

The warmth of the whisky was spreading through my chest. 'Having a date was on your list anyway. Why am I having to do it?' And why was he so keen for me to go out with people? I didn't want to think about that.

'I'll do it. When she's back from her yoga holiday.'

'There are other people, you know.'

'Who'd want to date me? I haven't been out in five years and I know all the words to the *Postman Pat* theme tune.'

I thought that actually quite a few women would want to date him, given he was handsome and kind and knew how to cook scallops, but I didn't say this. If I'd learned anything from the Barry fiasco, it was that you couldn't rush things. Like a fine whisky, you had to leave yourself in the cask until you'd matured. For me, I suspected that was going to be a long time yet. Instead I would just stay in the lovely house, drink wine, play board games, watch Disney films and continue with the crazy lists.

I wasn't sure what I was doing... I was drunk, that much was clear. I could tell from the heavy way I'd sat down on the loo, which had no soap and smelled not faintly of urine. I also appeared to be on another date, when I'd sworn right off them. Damn Patrick and his following through with plans. He had indeed asked out Ben the accountant for me.

But God, it had been something of a shock when I'd first seen him. After my experience with Top Bantz Barry, as I called him in my email to Cynthia and Emma, I made sure to be ten minutes late to our date in the cocktail bar, the kind of place with knowing innuendoes in the names of the twelve-quid drinks. Ben was already there, which was a good sign. He looked a little nervous, scanning everyone who came in and glancing at his watch. I'd waited outside for several minutes, trying to fight my legs, which seemed to want to walk away. 'Come on, you guys,' I pep-talked them. 'We knew it would be like this. We're over thirty— all of us, though you weren't much use to me until I was two—and you have to pan a lot of mud to find gold.'

But the gingerness. The sexism!

'Yes, yes, but I tested this one with some remarks about the Beauty Myth and he didn't slag it off.'

OK, then. Reluctantly, lefty and righty agreed to carry me in the door. I did the awkward, 'yes, it's me, I'm trying not to see you judge me as I arrive' walk and smile. He smiled back—he was nice! Not a hunk, but sweet. Then he stood up. Except, at first I didn't realise he had. Surely Patrick had said he was five foot eight. Being a short arse myself, it was one of the first things I checked. It wasn't my fault I only fancied taller men. That was just basic biology. Ben didn't look much more than my five foot three.

Again, I put on my 'date' smile—something similar to a grimace of horror—and did my best to muster the dating generals Small Talk, Weak Jokes and Hair Flicking. 'Hi,' he said nervously. 'Would you like a Sloe Comfortable Screw?'

'What?'

'Er, it's a drink.' He fumbled the menu over to me. I decided the only way to get through this was with a Screaming Orgasm, Sex on the Beach and perhaps even a Slippery Nipple.

Some awkward conversation and tired innuendo later, Ben was describing his co-workers in the accountancy office. 'They're all so dull, they think it's wacky if they get things that plug into their USB. That's the single biggest expression of personality they have. USB hand-warmers, USB pencil sharpeners, USB coffee mugs...'

'I never knew what USB stood for,' I said. 'Isn't it funny, we use these every day and don't know what they mean.'

'A lot of people think the "V" in DVD stands for video,' he said. 'But it doesn't.'

'Really? That's so interesting.'

(I know exactly what this sounds like. Believe me, I lived through this.)

'Excuse me, Ben.' I got up, legs suffering from the copious amounts I'd been drinking to quell my nerves, and went to the ladies', where I took out my phone and texted Patrick. *You owe me big-time.*

He texted back. *Not good?*

At least have got some good tips on my tax return.

I flipped open Facebook, searching for Dan's profile. I could see only a bit because he'd unfriended me, but a new picture was publically visible. *Cooking dinner for a special lady.* I recognised that table. I recognised that plate. I recognised my own recipe for beef stew. He was entertaining another woman in our house.

I sat in the cubicle, my knickers round my ankles, taking deep breaths and trying not to cry. So it was real. I'd been hoping, in some desperate secret way, that Jane had been wrong, or just trying to goad me into going back. But Dan really had moved on. It was only me who was stuck, with no job, no man, nowhere to live.

I got up, washed my hands, splashed water on my face and strode out to where Ben was fiddling nervously with the beer mat. He looked up.

'Can we go to yours?' I said.

Next thing there was a taxi, and the cold air on my face, and then I was in his—unmade; Superman sheets—bed, and he was taking his shirt off, apologising for the fact he'd put on weight. I blinked up drunkenly. He wasn't kidding. He was so pasty and chubby that all I could think of was a piglet. And believe me, you don't want to start thinking of farmyard animals in the context of the man you're going to sleep with. And his pants were also Superman-themed.

I know. This actually happened. I went home with a man who thought a good first-date approach was to wear underpants based on a fictional, slightly camp character.

'Are you OK?'

'Yes, I just… Sorry. I was distracted by that cobweb. I'm a bit scared of spiders.'

He looked up. 'Oh, yeah. Mum usually cleans in here, but she's been struggling with her back a bit. I'll have a word.'

'Mum?'

'Yeah. She'll be in bed by now though, don't worry. She'll do us breakfast in the morning if we ask nicely.'

'I'm sorry.' I struggled out from underneath the slightly foetid duvet and scrabbled for my jeans on the floor among the tubes of Pringles, crumpled gaming magazines, and layers of dust and dirty tissues. 'I can't do this.'

He sat up, looking like the saddest little pig who was going to the slaughterhouse. All I could think about was *Charlotte's Web*, an impression reinforced by the many cobwebs festooning his ceiling. 'Will I see you again?'

I was putting my shoes on, hopping about in my haste

to be out of there. 'I don't think so... I'm sorry... Just not ready... Divorce...'

And I dived out the door, trying in my fuzzy-headed state to work out how I would make it home from Hackney, tottering on my stupid date shoes. As I stood at the bus stop in the biting wind, squinting drunkenly at the map, and trying not to think about the horrors I had just witnessed—he had a *Star Wars* poster; he was thirty-two—I found myself remembering nights back home with Dan, shutting the door on the cold, putting on a DVD, lighting the gas fire. Was this really so much better than what I'd left?

List of stupid things I do when I'm drunk

1. Make everyone listen to YouTube videos of Kelly Clarkson singing 'Since U Been Gone'.

2. Try to analyse the words of same. Is she glad he went? Sad? Is the song an example of unreliable narration?

3. Make up dance routines to 'Survivor' and/or 'Single Ladies', shouting loudly on the bits that go "cos my momma taught me better than that!" even though she really didn't. She'd *totally* be dissing people on the internet if only she knew how to work it.

4. Decide it's a really good idea to mix up all the alcohol in the house and drink it. This was how I made up the 'Berocca and Roll' cocktail, which contains both your poison (much vodka, tequila, peach schnapps) and your cure.

5. Send ill-advised drunken texts, which sometimes just consist of punctuation: ?, !, etc.

6. Agree to go home with men I absolutely do not fancy in any way, shape or form.

Rachel's List of things to do to avoid the
post-split, pre-divorce slump

1. ~~Do stand-up comedy~~

2. ~~Learn to dance~~

3. Travel somewhere on a whim

4. Do yoga properly

5. Sleep with a stranger—*definitely not ready to do this!*

6. ~~Eat something weird~~

7. Go to a festival

8. ~~Get a tattoo~~

9. Go horse riding

10. ~~Try an extreme sport~~

Chapter Eighteen

'So it didn't go well with Ben, then. Shame.'

'Er, no, it didn't. Because you set me up with someone who thinks it's fun to tell stories about USB pens.'

'But he's a great guy! He's really close to his mum, for example.'

'That's because he LIVES WITH HER.'

Patrick shrugged. 'I don't understand what women want. He'd be nice to you.'

'We don't want much. Someone confident, but kind—not a tosser. Someone funny, but sweet. Someone with good abs, and all their own hair. Someone with a good job, but also creative and fun. Someone who can cook.'

'Right. That person you described—Peter Perfect the Perfect Date—he doesn't exist.'

'I bet he does.'

'No.' He shook his head. 'Everyone has something that you won't want.'

'But you're—' I stopped myself.

'What?'

'Well, you're nice, and you have a good job and can cook—and you're funny.' He also had good abs, but I was pretending I hadn't seen them at the tattoo parlour.

Patrick did a funny expression. 'That's sweet of you. I'm also getting divorced and have a small child. Not most people's idea of perfect.'

'Well, what about me? I'm getting divorced too and I don't have a house or a job, or even nice hair now that the mysterious hair-product pixie has been stealing my Frizz Ease.'

Patrick ran a nervous hand through his suspiciously lustrous curls. 'Um, but you've got a great sense of humour.'

'Oh thanks. That's what you say to people who live exclusively off biscuits.' He looked pointedly at my hand, in which I was holding an Orange Club bar. I shoved it gloomily into my mouth. 'What do you want anyway? Out of dating?'

'Oh God, who knows. It's hard to imagine starting again, when I've been with Michelle for so long. I guess ultimately I just want someone to make me happy, every day.'

'Just that?'

'So simple. But so hard.'

'Hmm.' I put down my Club bar wrapper, feeling suddenly overwhelmed. How would Patrick and I ever get past all this?

'So see you later for climbing?' He tidied my wrapper away.

'Yeah. I have to meet Cynthia first. Grovel and make her like me again.'

'But you didn't do anything wrong, did you? Sounded like it was just tempers fraying.'

'I was brought up by an Irish mum, Patrick. If you ever think you haven't done anything wrong, you just aren't looking hard enough.'

'So have you replied to Emma?' After the dinner party incident Emma had sent us an email to say sorry for over-reacting, she was just worried about something at work. I'd immediately accepted and sent my own grovelling apologies, but Cynthia was still holding out. Emma had even liked something she put on Facebook about pandas on a slide, but she ignored that too. This made me very anxious. I hated people not getting on.

Cynthia prowled ahead of me through the department store, picking up what looked like some string and masking tape lashed together. 'Oh, you know Emma. She thinks she can say whatever she wants, ruin my nice dinner, then we'll all come running when she deigns to say sorry. What about these?'

'What are they?'

'Pants, of course.'

I was experiencing almost as much fear as I had during the skydiving. After my email, Cynthia had agreed to meet me for a make-up lunch near her office. Unfortunately, this translated into 'no actual food, instead shopping for sexy underwear'. I was so hungry I was seeing spots—though it could have just been the polka dots on the hundred-pound bra in front of me.

'What's all this for, Cyn?' I looked longingly at two bra inserts, imagining they were real chicken fillets. Maybe in a Caesar salad or a fajita…

She had gathered up armfuls of the stuff, pants that were just strips of ribbon you wrapped around your thighs, bras that were more hole than material. Did people actually wear these things? Surely there was only a two-week window in any relationship where they might be seen? Then you'd be undressing yourself and getting into bed in your jammies. It wasn't worth the expense for just two weeks, I thought. You could get a lifetime's supply of M&S pants for that.

List of types of pants women own

1. Pants we pretend to wear

2. Pants we really wear

3. That's it.

'I'm taking your advice,' she said, chucking some dental-floss thongs into her basket without even looking at the price tag. I could imagine what Emma would say to those. *These pants are the pants of oppression!* It gave me cystitis just looking at them. 'I've finally persuaded Rich to come away for the weekend. So I thought I'd...'

'Oh. Good idea.' I didn't want the mental picture of Rich post-coital, or coital, for that matter. 'So you haven't spoken to Emma at all?'

'Hmm?'

'Emma.' You know, our best friend...

'Oh, I'll talk to her soon. Let her stew for a bit.' Cynthia heaped her undies onto the counter with the confidence of a woman who knows she can afford to take whatever the hit may be.

'I'm not good at that. I want everyone to like me.'

'Well, you need to stop it. Stop giving away your power.'

'Have you been reading— Oh!' I gaped at the price tags being racked up by the salesgirl, who wore so much make-up she looked as if she'd been vacuum-sealed. 'Is that right? There isn't an accidental extra nought?'

The cashier gave me a contemptuous look. Cynthia flashed a gold credit card. 'It costs what it costs, darling.'

'I could buy a new laptop for that,' I murmured sadly. Who would have thought that strips of rubber and lace could cost so much? Perhaps they were made of platinum or moon rocks or something? 'Anyway, will you talk to her? Please?'

'Why should I? She was the one slagging off my house and my fish knives, and after I'd gone to all the trouble of making, well, ordering, a lovely dinner.'

'I know, but we're friends! This isn't right.'

'You can't fix everyone, Rach. You need to fix yourself first.' I wondered if Cynthia had been watching *Working Girl* on repeat again. There was an edge to her voice, and more than a suspicion of shoulder pads under her suit.

I looked at my watch. 'I have to run. It's another task today.'

'Oh. I thought we could get lunch after this.' I was sensing a distinct waning of enthusiasm in Emma and Cynthia for the list, even though it had been their idea. It seemed to be me and Patrick doing all the tasks now, and Emma was barely even checking we'd done them, as List Arbiter.

'We're booked in for climbing though. Please, will you make up with Emma, for my sake?'

'I'll think about it,' said Cynthia, holding up a near-invisible thong to the light. It could almost have been garrotte wire.

I had made a mistake of epic proportions. I'd been so much at pains to ensure none of Patrick's tasks involved big-toothed chompers of the piscine variety, I had forgotten to clarify that I was also afraid of something else, which you were much more likely to encounter within the confines of the M25—heights. And, due to this oversight, I was now dangling over a large precipice with only a small harness keeping me from certain death. The harness actually bore a striking similarity to the scary bondage-style undies Cynthia had been viewing, which only made me feel more uneasy.

OK, it wasn't exactly *Touching the Void* or the start of *Cliffhanger*. We were in a warehouse somewhere near Woolwich, not in the Alps. The climbing wall was only ten metres high—only!—and there were no friendly Sherpas or frozen bodies attached to it, but all the same, I was gibbering with fear.

Of course Patrick liked climbing. I should have seen the signs—sturdy walking boots in the hall cupboard, ownership of more than one North Face item, sensible socks—but it had been masked by his North London, posh-cheese-eating, biscotti-crunching facade. And now here I was, having agreed to join him in his lunatic schemes, which all seemed to involve getting as close to death as we could while still using our Oyster cards.

I looked down the climbing wall. 'So we go…over?'

'Of course. Haven't you ever been abseiling?'

'You said climbing. As in, going *up*.' I'd imagined something like a child's climbing frame, which to be honest would have given me palpitations in itself, but which I could hopefully go up to within sensible, not-dying levels and then come down. I practically got altitude sickness going up Primrose Hill. But this was the opposite of climbing, a total denial of every instinct evolution had taught us. We were going *over the cliff.* With only some flimsy ropes between us and certain death, or, you know, really vicious ankle sprains.

'It'll be fine,' soothed Patrick. 'It's really easy. Kids come here for their parties. Look.' He indicated the other wall, which was swarming with toddlers.

'Maybe it's easier for them. Did you ever think that? Maybe they haven't learned sensible evolutionary fear yet.'

'Evolutionary fear?'

'It's a theory I have.'

'Tell me later. It's time!' Patrick was grinning, his curls sticking out from under his hard hat, as he launched himself backwards into space. I made a little noise like *gaaaarrrr!* and shut my eyes. When I opened them, I saw him rappelling—cool technical climbing term—down the wall as if he was born to it.

I stood up, my back to the ground. My hat was digging in under my chin, giving me a headache and amplifying the sound of my panicked breathing.

I didn't move. My legs were going, *No, she's lost it this time. We aren't going to walk off a* cliff. *Are you mad?*

Go on, I urged them. *Toddlers can do it.*

They are clearly insane. We'll save you from yourself.

The acned teen instructor was watching me, surprised.

'I can't do it,' I said. 'My legs won't move. They just won't do it.' And they wouldn't. I was totally frozen on the ledge. I was like someone in a film who'd had a bad climbing accident, my brain going *NOOOOOO! You have so much to live for!* Heart pounding, sweating into my erotic harness, having hideous flashbacks, except I'd never actually had a climbing accident, so it was just flashbacks to falling off the monkey bars in Devon aged four.

'Come on.' I heard Patrick's voice in my ear—he had

climbed back up. 'You just have to overcome all your body's instincts.'

'Oh, well, that sounds easy! I'll just tell it to stop… peristalsis too, then, shall I?'

'Good word. Come on.' He was holding on to my legs. 'Just lean back into me.'

'Nope. No way. Read my lips—N. O.'

'I can't see your lips, Rachel. You're in front of me. Just come down a centimetre at a time. It's like jumping in during diving.'

'I hate diving.'

'I know.' He must have been very close; I could feel his breath tickling my ear, and his solid body behind me. Instinctively, my shoulders relaxed. I knew he wouldn't let me fall. 'But look at it this way—there are definitely no sharks on the beginners' climbing wall. Just lean back.'

Just. Why do people say 'just', when it's followed by the most terrifying thing you can imagine? Just put your hand in the shark's mouth. Just leave your husband.

I felt one of Patrick's arms round my waist, solid as a sailing boom. The other was gripping on to his rope. 'I've got you. Just lean back and I'll help you down.' He eased me down so I was standing against the wall, my feet braced. He took his arm away and I felt a quick odd pang. 'Now you can't fall—you're tied up—so all you do is lean back and walk down.'

'Rappel?' I said, through shaking teeth.

'That's it. Hey, we'll make a climber out of you yet.'

I wouldn't say that, but I did make it down without crying or falling off. Feeling firm land under my feet again made me want to buckle down to it and kiss the rubber mats.

'Now we go up again,' said Patrick cheerfully.

'...?' I said, crumpling.

He put out a hand to me. 'Only kidding. It's Alex's turn now.'

This was a sport that Alex could actually do—he wasn't likely to get hurt or knocked and he wouldn't fall as he was all hooked up. All the same, I could feel Patrick's strain as he stood beside me. 'That's great, mate. Keep going.'

Alex was concentrating so hard, putting his little feet on each outcrop, his tongue poking out with the effort.

'He's so brave,' I said to Patrick quietly. 'Puts me to shame.'

Patrick kept his eyes on his son, perfectly still but following every move Alex made. 'I think we forget it, as we get older.'

'What?'

'How to be brave. It's a habit, like anything else. The more you practice, the more it's there and ready when you need it.'

Alex was at the top now, and we clapped him enthusiastically as he was helped back down the ladder.

'Well done!' I said, patting his too-large helmet. 'You were much better than me. I was so scared Daddy had to help me over the edge.'

'You shouldn't look down,' Alex said seriously. 'If you just shut your eyes, then your feets don't know they're up high.'

I felt there was probably some great wisdom in this, and I resolved to write it down in my notebook after we'd adjourned to the café for chocolate milk and banana cake.

'How was it, on the whole?' Patrick clapped me on the back companionably. I was still wearing my harness, and walking like John Wayne.

'Oh, you know, I looked into the abyss, and the abyss looked into me. It's just embarrassing that everything scares me so much. I mean, nothing gets to you.'

'Wait till you see me around horses. I also don't like boats much. Not keen on the whole drowning thing.'

'That's daft. You'd be able to get off in time.'

'Er, haven't you seen *Titanic*? The captain sailed it too fast into the iceberg because that guy with the moustache wanted to break the records. It was their ambition that brought them down. That and the iceberg.'

'You do know that wasn't actually a documentary, yes?'

'What?' He did a mock surprised face. 'Next you'll be telling me Rose and Jack weren't really in love and he didn't save her, in all the ways a person can be saved.'

'You're right, there is a very high risk of dying on a raft in the middle of the Atlantic, just because someone is too selfish to let you share it. "Sorry, Jack, I need the room for my elaborate frock. You'll have to stay in the water. Soz, but it is dry-clean only. It'll cost a fortune to get the sea-water out."'

'Also, if we got shipwrecked, I might have to eat you, and you're not very meaty.'

'Do you mean that?' I was absurdly flattered.

'I can honestly say, Rachel, that if we were in a ship-wreck, I would hesitate to eat you, because you don't have enough body fat to make it worthwhile.'

'Thanks. I think that's the nicest thing you've ever said to me.'

He patted my helmet, as I'd done with Alex. 'Come and choose what kind of cake you want. I need to fatten you up so I can snack on you if there's even a short delay during boarding.'

Patrick's List of things to do to avoid the
post-split, pre-divorce slump

1. ~~Climbing~~

2. ~~Skydiving~~

3. ~~Play on stage again~~

4. Get drunk

5. Go on a date

6. ~~Learn to fillet fish~~

7. Enter Max into a dog show

8. Buy a nice car

9. Take Alex overseas

10. ??

Chapter Nineteen

'It's looking at me funny,' said Patrick nervously.

'You should ask it why the long face? Get it? Long face, ha ha.'

He glared at me. I was mildly giddy with the euphoria of not being the one who was absolutely terrified at this task, and also with the fact I'd finally persuaded Patrick to visit his parents and sister in Kent. His parents were posh, raggedy types, his mother, Susanna, feeding her three dogs and chickens in wellies and a gilet, his father, Hamish, showing me his collection of war drawings after hearing I was an artist. After a huge lunch of their own eggs, home-grown salad, local ham, chutneys and three types of cake, I was feeling a bit sorry for the horses we were going to ride at Sophie's stables.

List of things posh people talk about

1. Horses

2. Dogs

3. Foxes and the evil thereof

4. Cheese

5. Members of the cabinet, with whom they were at school

6. Schools

7. The merits of different types of welly boots

'It's just a little pretty pony. Ten-year-old girls ride them and braid their hair.'

'How would you like it if I'd said we had to ride sharks for one task?'

'No one rides sharks, Patrick. And, if they do, they're dead. It's Darwinism in action.'

'Well, swim with sharks, then. I could have put that on my list. I still could, in fact. I don't have my number ten yet.'

'There aren't any sharks in England. Except in aquariums and you aren't usually allowed to dive into those.'

'Aquari-*a*.'

'Pedantry won't save you from the horses, Patrick.'

'It really is looking at me funny.'

I reached out to stroke Clover's nose. 'It' was a sweet little grey pony, barely taller than me, chewing peaceably on some grass. Sophie was 'tacking up' or 'leading out' or some other mythical horse-related activity in the stables, getting Patrick's 'mount' ready. Every time she called it that I sniggered and he looked cross. If there was one thing I was realising about doing all these activities, it was that people who do activities liked to describe things in the most secretive, nonsensical language possible. I suppose it was a way of making sure outsiders didn't get involved in their precious hobbies.

Eva Woods

Patrick was glaring at the pony. 'Careful. She might take a bite out of you.'

I laid my head against Clover and hugged her. She barely moved. 'Oh, sweet Clover, you're such a lovely girl.'

'I could do that to a shark. A hammerhead maybe.'

'People don't play with sharks for fun, Patrick!'

'Did you know horse riding is much, much more dangerous than sharks? It's the cause of about ten per cent of A & E admissions every year! How many do you think are caused by shark bites?'

'Have you been reading up on this?'

'Maybe. I wanted to know how likely I am to die, horribly trampled by the hooves of My Little Satanic Pony.'

'People die skiing all the time,' I pointed out. 'You still want to do that.'

'That's different. I can control the skis. They aren't going to turn around and take a bite out of me.'

'I think you're confusing "sweet pony" with "rabid Rottweiler". Look at her, she's lovely!'

'Hmm. What am I going to be on?'

There was a sound of clopping hooves. Only this time it was less 'joyful coconuts banging' and more 'deafening hoof beats of the Apocalypse'.

'Here's your mount, Patrick,' said Sophie, trotting up on her own shiny brown horse, Edison. Mount. I sniggered reflexively.

'Jesus wept,' said Patrick, quietly. His horse was massive, jet black, with an evil turn in its eyes. Its flanks were white with sweat and its mouth foamed.

'This is, like, Lucy,' said our bored stable hand, chewing gum. 'He's a bit feisty, but fast.'

'Lucy? For a he?'

'Short for Lucifer, like,' she said, snapping gum as she fiddled with the stirrups right within crushing distance of Lucifer's massive blade-like hooves.

'Are you sure about this?' Patrick gazed up at the horse. 'I mean, he seems a little...angry.'

'He's the only one we have big enough for a tall man, like. And he's a sweetie. You just have to show him who's boss.' And the fourteen-year-old girl in the Miffy T-shirt and no bra kissed the snarling beast between the eyes. I was noticing that these stables were full of disdainful teenage girls with ratty long hair and jodhpurs. There were no men to be seen anywhere—perhaps they sacrificed them to the gods of the horses?

I gave Patrick a look that said, *If she can do it, you can too.* 'Saddle up, cowboy.'

'Oh God.'

I watched him put a foot in the stirrup and pull himself up, like a character from a fantasy epic. 'Think of it as Shadowfax,' I said, trying to be helpful. 'Wasn't that Gandalf's horse?'

'Shadowfax was white and lovely and a beacon of hope for mankind. Lucifer is...well...nice, I'm sure.' He gingerly patted the horse's neck, then jumped as it snapped round at him.

'Behave, Lucy.' The riding girl swatted the horse with her whip.

Clover was so small I could practically step onto her. 'How come your sister is so into horses and you're scared of them?'

'He fell off once,' said Sophie, trotting up beside us in her smart riding gear.

'I didn't fall off. I got thrown. By an out-of-control animal. We could have sued.'

'Out-of-control seaside donkey.'

'It was huge! I was only little!'

'He landed on his ice cream and he cried, Rachel,' she said to me. 'He's never been on a horse since, until today. So well done, you.'

'I jumped to almost certain death from a plane for him. It's the least he can do.'

'I fell off. I'm traumatised!'

'Right, and this was when, last year?'

'I was three. It was horrible.'

Sophie snorted, riding her shiny horse ahead of us. 'Right, everyone ready? We're going on a hack.'

'It's so nice you came down,' she said, after a while of riding through the beautiful countryside, the horses' hooves churning the ground to mud, the sharp taste of winter in the air. Patrick was far ahead, being carted on by Lucifer's straining flanks. 'After what happened, I was afraid that might be it for Patrick and I. We were never that close, but to not speak for months…'

I was silent. 'Sophie, I don't actually know what happened. Patrick doesn't talk much about it.'

'Oh.' She rode on for a while. 'Well, I don't believe in keeping secrets, so I may as well tell you. It was me who told him. About Michelle and her…boyfriend.'

'And how did you…?'

'I called round. Sometimes I'm in town to see my accountant or so on, like the other day. I popped over one day, and she was there with him. Alan, I believe his name is.'

'Oh.'

'So when I saw you there, I thought— Well, it brought back some unpleasant memories.'

'I see. But why was he angry with you?'

'I told him right away. I couldn't even have thought of concealing it. I think he felt it wasn't my place, that perhaps I should have spoken to Michelle first, but I didn't know her that well. I think he blamed me, for a while, that she left.'

I remembered how he'd said it all fell apart in days. I could imagine it all too easily, how it was for Patrick—putting the question to the person you thought you'd be with forever, sure you'd get an answer, an easy explanation, a soothing word, and then hearing quite the opposite. I knew because it had happened to me.

'Sophie.' I nudged Clover on a bit as she stopped to eat some of a hedge. 'I know you feel you didn't do anything wrong, but if you want to make up, have you thought about maybe saying sorry?'

'You think people should say sorry when they aren't?'

'Sometimes. If it means they can be friends with their brother and help him when he needs it. And see their only nephew.' I held my breath, waited for her to tell me to mind my own business.

'Hmm.' She eyed me. 'You surprise me, Rachel. I got the impression you were the type of gel who'd rather hide under the table than confront someone you barely know.'

'Oh, I am. That's exactly me. But…'

'Yes?'

'He's really struggling, Sophie. Before I came, he was getting desperate. He can't afford a nanny and he's afraid to leave Alex with babysitters unless they understand his condition. So he just hardly ever goes out. If you could ever help out with him… I know Patrick would trust you.' We rode on in silence for a moment, the horses slogging up the hill, and from over the brow of it Patrick's shouts as Lucifer dragged him about the place. 'Sorry,' I said hastily. 'Not my place. Er, just trying to help. I'm very fond of him.'

'Yes,' she said, eyeing me. 'I can certainly see that.'

'Well, he's a great person. A good friend.'

Sophie looked me over with her penetrating gaze. 'Friend. Yes.'

Blushing, I stared down at my saddle, but I could still feel her looking at me. Luckily, at that point, we were interrupted by a rider coming up the track behind us, galloping a beautiful white horse. I didn't know much about riding, but even I could see the person was very good at it, their body moulded to the horse, urging it on, both of them totally in tune. They soon reached us and the horse stopped smartly, shaking its mane. The rider took off her helmet and rubbed her forehead, also shaking out long fair hair, streaked with grey. She was in her forties, I thought, weathered from being outside, but all the same exuding a glamour and confidence that made me shy. 'They're here,' she said to Sophie.

'Wonderful.' Sophie nodded to me. 'This is her.'

The woman smiled widely. 'Rachel! Hello, I'm Mathilda, Sophie's partner.'

'Oh, hi. It's a great stables. You must be doing well.'

Mathilda looked puzzled for a moment. 'Anyway, it's all set up for the surprise. They're getting ready.'

Sophie said, 'And Patrick has no idea?'

Mathilda shook her head. 'None.'

I looked between them. 'What surprise?'

'You'll see.' Sophie gave a wicked smile. 'I'm actually rather chuffed I thought of it. You'll see. Not a word to Pat now.'

'Hmm. OK.' I was still unsure. I was pretty sure Patrick

felt as I did, that surprises nearly always involved tears, vomit or some other involuntary expulsion of bodily fluids.

'See you back there.' Mathilda put back on her helmet and kicked the horse off, disappearing in a shower of earth like Liv Tyler in *Lord of the Rings*, only with slightly more attention to riding safety.

'Let's head back,' said Sophie, tugging on Edison's reins.

Soon we were at the end of the hack, the stables in sight. Patrick had reached there before us and was clinging weakly to Lucifer's mane. 'Hey! You're still on!' I called.

'I don't know how. It seems to defy the laws of gravity.' He was looking grey-faced, like someone who'd just survived a war.

'Well done,' said Sophie briskly. 'I said it would be easy. Lucy's bark is much worse than his bite.'

'He bites?' Patrick looked at him nervously. 'Anyway, can I get down now?'

'Don't you want a picture or something like that? For Instabook or whatever it is? People usually do.' She said this as if I would comment on someone taking a photo of themselves doing dishes—can you believe it? They thought getting on a horse wasn't an everyday occurrence?

'All right.' I fumbled my phone out of my pocket and passed it to her.

'Get the horses together, then.' We shuffled on the reins until Clover and Lucifer were side by side, comically mismatched, like Patrick and myself. I leaned over so we were almost but not quite touching. He glowed with adrenaline and heat.

'Smile!' said Sophie. 'Oh. How do you work this thing?'

'Press the camera button.'

'Which one? Oh, I've come out of it. Is that a picture of Beyoncé?'

'Press the camera icon,' I called hastily. 'It's there on the left.'

'The camera icon,' Patrick joined in. 'Come on, Soph. I really want to get off.'

Unfortunately, at that point, one of the stable cats, which had clearly been stalking me all along, dive-bombed from the roof onto my back and then landed on Clover, who kicked out in fear, catching Lucifer in the side. And Lucifer did not like being kicked. He bolted suddenly, and the look on Patrick's face as he was whipped away would have been funny if I hadn't also been in the process of falling off Clover and right onto the ground. Thankfully, there was some grass, and she wasn't very big, but it was still pretty sore.

'Say "Camembert"!' said Sophie. She looked up in surprise from the camera phone. 'Where's Patrick?'

By the time we caught Lucifer and coaxed him back with some apples, Patrick was frozen to the saddle.

'You can come down now,' said Sophie, holding the horse's bridle. 'He's just been a naughty boy.'

'It wasn't Patrick's fault Lucifer bolted.'

'I meant the horse.'

'Oh. Come on,' I said to Patrick. 'Look, there's the mounting block. Just put your leg over.'

His face was ashen. 'I can't... Life flashed...before eyes...'

'It's good though—you got to gallop, and you stayed on! That's, like, lots of lessons you just skipped right there.'

'That's, like, years of my life I just skipped right there.'

'Come on, soldier.' I helped him off. He was shaking. 'I fell off, you know, and you don't see me complaining.'

He looked behind me. 'Is that…a cushion tied onto your bum?'

'It was quite sore,' I said with dignity. 'I could have broken something.'

'I've broken my spirit,' he said sadly. 'That doesn't heal.'

'Oh, stop moaning. I jumped out of a plane. Anyway, come on over to the paddock. Sophie's got something that will cheer you up.'

'Is it a minced horse burger?'

'I was nearly a minced human burger.'

'Oh, stop moaning.' We had to lean on each other to limp over the paddock, like two survivors of a battlefield, me with my bruised coccyx and him with his shell shock. 'Why are we doing this, Rachel?' he said, as we hobbled. 'I mean, is the idea that the tasks make life fly by because it's *actually* flying by, i.e. we kill ourselves in the attempt?'

'It was supposed to make us feel more alive. Feel the wind in our hair, stop and smell the roses.'

'Why isn't that on the list? That doesn't sound like it would lead to me being smashed under a ton of horseflesh.'

'Well, it's over now. And, personally, I think dangling off a cliff is scarier than a horse, but there you go.'

'The ropes don't have teeth. Anyway, what is this you're dragging me to see? Is it a comfy chair and a cup of coffee?'

Sophie and her mum and dad were waiting for us by the fence of the paddock. 'Look,' she said proudly. 'Surprise!'

In the paddock, a small fat pony was being led around by Mathilda, several of the pouting glamorous girls hanging about. I wondered at what point the sulky stable girls morphed into these brisk, vaguely terrifying women. On top of the pony was Alex, in a riding hat that was slipping down over his curls. 'Daddy!' he called. 'I'm riding a pony! His name is Pickles!'

I gasped in delight. 'Oh wow, this is amazing! He loves horses, you know, and it seems like a good chance for him to try...'

I looked at Patrick's face. It had changed from white to red. He was stock-still, staring at his sister. 'You put my son on a horse?' he said quietly. 'My son, who might die if he gets even mildly injured, you put him on an unpredictable animal?'

'It's the easiest pony we have—look, he's smaller than Rachel. I—'

Before Sophie could say any more, he had vaulted over the fence and was half running, half walking, calling out. 'Tilda! I'm sorry, can you stop the pony, please? Is it safe?'

Mathilda stopped, as did the horse, who had been going about as fast as an elderly slow-worm anyway. 'Alex?' Patrick approached carefully, as if his child were on top of a marauding tiger. 'You need to get down now, mate. Just sit tight, OK.'

'But, Daddy, I'm having fun!'

'You can't ride horses, mate. We've talked about this. There's just some things you can't do. Your blood is too runny for it, remember?'

'But, Daddy!'

Patrick lunged in and dragged him off, carting him away from the pony as quickly as possible. The little horse shook its head and began to eat the grass.

Patrick stopped in front of Sophie and his parents, Alex clutched in his arms. 'No matter how many times I tell you, you never listen! He isn't like other kids! I'm sorry if that disappoints you, if he won't be your perfect ideal grandson, but this is how he is and he has a hard enough time understanding that without you undermining me.'

'Pat,' his mother cried. 'We didn't—'

'Oh, leave it.'

'Don't speak to your mother like that,' his father harrumphed.

'I mean it, OK? We're fine without you. Just leave us alone.' He carted Alex off to the car, the kid's little anguished face peering back at me.

To me, he didn't say anything at all. He didn't even look at me. I was stranded at the stables with Patrick's family, seventeen horses, a cushion strapped to my bum and a stable cat that was clearly out to get me.

Sophie drove me home. 'He really shouldn't have left you behind. That's just not cricket, is it?'

I was silent beside her, in her car that smelled of horses and had jodhpurs flung about the back seat. 'I didn't realise he would… I shouldn't have…'

'Rachel, Alex is my only nephew. When he was born, I researched everything I could about haemophilia. We even have an uncle who's a doctor and he agrees. Trust me, Patrick is far too protective. He's taken his cue from Michelle. Alex needs to be more careful than other children, yes, but he doesn't have to miss out on all games and activities.'

I said nothing. I just kept seeing Patrick's furious face, and Alex's little stricken one, being carried away. I shifted my legs, which were starting to ache from the saddle. Tomorrow I would be in agony all through my bum, thighs and stomach. Tomorrow I might also be homeless, if Patrick were really annoyed at me.

She saw my face and said kindly, 'Don't look so worried, Rachel. My brother has a bad temper sometimes, and he's as stubborn as an unbroken horse, but he'll come round.'

'I just…'

'You haven't done anything wrong.'

I said nothing. I wished I could be as sure as her. After all, it was my idea to go riding and bring Alex along.

When we reached London, Sophie had driven so fast that Patrick was only unloading Alex from the car. The little boy looked sleepy and sticky, as if he'd been crying. I smiled at him, but he just looked confused, trudging into the house with Roger trailing from one small hand.

Sophie put her hands on her hips, regarding her brother. 'I think you left something behind, Patrick.'

Patrick locked the car. 'Thanks for dropping her back. I shouldn't have… I'm sorry, Rachel. That was very thoughtless of me to forget you had no way home.' He didn't meet my eyes.

'It was all my idea,' declared Sophie. 'You mustn't blame Rachel. She's only trying to help, stop you burying yourself and poor Alex away here in this gloomy house. She's done wonders, poor girl. I gather you haven't been going anywhere since Michelle left.'

I tried to adopt a 'noble yet suffering' face, as if I might be played by Kate Winslet in a film.

'You had no business doing that,' Patrick said to Sophie. 'He could have been badly hurt.'

'You know me. I can't help interfering. It's because I care, and I hate not seeing my only nephew, and I hate that he can't do the things he loves. He was so happy, Pat. It would have been OK.'

'Maybe, but I can't…'

'It will always be this way,' Sophie said gently. 'You'll always have to choose between keeping him wrapped in cotton wool and the small chance of him being hurt. Like any child.' She patted his arm. 'You know Uncle Herbert thinks it's perfectly fine too.'

Uncle Herbert? God, they really were posh. I wondered what his parents had thought of me saying 'dinner' and 'napkin'.

'I see you've all been chatting about it,' said Patrick frostily. 'You didn't happen to tell Mum and Dad about your own living arrangements while you were doing all this talking?'

Sophie looked boot-faced. 'That's different.'

'Is it? You were pretty quick to tell them my wife was cheating on me, but you've never found the time to say, oh, you're gay, and by the way you live with Mathilda?'

Of course! Not business partners, partners partners. God, I was dumb. I cringed retrospectively.

'I'll tell them when I'm ready.'

'It's been eight years! Don't you think Tilda feels bad about that? Just tell them, Soph. They probably know already. For God's sake, you go on pottery weekends together.'

Sophie drew herself up. 'I hear what you're saying. And I would like to say I'm sorry for what I did. About Michelle. It seemed like the right thing at the time.'

'Well, look what it did.' He swept an arm. 'She's gone, and Alex is growing up without his mum.'

'I'm sorry,' said Sophie again, with dignity. 'I want to help. Let me look after him sometimes, Pat. I'd love to. And I promise I won't put him on horses, or take him mountain climbing. I mean, if you don't want me to.'

Patrick sighed, running a hand through his curls. He had

a bit of straw in them, I noticed. 'Let's just leave it for now. I'll see you at Christmas.'

'Sorry,' she said. Then she cleared her throat and her brisk ringing voice was back. 'Thank you, Rachel. You were a hit, and you've got an excellent seat for a beginner. Goodbye.'

'Bye,' I muttered. When she drove off, it was just me and him. 'I...'

'Let's not talk about it. My sister can be very persuasive, I know.'

'I really didn't...'

'I know. Can we just leave Alex out of our list plans for now, please? I'm just not ready. He might be, but I can't cope with the worry. I'll try though.'

'Of course. Of course.' I was just so relieved he had said 'our', I'd have agreed to anything. 'So you aren't kicking me out?'

'Of course not. Who else will walk Max and make ice-cream cake? Come here.' He took me in an awkward hug, and I leaned into his solid chest, smelling hay and horses and his lime aftershave. I reached up and took the bit of straw from his curls.

He blinked. 'I'm sorry I left you.'

'Sophie said it wasn't cricket. No doubt Uncle Herbert would say it too. I wonder if he also wears cords.'

'Ah, shut it, serf.' He smiled at me, and my heart soared, because everything was OK again.

Rachel's List of things to do to avoid the
post-split, pre-divorce slump

1. Do stand-up comedy

2. Learn to dance

3. Travel somewhere on a whim

4. Do yoga properly

5. Sleep with a stranger-???

6. ~~Eat something weird~~

7. Go to a festival

8. ~~Get a tattoo~~

9. ~~Go horse riding~~

10. ~~Try an extreme sport~~

Chapter Twenty

There's nothing about Christmas that should make it any harder on the soon-to-be-divorced lady of a certain age (pushing thirty-one). It's just another day, after all. It's not even when Jesus was born. That was probably sometime in March. No reason to slide into a lower life state, as my Buddhist friend Sunita would say.

I was telling myself all this from my vantage point in the upper deck of a National Express coach headed to Exeter, but it wasn't working. Christmas. My first without Dan, having to face my extended family and say, hey, thanks for those spoon rests you got us as a wedding present, but it hasn't worked out. Were you supposed to give things back if the marriage failed within a certain time frame, like a mobile phone handset? I kept imagining Dan at home with Jane, the two of them in the silent living room with their presents, eating with just the chink of cutlery and the tick of the grandfather clock. Maybe his grandma would be there too, a woman so Victorian she thought that gels wearing trousers was a bit racy. She'd once dropped her glass of sherry when I appeared for Christmas brunch in my pyjamas. There was, of course, a worse scenario, which was that Dan's new 'special lady', whoever she was, had whisked him away on a Christmassy minibreak. They'd be throwing snowballs at each other, then falling over in the ice, and he'd roll over, brush the hair from her cold cheek, and...

God. My imagination had clearly been mainlining Mills and Boon. I'd hated spending Christmas in someone else's house, missing Mum and Dad and Jess and the kids. And now I was on my way to an uninterrupted family Christmas, as I'd wished for, probably for the rest of my natural life, and I was mired in horror. Dad would lock himself in the shed when it all got too much. Mum would throw a strop over the gravy. Jess would be displaying her perfect children and happy marriage and I'd be all alone.

ALONE, ALONE. The wheels of the bus seemed to sing it out for me, or perhaps it was the tinny music emanating from the speakers of the teenage boy in front. Outside, a drizzly Christmas. Ho flipping ho.

Patrick was taking Alex to his parents' for Christmas. I'd asked if Michelle would be over to see her son, but Patrick said she had only one day off work. She would try, but if the weather continued snowy and stormy, it seemed unlikely. I wondered how Alex would feel, not seeing his mum at Christmas. Emma was with Ian's lot in Manchester—all Trivial Pursuit marathons and walks in the Peak District. She had sent me a text two days before, saying she'd see me at Cynthia's New Year thing. I took this to mean the two of them were now speaking again. Cynthia and Rich were hosting both families this year, because that was how together their lives were—they were at the point where they could say to their parents, *Hey, we've got it from here. We're the responsible adults. You can relax now and start playing golf or joining book groups.* Whereas I'd had to ring my mum to make sure I was getting chocolate coins in my stocking this year. She'd made some vague noises. 'Oh! I don't know about stockings, darling.'

'What? You "don't know" about stockings?'

'It's just Jess will be doing the boys and you are thirty now...'

'Mum! I've had a really hard year, and I just...'

She'd sighed. 'All right. As if I don't have enough to do.'

I'd hung up. A grudging stocking was almost as bad as no stocking at all.

Dad was waiting when I disembarked the coach several hours later. Someone had thrown up around Bath and I'd almost gagged myself at the smell. I toted my rucksack over to him. As part of a new grown-up life strategy, I had to get a smart wheely case, I'd decided. And stop travelling on coaches. 'Hi, Dad.' I hadn't seen him since I'd gone home to tell them Dan and I were on the skids. 'How's everything?'

'Oh fine.' He fidgeted with the car keys. 'You?'

'Well, you know, it's not been easy. Work's tough, and moving out was hard, and it's just...a struggle sometimes. You?'

He paused for a while. 'The snowdrops are about to come up, I think. A whole month early! Imagine.'

That was as close as Dad got to an emotional heart-to-heart.

Back at the house, the madness had begun. I could hear the noise as we parked in the driveway. 'Jess is here?'

Dad just nodded, a pained expression on his face. 'They've already broken the *Bounty* Airfix.'

'Oh, Dad! You spent weeks on that.'

He nodded bleakly. 'Three months. I was going to put it into a bottle for your mother for her present. Had to buy her some perfume from the market instead. This man was selling that stuff she likes, that Chanel No. 4. A real bargain though.'

'Wait, Chanel No. 4?'

'That's right. Isn't it?'

'Well, I'm sure she'll make the best of her loss.'

The house was approximately the temperature of Southern Sudan, exacerbated by the oven going full blast with frozen pizzas—Mum can't cook. The TV was on, blaring out *Cars*, even though no one was watching it. A miniature elf attached itself to my foot.

'Hello! Is this Santa's workshop?'

'It's me, Auntie Rachel.'

'Who's that? An elf?'

'Justin!'

'Oh, hello. Where's my Christmas cuddle?'

Justin, nephew number one, aged four, doled it out. He smelled of biscuits and crayons. I kissed him. 'Happy Christmas. What's Santa going to bring us, eh?'

Justin shook his head at me pityingly. 'He isn't coming to you, Auntie Rachel. You're too old.'

Even the kids were in on it.

'Justin, let Auntie Rachel come in.' Jess appeared in the doorway holding nephew number two, Archer. I assumed they'd considered and rejected other archaic-profession-based names before choosing it. Fletcher, Cooper, Plague Victim, etc.

'Hi.' I leaned in to kiss her but got tangled up in the mini-Boden model child. Jess spent more on her kids' clothes than I spent on mine, but I suppose that was fair, since she and her husband, Andy, had more than enough. He was a solicitor and so was she, or she had been before Archer. They lived in Exeter, conveniently close to Mum and Dad, and Facebook was always filled with shots of them on days out together or round for Sunday lunch or Andy and Jess out for meals while the parents babysat, clinking cocktail glasses and Instagramming their food with hashtags like #nom #blessed. Suddenly, I missed Dan, even though last Christmas had been excruciating. At least he'd been, nominally, on my side, someone to play with me in the infamous Game of Life marathon of Boxing Day or pass me the ear plugs when one of the kids kept us up with lusty late-night screeching.

Jess was wearing skinny indigo jeans, a long soft cardigan and knee boots. Her fair hair fell around her face in wisps. What with the flawless skin and lovely rosy-cheeked child in her arms, she was straight out of a catalogue. My sister was four inches taller than me and eighteen months older, but we may as well have been from different species.

'Hi, Rachel.' Andy appeared, corralling Justin as he did so. I hugged him—that was one thing I used to have on Jess; my husband was tall and hers was barely five foot seven, but of course I didn't have a husband at all now, so she'd pretty much come from behind and taken the gold in that too. *Typical.*

I hefted up my rucksack. 'Am I in my old room?'

Mum shifted in the kitchen doorway. 'Well, no, the boys are in there. They'll be going to bed earlier, so we thought...'

'And Jess and Andy are in her old room?'

'Of course.' Mum wasn't meeting my eyes.

I could see where this was going. 'So where am I?'

'The back room.'

It had come to this. The back room wasn't even a room. It was a dodgy shed-like extension Mum and Dad had put on after they bought the council house in the early nineties. It still smelled of the dog who'd died in 1996—RIP Fluffy, if only you'd seen that milk float coming—and had a lino floor they had shoved a camp bed on alongside Dad's collection of models and *Trainspotter* magazine back issues.

'It's a shed!'

'Don't be silly. We only use the shed when there's really overspill.'

'But…but…' Last year Dan and I'd had the good room, the one that used to be mine for one glorious year when Jess left for uni, because Mum and Dad were slightly in awe of him.

'Rachel.' Mum gave me one of her Looks. 'Don't make a fuss. It's nice to all bunk in together. We're a family.'

So it had come to this—I was nearly thirty-one and spending Christmas in a glorified lean-to at my parents. I tried to remember what Cynthia had said about not having fallen off the ladder, because I felt I was staring up from the bottom of dozens of them. This may have been because there was an actual ladder propped up in the corner of my so-called room. I arranged some of my things on it like shelves and went back to the main house.

I remembered the first time Dan came here. After his six-bed mansion, where he'd been the adored only child and encouraged to keep very quiet indeed, he'd found it hard to hide the horror on his face. Dad had picked us up from the coach and I could see he'd been horrified too at having to make conversation with a boy, an actual boy who might have come within two feet of his younger daughter. Worse,

Dan had no interest in birdwatching, Airfix or the history of the Morris dancing movement. Conversation flowed like a glacier—that is, extremely slowly and very coldly. When we'd entered the house, he'd been assailed by the smell of Mum's gravy and the sound of her screeching. Dad had a slight hearing problem—so he said anyway; I had my doubts, I reckoned if you had to live with Mum you might start faking one too—so she spoke twice as loud as normal all the time. And then there was the state of the place. My parents weren't exactly slobs. It's just that Dad was afraid of DIY, and even more afraid of tradesmen, so he always let them do a totally shoddy job—cf. the back room/lean-to I'd been relegated to—and Mum wouldn't deal with them because it was 'man's work', so she let it go ahead, then spent the next twenty years moaning about it instead.

I had been in the kitchen for a full five seconds before Mum had plonked a caramel-coloured cup of tea in front of me, along with a slice of Christmas cake. While doing this, she had not paused once in berating Dad about the Christmas tree lights. 'I was reading in the paper how this kiddie got electrocuted by one last year, so you need to make sure the plugs are higher up, you know Archer is into everything right now, so you need to move them tonight, Raymond, are you listening to me, you never listen, do you, Rachel, don't get crumbs on that table and don't spoil your appetite, we're eating early tonight for the kids, Raymond, are you listening?'

Dad had his back to her as he fiddled with some masking tape; I suspected trying to raise the sunken *Bounty* from its sad demise. 'What was that?' he said.

Jess appeared in the doorway, flushed and pretty. 'It's

OK, Mum. Andy's rigged up a plug guard. Should be fine. As long as Archie doesn't pull the tree over or something.'

Mum looked torn between relief and yet more worry. 'He is good, Andy. Nice to have ONE man around here who isn't totally USELESS.'

She meant Dad, of course, who was once again feigning deafness as he practised model marine salvage, but a sudden wave of sadness hit me as I realised they'd probably never really liked Dan, not since the day I brought him home and he refused Mum's apple turnovers because he was 'in training for football season'. Not on our wedding day, when he'd made a few cutting jokes in his speech about the size of the house and how hot it always was. Not when they first came to stay in our new house and he was too busy trying to get to the next level of Angry Birds to speak to them. They loved Andy though. Super Andy, the perfect son-in-law, to go with Jess's perfect kids and perfect home and perfect pore-free skin.

I had a sudden urge to text Patrick, but my phone was in my bag, and the subsequent grilling wouldn't be worth it.

'How's that landlord of yours?' said Mum, and I gulped. She could always read my mind.

'Eh, he's OK. Nice.'

'Seems a bit odd, letting a young girl stay with him rent-free.'

'I'm thirty, Mum. And he just needs a bit of help. His wife left him alone with their little boy.'

She softened. 'Poor man. Why was that?'

'She went back to America, where she's from. A work thing. Just for a bit.'

'Well, that explains it, doesn't it? Very heartless people I always thought, Americans. Look at Iraq.'

Dad looked up. 'There's only three hundred million of them, Susan. I'm sure some of them are nice. I mean, look at Walt Disney or Obama.'

Mum had a crush on Obama. Something to do with him being a kind funny man who also had his finger on the nuclear-deterrent button. 'Well, *someone* can hear well enough when they want to, can't they?'

Then there was a loud clatter as Archer 'got into' the tree and several baubles fell off, prompting widespread drama as Mum and Jess looked for broken glass and Archer screeched and Dad just shook his head and continued his attempts to Raise the *Titanic*.

And so it went. For the next three days. Without. A. Break.

Chapter Twenty-One

Christmas morning dawned, watery and chill. I woke up at 3 a.m. with a child's voice shouting, 'HAS HE BEEN YET?' somewhere upstairs. There was no weight of stocking at the end of my bed, so I went back to sleep, to be woken again a few hours later by the shuffle of Dad's slippers on the lino. 'Morning, Dad,' I said, without opening my eyes.

'Er, just bringing you some tea.' Something heavyish was laid on the end of my bed. I opened my eyes.

'Oh look! A stocking!'

'Where did that come from?' he said innocently.

'Magic, eh?'

I sat up and took the tea in my 1998 *Dawson's Creek* mug, as Dad perched on the ladder/shelves. 'How are things out there?' I asked.

He winced. 'It's like the battle of Ypres, only without the poison gas.'

'Well, wait till Mum opens her perfume set from the market, should take care of that.'

'Are you getting up, love? Your presents are there from us, errrr, I mean, Father Christmas.'

'Thanks. I'll finish this tea first.'

He got up and paused with an expression I knew from the once every five years it came around. It was 'about to say something vaguely related to the emotions'. I braced myself. 'Are you feeling OK, love? I mean, are you missing him?'

I ducked my head. 'No. And yes. I don't know. It's strange being alone. But it was the right thing to do.'

He mulled this over for a moment. 'It's nearly a new year. You never know what the future will bring.'

As he went out, I eyed my mug, reflecting that the cast of *Dawson's Creek* would undoubtedly agree with his wise point. Who'd have thought Michelle Williams would find stardom and heartbreak, while Katie Holmes would marry then divorce Tom Cruise, and that Dawson himself would still have a big head? Dad was right. You could never know.

Except for the fact that two small children on Christmas morning will produce a large amount of carnage. You can pretty much be a hundred per cent sure of that.

Later that day, we were all sunk under the weight of Christmas dinner—we begged Mum to buy it all from M&S, but she wouldn't, so every year we had tooth-shattering mince pies, turkey that was as dry as the Sahara during a drought and Brussels sprouts so soggy you could ship them into said Sahara as part of a drought relief programme. All the same, I always ate so much I had to be crane-lifted into a chair after.

I was slumped in front of Christmas *Top of the Pops*. The kids were napping, Dad was doing the washing-up and Mum was 'getting her head showered'—i.e. consuming a can of gin and tonic in the bath. Jess passed through the living room, scooping up toys and wrapping paper. Her own house was similar to Cynthia's, a temple of white and salvaged wood, pictures of the boys in different cool frames, candles everywhere. She did everything right. 'Peace at last,' she said.

'Where's Andy?'

'Helping Dad.'

Of course he was. Perfect, nice, bland Andy. Last year, Dan had gone for a nap after dinner and not helped with anything. My phone beeped—Patrick's reply to my text of earlier wishing him Happy Christmas.

Sophie driving me mad, he said. *Sixteen rounds of charades later. Come back soon. We could crush them.*

Then: *She has told them about Tilda, by the way. They said 'Oh, that's nice, dear. Like that Sue off the* BAKE OFF'.

I smiled. Jess was blatantly snooping over my shoulder. 'Who's Patrick?'

'Does no one in this family understand the concept of privacy? Honestly. It's like living with the NSA.'

'They've got nothing on Mum. She looks through my cupboards when she comes round. Pretends she's trying to help, but I know better. So who is he?'

'He's my landlord. My friend.'

'Oh yeah. Mum said you were living in some weird house share.'

'It's not weird. I'm just staying there to help him. Like an au pair.'

'You don't get paid though.'

'No, but I don't pay rent, and I don't do much, really. Just bits.'

My sister's pretty face looked concerned. 'You're sure

you're not being asked for too much? Because you know
Andy could draw up a contract—'

'I'm fine. He's my friend, for God's sake. You don't have
contracts with your friends.' Though Andy probably did.

'You don't know him that well,' she said. 'I'm just saying—'

'Well, don't just say. Please.'

She paused. 'It's the little boy I'm thinking of. He's four,
you said.'

'Yes. Nearly five.'

'So, I know if, God forbid, I went away, and Andy got
someone else in to live…well, Justin would be really confused. It's hardly fair on the kid, is it? He must not have a
clue what's going on.'

'Are you saying I should move out for Alex's sake?'

'I'm just saying, think carefully about it. Maybe look at
some other options. Have you even signed a lease?'

'No.'

'Well, there you go. This man could put you out on the
street tomorrow. Didn't you say the wife could be back at
any moment?'

'He wouldn't do that.'

'You didn't think Dan would either.'

For a moment I couldn't speak.

'Rach. I'm just worried about you. I mean, you seemed
so sorted, you were together ten years, and then suddenly
Dan's kicking you out? We couldn't believe you'd just go,
leave all your stuff—I mean, Andy or I could have helped.
You were entitled to something at least.'

Ah, that old phrase. *I'm worried about you.* Just another
way of saying, *I think you've made a complete and total
mess of your life.*

'I don't need you to worry about me.'

'But look at you—you're living in someone's box room, you're single and you said yourself work wasn't going well. I mean, what happened? You and Dan, you seemed happy.'

'We weren't. Dan and I...we just weren't working. It's...' I looked at her. She was so pretty, so together. She even looked slim after the post-Christmas dinner bloat. There was no way I could tell her what had happened to Dan and I. She would never understand, with her perfect life. 'You and Andy. What makes you work?'

She thought about it. 'I suppose...he's on my side. Whatever I do, however many mistakes I make, he has my back. You remember when we were little and we got in trouble at school, Mum always used to go and shout at them, even if we were at fault?'

'You never got in trouble,' I pointed out.

'Well, OK. Remember when you did, then. It's like that. I know I can lean on him.'

I wondered if it was really just that simple. 'Dan and I—we stopped being like that. We couldn't lean on each other at all, and eventually we just collapsed.'

In the living room there were about a hundred pictures of Jess and Andy's wedding, her in strapless white silk with her hair up, them laughing in a shower of confetti, them nuzzling each other in a field, them playfully looking at each other round a tree—I mean, really. Even if I weren't getting divorced, I'd be struggling to hold down my Quality Street in the face of so much coupled-up bliss. But previously there had also been two photos of a different wedding—mine and Dan's. There was me in my vintage lace ballerina dress and him in his old-fashioned suit and waistcoat with the pocket watch, grinning in front of a crowd of all our guests, and another of the two of us, caught unawares in the church, him passing me a tissue to wipe my eyes. Now both were gone. In their place was a picture of Archer and Justin, and also one of Mum and Dad's seventies wedding, all dreadful kipper ties and Juliet caps and princess sleeves, everyone arranged badly like a shelf of disorganised books.

Mum had seen me notice this change earlier. 'I thought it was best...you'd not want to be reminded.'

I'd swallowed. 'No. It's OK.'

There was no trace of us at all. Soon, that day in April two years ago would be as if it had never happened. Easiest way to waste ten grand I could think of.

I came back to London three days later, desperate to get away and to a place I could nominally call my own, even if it was just a room in someone else's house, as Jess had so delighted in telling me. I had avoided being alone with her as much as possible after her little pep talk. I wasn't going to give her the satisfaction of knowing she was right, I really was adrift.

Alex threw himself on me as I came in the door. He was attired in yet another trendy onesie. 'You were AGES. Where did you GO?'

'I had to see my mummy and daddy. They like to see me too, sometimes!'

'Oh. You can share my daddy, if you want.'

I started laughing, until I saw Patrick's face. 'Well, that wouldn't really work, mate. How was your Christmas?'

'I got *Star Wars* Lego.'

'Good stuff. And a new outfit, I see.'

'What's *outfit*?'

'Er, what you have on. Want to see what I got?' I opened

up my rucksack and extracted Patrick's gift, a striped onesie. 'Pretty snazzy, eh?'

'Did you like it?' Patrick said anxiously, hovering.

'I hardly took it off.'

Alex was tugging at my hand. 'Put it on now, Rachel. We'll be the same.'

'If you insist.'

'Daddy too.'

'OK, OK.' I turned to Patrick as Alex ran off to find a DVD. 'So did she...'

He shook his head. 'Storms, no flights, no time off work. She says she'll come in January.'

I didn't know what to say to that. Part of me, a terrible part, was glad I could come back and find nothing unchanged, move into my lovely tower room and hang out with this ready-made family, forget they weren't mine and everything else Jess had said.

And the three of us spent my first night back watching *Finding Nemo*, all in our new matching onesies, eating popcorn, and it was lovely, and when Alex fell asleep during the jellyfish-hopping bit—luckily avoiding the traumatic near-death experience of Ellen DeGeneres's fish—Patrick picked him up and put him in bed. Max trailed us as far as the stairs, then stopped, looking up at us with a sad face, so I lifted him and carried him up too. I stood in the door with the dog in my arms as the child was put down, safe in his bed, his night light softly burning.

Patrick came out to find me on the stairs, practising 'paw' with Max. He looked tired, his hair sticking up in all directions.

I smiled at him fondly. 'He's down?'

'Yeah.' Patrick paused. 'Rachel...'

'Yeah?'

'Nothing. It's good to have you back.'

I said nothing. It was good to be back.

Downstairs, it was all candles burning and fire crackling and wine pouring. The sounds and smells of home. 'Fancy a game of Scrabble?' Patrick asked. 'I got a little gizmo for Christmas. It calculates the score automatically. You know, so we won't encounter that "accidental" adding-up problem you had for a while there.'

'I can't believe you're still moaning about that. You won, didn't you?'

'I did. Fifteen times in a row now and counting.'

'I won't play with you if you're going to be insufferable about it.'

'Oh come on! It's just a game. Honestly, Alex loses more graciously than you.'

Things I should be old enough to do by now, but am not

1. Lose at games: In my family, board games were dangerous territory since the Great Mousetrap Incident of 1994, so when I lost at Scrabble, pub quizzes or just the Post-it name game, my response was still that of a twelve-year-old: 'You must have cheated! What's a "zo" anyway? You can't just MAKE UP WORDS. I'm telling Mum.'

2. Say no to nights out: Even Carrie Bradshaw stayed in occasionally, to flip through issues of *Vogue* and ponder life's great questions like: can we ever have too many shoes? Sometimes we all need downtime, and yet if I ever say no to an event, I will be stricken down by Fear of Missing Out (FOMO). And it will be the best night out

ever, which will fill the conversations of my friends for months to come. 'Remember that thing with the rabbits and the top hat? Ha ha ha! Oh wait. You weren't there.'

3. Open Tetra Paks: Carton open. Soup everywhere.

4. Bulk-buy toothpaste: or soap, dish sponges, batteries or any of those little things that always run out. I still bought loo roll in those dinky two-packs, because otherwise you have to haul home that massive twelve-packer, and people might think you're sharing your home with incontinent sextuplets, or one adult rugby player.

5. Plan ahead: Always making sure I have cash on me. Automatic Oyster top-ups. Downloaded tube maps–the art of planning ahead was really part of being grown-up. I still liked to use the 'I'll just hop on this bus and see where it's going' method of getting home from nights out, whereas my more organised friends had pre-booked minicabs and negotiated down the fare. My approach did often work, and you could have adventures–if you liked adventures that smelled of regurgitated kebabs.

'Oh hurry up. Continents have separated in less time than it takes you to play a word.'

'Is that one?' I placed some of my letters, frowning hard.

'SPOX?' he read. 'Er, no, it's not.'

'Are you sure?'

'What would it mean?'

'I don't know. I don't know *all* the words.'

'It sounds like those holding-in pants you wear.'

'Spanx? I don't wear those.'

'Rachel, I hang out your laundry.'

'Actually, it does sound like Spanx, only for your feet,' I

said. 'Spox. Like holding-in socks. I wonder if there's much of a market for them.'

'Do women worry about having fat feet?'

'They would after I'd marketed Spox at them. That's how you do it, see—you take a totally imaginary bodily problem, like your nails being too pale, or your ears being chubby, and then you persuade all the women they need to buy it. It's sexist, is what it is.'

He got to his feet. 'I'm going to need more wine for this.'

While he was gone, I stared at my letters with fierce concentration. I had to beat him. He was totally insufferable about beating me, and despite getting close I had never won once. I needed to use all my letters at once and get the extra fifty points. I typed some words into the Scrabble gizmo to check them.

'Sorry,' it beeped. 'I do not recognise CLIT.'

I sighed. 'Well, you're not alone there, Scrabble computer.' I gave up and put down CLAP. 'Your turn,' I called.

He did a comedy double take as he came back in with another bottle.

'What is it?'

'Good God, Rachel. I never noticed before. Your feet are just…so fat.'

'I'm sorry. Obese feet are a real problem nowadays.'

He held up a packet of dusters. 'Have you ever thought of trying Spox? It's Spanx, but for feet.'

'Now I can fit into those cute wedges for my date with Curt!'

He gave a cheesy wink to an imaginary camera and I fell about laughing. 'Come and go, I did a rubbish one.'

Patrick gave the board a cursory glance and put down TORCS on a double-word score. 'Not looking good for

Kenny in this game. Yet another victory for Gillan seems assured—this is starting to seem a little boring, isn't it, Alan?'

'Alan Shearer doesn't do Scrabble commentary.' I was staring at my new letters. Was it... Could it really be?

'I wish he did. Come on, put down your little four-letter word so I can win and get this over with.'

Excitement began to buzz in my stomach. Very slowly, not wanting to jinx it, I picked up my tiles and laid them nonchalantly on the board. The 'S' was part of another long word, and it crossed a triple letter and a double word. 'Oh, like that, you mean?'

Patrick glanced, then sat bolt upright. 'What the hell?'

'Oxidates,' I said smugly. 'Pretty sure that's a word, isn't it?'

'How did you get that?'

I shrugged. 'I've been hustling you all this time.'

He was tapping at the computer. 'That's... Wait...'

'Ninety-five points, I think you'll find. That's right, I can do mental adding-up too.'

'It's not fair.'

'T-O-U-G-H. That'd be eight points right there.'

'I've created a monster,' said Patrick sadly, as I went on to win the game with ease.

Chapter Twenty-Two

I don't know what it says about our culture that, just as you've survived Christmas and managed not to stab your in-laws or die of a burst colon through excessive turkey consumption, after a few days' respite, when you start thinking about salad and healthy walks, you have to plunge yourself back into the horrors of Hogmanay. That we're gluttons for punishment, I suppose. Or that it's best to get them both over while the alcoholic haze means you have a chance of not remembering most of it.

New Year's Eve—my nemesis. As I ransacked my wardrobe trying to figure out what to wear that night, past ones reeled through my head like a slow-motion montage of vomit, karaoke, drunken rows and crying in strange houses. Maybe I'd throw up in a sink. Again. I had an actual subset in my list of 'Terrible New Year's Eves' called 'throwing up in sinks (not my own)'. As in, it had happened more than once. That was how bad it got.

List of worst ever New Year's Eves

1. The time I got groped by a horrible man called Nigel at a cheese and wine party, and while running away trod in some really smelly Brie, and everyone on the bus looked at me like it was dog poop or I just hadn't washed in days.

2. The time I went back home with a uni friend (Ros of the suburban babies) and we went to a party at a school friend of hers, and I was so nervous and out of place I drank a whole bottle of Goldschläger and threw up in their sink and the random friends shouted at me, and for days afterwards my pee was gold-tinged, like a crazy millionairess.

3. The time Dan and I were on holiday in Egypt, trying to 'spice things up', and at midnight I jumped into the swimming pool fully clothed, because this seemed like a cool and crazy thing to do, until I realised another guest had really bad food poisoning and had thrown up into it, so then I was sick too and spent the rest of the night in wet pants (in fairness to me, this was one time when the vomiting was legitimately not my fault).

4. The year we went skiing and got lost in the tiny town we were staying in and spent three hours walking around in the cold, only to find the next day that we'd been going in circles within three streets of our hotel. I caught a cold and was cross with Dan for the rest of the holiday; he fell on some ice and couldn't even ski for the rest of it.

5. The time, aged seventeen, when Lucy Coleman and I tried to get into a big club in Exeter with fake IDs, and they let her in and not me, presumably because the sheer weight of make-up pulling her face down had aged her ten years, and she met a man in the queue who had a

leather jacket and mobile phone in a holster, and went in with him, leaving me outside in the cold. I had to ring my dad to pick me up and it was an hour's wait in the rain and I was grounded for three weeks afterwards, since I was supposed to be at a sleepover.

Oh God. I didn't want to go out. Damn Emma and damn Cynthia and damn her big fancy house and catered party with champagne in the bath, and damn them for forcing the issue that I 'couldn't be alone' on New Year's, and damn me for my FOMO and ridiculous lack of backbone. I had less backbone than the fish I had filleted at sushi class.

Patrick was in the kitchen when I went down for breakfast, spooning up organic granola. 'So you're off out tonight?'

'Yes. Got a party at Cynthia's.'

'Sounds nice.'

'No. No, it doesn't sound nice. It'll be all lawyers and people from university, plus, even worse, lawyers from university. They'll talk about house prices all night and I'll drink too much champagne and end up vomiting in a sink. Again.' At least Cynthia had plenty of sinks. I was going to aim for the one in their en suite.

'Doesn't sound like Emma's thing.' Patrick had taken to talking about my friends as if he'd known them all his life. It was quite sweet.

'I haven't told you the worst bit yet. Guess.'

'Um, there's karaoke?'

'No, sadly. Rich wouldn't allow it.'

'The champagne is really cava from Aldi?'

'As if. Cynthia wouldn't use that to clean her jewellery.'

'Um, they've got a blind date planned for you with an actuary called Keith?'

'No, I… Oh God, they might though. No, it's fancy dress.'

'Bad luck,' said Patrick sympathetically. 'Costume hire? They might be open today.'

'Oh, no. Nothing so easy. Emma says we have to make our own or it's cheating. It's a bit competitive.'

At uni, we did a lot of dressing up. I had a series of photos of me dressed as: pirate, fairy, Giant Peach—I was pulling a boy called James—wartime pilot and 'trampy vicar'. The only thing that was the same was the pissed-up expression on my face in each.

'I'll help,' he said, rinsing his bowl and putting it in the dishwasher. 'It could be fun.'

'You can do costumes?'

'I'm the single dad of a four-year-old whose school is very hot on "creative expression", but who can't use scissors. I could do an A-level in cutting out and Pritt Stick skills.'

'Thanks.' A thought came to me, shamefully late. 'Do you have plans tonight?' I should have asked him before, but I'd imagined he'd be doing something involving wine tasting and fine cheeses and his cultured work colleagues at the architecture firm. I didn't think he'd want to hang out with lots of drunk lawyers. Hey, I didn't even want to do that myself.

'Oh, no. A babysitter on New Year's Eve is worth the national debt of some countries. No, it's just me and a nice Ardbeg and hoping next year is better than this one.'

'You should come.'

'I can't.' But he hesitated. 'I'd like to though. So you better describe all those Hooray Henrys for me.'

'You could always just look in a mirror.'

'Do you want me to help you or not?'

'Yes, please.'

'So what's the theme? Is there one?'

'Of course. It's the most organised party in history. We wouldn't want the anarchy of non-themed fancy dress. It's "who you want to be when you grow up". Sort of cutesy, since there won't be a person there who's under thirty, probably.' The invite—yes, Cynthia sent invites, in the post; she ordered them online just to spite Emma and her crafting mania—had been charmingly adorned with a picture of a little girl in high heels.

'OK, so who were your heroes when you were little?' He tapped his chin. 'Amelia Earhart? Marie Curie? No, I bet it was an artist. Frida Kahlo? Can you grow a monobrow by tonight?'

'I was thinking of someone more recent,' I said shyly. 'Um. From the world of music. My ultimate icon.'

'Oh, I see. But how would we make a Meatloaf costume?' I threw the tea towel at him. 'You want to be Beyoncé?'

'Yes,' I said defiantly. 'I know I'm nowhere near as tall or beautiful as she is—I mean, duh—but it's fancy dress, shouldn't you be allowed to look nice?'

'Of course. Let's see what you have, then. I do think Meatloaf was a good fallback option though.'

It was strange leading Patrick into my room. Even though it was technically his, along with all the rest of the house, I'd put my stamp on it, largely through untidiness and forgetting to dust the skirting boards. 'Sorry,' I said. 'I was going to tidy before I went out.' I hadn't unpacked my Christmas suitcase, and clothes were strewn about it and on the window seats, chairs and bed. The bedside table had three dirty mugs on it, and my desk was a mess of paper and drawings. 'Eh, sorry,' I said lamely again. 'I'm just not very tidy.'

'Is it an artistic thing?' He stepped delicately over a bra I'd left on the floor.

'I'd like to think so. But I bet Beyoncé's room doesn't look like this.'

'She does have minions though. Is that what you need? Or just more cupboard space? I could buy you a tallboy or something.'

I thought of making a lame joke about needing a tall boy, then thankfully stopped myself. 'That would be good, thanks.' I wanted to change the subject—partly because I didn't like it when he slipped into landlord mode, and partly because the real reason wasn't a dearth of storage solutions; it was just my chronic untidiness. Dan's words were ringing in my ears—*I'm working all hours, the least you could do is pick up your bloody socks off the floor.*

'So what are the options?' Patrick said, clearly trying to block out the mess. I wondered if Michelle was really the obsessively tidy one or if they were both as bad as each other.

'Well, she has lots of great outfits obviously. There's the black Lycra one from "Single Ladies". Or something gold and spangly. Or hot pants.'

'Do you own anything that's Lycra or spangly or hot panty?'

'Eh, no.'

'How about that video you made me watch the other night, you know, the one where she's trying to make some kind of statement about the beauty industry, or so you said anyway?'

'"Flawless"? That's a good idea. She's just in denim shorts and a check shirt. I have both those things!'

'Great. People might not know you're meant to be a superstar though, and not just...Rachel. Wait here.'

He dashed off, and I could hear his footsteps pounding on the stairs. I began to scoop up armfuls of clothes, thinking

I really should make more of an effort. He was letting me live here rent-free, and I was starting to take it for granted. That was probably a mistake.

He was back in minutes, clutching what looked like headphones with something sticking out the front. 'Here', he said, out of breath, placing it on my head. 'It's a hands-free set I sometimes use in the car, but now it's…a radio mike!' I looked at myself. Rather than Beyoncé, I now just looked like a scruffy, make-up-less, five-foot-three woman in pyjamas with a headset on, but it was a start.

'Where's my keys?' I was running about the hall, upending every bag and coat I had. Three days without leaving the house meant I'd completely forgotten how to function in the outside world. I had finally located my Oyster card, purse, phone, lip balm and dry shampoo, and now the pesky keys were defeating me. 'I really can't find them!'

'Are they in the bowl there on the side?' Patrick was at the kitchen table with his little cafetière of Moroccan Roast.

'Yes! You're a key-finding genius. Now, where's Alex? I want to wish him Happy New Year, since I won't see him later.'

'He wants to stay up for the bells. Some kind of latent Scottishness coming through, I suppose.'

'Isn't he too young?'

'Yes. I have a cunning plan though. I recorded last year's fireworks on TV and I'll play them to him, then wish him Happy New Year. He'll never know it's only 8 p.m.'

'Lying to small children? I'm starting to think you're not as wholesome as you make out.' I was teasing, but Patrick's face fell.

'Hmm.'

'I didn't mean...'

'It's just something Michelle used to say. That I was wholesome. She meant I was like her—obsessed with re-cycling and walking ten thousand steps a day and eating quinoa. Boring, in other words.'

'I don't think you're—'

'It's fine. Have fun. You look...' He gazed at me in my short shorts and radio mike and massive hair.

'Stupid? Like this might just be my normal clothes? Borderline offensive?' I'd fallen into a panic about whether it was all right for me, as white as dried coconut, to im-personate Beyoncé.

'You look like...he should have put a ring on it.'

'He did. That was the problem. Shame they can't fit, "if you like it, then you should have cherished it in a fulfilling adult relationship" into a song, eh.'

Patrick paused. 'I always thought that song was about pigeon fanciers myself. Is it not?'

Cynthia's party was exactly as I'd feared. I was barely in the door when I'd seen three men dressed as Don Draper—i.e. their work suits plus cigars that weren't lit because no one smoked any more and their wives had them on raw juice diets. I didn't think many of the Dons were far off drinking too much and sleeping with their secretaries.

I waded through the packed room, looking for some-one vaguely human, avoiding those of Cynthia and Rich's friends I'd met before and had no wish to meet again, even if they were the last tax lawyers alive on earth and we had to repopulate the remuneration code together. I had to hand it to Cynthia, she knew how to throw a party. Everywhere twinkled with fairy lights and Diptyque candles guttered in storm lanterns. The champagne was already flowing and everyone was talking a little bit too loudly. The music was inoffensive Christmas jazz, Michael Bublé, I thought, and I could see Ian making retching noises about it when I located him and Emma in the kitchen next to the humungous buffet. The centrepiece was fir branches frosted in fake snow and artfully draped with lights.

'I'm eating alphabetically,' Ian announced. 'So far I've had avocados, brown sausage rolls, and now I'm on carrot sticks. Next is devilled eggs though, so that's good.'

'Isn't brown cheating? And you could have just done canapés for "C".'

He looked morose. 'I knew I missed you.'

'He's already stinking of egg,' said Emma, hugging me and poking me in the eye with the Barbie doll she had dismembered and stuck to herself. 'I'm glad you're here so I can talk to someone normal.'

I surveyed her costume, which seemed to involve a blonde wig, massive Army boots, and a lot of tinfoil and pages from books pasted onto herself along with empty pill packets and even a nappy. 'You're...'

'I'm the utopian future of womankind,' she said, straightening up proudly.

'Of course. Of course. And Ian—'

'I'm Barbie,' he said. Which explained the pink leotard and the blonde wig.

'I see.' I didn't.

'I told you,' Ian said crossly to Emma. 'Abstract ideas don't work as costumes. You should have been Ken. That would have made the feminist point and also fulfilled the criteria of instantly recognisable costumes.'

At least I think he said that. His mouth was full of egg again.

'How was Christmas?' Emma asked me.

'OK. Quiet. Mum and Dad treating me like glass, aunties asking have I considered freezing my eggs—hey, more eggs!—Jess gloating about her perfect children. You?'

She winced in a way that meant she'd tell me later. 'Who are you meant to be, by the way?'

'I'm Beyoncé!' I struck a pose. 'Like in the "Flawless" video. I woke up like dis!'

'Did you? Wasn't it hard to sleep with the mike thing?'

'No, it's from the video… Never mind.'

Ian sprayed food. 'Did you arrange that with Cynthia?'

'Snuggles,' Emma warned.

'What do you mean?'

Too late, I saw what he meant, as Cynthia finally appeared in the door. Because there's only one thing that'll make you look sillier than being Beyoncé when you're as white as milk and five foot three, and that's being Beyoncé when your stunning, tall, half-black friend is being Beyoncé too, only in her spangly hot-pants incarnation. Bollocks.

'Oh, hi, love,' she said, hugging me in a cloud of expensive perfume and sequins. 'You look comfy. These heels are killing me. Who are you?'

'She's you,' Ian said, paying close attention to the buffet, where he had now moved on to eggs (Scotch).

I did the pose, half-heartedly. 'You know…"Flawless".'

Cynthia started to laugh. 'Awesome. We're both Beyoncé. We'll have to duet later on when I get the karaoke out. Sod Rich.'

'Where is Rich?'

'Oh.' She moved her head vaguely. 'Think they went

outside to smoke cigars and be all *Wolf of Wall Street*. *Chihuahua of Wall Street*, more like.'

'Now, there's a film concept,' said Ian, who was basically inside an egg.

'Would you stop,' Emma snapped. 'Anyone would think you hadn't eaten in weeks.'

'I haven't. Well, not like this. This is like from *Waitrose* or some classy place.'

Cynthia gave me a look. I shrugged. I didn't know what was going on with those two. 'Anyway, have fun, guys, I have to mingle.' Off she trotted, tall and beauteous.

It was a nice party. Nice music, nice food, nice decoration, plenty of nice booze. But, all the same, I was bored. I stuck close to Emma and Ian, who bickered incessantly, shoving Kettle chips into my mouth while Cynthia flitted about being fabulous. She'd invited everyone from her work, and there just wasn't much conversation I could make with corporate lawyers. Rich's friends were beyond the pale. Most of them wore quilted jackets and read *The Telegraph*. I'd have more in common with Masai tribesmen than them. And, as I listened to them braying about house prices and ski trips, the thought of a nice mud hut was quite appealing.

List of things to say to people at parties when you have nothing in common with them

1. How do you know Cynthia/Rich? (insert name of mutual friend as needed)

2. Do you live locally? FOLLOW UP: Where are you based?

3. What do you do?

4. That sounds interesting. Said with upwards inflection

to encourage them to tell you more about accounting/IT/ marketing

5. These crisps are nice, aren't they? (only in desperation)

6. I have yet to think of a number six.

As Emma and Ian set to on a sotto voce conversation about how and when they should go home—'Don't be stupid, the buses will be rammed until at least 2 a.m.', 'Well, we can't get a taxi, we're still paying for that stupid motorbike cover you bought'—I wandered through to the kitchen and onto the outside decking, where Rich had set up an environment-ruining patio heater. I hugged my flannel shirt around me and looked up at the sky. I couldn't see any stars, due to light pollution and clouds, but surely they were there all the same. I just had to wait for it to clear, and things might get better, as Dad had said.

What a year it had been. Divorce, homelessness, massive backwards steps. Earlier, on Facebook, most people had been posting things like, 'Feeling soooo blessed right now, not only were the beautiful twins born this year, but I lost twenty pounds and my online macramé business is really taking off, we closed on the house and I learned to samba!' Even the site itself was getting in on the act, showing me my 'highlights' of the year. As I didn't have any highlights, no exotic holidays or babies born or houses bought, these just consisted of blurry Instagram pictures of me trying to dance and do stand-up comedy and falling off Clover. Facebook was basically the new round-robin Christmas letters. Only ALL. YEAR. LONG.

Far up ahead, one star glimmered through the haze. Or possibly it was a plane heading to Heathrow. I wished on it for a moment—happiness. Love, if possible. Just for things to be better than they were right now. *Please*. I didn't even know who I was talking to.

The door opened, bringing a gust of noise and warmth. A man had staggered out. He pointed to me, squinting. 'Female lumberjack.'

'No.' I smiled weakly.

'Er, someone from a programme about Canada?'

I sighed. 'I'm Beyoncé. Only really pale and not tall or beautiful.'

'Should he have put a ring on it?'

'What, that pigeon-fancier song?' I repeated Patrick's stupid joke, which had made me almost wet myself earlier.

'Eh?'

'You know…a ring on its leg…like to stop it going missing.' An awkward pause. 'Anyway! Yes, I'm Beyoncé, only not beautiful.'

'I don't know about that.' OK, it was dark, and the way he was squinting at me suggested a few too many Don Draper martinis, but I looked at him properly. Not bad. A little on the short side, but a nice face, brown hair, smile dimples. He was dressed in a *Top Gun* outfit. Not that original. But still, it was a New Year costume party in Chiswick. Opportunities for artistic expression were limited.

'Why are you sitting out here?'

'I was looking at the stars.'

He gazed up. 'There aren't any.'

'There are. We just can't see them sometimes. They're always there.'

'That's deep.'

'Yeah. I might get it put on a T-shirt.'

He laughed. It was a nice laugh. 'So how do you know these guys?'

Question number one—strike to him. 'I was at university with Cynthia.'

'She's pretty wow, isn't she?'

'Yep.' This was my curse as her friend—everyone I meet would always be more in love with her than me. The only person unaffected so far was Ian.

'Bit tall for me though. Sadly.'

I shuffled so he could clearly see I was a short arse. 'How do you know them?' Question one back to him. It was like *Blind Date.*

'Oh, I did some web design for Cynthia's company this year. I think she was inviting everyone she'd ever met.'

'You're a web designer?' Question three. Tick. I started to panic we'd run through all the small talk too quickly.

'No, but don't tell anyone, will you? I think I'm getting away with it so far.'

I laughed. That was a first. I'd almost forgotten how it sounded. Look at me, sitting talking to a fairly funny, not horrible, reasonably heighted man! 'You came though—no other web designer parties to be at?'

'Plans fell through. Break-up with my girlfriend and that.' He did a sad head wiggle. 'It tends to upset the New Year plans.'

Dan and I had discussed going away for New Year. Skiing. Clinking glasses in front of the fire, throwing our heads back laughing, while outside the avalanche of doom gathered itself. 'I hate New Year,' I said out loud.

'Me too.' He held up his paper cup. 'I'll drink to that.'

'I don't have a drink.'

He did a horrified face. 'We must get you one. Come with me, if you want to live.'

Funny and film quotes! I could get on board with this.

I cast a quick upward glance to the star/747 in gratitude—that was fast work—and I followed him into the kitchen, where he poured us both more Prosecco and then led me to the stairs. I've always liked sitting on the stairs at parties. I think it's a sign of a good one if several people are up and down them arguing/crying/snogging. And we talked. His name was Steve, he really was a web designer, he lived nearby with three other boys, he was twenty-nine—could I still pull someone in the decade below me?—he liked football and could cook—though in my experience, when men said this it meant 'can heat up'—and though he wasn't that handsome under the lights—he looked older than he was and I could detect the aroma of cigarettes which suggested why—he was OK. I was letting my knees drift close to his hands as we sat on different steps. Then it was midnight, and people were chanting, and whooping, and it was a new year, a chance not to mess up this time, a clean slate. Steve the web designer leaned over and, as if it were the most natural thing in the world, pressed his lips to mine. 'Happy New Year, Rachel.'

His lips were a little dry, but warm. I should kiss him back. I was. We were kissing. It was fine. It was nice, even if he tasted of smoke and sausage rolls. He pulled away, his hand rubbing my cheek. 'Would you like to come back with me?'

This was how it worked, wasn't it? It could be easy. You met someone, you liked them, you went home with them. I thought of my list—*sleep with a stranger*. It was on there for a reason, wasn't it? New year, new start. I found myself nodding.

He leapt to his feet. 'Great! Let's go.'

'I just need to tell my friends I'm going.'

'OK. Hurry.' He planted another kiss on my mouth, his tongue probing inside. I pulled away slightly. It was fine. It would be fine. I was going to tick another item off the list.

Chapter Twenty-Three

List of things that happen at a good party

1. Dancing in the living room

2. Someone passed out on a sofa

3. Deciding to drink all the random alcohol you brought back from holidays

4. Sitting on the stairs having a heart-to-heart

5. Sausage rolls

I couldn't see Emma or Cynthia downstairs, so I went up to the first floor, where it was quieter. I padded down the corridor, peering past open doors into the lovely tidy bedrooms inside—until I heard someone talking. 'Cyn?'

Rich appeared round the door of their room, his phone in his hand. He was wearing a suit, as if he'd just come from work—this was his costume. 'Oh, hi, Rachel. Just making a call.'

'Do you know where Cyn is?'

'Oh, she's around. Listening to that godawful music you all like, ha.'

'Right. Happy New Year.'

'Yes, same.' He shut the door in my face. I blinked and went the other way, where I encountered Emma coming out of the bathroom, getting stuck in the doorway by the bits of her costume. She had her phone in her hand, a cross expression on her face.

'Bloody cabs, of course I know it's New Year, that's why I want one, hello…' She looked at me. 'What's up? Where's that guy I saw you with?'

'Oh, he kissed me.'

'That's great!' She saw my face. 'Or not.'

'Oh, no, it's fine. He asked me to go back with him.'

'All right. And do you want to?'

'Yes? Yes.'

She was looking at me keenly. 'What about Patrick?'

'Er, what about him? He's got a date with that annoying American soon.'

'And you're OK with that?'

'Em, we're just friends! He's the one always telling me to date.'

'OK.' She hugged me quickly. 'Have fun. I better go and find Ian. He's driving me crazy.'

'What's up with you two? You seem to be permanently in the middle of a massive row.'

'Oh, it's just…that stuff he does, the charmingly eccentric thing. It's not so charming when you have to be his mum, and he won't talk about anything serious, like, I don't know, moving to a better place, let alone getting married or anything else like that. Christmas was a nightmare. His bloody family all trying to be the funniest and throwing strops over the rules of the Post-it name game. As if it even has rules! It's a MADE-UP GAME. For God's sake. And he spent a fortune on stupid presents, even though I told him just to get me a box set of *Mad Men*. We don't have money to be throwing away.'

Through the banisters I could see Cynthia, in her shimmery top and hot pants, laughing at something Ian was saying, laying a hand on his arm. He was grinning.

Emma muttered something that sounded like, 'Not this shit again.' She turned back to me. 'Go on, Rach. Nothing good happens after midnight on New Year. Have fun. I'll tell her you went.'

'Happy New Year,' I called despondently. 'It's got to be better, hasn't it?'

She grimaced. 'Let's hope so.'

Steve and I didn't speak during the short journey home. He walked quickly, hands in the pockets of his Superdry jacket, and, even in flat shoes, I struggled to keep up. 'Is it nearby?'

'Yeah, yeah, just round the corner.'

This transpired to be a good twenty-minute trek in the cold, to an ex–council house with weeds in the garden and bikes propped up in the hallway. I climbed over them, noticing the dirty carpet and pile of huge men's shoes. Once we were in the living room—a jungle of electric cables, an *FHM* calendar on the wall, dirty dishes heaped everywhere—he started to kiss me again, pressing me against the wall. His tongue was insistent and I pulled away, laughing a bit. 'Hey, hey, slow down.'

'Sorry. You're just really sexy.' It was a long, long time

since anyone had told me that. I started to kiss him back. It was always going to feel weird the first time. I just had to get this over with.

Very soon we were in his bedroom—musty futon on the floor, football kit in the corner, Pot Noodle pot full of fag ends—and I was down to my underwear. He'd pulled off my tights with some very unsexy rooting around and was now taking off his shirt and jeans. His pants, thankfully, were not Superman ones, just unremarkable blue-and-white boxers. I averted my eyes like a Victorian spinster from what might be beneath—was I ready for this? After ten years of only Dan, his familiar body, our shared shorthand of what we liked?

Steve was breathing hard. 'You're really sexy. Proper fit.'

Did people still say that? 'Thank you,' I said automatically. He was steaming ahead. There was some fumbling about for a condom, and then my underwear was off and without any further ado—I'd have liked some ado, to be honest—it was happening. I was doing number five. Sex with a stranger. Except there were no friends to tell me this was a good or bad idea, no one to help me tick it off, no Patrick to…

Patrick.

I pushed Steve off me and sat up suddenly. The look on his face would have been almost comical in other circumstances. He put his hand behind my head, yanked me back to him. His mouth felt wet. 'Stop!'

'What's wrong?' He looked puzzled, as I pushed him away, shaking.

'I'm sorry. I can't. I'm not ready for this. I…'

'Then why did you come back with me?' The pleasant,

ordinary-bloke expression he'd worn had slipped into something harder.

'I...I was having a nice time.'

'You've been flirting with me all night.'

'I'm sorry.' I stared into his unwashed pillow, trying not to cry. 'It's just I'm getting divorced and I...'

'Then maybe you shouldn't be at parties, teasing people.' He pushed himself up and stomped off into the kitchen.

I quickly got dressed, feeling cold and grubby, and, with my shoes in hand, went into the hallway. He hadn't even offered me a glass of water. Steve was slumped on his sofa, in just his pants, with the TV on. 'I'll just...'

'Yeah. Go on. Leave.'

I fled, like Cinderella, except in sensible shoes—how many fairy tales would be different if that were the case? Cinders just needed better shoes; Rapunzel, a pixie crop; Sleeping Beauty, more coffee; Snow White, the Atkins diet... I was halfway down his road when I realised I had no idea how I was getting home. I was sober enough to find a bus stop but not to figure out what circuitous route I'd need to take to get from Chiswick to Hampstead. My chances of a cab were minimal and I was miles from the tube. As I stood on the pavement, slightly lost, it began to rain.

I trudged along.

What would Beyoncé do? Well, Beyoncé would never be in this situation, as she'd have a limo/helicopter on standby, and anyway Beyoncé was married with a child and called her last tour after her husband—even she was a total letdown. I stared mournfully at my phone. If you liked it, then you should have put a taxi number on it. There was only one thing for it. I would have to ring Patrick.

* * *

I could have gone back to the house, but I couldn't face seeing Steve again, so I walked along in the rain, having arranged to meet Patrick at the station, traipsing in my Converse and thinking of the year that had gone, me moving out, lying on the floor crying, Dan's face the last time I'd seen him, the disappointment in Jane's eyes as I'd handed her back the engagement ring. And Patrick, confronting Michelle, hoping she'd deny her affair, then to hear she was leaving, leaving him and their home and Alex too. I realised some of the wet on my face wasn't rain. Well, this was a good start to the year. And that's the fundamental problem with New Year—unless you go to bed early, with someone you love, and all is already right with your life, you aren't going to wake up feeling full of joy and positivity and ready to shed those bad habits. You're going to wake up in the horrors, in dire need of a bacon sandwich and possibly with wet pants. Which just goes to show that the only people who can truly enjoy New Year are the ones who don't need it in the first place.

I had reached the station now. Ahead of me, like a beacon through the rain, like lights guiding Beyoncé onto her stage, were the headlamps of Patrick's car.

'So this guy just tried to sleep with you then wouldn't take no for an answer?' We were whispering, as Alex was in the back in his car seat, asleep. Patrick had lifted him out of bed, pyjamas and Roger and all.

'Well, not exactly, but he wasn't pleased when I asked him to stop. He said I'd teased him.'

'Your fault, really. You should have realised the party was in the 1960s, when people last said things like that.'

I managed a weak smile.

'Steve? Was that his name?'

'Yeah. Evil Steve.'

'Stevil.'

'Ha.'

'I'm sorry, Rachel. Not everyone will be like that.'

'Won't they? Or will they just smell of garlic, or have Superman bedspreads, or be twenty years older than me? I'm going to be alone forever.' My voice wobbled. 'I don't even know where to buy turbans either.'

He put his hand over and held mine briefly. 'It'll be OK.'

'How will it?'

'I don't know. Because we can't go back, so we have to go forward. And you won't be alone. Your friends would do anything for you. I wish I had that.'

'What do you mean?' The only sound was the car engine, the heater roaring and the windscreen wipers battling with the rain outside. He was still holding my hand in his, warm and dry.

'Before all this, I was really alone—Michelle was gone, I wasn't speaking to my family and I'd managed to let all my friends go over the years, what with work and marriage and taking care of the little guy. I was properly alone, except for Alex, and I have to look after him. He can't look after me.' Patrick changed gear, dropping my hand. I wondered if I could ask him to take it again. 'You know, I read in a book about this condition called anhedonia, where you forget how to enjoy anything. I think I was a bit like that. And then you came, and now I'm doing all these crazy things, even playing bass again, seeing the guys, and it's... You don't know how much you've helped me. I was so wholesome, like Michelle always said. Boring. I was too boring even for her in the end.'

I patted his hand. I was afraid of what might happen if we said any more. 'We're helping each other. And, Patrick—you aren't boring. Not in the slightest. You made me laugh so much the other day tea came out of my nose.'

'Thanks. And ew.'

'Thank you for coming to get me. I'm sorry you had to drag Alex out too.'

'Oh, he's OK. Didn't stir.'

'In a few years you'll be waiting for him outside discos.'

'You think so?' Patrick seemed to find it reassuring to hear that Alex would have a normal life.

'Of course. He's going to be a heartbreaker. Look at him.'

We looked at the little boy for a while, conked out with his teddy in his hand. 'You lift him and I'll lock up,' I whispered.

As Patrick unbuckled him, Alex said, without opening his eyes, 'Happy New Year, Daddy and Rachel.'

I smiled, scrunching the tissue in my hand. It was bliss, after that rain and tears and uncomfortable clothes, to be in bed in my onesie.

Rachel's List of things to do to avoid the post-split, pre-divorce slump

1. ~~Do stand-up comedy~~

2. ~~Learn to dance~~

3. Travel somewhere on a whim

4. Do yoga properly

5. ~~Sleep with a stranger~~

6. ~~Eat something weird~~

7. Go to a festival

8. ~~Get a tattoo~~

9. ~~Go horse riding~~

10. ~~Try an extreme sport~~

Chapter Twenty-Four

'Now, are you sure you've got your Spox on? Women really hate fat feet in a man. It's so unsightly.'

'Don't joke. I've already thought about borrowing your stomach holding-in corset thing.'

It was a Saturday night in January, and Patrick was getting ready for his date with Arwen the hot American, who had finally found some time in her 'schedule'. I was betting she was a *Lord of the Rings* enthusiast who'd been born Tracey.

'You're sure you don't mind babysitting?'

'I said it was OK. Alex will be in bed soon anyway.'

'It's just I'd hate to be keeping you from any plans… You're young and hip.'

I burst out laughing. 'I'm about as hip as your granny. My plans involve putting on my Christmas onesie and eating peanut butter out of the jar.' He looked alarmed. 'Don't worry, I won't get any on the sofa. In fact, I'll eat it over the sink. That's the most relaxed way to snack, I always think.'

'I didn't mean… You've just been in a lot recently. Is something up?'

'Oh.' I picked at my socks. 'I had a bit of a thing with the girls before Christmas. Things haven't been quite the same since.' I hadn't heard from either since the party. Irrationally, I wondered if Cynthia was annoyed I'd turned down sex with her web designer. I was thirty. Maybe this was just how people courted nowadays and I was woefully behind.

'What? Are you OK?'

'Yes, yes, calm down, Mum.' She used to put on exactly the same expression when I fell out with Lucy Coleman at school, which was approximately once a week. *Oh God, you'll never have any friends. You have to* mix *more, Rachel!* 'I'm just having some downtime, is all.'

'Chillaxing.'

'That's it. It's January anyway. It's a time to hibernate.'

'What am I doing, then?' He squinted at himself in the mirror. He had shaved, revealing the chiselled jaw Cynthia was such a fan of, and wore a dark blue shirt and red tie. 'Give me some advice. You've been on dates recently?'

'If you can call them that.'

'Well, prearranged romantic occasions in a mutually convenient location?'

'Er, yeah.'

'What do hip people wear on dates? Is this…?' He indicated his clothes. I recognised the signs of full-on outfit paralysis.

'Well, it depends. Some people wear their old smelly gym clothes and don't brush their teeth. Some wear Superman pants. Some wear jeans and lumberjack shirts, accessorised with redneck beards and tattoos.'

'I've got one of those! Should I wear a polo shirt to show it off?'

'No, keep it mysterious.' I was going to say wait till it comes up, but that made me think of him taking his shirt off in Arwen's no-doubt cool penthouse apartment with distressed wood floors—I don't know why they'd be distressed, maybe she walked on them a lot with high heels. 'Where are you going?'

'Restaurant. Some fusion place. I found it on Trip Advisor. Do you think…?'

'Lovely. She'll appreciate that you organised something, and researched it. Trust me.'

'And do I pay?'

'You offer, then accept if she wants to split. Or if it's gone well, say she can get "the next time". She'll like that.'

'What else?' He was frantically knotting and re-knotting his tie. I could smell his Penhaligon's English Fern aftershave.

'Um, don't lecture her on gender politics, don't have a Pot Noodle pot by your bed and be sure to have a mint.'

'Oh, Rachel. You've had some bad times.'

I shuddered. 'You weren't there. You can't know, man. Listen. Patrick…'

'Hmm?' He was still fiddling, looking for his wallet and keys.

'If you want to stay out later, it's OK. I mean, I'm not going anywhere and I can easily explain it to Alex when he gets up.'

'What do you mean?'

'You know, if you…'

His eyebrows shot up. 'It's a first date!'

'That's what happens now. It's the age of instant gratification. Click, meet, shag in a toilet, move on.'

'God. That sounds—'

'Amazing? Perfect? What you'd have loved in your twenties?'

'Well, I would have then. But no, it sounds scary now. I mean, a long time with the same person, it's sort of like not doing it at all, isn't it?'

I thought back to my scarifying experiences with Ben and Stevil from New Year. 'Yeah. You'll be OK though.'

'Will she expect me to do...that?'

'She might. But I'm sure she would respect your boundaries too.'

'I wouldn't want to disappoint her.'

'It'll get all round her locker-room buddies that you don't put out, and she'll go out with the slutty bartender with the come-to-bed eyes instead.'

Patrick was looking pale.

'It'll be fine! I'm sure she'll appreciate some sweet old-fashioned courtship.'

'I'm not taking her on a date to 1943,' he said crossly. 'I'm not sweet. I'm hip.'

I surveyed him. 'Better ditch the tie and lead with the tattoo, then, if it's getting tough.'

'That's right, I do have the tat. I'm a badass. And I'm in a band. Well, sometimes, when Ed's been playing too much lawn tennis.'

'Totally. Do you want to take Thomas for moral support?' I held up the toy train.

He threw his tie at me.

'Text me if you need an out. I'll call and say Max has set fire to himself again or something.' This had happened the previous week due to a misunderstanding with a vanilla-scented candle. Since then we had instituted a new house rule—no buying things that smell like food but which also go on fire.

'Thanks.'

When the door shut, leaving behind a cloud of English Fern, I felt oddly bereft. Towards the end, Dan and I never went out on weekends. He would always complain about the noise in bars and the expense of drinks and food, and it got too much of a hassle to take the train up to London and run for the last one. In the end, we just got takeaways and watched films, or I read and he played computer games. That was loneliness. Being alone by choice, with a cute kid and dog, that wasn't lonely. Or so I told myself.

Patrick had been gone five seconds when I heard a little pitter-patter on the stairs and from the kitchen. Alex and Max hurled themselves onto me on the sofa, Alex saying, 'Can we watch *Thomas*? Can we make popcorn? Can I show you my ninja moves?' Max saying, 'Feed me dog biscuits! Scratch my tummy! Walkies!' Or so I translated.

'You're supposed to be in bed,' I chided Alex.

'It's only this time.' He held his hands in the shape of a seven.

'Well, OK. Let's watch part of a film, and then it's time for bed.'

In the end, we made popcorn and watched *Monsters, Inc.*, and when I got a bit tearful Alex patted my hand. 'Don't worry, Rachel. It's just a drawing, like you do.'

Max was asleep, popcorn caught in his fur, snoring loudly. Alex fell asleep too before the end and I picked him up and carried him to bed. He was quite heavy and I was sure he'd wake as I huffed up the stairs, but he didn't, just slept trustingly with his head on my shoulder. I hugged him tight, feeling his warmth, his weight, the utter peace of his sleep. He smelled of butter and baby shampoo, and I tumbled him into bed as floppy as a pile of washing. I tucked him in, made sure he had Roger and put his night light on. I decided his teeth could wait until morning. How I wished there was someone to do this for me, make sure I slept peacefully with soft ocean light playing over the ceiling.

'Night, Alex,' I said quietly, going to the door.

'Night, Mummy,' he mumbled.

Oh.

As I watched the end of the film, I rubbed my face and found it was wet. Stupid me, crying over a kids' film and a confused little boy whose mum was miles away and dad was out with some sexy American stranger. All he had was me, another virtual stranger, squatting in his house like an unpaid babysitter. Basically, I was less fiscally aware than a teenage girl. The Babysitters Club would have kicked me right out for crossing the picket line. I sighed and rummaged around in my DVD collection for something else sappy and light-hearted. *Bridget Jones's Diary*, *Titanic*, *Legally Blonde*... My collection was a tragic story in itself.

To cheer myself up, I decided to write some New Year's resolutions. After all, January was the perfect time to start again.

List of New Year's resolutions

1. Get into obscure Korean revenge cinema. Throw away all DVDs with pink on the cover or Renée Zellweger in them

2. Find a nice man to date who keeps his room clean, doesn't live with his mum and won't call me a 'tease'

3. Develop my freelancing. It was going OK—that was something to be thankful for. And I had my friends. And my health...

4. Find somewhere else to live?

I sighed and put the pen down, looking round at the lovely living room, fire crackling in the grate, candles everywhere, framed pictures, silk wallpaper—the truth was I didn't want to find somewhere else to live. I wanted to stay here.

Around ten the door went, and I jumped, frantically sweeping bits of popcorn into the bowl and pulling off my sweatshirt. The vest top underneath was at least a bit nicer. 'Hello?' I paused the DVD.

'It's me.' Patrick was brushing rain out of his curly hair, hanging up his jacket.

'That was early. I wasn't expecting you.'

'Yeah.' He sighed, leaning against the door frame. 'It was... Well, it was OK. She reminded me of Michelle.'

'But isn't that...'

'No, not in a good way. All that glossy hair and make-up, and the goal-orientated discussions. What are your career plans? Are you vacationing this year? Do you ever put your kid in summer camp? Oh, I know a great one for kids with handicaps in Montana. Are you dating anyone else? Do you snowboard? It was exhausting.'

'I'm sorry.' I wasn't sorry. 'And you missed out on some exciting scenes here. For a moment it looked like Sulley wouldn't find the right door, then...guess what?'

'He found it.'

'Aw, spoiler alert.'

Patrick peered at the TV, which was still on pause. 'What's that?'

'Oh, just a…documentary about the closures of the coal mines.'

'That's Hugh Grant.'

'No, it's Arthur Scargill. The two are often confused.'

'You're watching *Four Weddings* again? Oh, Rachel. Do you need an intervention?'

'I like it! Anyway, I'm a single woman without a date on a Saturday night. I'm just fulfilling stereotypes. It's not my fault.'

'Have you got to this point yet?' Patrick fluffed up his hair and opened his eyes wide, putting on a fake American accent. 'Is it still raining? I hadn't noticed.'

'Stop slagging off Andie MacDowell. She's a brilliant actress. I mean, look at those L'Oréal ads.'

Max, who was sprawled out beside me, shook himself, coughed and spat out a piece of popcorn, then trotted back to his basket. 'It's non-stop glamour round here,' said Patrick, scooping it up, then washing his hands at the sink. 'You tired?'

'Not too much.'

'Drink?'

'Sure.' I settled back on the sofa, brushing popcorn from my cleavage, such as it was. 'Sounds good. So tell me about the really important thing.'

'Um, you mean… No, we didn't kiss or anything like that.' I could hear him rummaging in the kitchen.

I felt some strange relief at that, which I chose to ignore. 'Not that, silly. The food. Tell me everything you had.'

'Ooh, well, tuna carpaccio with ginger and soy to start. Then seared Wagyu beef with noodles. Everything's seared now, isn't it? Nothing is just cooked. Also, cocktails, and a plate of little mini desserts. God, they were good.'

'Petits fours?'

'Yep.'

I groaned. 'My favourite.'

'Just as well I nicked some, then.' He placed a plate in front of me, containing three little sweets in frilled wrappers.

'Oh my God. You're the best. And what did she have?'

'One lettuce leaf, I think.'

'Ah. You didn't do task number four, then?'

'Get drunk? No chance. She was off alcohol for January and doesn't drink much in any case. She thinks the British have "an unhealthy reliance on stimuluses".'

'Well, I hope you corrected her grammar. Stimuli, surely?'

'I wanted to, but apparently women don't actually like to be constantly corrected.'

'Amazing. No one told me.'

He held up a bottle of gin. 'Fancy some unhealthy stimulus?'

'Really?'

'It's only ten-thirty. I've been known to stay up past midnight on special occasions, I'll have you know.'

'Like when people are playing cricket, or there's a sale on at Brooks Brothers?'

'Hey, do you want some gin or not?'

I switched off the TV. 'Yes, please.'

Several hours later, Patrick and I were in the kitchen. 'This one.' His iPad was on the dock and he was drunkenly jabbing his way through it.

I was waving my hands, still trying to dance even though there was no music. 'Girls Aloud! Pleeeeease! "Biology", you'll love it. 'S a great song.' I'd had four gins in the past hour. I was well on my way to being stocious.

'Wait. Shhhh. Ah!' He smiled as notes filled the air, jazzy, jivey, making you want to get up and spring around as if you were at a high school dance in the fifties, minus the nuclear threat and fear of Communism, of course.

'What's this?'

'"Runaround Sue". Dion and the Belmonts. Nineteen sixty-one.'

'Aw, it's nice when you play me music from your youth. You'd have been, what, eighteen?'

'Shut up.' He was shimmying. Patrick was actually shimmying. He was man-dancing—playing imaginary bongos, waving his hands from the wrist, shuffling his feet without actually lifting them off the ground.

'That's not dancing!'

'No?' He stopped. 'Well, you show me how, then.'

'Me?'

'You're the one who went to the class.'

'But I don't have my dancing shoes.'

'Live on the edge, Rachel.' He was shimmying again. 'Be an edge-liver!'

'Come here.' I held out my hands and he took them, his warm and rough. And then we were dancing in the kitchen, out of time and laughing manically. We did the moonwalk. We did 'Thriller'. We did the 'Macarena' and 'Saturday Night' by Whigfield and the dance to the Spice Girls' 'Stop'! We did the tango, really badly, and I almost cracked my head doing the bend, but somehow that was just funnier. We did the jive and the Harlem shake and the charleston, and I explained what twerking was, and he was appalled.

All the while he was so close I could feel his heart beating, the warmth of his skin.

'Wait!' He held up his finger, then disappeared. I flopped down at the kitchen table, panting. I hadn't exercised so much in ages. I was sweating, and my hair was falling out of its plait, but when I caught sight of myself in the mirror I had a massive grin on my face.

'Ta-da!' Patrick had appeared. In his hands, a guitar.

'You got the guitar out!'

'I told you, I'm living on the edge. Here we go.' He strummed a note and put on a cheesy DJ voice. 'This one is especially for Rachel Kenny in Hampstead, and she asks if we can play it because it represents the pinnacle of musical achievement for humanity.' And he launched into an acoustic version of 'Single Ladies'.

'Do the dance! Do the dance!' I clapped along manically. 'Wait!' I scrabbled for the iPad, found the song and pressed play. 'Do it!'

Patrick put down the guitar and assumed the position, hand on hip, finger extended, bottom wiggled. It was all the funnier because he had changed into his onesie. 'Acting tough, shouldn't chase muff, I don't really care what you think…'

'Those aren't the words!'

'I don't care. I'm living on the edge!' He went into the tap-dancing bit and I almost fell off my chair laughing. I was still struggling to draw in air when the song ended and he sat down, panting and grinning.

'Bravo!' I threw imaginary flowers at him. 'Women are now liberated, because you wiggled your arse in hot pants!'

'I'd like to thank my husband, Jay Zed, that's Mr Zed to

you, and my daughter, Pomegranate Noir, and most of all, Jesus Christ!'

At this the dog flap rattled and in came Max. He stood there looking between us, an expression of disdain on his furry face. 'Woof!'

'Everyone's a critic,' said Patrick.

I fell about laughing again. 'If only you'd had a list task that said, make a total twat of yourself dancing to Beyoncé songs.'

'Oh, I wouldn't call that a task, more of a life philosophy.' He leaned back in the chair, stretching. 'This was fun, Rachel.'

'Better than being out with Miss America?' I don't know what made me ask it.

'Yeah, it was. A lot better. Which doesn't bode well for my future dating, if I'd rather be here with you in my pyjamas.' He stretched again, the buttons of his onesie gaping so I could see his flat stomach underneath, stippled in hair and still tanned from summer.

'Why's that?' I asked, keeping my voice light.

'I suppose it's just more comfortable.'

'Oh.'

He yawned. 'I better get to bed. Alex will be up at six, bouncing on my kidneys. Thanks, Rachel.'

'Night.' I stayed in the kitchen, suddenly cold and very sober. Comfortable, he'd said. Dan and I had been comfortable. And we all knew where that ended, and it wasn't in hot steamy romance, but rather reheated pizza, separate beds and then divorce.

Patrick's List of things to do to avoid the
post-split, pre-divorce slump

1. ~~Climbing~~

2. ~~Skydiving~~

3. ~~Play on stage again~~

4. ~~Get drunk~~

5. ~~Go on a date~~

6. ~~Learn to fillet fish~~

7. Enter Max into a dog show

8. Buy a nice car

9. Take Alex overseas

10. ??

Chapter Twenty-Five

The idea of 'just turning up at the airport and getting on the next flight' was a lovely one in principle—if you were in a film or a millionaire—but in real life there were other considerations. Alex, for example, and his need to be within racing distance of a competent hospital. Cost was another—I was still mostly broke, and Patrick was feeling the pinch too with legal fees and the mortgage and Alex's school. Last but not least was packing—you couldn't go to Iceland, for example, if you'd turned up with a suitcase full of bikinis and straw hats. The fishermen would laugh at you. So we settled on the 'random yet controlled' manner of writing down suitable places, then plucking one out of a hat. The hat in question being Alex's train driver one, of course.

'Controlled fun, the best kind,' I said, settling in. It was very dramatic. Patrick and I sat at opposite ends of the table, arms folded. Alex knelt on a chair, sifting through the entries, glaring at us both with the suspicion and gravity of a customs officer going through your luggage, or Ant and

Dec telling you not to vote yet as it wouldn't be counted but you might still be charged. I tried to catch Patrick's eyes— I desperately didn't want to end up with somewhere cold and horrible.

'Come on, mate. Do the draw.'

'It has to be secret.' He scowled at us both. 'So when I pick the place, we'll go there?'

'Yep.'

'Even if we don't like it?'

'That was the plan,' I said uncertainly. 'I'm not sure why.'

Alex fished around for a while, with the rapt concentration of someone splitting an atom. He had a piece. He unfolded it carefully, trying to spell out the letters.

I crossed my fingers. *Not Brussels, not Brussels...*

'I think it says "Flo-ri-da",' Alex read laboriously.

'Get in! Mickey Mouse for the win!' Patrick punched the air. 'Sun and sea!'

'Gun culture,' I said. 'Racism. Old people.'

'All-you-can-eat buffets,' he countered. 'Disney World.'

'Hanging chads.'

'Dolphins!'

'*Sharks.*'

'Come on, Rach. Have you ever been to a Disneyland?'

'No. We almost went to Euro Disney when I was fourteen, but instead we had to go to the Eiffel Tower because my sister was doing French for her GCSE and needed to practise saying *"Où est la Tour Eiffel, s'il vous plait?"* Even though we were *underneath it.*' That one featured prominently on my list of things Jess had done to slight me.

'Then you'll love it. You *love* Disney stuff. You're like a five-year-old.'

'I have *slightly* better control of my bladder. I think.'

'Daddy?' We turned then to the actual child, who had emptied out all the bits of paper and was opening them one by one, the hat on his head. 'Are all these letters the same?'

'Of course not,' blustered Patrick. 'Let's tidy these up now.'

'They look the same, Daddy.'

'What?' I lunged over.

Patrick was gathering them up. 'Come on, don't listen to Alex, he can barely read.'

'I can so! Look! The same!' Alex held up a crumpled handful in the manner of a pint-sized Columbo, and I could see they did all indeed say 'Florida', in Patrick's large square writing.

I turned to him open-mouthed. 'You big cheat! What kind of example is that for your child?'

'A bad one. Don't cheat, Alex. Look, I just didn't want to go to Belgium. I haven't seen the sun for five years, Rachel. Five years.' He looked awkward. 'Also, I may, just possibly, have already found a good deal and booked it.'

'Patrick! That is totally against the spirit of the list!'

'I know, but, Rachel, the list involved fish guts, and falling off a horse, and getting hit on by slimy men—that was you, I hasten to add, not me—don't we deserve a little fun?'

'When are we going?' I said, sulkily.

'Well, errrr, are you free, say, next week, for example? I probably should have asked that first. You might have important plans.'

'Am I free next week? Well, let me see—I'm an underemployed freelancer with no love life and friends who are suddenly too busy to see me. Yes, I'm free.'

'That's good. Because we're going next week.'

In the end I forgave him, but only because I really didn't

want to go to Belgium either, and also he promised to buy me a *Finding Nemo* toy in Disney World.

I'd never realised just how many preparations were needed for transporting a four-year-old with a health condition to a different continent. After three days of packing, and checking lists, and stockpiling Alex's medical paraphernalia, and getting a letter from the hospital so he could take it through customs, I was exhausted, and we hadn't even left yet. My own list-making had gone into overdrive. I was taking three different pairs of sunglasses and four types of sun cream—face, 50, 30 and 20. But now we had run into a slight snag. I came into the kitchen the day before we were going with the phone in my hand, to find Patrick frowning at a display of medical equipment from the locked cupboard. I remembered how I had once speculated this might contain murder tools—we'd come a long way, though I wasn't too far wrong.

'I feel like Walter out of *Breaking Bad* here. Maybe I'll shave my head and start a drugs lab.'

Ordinarily, I'd have laughed, but I was too worried. 'Listen, Patrick, I just spoke to Jess about us going…and she said, well, you might not be legally allowed to take Alex out of the country without Michelle's permission.'

'What? That's ridiculous! Why?'

'Because you haven't arranged anything between you, and there's no custody order in place…well, it's to stop abductions and things like that.'

Patrick's face was like thunder.

'I'm sorry! I just thought it was better to know now, before we got stopped at customs.' I had visions of Alex being carried off, Patrick and I holding up numbers for mugshots, like a gangster and his moll. Or Hugh Grant and his...you know.

'Did she say what I'd need?'

'A letter from Michelle would help, she said, just in case we do get stopped.'

'But it's absurd. I'm actually taking him into the country where Michelle is!'

That made me think something else. 'Do you think... Well, should you take him to see her, maybe?'

'We don't have time to divert to New York.' Patrick was suddenly very busy packing syringes into a cool bag.

'Yes, but maybe she'd like to come down, or... It's none of my business, I know! It's just...he misses her. He... Sometimes he calls me "Mummy". Like when he's half asleep.' This was greeted with total silence. 'I'm sorry,' I said again lamely.

Patrick was staring out the window. 'Does he really do that?'

'Sometimes. I know they talk on Skype and that, but it's not the same, is it?'

He sighed and looked at his watch. He held out his hand. 'Give me the phone.'

I busied myself repacking everything, checking the lists once again and trying not to hear anything from the next room. We had three lists, in fact. One for me—sun cream, books, large hats; I sizzled like a vampire in the sun. One for Patrick—in-flight cheese, dad-like deck shoes, maps. And one for Alex—Thomas the Tank Engine, Roger, fourteen butterfly needles.

List of things I always take on holiday, then never use

1. First-aid kit

2. Passport holder

3. Set of travel toiletries

4. High heels

5. Seven summer dresses, four T-shirts, three pairs of espadrilles

6. Travel hairdryer

7. Mini padlock for case

8. Sun cream (see more on this later)

Patrick was soon back, hanging the phone up on its cradle. 'You're right, apparently. She wasn't too pleased I didn't tell her about the trip. I had to persuade her there was no danger.'

'Oh.'

'But she'll fax over a letter, she said. And she wants to fly down and see him.'

'Oh. Well, that's good, isn't it?' My mind suddenly tried to picture the scene—Patrick and Michelle and Alex and me in Florida. For some reason I was wearing Minnie Mouse ears in the image. Nothing about it was right.

'The thing is, Rachel…'

'Yes?' The words 'the thing is' are never followed by anything good, are they? They're much like 'we need to talk' and 'you should sit down' in that respect.

'She might not like you being there, you know—she doesn't know you.'

'Oh.' I tried to rally myself. 'Well, that's OK. I can easily amuse myself while you meet up. It'll be nice. I'm sure she misses him.'

'She left him. She left us. It's a bit rich of her to then complain about it.'

For a smiley man who liked dancing to Beyoncé, there was still a lot of bitterness in Patrick, I reflected, checking the list for a third time—I was even more thorough than Santa in this respect.

Chapter Twenty-Six

I woke up with my face in a puddle of sunlight. This was so unlike rainy London that I just lay there for several minutes, basking in it as Max would do. He was staying at Sophie's while we were gone, and no doubt being terrorised by the evil stable cat. I had no idea what time it might be—the long flight across the Atlantic had confused my body. My stomach definitely thought it was time for some kind of meal though. I could smell pancakes and bacon.

Outside the door, I could hear Patrick and Alex having a typical morning conversation. 'You see, I can call you mate, but you're meant to call me Daddy.'

'Nobody *else* calls you Daddy. They call you *Patrick*.'

'I know, because that's my name. But I'm your daddy. No one else's.'

'Can I call you mate too?'

'Well, no…'

'Why not, mate?'

I smiled to myself.

'Daddy, should we wake up Rachel? It's VERY, VERY LATE.'

'Actually, it's pretty early, mate. But we should wake her, because today we're going to DISNEY WORLD.'

I stretched and called out groggily, 'OK, I get the message. You two could wake up Sleeping Beauty with that noise.'

There was a grudging attempt at a knock, and Alex's face appeared around the door. 'We have to go and SEE Sleeping Beauty today. Get up, Rachel!' He added as a polite afterthought, 'If you're not tired. Thank you. Morning.'

'So, Rachel, you know how you're scared of heights?' said Patrick.

'Yes, and sharks, and needles—basically Darwinism should have finished me off by now. I'm too tender for this world.'

'Well, the height thing, does it extend to roller coasters?'

'Of course, but there aren't any here, are there?' I hadn't spotted any telltale twists and loops as we'd walked about. I was pretty sure nothing scary or horrible was allowed in Disney World. Everyone was smiling, the sun was shining, the castle was sparkling and the place smelled of popcorn and hot chocolate. The rides were surely all going to be gently spinning teacups and slow-moving kiddie trains and so on.

Patrick was suddenly evasive. 'Well, not technically, no.'

We were in the queue, the very, very long queue, for something called Splash Mountain, which sounded pretty tame and nice. The queue was inside the ride, snaking through tunnels that were all decorated in a cutesy Old Frontier way, with talking beavers and the like. I was glad to be indoors—my pale English skin had already turned the colour of Ragú sauce, despite the slathers of cream I'd applied. I now looked like a raspberry ripple ice cream, and I was wearing those trainer-sandals that you somehow think are a good idea on holiday, then see the pictures and realise you look like a hundred-year-old woman on a coach trip to Bognor. I had also bought an Indiana Jones–style hat to keep the sun off, which wasn't working.

Patrick wasn't faring much better in the style stakes. He'd decided to wear those clip-on sunglasses you can get over his own glasses, as he hadn't been able to find his prescription ones in the packing madness. His nose was also red as Rudolph's and he was wearing a hat shaped like Goofy, which I imagined was quite sweaty in the heat.

Alex, who up until now had been having the best day of his life—on first spotting Mickey Mouse he'd just run around him in a circle for five minutes shouting 'Mickey! Mickey!'—had chosen this moment to droop. '*Why* can't I go on this one? Is it cos of my runny blood?'

'No, it's because you're too short,' Patrick explained. 'You'd shoot right out of the belt once it starts twisting and turning. No kids can go on it.'

''S not fair.'

I wasn't liking the sound of this twisting and turning business. 'This is a kids' ride though, isn't it?'

'Of course. Look, fun beavers, happy racoons! It's just for older kids, that's all.'

''S not fair.'

Patrick bent down to him. Alex was so covered in sun cream that if he'd made a run for it and we'd tried to catch him, he would have slipped right through. 'After this we'll get lunch, OK? Chips and a burger, because we're on holiday. And then we'll have a little rest.'

'Don't want to rest!'

'Well, OK. Just lunch, then.' Patrick rolled his eyes at me as Alex pressed his face balefully into his stomach, leaving an imprint on his T-shirt like the Shroud of Turin. All around us, families were having similar discussions with their smallest members, as adults and children alike became tetchy with the heat and long queues and smell of fried onion strategically drifting in to us. A woman smiled at me from under her Disney Princess hat and I grimaced back in solidarity; her child was trying to climb up her front.

'Mommy, I don't wanna!'

'Well, you don't have to, honey.'

'But I wanna!'

'But you can't, honey.'

'But I don't wanna!'

She turned to me. 'They sure are a handful in the warm weather. How old's your little one?' She nodded to Alex, who was sulkily trailing his hands along the fake mine-tunnel walls.

'Four,' I said, without thinking.

'He looks just like you.'

Patrick shot me a funny look. I smiled back hastily at the woman. It was too hard to explain that Alex wasn't 'my' little one. 'Hope you enjoy it.'

'You too, hon. Y'all have a nice day.' *Have a nice day.* They all said it. So simple, yet so nice. I tried to imagine how a Londoner might react if I struck up a conversation with them on the tube platform. I'd probably be in a secure facility by nightfall.

We were nearing the front now. 'So you go first,' Patrick

instructed me. 'I'll wait here with Alex, then you come back through the back way and I'll swap him over to you. Meet you outside at the lunch place?'

'OK,' I said nervously. 'It's tame, right?'

'It's not a roller coaster. I promise you that.'

'OK, then.' I let myself be strapped into the fake-log ride by the bizarrely grinning Disney staffer—what were they on?—and heard the crank of the machinery get going. It smelled like a swimming pool—a water ride, that made sense, given the name. It might be nice to get a little splashed in this heat.

'Hey there,' said my seat mate, a man so large his thighs were about the size of my waist. 'Chad's the name.'

'I'm Rachel,' I said, nervously glancing about me as we started to move.

'Good to meet you.' He stuck over his meaty hand to shake, and I took it awkwardly over our harnesses.

We travelled through the ride. This was OK. It was cute! There were little animals singing, and abandoned mine-shafts, and all kinds of japes. I began to feel pretty smug that it was a normal Wednesday and I was here in Disney World while everyone else was slaving away in offices and classrooms. I grinned at Chad. 'It's fun!'

'Yup, I've rode this here ride two hundred twenny-four times.'

'No kidding?'

'No, ma'am. It's a darn good ride.'

We were being cranked up a little hill now and I braced myself at the mild g-forces. 'You like kids' rides, then?'

'I wouldn't call this a kiddie ride, ma'am, what with the drop and all.'

'The what?' I was having to shout now, as we were being winched up a big track. I could see light at the top.

'The drop!' yelled Chad. 'Hang on to your hat, missy! Woooooooo! Here we go! Yeeeee-haaaaw!'

So it turned out, when he said 'the drop', he meant we were actually being dropped off the top of the track, sliding down vertically and landing in a big pool of water. I closed my eyes and uttered a small prayer.

'AAAAAAAH!'

'WOOO! U-S-A! U-S-AAAAAARGH!'

We'd landed in the water, and about half of it had come into the boat with us. I turned to a streaming, spluttering Chad. 'Hell of a ride!' he shouted, trying to high-five me through his harness.

I managed a weak, 'Meeeeh.' Like a slowly deflating water balloon.

'Flattering.'

'Shut up. You didn't tell me there'd be water!'

'It's called Splash Mountain, not Splash Mild Gradient! Did you think it would be kittens blowing straws at you?'

'Not…entirely. Anyway, you said it was tame. You're a big fat liar, pants on fire. First the trip and now this. You can't be trusted at all. I'm going to report you to the Truth Police.'

'Aw, Rachel. Let me buy you this picture as a memento.'

'Don't you dare.'

'But you look so lovely.'

Turned out Disney took a photo of you at the moment you got thrown over the top. With my sunburn and the g-forces, I looked like a wet tomato being pressed against a window. The unfortunate way Chad was cheering made it look as if he was about to take a bite out of me. Patrick examined it. 'It's so nice you met your future husband on the ride as well. You'll have beautiful children.'

'Alex,' I said loftily. 'Unfortunately, your dad is very childish and untrustworthy.'

'What's "untrustworthy"?' said Alex sulkily.

'It means he'd say he was going to buy you chips, say, or a *Finding Nemo* toy, and then he just wouldn't.'

'Of course we're getting chips!' Patrick scooped up the small, cream-smeared boy. 'Let's go and get some now. And we need to buy Rachel a new hat.'

'Do we?' I felt the top of my head, which was bare. The Indiana Jones one had—ironically—been left behind in the flood.

List of things you buy in Disney World,
and then get home and realise you've gone mad

1. A hat shaped like an animal's head, to wear on top of your own head

2. A rain poncho that costs twenty dollars and is essentially made of a bin bag

3. A life-size replica frontier gun, which you will definitely not be able to get through airport security without someone gaining intimate knowledge of your innermost parts

4. A ten-dollar portion of chips

5. Dolphin earrings, such as those sported by a teenage girl in 1995

'That was a good day, wasn't it?'

'I think it was maybe the best day ever.'

'Even though it involved getting chucked into some water?'

Eva Woods

'I needed to cool off. And it also involved fireworks, a parade, a hot dog, three ice creams and two burgers, so that makes up for it.'

'Do you think he enjoyed it?' We were looking at Alex in the back of the hire car, where he'd conked out as soon as we put him in. His *Monsters, Inc.* Mike hat had fallen over his face, so the crazy round eyes stared at us.

'He loved it. All kids get a bit tired and hot in the middle of a day like that.' I shifted in the seat; the leather was sticking to my sunburn. 'So what's tomorrow?' Michelle was coming down the day after that, I knew, so it was our last one together.

'Well, tomorrow I've got a surprise for you.'

'A nasty one? Like the time Max was sick in my wellies?'

'Not like that.'

'Is there any vomit involved?'

'I can't promise there won't be any vomit, no. But you'll like it.'

'Hmm.'

'Just be ready at 8 a.m. tomorrow, and pack some camping stuff, plus a raincoat and your wellies. Assuming you've got the dog vomit out.'

I tried to think of instances when I'd enjoyed vomit-featuring events—the birth of my nephews, my fifth birthday party, my thirtieth birthday party.

'Are you going to tell me why?'

'No. It's a surprise.'

I was dubious. In my experience, surprises tended to be more of the 'and guess what, the whole electrics need redoing' or 'and so I think we should get divorced' kind than 'hey, we're going on a minibreak in Paris!'

* * *

'Are we there yet?'

'No. Shut up.'

'I wouldn't have to ask if I knew where we were actually going.'

'It's a surprise!' Patrick's temper had begun to fray when we woke up to heavy tropical rain that morning, lashing the windows and bending the palm trees. Now we were stuck in traffic on a partially flooded freeway, it had snapped like old knicker elastic.

'Do you think it'll be OK, you know, with this weather?'

He gripped the steering wheel. 'It's a tropical climate. It gets rain most days, they said.'

'You know what it also gets though? Tropical storms. And hurricanes.'

'This isn't helping. It's just rain.'

'Is it still raining? I hadn't noticed.'

Patrick glared at me. 'Even less funny than in the film.'

'I mean, we're going to a festival, aren't we? Is it the Angry Grape concert—the festival in Tampa? It must be. Number seven on my list.'

'Stop guessing.'

'How'd you get tickets? They were all sold out, it said. Though maybe people were reselling them when the bassist broke his wrist last week. Sounds like quite a dodgy injury to me—"carrying too many protein shakes". Uh-huh… I'd make a joke about shakes, but Alex is here. I do like Angry Grape though. Is that where we're going?'

Patrick exhaled slowly. 'Just hum some songs to yourself. Enjoy the mystery.'

'Patrick?' I said after a while.

'What?'

'I need a wee.'

Patrick made a noise of exasperation and switched on the radio. A nasal voice said, 'As Tropical Storm Tim diverts to Orlando, all outdoor activities are cancelled in the Panhandle area. People are advised to get home to shelter, cos it's gonna be a bad one, folks. Now, here's Earth, Wind and Fire, as a little tribute to Tim.'

He snapped it off. 'Crap.'

'That's a bad word, Daddy,' Alex said from the back.

'Yes, well, I'm afraid it's bad news, mate. We have to go back to the hotel. Looks like the thing we're going to is cancelled.'

'Sorry.'

'It's not exactly your fault the entire Gulf is now being dropped on the roof of our hotel room.'

'No, but I really wanted to take you to the…thing.'

'You can tell me now. Since it's not happening. The festival, right?'

'Yes. You were right. Only Angry Grape weren't playing any more, because of the bassist's dodgy injury. It was going to be…someone else.'

'Who?'

'I don't want to tell you.'

'Oh my God. It wasn't… Was it…*her*?'

'Yes. She was going to step in. I'm sorry.'

Oh my God. I could have been seeing Beyoncé, and instead I was sheltering in a hotel bathroom trying not to think about how hard the wind was blowing outside. We were doing our best to keep cheerful for Alex's sake. We were playing the radio through Patrick's iPad and had arranged

Alex on lots of pillows with colouring books and Roger. Every time he looked up at a particularly loud gust of wind, or something that sounded suspiciously like roof tiles being torn off, one of us would feed him an M&M. Patrick was sitting on the loo with the lid down, trying to get a signal on his phone, and I was sprawled beside Alex on the cushions.

'Let's play a game,' I said. Anything to try to forget about Stormageddon and Beyoncé and I missing our one chance to bump into each other in the Portaloos and become BFFs. 'I spy?'

'Cistern. Tap. Complimentary Fruits of the Forest Shower Gel. That isn't going to take up much time.' Patrick rubbed his head grouchily.

'Well, what do you suggest, then?' We raised our voices as the noise from outside swelled again. The bathroom was windowless, and it felt as if we were in a boat tossed on the sea, just the three of us.

'Cards? I don't think Scrabble would be fair.'

'On Alex, you mean?'

'On you. You're the woman who thought "spox" was a word.'

I threw a loofah at him. 'We can do cards, but you'll have to teach both of us a game. I can never remember any of them. What game? Snap or something? Not Old Maid, please, or I'll take it as a personal slight.'

'Oh, no.' Patrick reached into the emergency fun bag we'd packed for the trip and produced a deck of cards. He snapped them like a card shark, an impression that was slightly ruined by the fact they had Scooby Doo on the back of them. 'Not Snap. You're never too young—or too old—to learn poker.'

Sometime later, I had lost my entire stash of M&Ms to

Alex and was having another full-on board-game strop. 'Isn't gambling illegal in America anyway? I could have you both arrested.'

'Why don't you ring the police, then? I'm sure the emergency services are taking it easy right now.'

I sulked. To cheer me up, Patrick braved the hotel lobby and got us some hot dogs out of a vending machine that did hot food. I wondered if I could install one in my bedroom. The curtains might smell like mustard though. When he arrived back, arms full of meaty goodness, he gestured to me to come out into the bedroom.

'Stay there, Alex,' I instructed, but he wasn't really listening anyway. He was busy watching *Ratatouille* for the thousandth time on Patrick's iPad. Almost but not quite ruining my appetite for vending-machine hot dogs.

Outside the bathroom door, the noise of the storm was even louder. The windows were dark, lashed by rain and the occasional flash of lightning. 'They say it's quietening down.'

'Um, do they?'

'Happens all the time, apparently.'

'Rather them than me.'

'Listen, my email got through when I was out there. Michelle isn't going to make it tomorrow. Too stormy—there's no flights in or out.'

'Oh.' I peered back in at Alex, his face lit up by the glow of the tablet. 'So he isn't going to see her.'

'Not this time. She says she'll visit us in London soon. Let's not tell him, OK? I was vague with him anyway. I thought something like this might happen.'

'You thought there'd be the worst tropical storm for a decade?'

'No. But let's just say that Michelle has made it clear where her priorities lie.'

I didn't know what to say to that. I didn't want to judge this woman I'd never met, but I didn't understand how someone could stay away from Alex for so long. He wasn't even my kid and I missed him when he was at school.

We went back in. 'Daddy,' said Alex, his face covered in ketchup as he happily ate a meal that involved meat, bread and chocolate, his favourite things.

'Yes, mate?' Patrick also had ketchup on his face, which matched his sunburn in an oddly endearing way. I thought how strange it was that a few months ago I hadn't even known they existed, and now here we were sheltering from the storm in a life-and-death situation—well, not really, but we had almost finished all the M&Ms and that was an emergency in my book.

'You know how yesterday we had a nice day?'

'Yep.'

'Well, today I had a nice day too.'

Patrick looked incredulous—we'd spent the entire day stuck in the bathroom, shutting our eyes and humming loudly when someone needed to pee, playing games and eating unhealthy snacks. But I understood. 'Me too, Alex.'

Soon Alex was asleep on the cushions, and the storm was still raging. Patrick and I dragged our mattresses in and set up camp on the bathroom floor. I changed into my pyjamas with the shower curtain drawn and settled down beside Alex. I brushed some breadcrumbs from his curls. In sleep he looked so little, clutching Roger to him, his thumb resting against his open mouth as if he might start sucking it. 'Are you coming to sleep?' I whispered.

Patrick was perched on the bath with his iPad. 'In a minute. You nod off.' I cuddled up to Alex, who smelled of ketchup and sun cream, and I tried to sleep.

Sometime in the night, I woke up. Patrick was lying alongside me on the mattress. He was so tall he couldn't manage it without touching me. His bare feet were tangled in mine, the skin warm. He shifted, trying to get comfortable, and very gently laid his arm over me. I froze, hardly breathing. I could feel his breath on my neck, the weight of him on the mattress. I didn't move away. 'Rachel?' he said very quietly. 'Are you awake?'

For what felt like a long time we lay there, me in his arms, neither of us moving. I could feel he was holding himself tense. Then I closed my eyes and pretended to be asleep.

Rachel's List of things to do to avoid the post-split, pre-divorce slump

1. Do stand-up comedy

2. Learn to dance

3. Travel somewhere on a whim

4. Do yoga properly

5. Sleep with a stranger

6. Eat something weird

7. Go to a festival-*postponed due to weather*

8. Get a tattoo

9. Go horse riding

10. Try an extreme sport

Patrick's List of things to do to avoid the
post-split, pre-divorce slump

1. ~~Climbing~~

2. ~~Skydiving~~

3. ~~Play on stage again~~

4. ~~Get drunk~~

5. ~~Go on a date~~

6. ~~Learn to fillet fish~~

7. Enter Max into a dog show

8. Buy a nice car

9. ~~Take Alex overseas~~

10. ??

Chapter Twenty-Seven

One of the last things on Patrick's list was to take Max to a dog show. Although I found this idea ridiculous—we couldn't even train Max to stop regurgitating half-chewed biscuits on the beds—he had already found one that allowed amateur entries, and we were all signed up to attend the unfortunately named 'Mufts'.

'And how are we going to get to, eh…Mufts? You said it was in Berkshire.'

'I told you, it's a play on "mutts" and "Crufts". At least I think it is.'

'Well, OK. How are we going to get Max there? He won't go on the train. He's afraid of bicycles even if they go too fast.'

'I've got an idea.' He tapped his nose. 'Surprise.'

'Oh God. I hate surprises. It better not involve vomit or sharks, is all I can say.'

'Oh, you busted me. I was totally planning to get to Reading on a vomiting shark.'

'I hope for your sake that's not true.'

We had been back from Florida a week, to a cold and damp England in February, and neither of us was in the best of moods. On the morning of the dog show, I was pondering what to wear—something very old and shabby, surely, if the other dogs were as moulty as Max, but then what if the owners were also judged on presentation? I settled in the end for jeans and a white shirt that had grown too tight thanks to my excessive baking schedule, and squeezed my chest area rather snugly. I tried to do up another button, but it looked close to popping. Oh well. Maybe dog shows were hotbeds of pulling action and I'd score with a Bichon Frise breeder. I was trying not to think about the fact that neither Emma nor Cynthia had even replied to my email about coming along to the show—despite it all being their idea, they were clearly giving up on the list. Well, I wasn't. I would see it through—we were nearly there, after all.

The door slammed; Patrick was back from whatever errand he'd been on and was shouting up the stairs. 'Rachel! We better go.'

'Coming!' I zipped up some knee boots, thinking they might be easier to clean if the place was a little mucky, and went downstairs.

His eyebrows went up. 'What?' I panicked. 'What do people wear at dog shows?'

'I've no idea.'

'So what's wrong?' I adjusted the shirt.

'Nothing, nothing, you're just… Erm. You look smart.'

Was Patrick blushing? I tried again to hitch the shirt up. Normally, my breasts were modest, well-behaved things that sat quietly where I put them. Not like Cynthia's, which she swore flirted with men of their own volition and were always having to be measured and clad in highly expensive muzzle-like underwear. But today, due to some unfortunate combination of a too-small old shirt and a new bra, mine seemed to be taking an active interest in proceedings. 'So how are we getting there?' I put on my coat.

'You'll see.' He held the door open for me. 'Ta-da!'

In the driveway, where I was used to seeing Patrick's old Volvo, was parked a gleaming silver car. It seemed to purr with money, with comfort, with speed. 'You didn't.'

'I did! Went to the dealership this morning.'

'You bought a Jaguar?'

'A Jaguar is a kind of leopard, Daddy,' said Alex, trotting out with his Octonauts backpack on and holding Max's lead.

'Not this kind.' I stared at it. Patrick was running a hand over its curves, like a sleazy man at a tango class. I realised suddenly that I hadn't seen him kick Alan's fence or throw coffee into his garden for ages. Maybe he was changing. Maybe we both were.

'Look at it. Nought to a hundred in five seconds. Alloy wheels. Power steering.' At least I think that's what he said. All I heard was 'blah blah blah blah car'.

'Are you seriously going to transport Max in a brand-new, very expensive car?'

'No, I thought I'd just leave it here and we'd take the bus.'

'Be sarcastic all you want. Don't blame me when your upholstery is covered in dog hair and puke.'

He frowned. 'I never thought of that. We better corral him in.' So we set off in heavy Saturday traffic, Max locked in his crate and the seats spread over with plastic sheeting, as if we were transporting a murder victim. Somewhere around Slough, the car filled with a dreadful smell and Alex said, 'Daddy, I think Max has been sick.'

It took all my strength not to say 'I told you so', as we crawled along the motorway with all the windows open, our hair in disarray and the sound of a groaning, sick and definitely not prize-winning Westie behind us.

'Don't gloat,' said Patrick.

'I'm not. I'm just trying to work out if I've actually enjoyed any of the tasks. I mean, there's been groping, vomit, blisters, horrific existential terror, bleeding, fainting, falling off horses...'

'What would we have done otherwise?' He shifted into second gear as the traffic moved slightly. 'Sat at home being sad about Michelle and Dan and eating cake?'

'We did that anyway.'

'True. At least it got us out and about, seizing life and so on. And we got some good anecdotes out of it.'

I said nothing. I was no longer sure that doing something for the comedy value was worth it. Ian would emphatically disagree with me, but then he was a man who kept bike parts in his bath and Peperami in the toothbrush holder, so I wasn't inclined to trust his judgement.

Mufts, the Home Counties' Premier Amateur Canine Companion Show, was being held in a large warehouse-like space off a ring road near Reading. By the time we got Max there, he was covered in vomit and glaring at us both balefully as if to say, *I could be in my basket watching the washing machine channel right now, and you've dragged me here?* I felt much the same myself. Luckily, there was a dedicated dog-grooming area—for all your pampered pooches—and we booked him in for the full shampoo, brush and manicure. The lady who took him, who had strangely long false nails and a fancy top for someone who was washing dogs all day—perhaps I was right about it being a hotbed of sexual tension here—wrinkled her nose. 'Oh dear. Has someone had a little accident?'

'*I* haven't!' said Alex crossly. He was very sensitive to any implication that he might not be able to use grown-up loos.

'She means Max was sick, mate.' Patrick steered him to the exhibits, where you could buy anything from a doggy coat to a gold-plated drinking dish. I hoped Max didn't get a complex and start throwing tantrums, demanding a higher grade of doggy biscuit.

'So what's the idea here?' I asked, browsing in the jewelled dog collars. There was more bling here than in a whole VIP box of footballers' wives.

'I've entered Max in the "amateur purebred" category. He has to run around an assault course and obey commands and so on.'

'Good luck with that. Isn't it a bit discriminatory, the whole purebred thing? You know, a wee bit Nazi Germany, circa 1938?'

'That's how it works with dog shows. Although, look, that one does look a bit like Churchill.' He pointed as a fat bulldog waddled by, its chins wobbling. I started to amuse myself by looking for dogs who resembled their owners. A graceful Afghan hound led by a lady with long blonde hair and a flicky fringe. A poodle shown by a little old lady with a blue rinse. An enthusiastic collie with a shaggy dark-haired man. All the same I was a little bored. The tasks seemed to be getting tamer, and I found myself wondering what would happen now we were almost at the end of the lists. What then? Just get on with our lives somehow? At some point I was going to have to face the fact that I couldn't live in Patrick's attic forever, like some mad paint-stained Mrs Rochester.

At least Alex was having a good time, running over to every dog he saw and throwing his arms around them, if we didn't stop him in time. Some of the dogs, like the Irish wolfhound class, were taller than him and it made my heart still to see his little dark head buried in the fur of some toothy beast. The atmosphere resembled that of Fashion Week—the bitchy glances as the owners whispered who'd eaten too many doggy treats that year, the oddly overbred dogs all legs and chins and long glossy hair, the hushed air of competition.

When we collected Max from his groomer, a shock was in store.

'Where's Maxxy?' Alex barrelled in, searching among the crates.

'Er...' Patrick and I had stopped in front of one.

'Oh God. What have they done?'

'Al,' called Patrick. 'I've found him.'

'That's not Maxxy. That's some silly poodle doggy.'

'Nope. It is Max. Just...different.'

Max stared out mournfully from the bars of his crate. His fur had been shaved in a ridiculous pompadour, with little ruffs around his paws and a sort of Mohican affair on his head. He gave us a look I recognised, because I'd worn it myself many times—the person who has just received the worst haircut of their life, right before a huge interview or meeting or date or indeed dog show debut. 'I'm sorry,' I said, bending down to him. 'It'll grow out in three weeks, I promise.' Max sniffed and turned away. If he were human, he'd have been assuring the groomer it was lovely and tipping extra, then going home to cry in front of the mirror.

'I hope this doesn't put him off his game,' Patrick was saying. 'Some of these breeders are really competitive. Max is quite literally the underdog.'

'Well, in films, they're always the ones that win.'

'I'm not sure we're in that kind of film here. It feels more like *Edward Scissorhands* than *101 Dalmatians*.'

List of the most ridiculously named dog breeds

1. The timber wolf (sounds like an intimate nickname for Justin Timberlake)

2. The Norwegian ridgeback (sounds like something from *Harry Potter*)

3. The American rat pinscher (I wouldn't want to meet one of those on a dark night)

4. The pookimo (sounds like a Japanese children's character)

5. The cockapoo (sounds like...well, you can imagine)

A short time later, or possibly a hundred years, depending on which of our party you'd asked—I was erring towards it being the longest day of my life—we were waiting ringside for Max to go in. In the ring, a perky chihuahua was bouncing around the slides and tunnels and hoops laid out for the dogs. Its owner, a fussy man in a green suit and tweed jacket, was visibly gloating as Fifi trotted out with only one fault for not being tall enough to jump onto the seesaw unaided.

'That's cheating,' Patrick was grumbling, sounding remarkably like Emma. 'A dog that small can get through anything. You may as well send a rat round the ring.'

'Shh!' We were getting daggers from some of the other

breeders. They'd clearly been coming to this for years, establishing hierarchies and alliances, and we had wandered in totally clueless with our vomit-stained and now be-poodled ageing Westie. I'd caught some remark about 'possible crossbreeding' and gave them the kind of stare I'd reserve for members of the BNP. These people were just dog racists.

'And now a new competitor,' boomed the plummy man who did the commentating. He had a fedora and red cords. 'It's Cosmos Magician Maximillian, kennel name "Max". Huh.'

A smattering of applause that seemed tinged with sarcasm, if it were possible to clap sarcastically. Patrick led Max in, smiling and waving like an Olympic gymnast about to mount the pommel horse. I saw some of the toothy older ladies, all jewelled sunglass chains and ski tans, adjust their specs to eye him up. Old hags. 'Come on, Max,' I muttered. We had to beat these smug bitches. And that was just the owners.

Poor Max still looked dejected but trotted obediently through the hoops and down the tunnels. I was actually quite impressed. But, like a beauty pageant contestant, he would have to perk up a bit to stand a chance. Smile, even though his leotard was up his bum and his high heels were chafing. Alex's hand was sticky in mine. 'Will Maxxy win?' he asked loudly.

'I don't know, Al.' I could almost feel the scorn around us. That was the trouble with doing lots of new activities. You could never fit into these worlds, not unless you'd been doing it for years. No wonder people found it easier to sit at home watching TV and drinking tea. TV and tea were

fraternities that welcomed everyone. I worried that I was
getting a bit sick of all this list stuff.

Max was almost round the course, bounding up and down
the seesaw with an agility that surprised me. I squeezed
Alex's hand—perhaps this wasn't totally hopeless. Patrick
was directing him, whispering words of encouragement, following alongside him in his green jumper and jeans. He'd
been nervously running his hands through his curls again,
and they could have done with a trip to the groomer's too.

Then, near the end, Max suddenly froze. 'Oh no,' said
Alex, beside me.

What was wrong? I heard Patrick say, 'Come on, Maxxy.
Nearly there. Good boy.'

Nothing. The little dog was totally still except for the
quivering of his nose as he stared into the crowd. Patrick
met my eyes and shrugged. Then Max gave a yelp and suddenly strained forward. Startled, Patrick dropped his lead.
Max was off, vaulting over the side and into the crowd,
where he cut a swathe through them.

'Oh I say…'

'…typical crossbreed behaviour…'

'And it looks as if "Max" has abandoned the course,'
boomed the announcer. 'What a shame for a surprisingly
strong showing. I'm afraid this will lead to automatic disqualification.'

Patrick had leapt over the barrier and was searching the
crowd. I grabbed Alex and ran over to help. 'What happened to him?'

'I don't know. He just took off. I've never seen him move
that fast.'

'Where is he?' Dogs everywhere, but none a short-shorn
Westie.

Just then we heard a cry of, 'Good Lord! Get this beast off my darling!'

Patrick and I looked at each other in horror, then sprinted off in the direction of the grooming area.

Max was standing between the glamorous groomer and a dog crate. He was barking loudly, which I'd never heard him do before. An overly made-up woman in leopard-print trousers was complaining. 'Get this little runt away! My Clemmie needs a cut before the show!'

Max went up to the crate and nuzzled the nose of the dog in it. 'He's trying to help her,' I said. 'Look, he doesn't want her to get the same bad cut he did! Oh, how sweet. Max must have fallen in love at the groomer's.'

'I won't have this thing near my Clemmie,' spluttered the woman, who presumably owned the dog in the cage.

'Excuse me, Max is a purebred West Highland terrier,' I said hotly. 'Not that it matters. You…dog racist.'

'I beg your pardon? How dare you!' She undid the cage and removed a pink-rinsed poodle, pre-clipping. 'There there, baby, Mummy won't let the nasty little dog near you.'

But Clemmie the poodle seemed to have other ideas, lurching out of Mummy's arms and frantically licking Max's face.

'Aw,' I said. 'So sweet. They're in doggy love.'

Alex was tugging on my arm. 'Rachel? Is that a girl doggy?'

'I guess so. It's pink.'

'Then why does it have a willy?' Alex's voice was the loudest thing in the room.

'It doesn't have a— Oh.'

Patrick met my eyes, stricken. 'Well, this is awkward.'

'Why? Don't tell me these people are dog homophobes too?'

'It's more what they're…doing.'

Clemmie and Max were expressing their newfound affection in the most natural way they knew. I automatically stuck my hands over Alex's eyes, but it was all we could do to escape with a disqualification, an official reprimand and one jewelled collar Alex had 'accidentally' stolen off the stall. Clemmie's owner declined to give us her dog's number, and so the canine Romeo and Juliet, or Rovereo and Poodliet, were forever torn asunder.

'Well, that was…interesting.'

We were driving away, with an even more maudlin, lovesick, yet presumably out and proud Max in the back, along with a very quizzical Alex. 'So that was a boy dog Maxxy liked, Daddy?'

'Er, yes.'

'But how come?'

Patrick looked at me pleadingly. I sighed and met Alex's eyes in the mirror. 'You know how in your class, Emily has two mummies?'

'Yeah.'

'Well, it's sort of like that. Sometimes boy dogs like other boy dogs.'

'But why was it pink?'

I said, 'Boys can wear pink. Look at Daddy, he has lots of pink shirts.'

'Does that mean he likes—'

'Anyway!' said Patrick loudly. 'Who wants to stop for a McDonald's, eh?'

The smell of burgers didn't add much to the vomit-scented interior of the car. I wrinkled my nose. 'Bet you wish you'd just bought a Vauxhall Corsa now.'

Patrick changed gear with unnecessary force. 'Yes, all right. You've not really embraced the spirit of the list today, you know that?'

'What's that supposed to mean?'

'You've been really moany and critical. I thought it would be a fun day out.'

I was speechless for a moment. Patrick had actually criticised me, not just banter but genuinely annoyed. 'Well, I'm sorry.'

'Fine. My list is done now anyway, so at least we can stop all this.'

'No. I'm going to finish mine. I promised myself.'

'It'd be a first,' he muttered.

'What?'

'Nothing. You just don't seem to follow through on a lot of things, that's all.'

'What do you...?'

'I mean, you still haven't even given me those cartoon samples for my friend at the paper, have you? I was trying to help you. Sometimes you're really good at shooting yourself in the foot.'

I folded my arms. 'All right. I'll just do the yoga, and then we'll give it all up. Stay home and watch TV and eat cake.'

'Fine by me.'

'Fine.'

Once the word 'fine' has been uttered more than twice in a conversation, it is verging dangerously on a row. I was about to open my mouth to say something conciliatory, but I noticed Patrick's eyes had dropped to my overly tight shirt. One of the buttons had popped under the strain of arguing, and my breasts could clearly be seen trying to join the party, like caged-up mutts at the groomer's. I thought of the dogs and their vigorous, er, affection, and suddenly I was absolutely mortified. The temperature in the car seemed to go up about twenty degrees, even though all the windows were open. I couldn't look at Patrick and didn't dare hitch up my shirt. I heard Patrick cough slightly and my face flushed redder than the ketchup Alex had dropped on the new leather seats.

'Daddy?' Alex piped up.

'Yes, mate?' Patrick said eagerly. Almost as if he wanted to change the subject.

'What were the dogs going to *do* with their two willies?'

Patrick's List of things to do to avoid the
post-split, pre-divorce slump

1. ~~Climbing~~

2. ~~Skydiving~~

3. ~~Play on stage again~~

4. ~~Get drunk~~

5. ~~Go on a date~~

6. ~~Learn to fillet fish~~

7. ~~Enter Max into a dog show~~

8. ~~Buy a nice car~~

9. ~~Take Alex overseas~~

10. ??

Chapter Twenty-Eight

'You don't have to come, you know.'

'I said I'd do all the tasks with you. You did mine, after all.'

'We haven't done the festival,' I pointed out.

Patrick had his head in the hall cupboard, rooting around. 'Yes, well, that will have to wait till the summer. I did try.'

'So after today, the lists are done? We're agreed? We'll leave the rest?'

'That's what we said.'

'What will we do, then?'

His voice was muffled. 'Oh, I don't know, actually enjoy our lives, instead of spending Saturday making animal shapes with a lot of lentil-eating hippies?'

'I said you didn't have to come!'

'And I said it's fine! Oof!' The exercise mat he'd been pulling on came out all at once, and Patrick toppled back against the cupboard door. He clutched it, wincing. 'Great! That's my back out.'

'Well, you're going to the right place. Yoga is excellent for your back.'

He glared at me. 'So is staying at home, and never moving or going out for the next five years.'

'Well, that can be your number ten,' I said crossly. 'Personally, I am going on the all-day yoga class, and you may come, or not come, as you so wish. Though I will say that your aura is horrible today.'

'My aura is horrible?'

'Yeah. It's all grouchy and dark and needs a good clean.'

'God, there's no need to get personal, Rachel. It's not very Zen of you to say it, is it?'

'You don't even know what Zen means.'

'I know it doesn't get you any points in Scrabble. You, however, do not seem to know that, seeing as you tried to play it three times recently.'

I shut the cupboard door with what might have been considered unnecessary force, reflecting that Patrick's downward-facing dog was going to be closer to upward-facing bitch.

The yoga day was the last thing on my list, apart from the festival, which we had at least tried to do. I had arranged to go with Sunita, who I'd met at a meditation class when I'd wandered into the church hall thinking it was a cake sale and then just been too embarrassed to leave. She worked in a shop in Denmark Hill that sold incense and books about chakras and inner eyes, and she always spoke in a soothing whisper. I had been to yoga a few times since and realised I was about as flexible as an ironing board. This was surely something I should remedy as I headed into my thirties. Plus, I could do with some inner love and peace.

Patrick had been really grumpy since the dog show trip, and I wondered uneasily if he was getting sick of having me around. But I was determined we were going to enjoy today. Emma had even said she would come—I think she was feeling guilty about not correctly moderating the tasks. The fiasco of the dog show had shown her we were hopeless without her guiding tutelage, or so I said when trying to persuade her. Cynthia was working, of course.

'Hey, Patrick, who am I?' We were unrolling our yoga mats in the draughty hall. I was wearing tracksuit bottoms and a baggy Dire Straits T-shirt. Emma had turned up kitted out in quite tight yoga pants, not really like her. The place was full of stretchy toned ladies who lunched, all limbering up and accessing their inner light. 'Who am I?' I asked again, bursting into song. 'La la la woman, it's all in meeeeee.'

'I don't know.'

'Chakra Khan! Get it?'

'She's worse than bloody Ian,' Emma said to Patrick. 'One day I would like to visit a country where absolutely no one has a sense of humour. No stupid jokes, no puns, just sensible discussions about the euro and different types of shelving.'

'You'd love my office, then,' said Patrick, stretching out his calves. 'Plus, people are always having tantrums and stealing each other's colouring-in pencils, so you'd feel right at home.' He was also wearing tracksuit bottoms, and a polo shirt that showed off his tattoo. I noticed some of the ladies checking him out from under their natural-look extended eyelashes. I was feeling a bit grumpy about that. I thought this was meant to be about inner beauty, not flawless make-up and tight stretchy clothes. If I wanted to worry about how I looked while contorting myself into weird shapes, I'd have done number five again, sleep with a stranger.

Sunita was doing a casual handstand. 'This is going to be fantastic,' she said peaceably. 'We're going to feel full of grace and light.' I saw Emma and Patrick exchange a sneery glance and felt even crosser. Sunita was lovely. You didn't need relentless negativity to be an interesting person.

'Welcome, everyone,' said a voice like liquid caramel.

'Oh my God,' Emma gasped. I followed her gaze. The teacher for the class was simply the most beautiful man I had ever seen. Lithe, toned, tanned, with green eyes, dark cropped hair and perfect white teeth. 'My name is Federico,' he said. 'I come here from Brazil to your lovely country to share the art of yooooooga. Let's chant together to begin with.' He closed his sleepy emerald eyes and sat in a perfect lotus position. Sunita followed suit, chanting 'OOOOOOOMMMMM' loudly and unselfconsciously. I murmured along. I could hear Patrick and Emma having a whispered conversation. 'I thought it was exercise, not like a mad *cult*.'

'I'm not doing it. I'm just going to sit here in protest. Like Gandhi.'

I opened my eyes and glared at them. 'Shh!'

Patrick didn't stop moaning all through the class. 'Why do they have such silly names? Warrior, for God's sake. Camel pose? What's that, looking humpy?'

Emma was snickering along with all his little snide comments, and the rest of the lovely hippy yoga people, though far too nice to say anything, were starting to notice. 'Let's all stay positive,' Federico said, with his gleaming smile.

'Even if you're just beginning your practice, bring an open heart and mind! Let the light into your soul!'

'Open the curtains, then,' muttered Patrick, and Emma giggled again. I was wishing she hadn't come. I'd barely seen her since the New Year debacle, and now she was taking his side. This whole stupid list had been her idea in the first place. She was so bloody bossy—they both were. I pushed myself into the Cobra pose, trying to let go of the resentment that burned in my stomach like the acid reflux from the lentil and chickpea vegetarian loaf we were having for lunch.

That was embarrassing too. OK, a lot of the yoga practitioners may have had long unbrushed hair, and some of them might have been called things like Rainbow and Wurzel, and yes, quite a few of them did dress in tie-dye or huge rainbow-knitted cardigans, but they were nice people. There was no need for Emma and Patrick to nudge each other every time someone made a comment about the spiritual awakening they'd had in India or how they'd given up meat because they were afraid they were 'eating the animal's fear as it died'.

'You used to be a vegetarian,' I pointed out to Emma. 'You picketed the student union to start serving Quorn sausage rolls.' I knew Patrick disapproved of vegetarianism on principle, as some people disapprove of UKIP membership or not eating chocolate.

'Well, maybe, but because of serious ecological and environmental concerns. Not because of this airy-fairy bollocks.'

'Can't you just be nice?' I hissed crossly at them both. At that point Sunita drifted over with a plate of organic gluten- and dairy-free carrot cake, a beatific smile on her face.

'Everyone's got such a nice aura during yoga. So clean and gleaming.'

'Do you spring-clean your aura?' asked Patrick politely.

'Oh yes,' she said earnestly. 'With chanting and fasting, of course.'

'I use Pledge on mine,' he muttered, sending Emma off again. Funny how she seemed to love Patrick's lame jokes, when her own boyfriend's drove her mad.

In the second part of the class, Federico had us do some more challenging 'asanas', including one where we stood on our shoulders and spread our legs wide.

'This is ridiculous,' Emma complained. 'If my children did this, they'd be in the naughty corner for a week.'

Federico was coming over and correcting people's poses, pressing down their legs or realigning their arms. 'Oh no, he's coming over,' she said.

'Er, didn't you say he was the loveliest thing you'd ever seen, and more delicious than a whole pyramid of Ferrero Rocher?'

'Federico Rocher,' said Patrick, a little sniffily.

'That's the problem! I can't have him touch me. I might… say something.'

But then he was upon her. 'Mees Emmma, you are new to this practice, I think?'

'How can you tell?' she said sulkily, opening her legs barely ten centimetres. Some people had theirs literally at right angles.

'May I open your legs a little, Emmma?'

Emma gulped. 'Well, I suppose so, eh… Oh Lord.' Federico was pressing down on her thighs. 'THANK YOU!'

she shouted. 'Er, I have, eh, sciatica, so we better leave it there. Thanks though.'

'As you wish.' He bowed and moved on.

'Pretty sure some people pay by the hour for that,' she muttered.

'Not me,' said Patrick quickly, as Federico approached.

'But, Patreeeck, if you would let me help with the alignment...'

'My alignment is just fine. Seriously. Not a finger. Please, mate.'

Emma started laughing again. I rolled my eyes, which was difficult to do with my head between my legs. Now Federico was with me. 'Rrrrachel. You are very good, very, very good. You try hard.'

I smiled smugly.

'May I push you a bit harder?'

'You may push me just as hard as you like, Federico.'

Then his liquid green eyes were hovering somewhere near my navel, his strong hands pressing on my thighs, and actually, oh dear, brushing my bum... Mmm. For a moment, I let myself imagine us in a different setting, no one else around, but doing a very similar position... 'Harder,' I heard myself murmur.

'Harder?' He looked puzzled.

'Er, no! That's fine, that's fine, thank you.' I hid my blushing face under my own legs and distinctly heard Patrick let out a snide 'huh' from under his.

List of the most comical yoga poses

1. Camel pose

2. Downward-facing dog

3. Pigeon pose

4. Sleeping tiger pose

5. Dolphin pose

When the class was over, we rolled up our mats. 'We're all going to the organic café for nettle tea,' enthused Sunita. 'You will come, won't you?'

I glanced at Emma and Patrick, who were making comments to each other out of the sides of their mouths. 'I think I better take these two away. I'm sorry.'

She looked a little stricken, biting her lip. 'Rachel, my dear, I hate to say anything negative, but are you happy?'

'Of course. I've got a nice place to live, company, lots of fun things to do...'

'And this is all what you want?'

'Eh, yeah? Yeah.'

'OK.' She gave me a hug. 'Come round for lentil soup sometime. Oh, hi, Federico.'

I blushed as he came up behind us. He'd changed from his baggy clothes into a green T-shirt that matched his eyes, and jeans that hugged his yoga-cised body. 'Hey, Rrrrachel. You did well today. You would like maybe to meet sometime, to practise the yoga?'

'You mean like a class?'

'I am meaning like just you and me.'

Oh. OH. I looked at his gorgeous face and eyes and smile and abs where his T-shirt rode up ever so slightly. The totally hot teacher was asking me, Rachel Kenny, out on a date. Then I caught sight of Patrick, suddenly paying attention to us, his hair a mess, his face grumpy, his top rumpled. 'I don't think so, Federico. Thank you though. Today was great.'

Buddhists are pretty easy to blow off, as they never harbour any resentment. 'As you wish,' he said, bowing his head. *'Namaste.'*

'Namaste,' I mumbled.

Sunita was looking at me strangely. 'Love will find you, Rachel, but not if you reject it when it comes. Remember you have to be like a love tree—take in whatever negativity you get, process it, turn it into love.'

'What? Oh, no, he's not really my type, is all.'

'He's bloody gorgeous,' she said. 'And he has a lovely aura, I mean. A deep spirit.' She gazed after him. 'And a nice bum...'

I squirmed. 'I'm just not ready.'

'Of course.' She hugged me again, then Patrick and Emma, who had the grace to look a little ashamed at their snideness. 'Lovely to meet you both. Bye!'

'What did the boy from Ipanema want?' asked Patrick casually.

'Federico? Oh, nothing. Just to say I had the best Warrior pose in the class, and he felt sorry for me with my horrible negative friends.'

Patrick put his arm around me awkwardly. 'I'm sorry, Rachel. It's just... Can I be honest?'

'Go on.'

'I'm really, really sick of the lists.'

'Me too,' I said.

'I was sick of them ages ago,' Emma said. 'I can't believe you actually did them all.'

I gaped at her. 'It was your idea! You said it would get me out of my disastropiphany slump!'

'Well, it did, didn't it? But no one ever actually completes those bucket list things. It's always just easier to sit at home and watch telly. I mean, there's a reason people never learn dancing or take up fencing or hike the Inca trail. Those things are nice, but they aren't life. Your life is the tax forms and getting the shopping in Sainsbury's and cleaning the loo.'

Patrick and I stared at each other. 'But…but what about all that stuff about embracing life, seizing the day?'

She shrugged, buttoning up her duffel coat. 'Depends on the day, doesn't it? I mean, if it's like a rainy Tuesday in January, I'm not too keen on seizing it, to be honest. It can do one.'

Patrick was shaking his head, as if his world had been shattered. 'I guess we were the ones stupid enough to go through with it. But can we stop now?'

'You never had a number ten,' I said sadly.

'Well, this can be it. Number ten is—stop the list madness and go back to normal.'

'OK,' I said, sighing. 'We're pretty much finished anyway.'

'Good,' said Emma, putting on her bike helmet. 'Next year I suggest we resolve instead to watch more TV, eat more cake and spend more time in bed. That's something we could all achieve with ease.'

Rachel's List of things to do to avoid the
post-split, pre-divorce slump

1. ~~Do stand-up comedy~~

2. ~~Learn to dance~~

3. ~~Travel somewhere on a whim~~

4. ~~Do yoga properly~~

5. ~~Sleep with a stranger~~

6. Eat something weird

7. Go to a festival-*postponed due to weather*

8. Get a tattoo

9. Go horse riding

10. Try an extreme sport

Chapter Twenty-Nine

Myself, I've never trusted time. I know that sounds like a mad thing to say, like not believing in gravity or thinking the world is a thousand years old and was designed by Care Bears, but bear—sorry—with me. Think about how long a minute can be when you're waiting for something to cook in the office microwave, with Impatient Joan from Accounts tapping her New Look heels behind you, or when you run on the treadmill at the gym, or wait for a tube that promises it's just round the corner. Then think about how time flits and flies when you're out with your best friends, or with someone you love, or on holiday. Don't tell me every minute of your life is the same length.

And so, just as the previous months had dragged, every day something else to grapple with, time suddenly began to speed up and I found I'd been at Patrick's for nearly four months.

It was a Thursday in February. I was feeling pretty good, in fact. I hadn't thought about Dan, or the ladders, or the gaping maw of the rest of my life, for quite some time. Since the yoga class and official suspending of the lists, we'd gone back to normal, working, cooking, looking after Alex and Max. I was managing to quell the little voices of doubt that whispered to me in quiet moments. *But does he want you here? Where will you go after this?*

On the day it all came to an end, I'd been to the shops and farmers' market, and I was thinking I might do some baking, surprise Alex and Patrick with a cake for after dinner. I'd bought a cheese called Vile Bellringer, which I knew Patrick would love, even if it made me smell as if I was transporting a dead body in my tote bag.

List of the weirdest cheese Patrick likes

1. Pantsygawn

2. Stinking Bishop

3. Ancient Ratcatcher

4. Slack Ma Girdle

5. Ticklemore

I knew Max would stand by my feet as I cooked, patiently gazing on everything I did as if I were crazy, but he was fond of me all the same. I was feeling settled. Life actually seemed good for a moment.

I should have realised, of course, that this was exactly when it all falls apart beneath your feet.

I let myself in, noticing in passing a quite posh coat hanging up. It certainly wasn't mine. Perhaps Patrick was finally giving Michelle's things to the charity shop. Lord knows she had enough designer gear stuffing out the cupboards.

I hung up my own student duffel coat beside it and

lifted my bundle from the farmers' market. What an idiot I was, in hindsight. Spending six pounds on cheese because I thought Patrick might like it. Forgetting I didn't have the money for it. For any of it. Forgetting none of this was mine.

A woman was standing in the doorway of the kitchen. Tiny, beautiful, with jet-black hair down the back of her red dress. I just stared at her for a moment.

'Who are you?' she said, frowning.

I would have asked her the same, except I knew. I'd seen her face in dozens of pictures around the house. 'You're Michelle.'

'I know who I am. What I don't know is who you are or why you're letting yourself into my house with a key.' I didn't know what to say. Surely Patrick had told her about me?

'I'm Rachel. I'm the lodger. Sort of.'

'Sort of?'

'I stay here.'

'With my son?'

'Yes, I—'

Then, with very bad timing, the front door shot open and Alex raced in, fresh from his carpool, bringing his smell of earth and crayons. 'Rachel! Guess what? Today we had a guinea pig in class! Only I don't know why it's called a pig, because it's only little and pigs aren't all hairy.' He came up beside me, nuzzling in under my arm, like Max when he wanted to be stroked.

'Alex,' I said weakly.

He glanced up, saw Michelle. The look of confusion that crossed his face nearly broke my heart. 'Mummy?' he said. As if he wasn't even sure.

'Hello, sweet pea,' said Michelle. 'Did you miss me?' She had a husky American accent. 'I missed you.'

Alex looked up at me, doubtful. 'Mummy's come back,' I said. I would have said more but didn't know what she was doing here.

'But weren't you over the seas?'

'I was. But I missed you too much, so I had to come back for you.'

Come back for him? What did that mean? I wished Patrick were here.

'What time does Daddy get home?' Michelle asked Alex.

Alex shrugged. He had no more concept of time than the dog did. I said, 'He's usually home by six. He'd come earlier though if he knew you were here.' I realised as I said it how wrong this was, that I knew where Patrick might be, but his wife didn't. 'Do you want me to call him?'

She looked at me coolly. She was stunningly pretty, her face like a doll's, her make-up perfect. 'I can call him. I know where he works.'

'Of course. I'll just...' I put away the groceries while she watched, acutely aware that this was her kitchen I was poking about in. I felt so stupid about the cheese.

She watched as I opened the fridge. 'Is that to eat today?'

'I don't know. I...'

'You should let it breathe if so. Patrick hates cold dairy.'

What a ridiculous thing to say. *My husband, who I left and haven't seen for months, and whose heart I broke, whatever you do, make sure his cheese is at the correct room temperature!* I had wondered about her priorities when I saw she'd labelled all the herbal teabags and put them in little snap-close jars, and this just confirmed it.

She folded her arms, standing against the sink. 'So you're staying here? You pay rent?'

'Not exactly. I help out. Round the house and with Alex.'

'Like a nanny?'

'Not exactly.'

I was getting pretty sick of strange women barging in here and asking me about the conditions of my lease. Although in Michelle's case I suppose she did own the place. And it probably wasn't very nice to come home and find a stranger there, looking after your child.

Alex came bustling in, handing me his school shirt for the washing machine, as he was used to doing. 'Can I have chocolate biscuits today, Rachel?'

'Er...' I looked at Michelle.

She frowned. 'Has Daddy been letting you eat sugar, sweet pea?'

Alex shrugged. I cast about. 'Um, how about some rice cakes for a snack today, Al?'

'Yuck.' I shared his feelings, but she was his mum. I was...no one.

After an excruciatingly awkward fifteen minutes where I tried to follow Alex's after-school routine of snack, homework, wash and clothes change, while Michelle stood over me saying nothing but just watching, the door went. Patrick walked in in his sheepskin jacket and with his hair all disordered by the afternoon drizzle. He didn't look at me but stared straight at Michelle. 'Hello.'

'Hi.'

Michelle was sitting in the lounge, her ankles crossed. I was hovering anxiously in the door of the kitchen. Patrick didn't meet my eyes. 'I wasn't expecting you,' he said to her.

'Last-minute business trip. We need to talk.'

'Where's *Alan*?'

Michelle looked away. 'Back home. I mean, in the States.'

'Rachel,' said Patrick formally, still not really looking at me. 'Would you mind giving us some time?'

I was being booted out. 'I can take Alex to the park if you like. And Max.'

I felt the little dog brush up against me, his breath on my legs. He was picking up on the weird atmosphere, I was sure.

'Thanks. That would be good.'

'Make sure he wears a coat,' Michelle said. How bloody dare she. I'd been looking after her son for months while she swanned around New York, ice skating and eating melts and whatever people did there (it's obvious I've never been).

'Max or Alex?' I said.

She stared at me. 'Both. If they need it.'

And with that, the lady of the house was dismissing me.

I'd always thought it was hard to be preoccupied when you were with a child—they needed your full attention to answer all their daft questions, like how do birds stay up, and to stop them falling into the road in the path of a bus, but today Alex wasn't saying much either. I had Max's lead in one hand and Alex's hand in the other as we strode towards the Heath. It was raining and almost dark, a chilly wind blowing in and freezing my face. I'd wanted nothing more than to settle into the nice warm kitchen and eat my farmers' market quinoa sourdough with overpriced artisan cheese. Alex was trotting along beside me in his wellies.

'You OK, mate?' I glanced down at him. He was walking very slowly, and with a suspicious crunching noise. 'Have you got something in your boots again?'

Alex nodded miserably.

'What is it? Crisps? No? Biscuits?'

Another sad nod.

'Oh, mate. You haven't done that in ages. What's the matter?'

'Mummy came back. From over the seas.'

'Yep. Looks like it.'

'Are you going now, Rachel?'

'What? Why?'

'You came after Mummy went. Are you going again?' His hand in mine was cold and limp.

I realised I didn't know the answer to that question. I knelt down in front of him, on the wet pavement, and put my arms round him. I could smell biscuits and baby shampoo, and feel his wet face press against my coat. 'I don't know, Alex. I'm sorry. I'll always be your friend though, whatever happens. Shall we get ice cream? Or a cake in the café, maybe?'

He shook his head. I thought he was trying hard not to cry.

'So? Is she...?' I was immensely glad that Michelle had gone when we arrived home, damp and down-hearted. Alex went straight up to his room to play, saying he didn't even want a hot chocolate, so something was definitely wrong.

Patrick leaned against the sink, rubbing his hands over his face. 'She's going to stay in a hotel.'

'I see.' Because that was the kind of person Michelle was—when you made a mess, when you smashed up your home, you could always go somewhere else, because you had money. Not like me, forced to live with my mistakes.

He rubbed his hands over his face again, straightening the dish towel compulsively. 'She wants Alex to live with her.'

'She's coming home?'

'No. She wants to take him with her.'

I absorbed this for a moment—Alex, disappearing onto a plane, carrying his little Octonauts rucksack with Max's head poking out. No. She wouldn't take Max. There was quarantine, and she didn't like dogs anyway. 'Can she do that?'

'She's his mother. They nearly always get custody.'

'But what about you?'

'I—' His jaw clenched. 'I think I might have to go too. I'd probably get a green card OK, with my experience. Since we're not actually divorced, that would help, Michelle being an American citizen and all.'

I just stared at him. 'You're getting back together?'

'No, I... Look, I don't know what's happening right now. I think she wants to live back there permanently. Her mother is quite ill, on top of everything, and she has a great job. Plus, there's...Alan.'

'Oh.' I swallowed hard. 'What about... When?'

'I don't know. She doesn't have long off work. She wants to see a lawyer tomorrow and hash things out.'

I stood there for a long time, feeling bits of my life crumble and fall to the ground round me. Bang. Bang. Bang. That was the sound of the ladder itself falling apart. 'I think I better move out,' I heard myself say. 'If there's a chance for you two.'

He didn't look at me. He was leaning on the counter so hard his knuckles were white.

'Patrick?'

'I don't know yet, but...well, yes, it might be a good idea if you started looking.'

Chapter Thirty

It's a truth universally acknowledged, as Jane Austen didn't say, that one area of your life suddenly falling apart means the rest goes too, like when you accidentally knock down a load-bearing wall (I watched a lot of DIY shows during the day). The day after this bombshell, Patrick and Michelle were still trying to thrash out their differences. I was in my room trying to get on with work as best I could, and failing, and pausing to manically Google flats, then remembering how hard I'd found it last time, and stopping to panic. Michelle had turned up that morning with a man in yellow cords, who I thought was her lawyer. He'd shaken my hand and peered at me over his glasses, getting a good look at my chest. 'Hello, my dear.' Sometimes I would hear raised voices, all the way up in my tower, and would try to ignore it. It was cutting way into my tea consumption anyway, and about the only good thing was I wasn't eating quite so many biscotti. However, what my teeth gained, the rest of my life surely lost. About lunchtime, Patrick came up to tell me they were going out.

'Henry wants to "get a good luncheon", apparently. He doesn't "do" sandwiches.'

'OK. How's it going?'

Patrick just shook his head. He looked grim. I felt sick dread coiling in my stomach. For the next hour or so I tried to get on with work, until far below, the doorbell went. I listened, but there was no sound of the door being answered, so I dragged myself down the three flights of stairs. They must still be out.

When I opened the door, I gaped.

'What are you doing here?' It was 2 p.m. on a weekday. Come rain or shine, come colds or nits—it happens—Emma was always in front of her class at this time. Instead now she was standing on the doorstep. She shook her head, as if unable to speak. I saw her face was very red. 'Em, are you OK? Look, come in, sit down.' I sat her down in the lounge on the sofa. She was still wearing her duffel coat. 'Has something happened?'

She laid something on the coffee table—a mobile phone. Not hers, that had a Greenpeace sticker on and was an ancient Nokia she had never replaced because of what cobalt mining was doing in the Congo. I recognised the phone though—the cracked screen and smudge of oil on the back could only have come from one person.

'You took his phone?'

She pointed at the screen, still speechless.

'You want me to look? Em, I don't know if I should...'

I quailed at the sight of her face and peered at the screen. It was a series of text messages to someone called 'Dave'. Only thing was, it didn't sound like a Dave. Not at all.

Thanx for last night. Really needed to talk. X
And Ian had said: *No prob. He's a stupid arse you know.*
I must be stupid. He's the one cheating. x
He's a fucking idiot to cheat on you. Sorry. X
Ian never used kisses on text messages. He said they were 'emotional blackmail in a character'. In fact, he'd even developed a list of what they meant.

List of what kisses in text messages mean

1. One kiss: I am a woman. I don't know you that well, or I'm cross with you.

2. Two kisses: I am a woman. All normal here.

3. Three kisses: I fancy you.

4. Four kisses: I am in love with you, or your cat just got run over.

Thanx, said 'Dave'. *Means a lot to me. Feeling really alone here.*
Ur not alone. Always here. XX
Then a follow-up message. *If you need to meet up I'm around tomorrow. XXX*
Immediately—*Can we? Amazing. Don't tell Em yet though.*
And back from Ian. *Sure. xxxx*
Bollocks. Four kisses. Who the hell was Dave? I looked at Emma. 'But—'
She held up a finger, then pulled out her own phone. She scrolled through her contacts then laid the phone beside the messages from 'Dave'. I looked at the numbers. And then, far too late, it all made sense.
I felt my head pop, like when you surface too quickly in diving. 'She wouldn't.'

Emma's voice came out, raspy and hollow. 'She bloody well did. They've been meeting in secret. He told me he was working late.'

I didn't know what to say. 'But maybe it's just...'

'Uh-uh. There is no maybe. It's over. I've asked him to leave. And as for Cynthia...well, you can tell her she's welcome to him. I'm never speaking to her again.'

Little things were falling into place. The way they'd been giggling at the New Year party. The way she stood up for him about doing comedy. The way he held a spoon for her to try his curry. Oh God. Not Ian. Not Cynthia.

Then Emma, my rock, my bossy, practical friend, who once broke a toe on a night out and didn't even notice until the next day, who'd faced down the abusive six-foot-five father of a bruised six-year-old, who *hadn't even cried at Toy Story 3*, put her head on her arms and burst into tears.

I put her to bed in my room, since she was in no fit state for the tube, and didn't want to go back to Ian anyway. Then I crawled into bed beside her, as we used to do at university when we had hangovers and essays to write on the nude in Western art (me) or causes of dissent in Weimar Germany (her).

I was still trying to make sense of it. 'I just don't understand it. Why didn't he delete the messages? And why the fake name? He's had her number for years, surely.'

'He must have just wanted to keep them. To reread.'

That made it even worse, somehow. 'And what was all that about cheating?'

'Oh.' Under the covers, she snorted. 'Rich has been seeing someone. Ian told me. He's getting all the secrets, apparently.'

'Someone at work?'

'Worse. I'll give you a clue—she probably wears leg warmers and heels in bed.'

'Not…the dance teacher from tango? Cockney Nikki?'

'The same. Took a shine to him, apparently. I'm sure that had nothing to do with his Savile Row suits and big pay packet.'

'Christ. Are they splitting up?'

'Guess so. So her and Ian can get together now. Cosy.'

'Oh, Em. I'm sure it isn't like that. Look, there's nothing there that's totally bad. It could be just friendly. It's inappropriate, yes, but not actually cheating.'

'Of course it's cheating! He lied to me.'

'Well, is that…?' I was on very shaky ground here and didn't want to say much more. 'Shouldn't you at least talk to her?'

Suddenly, she sat up, her bobbed hair all at right angles. 'All right, then. But I want you to come with me. To hers.'

'Now? Is that a good idea?'

'No. But it's what I need.'

'She won't be there! It's a weekday.'

'Oh, she will. She texted him earlier to say she was taking a sick day and they needed to talk.'

'Oh. Promise me you'll just ask her about it? Honestly, it could be nothing.'

'Could it?' She was out of bed, pulling on her shoes.

I took a deep breath. 'Em. Are you sure this isn't about your issues with Ian? What you said at New Year…'

'I wanted us to move forward,' she said, staring ahead into space. 'Is that so wrong? I wanted to get married. And yes, I know I said it was bollocks, all that honour and obey crap, but I'm thirty. I've been with him nearly twelve years—I just want to call him my husband. I want a baby, but he won't even discuss it, just wants to do this stupid comedy stuff and go out on his bike all the time and drink cider. So I guess she was just more…understanding.' Emma sniffed and wiped her hands over her face. 'Let's go.'

'How are we getting there?'

'Patrick has a car, doesn't he?'

'The Jaguar? Emma! He will kill me. I can't drive the Jaguar!'

She gave me a look that could freeze custard. 'Rachel Kenny. Listen to me. When you needed to move, I took a day off school—first day I'd taken off in five years!—and I rented you a van. When you drank too many Jäger-bombs on your thirtieth birthday, I held your hair while you puked—ditto with your twenty-first, twenty-second and twenty-fifth. I went *tango dancing* for you. I've put up with you being in this slump for months now, crying and panicking or else going on and on about how brilliant your new friend Patrick is. I did that because I am your oldest and dearest friend. Now drive me to see our other oldest friend so I can shout at her.'

I was about to say Lucy Coleman was probably my oldest friend, but we didn't talk much these days, since she worked behind the bar of the town Wetherspoons and had three kids with three different fathers, but, sulkily, I went to find the car keys in Patrick's not-so-secret secret hiding place in a vase in the hall. I told myself he would understand.

'You do remember I'm not the best driver?' I was nervously settling into the seat.

'You mean do I remember the time we hired a car to

go camping, and you got it stuck halfway up a hillside in Wales? I doubt those sheep have ever recovered.'

'Clearly you do. And you still want me to drive you? I've never really done it in London, you know.'

Emma just stared ahead, stony-faced. I felt like some hapless bystander being forced to drive a bomb into the White House car park. Luckily, Patrick had satnav, which told us in soothing tones how to get there. If only there was such thing as a lifenav, I mused. *Marry this man now. At the next exit, get pregnant. At the nearest possible convenience, make a life U-turn.*

'Weren't you supposed to turn there?'

'Was I? Oh well. The satnav woman will tell us when we go wrong.' She was quite like Emma in that respect, but I didn't say so, for fear of having my arm chewed off. She was staring ahead with gimlet rage, but this didn't stop her exclaiming, 'Wow! Close call!' every time we came ever so slightly into someone else's lane.

'So what are you going to do?' I asked, to distract her from the other cars that seemed to want to get up close and personal with the Jaguar, like a rich man passing through a cheap nightclub.

'Have it out with her. And she better not lie. I'm impossible to lie to. I spend all day with people telling me that, honest, it wasn't them who put their fingers in the green paint and then onto my cardigan.' She winced. 'Bicycles come close these days, don't they?'

'What? Oh.' I hadn't noticed. 'You're not going to, you know...'

'What?'

'Do a Nancy Hall?' This was a girl we'd known at university who had incurred Emma's wrath by dancing too close to Ian to the strains of 'Hot in Herre' one Wednesday night in Minty's, our student disco. Emma had 'accidentally' thrown a pint glass of Sex on the Beach over Nancy's short white dress, making her look like an extra from the prom scene from *Carrie*. 'She wasn't so bloody hot after that,' Emma had remarked grimly afterwards.

Emma sighed. 'No. It's just…I never thought it would be him. I mean, every other guy we know, yes, they fancy Cynthia. She's tall, she's gorgeous, she's nice to them—even Dan liked her, didn't he?'

'I suppose. He didn't really like anything, towards the end. I'd have been relieved if he'd shown interest in any woman other than Lara Croft.'

'But Ian…he never seemed to notice her in that way. He only had eyes for me. I thought.' She sounded so sad.

I accidentally distracted her by veering into a totally wrong lane and causing a bus to honk at me. 'Sorry!'

Emma closed her eyes. 'This is good. If we die getting there, I won't have to worry about finding somewhere else to live or what to do with the rest of my life.'

Chapter Thirty-One

'Come in.' Cynthia looked as composed as ever, her hair straightened and gleaming, wearing an orange dress and knee boots. The house was clean, the only sign of life one cup of herbal tea on the glass coffee table. Emma and I sat down, and it was so weird, thinking of all the times we'd spent here dancing to 'Survivor', spotting the ornament Emma had once knocked over and smashed doing the 'Macarena', remembering us with our feet on the leather sofas, talking a mile a minute. Now we sat in cold silence.

Cynthia spoke first. 'I can explain, if you let me.'

'Explain why you're seeing my boyfriend behind my back?' I had to admit Emma was right about the marriage thing—saying 'back off from my husband, bitch' would carry a lot more emotional weight.

'I wasn't seeing him. Not like that. I just needed a friend.' Cynthia twisted her wedding ring and I saw she was ashen under her make-up, as if she hadn't slept in days. 'Rich is leaving me. He's been seeing someone else. For a long time now, since that stupid dance class. They're moving in together. I thought something was up, but I only found out for sure the other day.'

'I'm sorry,' I said, wondering if Emma would kill me for being sympathetic. 'Why didn't you tell us things were bad though?'

She gave a short bitter laugh. 'I tried. Couldn't get it in between you panicking about being alone forever and Emma being furious at Ian for not getting down on one knee with a diamond, even though she's been saying for years that's all sexist rubbish, and anyway diamonds contribute to civil wars and trafficking and human rights abuses.' That was a pretty pitch-perfect impression of Emma, who was sitting in stony silence.

'It was wrong to turn to Ian,' Cynthia went on. 'I see that now. I was just so lonely. I mean, this house, yeah, it looks great, but it's so much space to be alone in.' She said this calmly. 'I'm not used to it. I grew up with kids hanging off every limb, noise, cooking, fights. Not...' She waved her arms about her, at the silent, clean, chilly house. 'That's why I was so upset when you came round for dinner. I mean, Rich has never been the most affectionate, but lately it's been like he doesn't even see me at all. I had no one to talk to. Ian was just...there for me.'

'So why did he put you in his phone under a fake name?' said Emma, still not looking at her.

'I have no idea. I didn't know. But if I had to guess, Emma...'

Oh oh. I could feel this was going to go down about as well as that power cut in *Jurassic Park* that time.

'...I'd say he felt worn down by your constant criticism. Ian, get a better job. Ian, shave off your beard. Ian, don't eat meat. Ian, stop making jokes. Those are the things that make him who he is. He's a hairy biker who likes eating pies. You used to want that, not some identikit commuter from the suburbs. He is a good thing, Em. The best. You two are the best couple I know.'

'Were,' said Emma frostily. 'It's over.'

I saw Cynthia bite her lip. 'Please don't. Not because of this. It wasn't anything, I swear.'

'"Don't tell Em", you said. Why did you ask him not to tell me, if it was so innocent?'

'Honestly? I couldn't bear you knowing Rich had left me. You've slagged him off from day one—his poshness, his job, his money, all your little digs about fish knives. Christ. Do you want us all to live in a commune and knit our own salads, is that it? I just thought you'd be gloating that it hadn't worked out, despite our money.'

I looked between them, stricken. What Cynthia had said was completely true. They were both right. I tried to intervene. 'Look, I can see you've both been having a tough time. I wish you'd told me, but we're all friends, and Cynthia says it was a mistake, but nothing happened.'

'She was texting my boyfriend,' Emma barked. 'How dare she try to take the moral high ground. She is…below moral sea level!'

'Well, is it really—'

'I will never forgive her. Never.'

'Typical.' Cynthia got to her feet. 'Saint Emma, saviour of the downtrodden. Tell me this, Em, if you love being poor and self-righteous so much, why were you pushing Ian to change jobs?'

'He had no right to tell you that!'

Oh dear. I bleated, 'Guys, guys, let's not… Please.'

'I don't know why you're taking her side.' Cynthia turned on me suddenly, and I could see the backstreet scrapper she'd been before university had polished her, all curry chips and nail varnish and hitting girls with her shoes. 'All this pining after Dan, months and months of it—you didn't even love him! You weren't even happy!'

'I...'

'I guess Emma doesn't know you also have a pretty relaxed attitude to what constitutes cheating.'

All the blood ran from my face. Oh no. Oh God. She wouldn't...

Emma was staring at me. Cynthia had her arms folded. 'Looks like Rachel didn't tell you about that. Even though you're such best friends.' Her voice wobbled with tears.

'You cheated on Dan?' Emma's face was white.

'I... No! It was nothing. Just...' I took a deep breath. 'I kissed someone. And Dan found out. And it was wrong, I know, but I made a mistake. People do, Emma. Maybe not you, but...'

'Fucking Simon.' Emma was shaking her head. 'I knew it. You told me nothing happened. You lied.' She got to her feet. 'At least I know now. I can't trust a single one of you. Not you, not her, not Ian.'

I heard her footsteps run down the stairs and then the front door slam. Cynthia put her head in her hands. 'Shit.'

I was shaking. 'I...'

'I'm sorry, Rach. I just... I was angry, and you were taking her side, and she's so bloody judgemental. I mean, that's why you never told her in the first place, isn't it? Because all she does is judge us.'

I stood up as well. 'I'm sorry about you and Rich. But Ian's not the answer. And, as you pointed out, I would know.'

My journey home was perfectly rounded off when I turned into the driveway an hour later, blind with tears, clipping Patrick's precious baby off the gatepost and shattering the front light.

List of terrible flashback moments in the life of Rachel Kenny

1. Crying on the floor the day Dan kicked me out

2. Dan confronting me about Simon (see below)

3. Wetting myself in primary school assembly, aged seven, during an extra-long rendition of 'Jerusalem'

4. That one. That one right there, when I realised that on top of everything else I'd lost my two best friends

Chapter Thirty-Two

The day after the big row and crash, I woke up late and cringed under the duvet. Oh God. Had Cynthia really... Had Emma... Had I actually crashed Patrick's car into the gate?

Yes, it was all true.

I hardly had time to brood about it all, because he was knocking on the door. 'Are you up?'

'Just about. Come in.' I pulled the duvet up to my neck.

He came in, dressed unusually smartly in a shirt and jeans, looking exhausted and pale. 'Patrick. I am so sorry about the car. It was... Emma made me, and I was so upset I just...'

'The car doesn't matter.'

'But you love it!'

He sighed. 'It doesn't matter. Look, Michelle is coming round soon with her lawyer.'

'OK. I'll stay here.' Even though I really wanted to sit in front of the TV and eat crumpets and jam and stare out at the driving rain. I thought of our stupid running joke—

Is it still raining? I hadn't noticed. Would we ever be silly together again?

'The thing is, she's said she doesn't feel comfortable with you in the house. Would you mind...?'

'You want me out?'

'Just for a few hours. Please.'

'Well, OK. I can find a café. I suppose I should be looking to move soon, should I?'

He didn't say anything. 'She'll be here in a minute.'

A home isn't a home when you aren't welcome in it. I had quickly gone from feeling as if I lived in Patrick's house, to feeling like a house guest who just won't take the hint that you want them to leave so you can watch *CSI*. Getting dressed, pointedly not washing my hair as Patrick was rushing me, I went downstairs, passing Alex on the stairs. He was hugging Roger morosely, as from downstairs the sound of tense conversation drifted up.

'All right, dude?'

He hugged the teddy tighter. 'What's happening, Rachel?'

'I don't know. I'm sorry.'

'Where are you going?'

'Just out...out for a walk. In the rain.'

'Can I come?'

'No, I'm sorry, mate. It's too wet. I'll bring you back some sweets.' I was pretty sure Michelle would disapprove, but the atmosphere of seething tension in the house was surely a lot more damaging to Alex than some sugar.

Michelle was already there, leaning against the sink drinking coffee, as if she owned the place. Which, of course, she did. She stared at me. She was wearing high heels, tights and a grey suit. On a Saturday. 'I'm going now,' I said mournfully, like Max when we made him go for walkies in the rain.

She turned away, ignoring me. I trudged out into the damp, walking aimlessly. I'd find a café and start looking at some flats. But I found myself walking and walking, once again trying to escape the wave of gloom. It was back. Turned out it had only receded in the same way a tidal wave did, gathering extra force to crash onto your head. I found myself in Kentish Town, back in the same café I'd been in on the day I'd gone round and met Patrick and everything had changed. I've always had an eye for melodramatic symbolism, so I went in and sat at the steamed-up window. I ordered some tea and prepared to brood.

List of things I liked about Patrick

1. The way he ran his hands through his hair, so it stuck up like Krusty the Clown's, and he never realised because he never looked in the mirror before he left the house. Unlike Dan, who owned seven types of hair gel.

2. The way he sniffed his weird cheese before eating it, practically licking it. 'Ah, a Tenuous Badger Blue. Lovely.'

3. The way he loved my cookery—again unlike Dan, who'd rather have eaten a large Papa John's with extra pepperoni.

4. The way I'd be upstairs and hear him all the way in the kitchen, at first grumbling 'for God's sake!' that I'd left the radio set to Absolute 80s, then singing along loudly and out of tune to 'Take On Me'.

5. The way he would do anything for Alex, to make sure he was safe, to make him laugh, even putting pants

on his head and singing 'Pantsman Pat, Pantsman Pat, Pantsman Pat and his black-and-white pants!'

6. The way he'd let Max jump onto his knee in the evenings and be so absorbed in reading the paper or his book he'd not even notice the dog surreptitiously licking his biscotti.

7. The way that when we were out, he'd always see some building he liked and snoop around it trying to check out the cornicing or something.

8. The way he laughed at my stupid jokes until tears came out of his eyes and sometimes snot spurted out of his nose (gross, but adorable)...

But no, that was no good. I didn't need to think of reasons why I liked him. That wasn't helpful at all.

List of things I didn't like about Patrick

1. Quite posh—wears cords, thinks £8 is an acceptable price to pay for bread

2. Grumpy on occasions

3. Likes doing too many scary activities

4. Kicked me out of his house

5. Er...6. That's all.

I was on my third Florentine when my phone rang. It was him. I debated not answering. He probably wanted me to pick up some quinoa yogurt or something. 'Hello?'

His voice on the phone sounded muffled. 'Rachel? Is Alex with you?'

'Hmm? No, of course not. I wouldn't just take him, not

without telling you.' There was a long silence, and I began to think we'd got cut off. 'Hello?'

'He isn't here.'

'What? Where is he?'

'He was in his room, we thought. Being quiet while we talked. Then when I went to get him, he wasn't there. His coat and shoes are gone too.'

I tried to make sense of this. 'But he can't even reach the door by himself.'

'He can,' said Patrick bleakly. 'I taught him how to use a stool to climb up. Just in case of a fire or something. I thought...'

'Oh.' I thought back to when I'd left the house—had I shut the door properly? Was it possible I'd missed the sound of little steps behind me? 'He can't be far,' I said, trying to sound reasonable. 'He's only little. He'll be nearby. Probably someone's got him safe in a shop or something.' I looked doubtfully out at the rain. Alex couldn't even put his shoes on the right feet—admittedly I had done this wrong myself in recent times, but usually owing to drink being taken.

'But what if he's... Rachel, what if someone took him, or what if he falls, or... He's only a baby!' I heard a choking sob down the phone, and I realised Patrick was crying.

'The Heath,' I said quickly. 'He has to be there. It's where we always go on our walks, or from school. Can you meet me there? I'm not far.'

'Where?' He was breathing rapidly, panicking.

'By the pub. You know. I'll go now. Oh—and bring Max.' I threw some money on the table and left, pulling my coat on without waiting for my change.

I must have looked demented. I imagine there were several calls to police that day about a madwoman running

through the streets of North London with wet rat's-tail hair
and canvas shoes totally unsuitable for the weather. I ran all
the way to the tube, even though I wasn't fit at the best of
times, and the pavements were shiny with rain. At Hampstead station, I couldn't bear to wait for the lifts, so I foolishly tried the stairs, ignoring the sign that said there were
over three hundred of them. Deepest station in the underground, apparently. That would have been a good pub quiz
fact to remember, had I not been tearing past it, panting, wet
shoes slipping on the steps. After thirty steps, I was seeing spots. God, I was unfit. After this, I would prioritise it.
Cardiovascular fitness all the way. After I'd given Alex the
biggest hug I could without damaging him that was.

I sprinted to the corner of the Heath, dodging posh
buggies and rich old ladies with pixie hoods. Patrick was
standing in the rain under his enormous yellow rain mac,
like a Nordic fisherman, Max shivering on a lead. I ran
over to him, holding my bag above my head. He just looked
at me, stricken. I could hardly speak after my run—I might
be having a heart attack once this was all over. 'Any...
news?'

'Michelle's at the police station. They said not to worry.'
He gave a shaky laugh. 'Great advice, huh? Here.' He'd
brought my red raincoat. 'I knew you'd have no coat. Plus,
if it's bright, he might see and...'

I nodded, putting it over my already sodden clothes. 'Let's
go. I know the places he likes.'

We pounded up the hill, my Converse rapidly clogged
in mud, which seeped in and squelched between my shoes.
Under other circumstances women might pay about fifty
quid for that kind of treatment at a posh spa, but right now,
in the howling wind and rain, it wasn't very pleasant. We

went first to the pond and running track, then the play park. It was deserted in the rain. 'Alex!' We accosted everyone we passed, from city types with golf umbrellas to small nannied children in quilted coats. 'Have you seen a little boy on his own? Curly hair, maybe a yellow mac on like this?' Gesturing to Patrick's grown-up version. No one had seen anything.

We panted up the hill to the café, me reeling off places Alex would know. 'The tennis courts—we sometimes watch people play and give them scores. The Primrose Hill bench...'

'He can't get that far on his own,' Patrick kept repeating. 'He's only four.'

The other horrible possibility—of Alex not being on his own—was pushed to the back of my mind. He would be OK. He would be OK because he had to be.

We raced all round that part of the park, even checking in the public loos, though Alex was too scared to go in there on his own. Nothing. The Heath was almost empty now, as sensible people got out of the rain, which had stepped up to a drumming tattoo on the hood of my coat. In the gloom and mist, it looked sinister, a different world from that of happy families and feeding the ducks, but rather a place of a thousand hiding places, where pop stars and cabinet ministers found their ruin.

Patrick was thumbing water from his phone. 'Michelle says they're sending out police officers. Not enough though. I think she's giving them a bollocking about Amber Alerts and so on. Oh God.' I could see his brain was dissolving into pictures of missing kids, abductions, wanted posters...

Think, Rachel, think. I tried to imagine all the days we'd spent together, Alex trotting in my wake with his incessant chatter—what I wouldn't give now to hear his light footsteps.

I crouched down in the rain to the little dog, who was twitching miserably as rain ran into his eyes. 'I'm sorry it's wet, Maxxy—please find Alex. Where's Alex? Where's your friend?'

Max stared back, uncomprehending.

'The bathing ponds,' I said suddenly.

'What?' Patrick had to shout over the increased pounding of the rain.

'He's fascinated by them. I told him the history, and about people swimming with no clothes on. He thinks it's funny—come on!' I seized Patrick's hand, cold and wet, and we raced off to the other end of the Heath, Max panting behind us on his little legs.

The ponds were mud-coloured in the gloom, the surface rippled by wind and drops of rain. 'Alex,' I was calling. 'Are you here? It's Rachel!'

I was almost giving up hope when Max began to woof, pulling on his lead. 'Patrick!' I shouted. 'He's smelling something!'

Max was ploughing through the bushes, his scrabbling feet caked in mud. I was thinking horrible things—how near we were to the water, how Alex couldn't swim—when Max stopped short, barking, his nose in a large wet bush. I pushed aside a branch. 'Patrick!' I'd seen a flash of colour. I was then on my knees in the mud, crawling into the green damp.

Alex was right up against the roots of the bush. He was covered in mud, his face pale and clammy. I saw with a lurch there was blood on his forehead, very red against the white of his skin. He was shivering. 'Hey, mate,' I said. 'What are you doing in there?' He said nothing. 'We were all looking for you. Look, here's Max!'

The dog was snuffling nearby, licking his face. Alex put out his arms and hugged him weakly. 'Don't want to go away,' he muttered.

'Hmm?' I could hardly hear him over the rain striking the leaves above.

'Mummy and Daddy. They said I had to go away and I couldn't take Max. Don't want to.'

Oh God. He must have been listening in to their discussions about residence and moving to New York. 'Come on out and we'll get it all fixed. Daddy's here too.'

Patrick was peering under the bush. 'Al, mate! We've been so worried. Please come out.'

'I bumped my head,' Alex said in a small voice. His words were slightly slurred.

'Oh. Well, you better come out so we can look at it.' Patrick was trying to speak cheerfully, but I could hear the worry squeezing his voice. If Alex had been bleeding into his brain, we had to get him to hospital right away.

I had an idea. 'Pull my legs,' I called behind me to Patrick. And I crawled further in and grasped Alex by his raincoat. 'Come on, mate. Let's get out of here.'

I put my arms round Alex, so small under his coat, and grabbed on tight as Patrick's cold hands closed around my ankles. We popped out like a cork from a bottle, both of us muddy and scratched. We were so close to the hospital that Patrick gathered Alex up in his arms and ran, me and Max bringing up the rear at a slightly slower pace. The hospital was the best place for me, I reflected grimly, as I pounded along, since I was pretty sure I was about to go into full cardiac arrest any minute now.

Chapter Thirty-Three

I still can't remember much about that day. There were the long blue corridors of the hospital, squeaky plastic floors and double doors and a cup of tea from a machine that was so hot and sweet I couldn't drink it. The doctors wouldn't speak to me because I wasn't family, so I sat in the waiting room while Michelle and Patrick were in with the consultant. Then Patrick came out white-faced and I could hear the sound of Michelle crying as the door swung back.

'But I don't understand,' I kept saying. 'Why don't they give him the clotting factor?'

'It isn't working. He's got a bleed in his brain and it's just getting worse.'

'But how—'

'It happens sometimes. It just stops working. It's called an inhibitor. They're giving him something else, but—'

I was freezing. My feet were so wet and cold I hadn't felt them in an hour. 'Can I see him?'

'He's not conscious. He's…he's in a bad way, Rachel. Thank God you found him.'

A sob tore out of me. 'He needs Roger. Did someone get him Roger?'

'No. You're right.' Gently, he took my arm. 'Come on, I'm taking you home. I'll come back with his things, but you should stay there. Please. There's really nothing you can do.'

Of course there wasn't. Because Alex wasn't my child. He wasn't my anything. And I had to go now and leave him with his parents, however much I just wanted to grab him in my arms and hug him tight.

Patrick and I walked the few streets back to the house, two feet between us, wrapped separately in miserable worry. I was shivering with fear and cold. When we reached the house, I saw a familiar car sitting outside. Navy BMW. 'Is that…?'

'I texted them,' said Patrick. 'You shouldn't be alone. Go on.'

I walked over to the car, dazed with everything that had happened that day. The passenger seat was empty. The window slid down, silent and sleek. 'Get in,' said Cynthia.

The windows were steamed up. I got into the car's warm interior. 'Are you OK?' said a voice from behind me. Emma.

Cynthia always said her life was changed by the discovery of salons for African hair. The reason for her luxuriant locks these days was that, even now, when she went to work with the flu and kept a set of knickers in the office, she still took one day off a month to get a weave done. So the second thing I noticed, other than the surprising fact of Emma being there at all, was that Cynthia had let her hair grow out. It was now several inches shorter, and fluffy. She was wearing jeans, and no make-up. I looked between them suspiciously. 'What's going on?'

'Patrick texted me,' Cynthia said. I saw that her hands on the steering wheel were bare—she'd taken off her rings. 'Is Alex OK?'

'I don't know. He's pretty bad, I think. They...' My voice hitched. 'They said I shouldn't be there.' I gulped back my tears. 'What are you two doing here? I mean...'

'She called me,' Emma said. 'And I realised...well, it wasn't really her fault. After all, it was Ian who used a fake name and arranged to meet her.'

'Even though I'm still sorry,' Cynthia said quickly.

'Yes, even though, but it's more...well, like you said, Rach. The problem is really with Ian and me. We just want different things. I want to grow up. He doesn't.'

'Has he gone?'

'He's sleeping on the sofa. We're trying to figure out how we can afford to rent two places. We can't, is the answer so far.'

'I'm sorry.'

I saw her shrug in the mirror. 'Turns out we're just like everyone else, after all. We weren't the perfect couple. We were just...clinging on.'

Emma and Ian. I couldn't bear it. Always the ones who had it sussed, who made each other laugh, who never spent a night apart. 'What about you, Cyn?'

'Rich has gone. Filed for divorce already. The house is on the market.'

'What will you do?'

'I'm going to Jamaica for a while.'

I blinked. She had never mentioned this before. 'To see your dad?'

'I'm going to try to find him, yes. I spoke to Mum, and she admitted— Well, she said my dad did try to get in touch with me a few times over the years. My grandma too. But she, Mum, I mean—she always thought it was best not to tell me. So I'd feel Frank was my dad. And I guess he was, but still...'

'God. So you're going?'

She twisted her hand, where her wedding ring used to be. 'He might not want to see me now—I mean, it's been thirty years—but at least I'll have tried. I'm leaving next week.'

'What about work?'

'She quit,' said Emma proudly.

'You never!'

'I did.' Cynthia almost smiled.

'Brilliant! Did you march in and tell Martin you'd rather have a job wiping Saddam Hussein's bottom than work for him and that he's worse than the Nazis who catch Richard Attenborough on that bus in *The Great Escape*?'

'Well, no, because I'll need a reference sometime.'

'Oh.'

'But in my head, yeah, I *totally* told him that.'

I snuffled a bit, wiping the rain and tears and mud off my face. 'I'm sorry, guys. I've been rubbish this year. Longer than that, I know. I've been so wrapped up in myself.' They were silent, and I knew it was true. 'Look at you both. Everything's falling to bits, and you needed me, and I didn't even notice.'

Emma spoke carefully. 'You did get a bit...wrapped up with Patrick and Alex.'

Cynthia said, 'I mean, we hoped the list would distract you from your disastropiphany, but we never thought we'd lose you entirely.'

I felt more tears prick my nose. 'You didn't lose me. I just lost touch a bit. I'm so sorry. I'm rubbish.'

Cynthia took my hand. 'You're not rubbish. Rach, we'd hardly even be friends without you. You're the peacemaker. You're, like, the glue holding us together. So we needed you, you see.'

'The sparkly glitter glue,' said Emma, patting my shoulder from behind. I reached around to grasp her hand.

I felt my nose sting with tears. 'I feel terrible. Instead of being there for you, I let myself get carried away with the stupid list.'

'The list isn't stupid,' said Emma. 'It's the best thing we've done for ages. I just wish we'd stuck with it too. We did, like, two things, then life took over. But you kept it up.'

'I jumped out of a plane.' I could hardly believe I'd done it.

'I know you did. You inspired me,' said Cynthia. 'To jump, I mean. From my job.'

Emma wrinkled her nose. 'Pretty cheesy, Cyn. I mean, you weren't actually ten thousand feet in the sky.'

'It's a metaphor!'

'A cheesy metaphor. A twenty-four Dairylea one. A whole wheel of Camembert one.'

'Oh, shut up. At least I don't have Pritt Stick on my bum.'

And just like that, we were back to normal. Except that Alex was in the hospital, so nothing would be normal again until he came out safe.

Cynthia had to go into the office to finish things up before she left, so Emma said she would stay in the house with me that night, but she fell asleep right away, and I couldn't doze off with her muttering and weird sleep-talking and kicking me with her cold feet. I couldn't have slept anyway. I kept my phone in my hand, pressing it obsessively so blue light filled the room, making Emma toss and turn and mutter more sleep-gibberish. 'Get the bin bags from Denmark! No, the other caterpillar, not that one!'

I wished they'd let me see Alex, even for a second, because I was picturing him all hooked up to tubes, a bloody bandage round his head. But what if the reality was even worse? Eventually, when the clock on my phone read 1.17 a.m., I got up and dressed quietly in my jeans and hoody, and crept out, leaving Emma to visit home supply shops in Denmark. When I passed the kitchen, I saw Max sitting sadly in his basket, wide awake, but perfectly still. I knew how he felt. 'He'll be OK, Maxxy,' I said softly, wishing I believed it. Max looked at me with big sorrowful eyes, slowly lowering his head onto the side of his basket. I stooped to pet him, then slipped out the door.

It wasn't far to the hospital, so I jogged in, seeing my breath mist out before me. Once inside, I found my way to the children's ward. The hospital was just as busy as in the day, lights blaring and doctors and nurses rushing about with lanyards swinging. It made me feel disorientated, jet-lagged.

In the waiting room, I saw a woman sitting alone with her head bowed. She was dressed in a crumpled grey suit, despite the late hour. Michelle raised her head and I saw she was crying. My blood turned to ice. 'Oh God.'

'He's OK,' she said, wiping her face. 'At least, he's the same. They're trying him with a different factor to see if he accepts it.'

I fished in my pocket for the flowered tissues Cynthia had given mc earlier and handed one to Michelle. Her hands were shaking. 'Thanks. I'm just so scared. He only ran away because we were fighting.'

I hovered awkwardly. 'I…I guess it could have happened any time.'

She stared at her hands and I saw she was still wearing her wedding ring. 'They talk about you so much. Rachel this, Rachel that. "Mommy, she's so cool and funny." I didn't even know you were living in the house—I'm sorry I was a little curt.'

I shifted from one foot to the other. 'I thought he would have told you. I'm so sorry. It must have been a shock for you.'

'Well. You've been there. I haven't. And now this has happened.'

I didn't know what to say to that. It was true, but I could see there was more to the story than I knew.

'It's all my fault,' she said. 'He wouldn't be like this if not for me. I gave him this horrible thing.' She bit her lip as tears welled up.

Still awkward, I sat down on the chair beside her. Even after crying for hours, she looked more poised than me. I'd just pulled on my muddy jeans and shoes from earlier and hadn't brushed my hair.

Michelle was clearly trying not to cry. 'I'm sorry. This isn't your problem.'

'Michelle,' I said quickly, 'I know it's not… I'm not… I know it's not my business, but most of the time Alex is totally fine with his condition. Honest, it doesn't affect him, or not much at least. This is just an accident.'

She kept staring at the tissue clenched in her hands. 'I bet you think I'm a terrible mom, right? I don't see my kid for four months… Well, I tried, Rachel. I tried to be a good

mom. When he was born, my career took a back seat—
Alex was sick so much as a baby, I was almost too scared
to go to sleep in case I lost him. I'd had this great job, and
it all just went—I took this massive demotion. Not Patrick
though. He worked twice as hard. We never did anything
that wasn't work, or worrying about Alex. Patrick hardly
looked at me except to talk about bills or chores or medi-
cine. And I didn't… It just wasn't enough for me. I needed
to go back to work. And this thing with Alan, the job in
New York—I was always going to come back. And I thought
Patrick would bring Alex to visit. I never thought it would
be this long. I just had to get away. I'd had enough. Try to
understand?'

She was crying again. I watched her, not knowing what
to do. I was realising it was me who'd wandered into this
family, taking up residence in their house and their lives,
without a thought for what I was getting into. 'It will be
OK,' I said. Even though I didn't believe it.

Michelle sniffed hard, trying to compose herself. 'Patrick's in there with Alex, if you want to see him.'

'Are you sure?'

She nodded. 'Alex would want you to. I'm sure of it.'

I stood up again. For some reason, I felt so terribly guilty.
'Look, Michelle, maybe you should go and get a coffee or
something. You look— Well, I know it's stressful.'

She shook her head. 'I'm afraid to leave.'

'Just five minutes. I'll come and get you the second anything happens, but I'm sure it won't. I promise.'

Shakily, she got to her feet. 'All right. Just five minutes.
I could use some coffee. I'm still really jet-lagged.'

As she went off, crying quietly into her hand, I took

a deep breath and pushed open the door to Alex's room. Patrick was sitting beside the bed, still wearing his damp clothes from earlier, his hair dried in corkscrew curls. He was holding Alex's limp hand in his.

I wasn't prepared. Alex did not look as if he was asleep— he was clearly out cold, somewhere else, not dreaming safely in his bed with the night light and Thomas bedspread. Roger was propped beside him, looking forlorn and bedraggled. Alex was paler than the sheets, and he had various wires coming out of him. They'd shaved some of his lovely curls on the side so they could attach a sticky monitor pad, and it was this that sent me over the edge.

'His hair!' I gasped. 'Oh God. Oh God.'

Patrick was on his feet. 'It's not as bad as it looks, honest. They're trying to keep him under to see if the new treatment works.'

I was sobbing uncontrollably. 'He's so little!'

'I know. I know.'

Then his arms were around me, so solid and warm, and I could breathe in his aftershave under the smells of the hospital and damp clothes and soil. 'I'm scared too. But he'll be OK. They said he would.'

I cried into Patrick's shoulder. 'I'm sorry. I shouldn't— I just didn't expect— I mean, he's not even my kid, and—'

'Come on. It's OK.' I tried to get a hold of myself, and Patrick mopped my face with his sleeve. For a moment, he stared at me, his hand holding my chin, and I saw how afraid he was. 'I don't know what I'm going to do,' he said, terrified.

I felt the words gush out of me. 'You should have taken him to see Michelle. And you should have told her I lived with you!'

'What?'

'You stopped him from seeing his mum. Whatever she did, it wasn't right, Patrick.'

Patrick pulled away angrily. 'She left us! She left him. It was her decision. We were fine before she ruined it, cheating on me.'

'Were you? Because, Patrick, I've been there, and things are never fine before they break. There's always a crack, just ready to shatter. You don't need to punish her and Alex forever because of it.'

'For God's sake, Rachel. I don't need this now. My son is…is…' His voice broke. I scrabbled for him, fear clutching my heart.

'I'm sorry! I'm sorry. I don't know what I'm saying. Oh God, what's going to happen?'

'Shh. He'll be OK. We have to be strong for him.'

We stood there for a moment, neither of us seeming to want to move, his hand still on my face, my arms around his waist. 'Rachel…' He was very close. I forgot to breathe for a moment. I could feel his mouth just millimetres from my wet cheek. Then I don't quite know how it happened, but just for a second, we were kissing. He was shaking. I was still crying a little and he was close to it. His hands were on my waist, and mine were around his neck, tangling in his hair.

Just then there was a noise at the door and we sprang apart. Michelle was standing there, cups of coffee in her hands.

Patrick blustered. 'He's OK. No change.'

Michelle stood looking at us both, then without a word went out again, letting the door close behind her.

List of terrible moments in the life of Rachel Kenny
(ongoing)

1. Yep. That one. That one right there.

Chapter Thirty-Four

The next day came. Patrick and Michelle were still at the hospital and I'd gone home after that supremely awkward moment. I tried to get on with work, tidying the living room, making little snacks to bring up to Alex and desperately trying not to think about what had happened, or not happened, beside his hospital bed. We were all distraught. It was natural that we'd say or do strange things. It didn't mean anything. Restless, I went out for a walk on the Heath, but it was raining and cold and all I could think about was that Alex wasn't there. Even Max seemed forlorn. He didn't even woof when we passed the café with its smells of fresh bread and cake. We came back to find Patrick in the hallway, as if he'd been waiting for me.

'Hi.' I took off my boots, still feeling awkward round him. 'Any news?'

'He's over the worst. He can come home in a few days, they said.'

'Oh, thank God. I'll make him a cake. We should get everything ready, put all his toys out...'

'Rachel. There's someone to see you.'

'Who's that?' One of the girls, I thought. Patrick stood back to let me into the kitchen. And I walked in and there was the last person I expected to see.

'What—er, what are you doing here?' I tried to speak causally, as if it was perfectly normal for him to be in Patrick's kitchen. My mind was having a hard time seeing them in the same room, like characters from two different TV series sharing a screen. 'How did you...?'

Dan stood up. 'I heard you were living here.'

'Oh. OK. But...'

Patrick coughed. 'I'll leave you to it. I'll just be upstairs if you need me.'

Dan was looking well, I thought. Less pasty, and he'd lost a few pounds. He was wearing a T-shirt I didn't recognise, and jeans. He'd grown a little beard, which was straggly and streaked with ginger. He looked so much older than the man I'd married two years ago, full of hope and joy.

'Nice place.'

'Yeah. I just live in the box room.' I wasn't sure if he thought maybe Patrick and I were...something.

'It's not home though, is it? Living in someone's spare room.'

'No. But I don't have much choice.' What was he on about? My home was still there. It was just that he was in it, so I had to be out. That was what happened when you got divorced.

'Rachey.' The pet name stung me like acid. 'I got these through.' He reached into his leather manbag, which I'd bought him, and laid out some papers. I peered at the text. Petition for divorce.

'It's to make it legal. We file for divorce—well, I do, or you can, but since you left it's easier if… And you transfer the house to my name and I give you the money.'

'OK.' The words seemed to swim before my eyes. 'So why are you…?'

'I wanted to make sure. Before we sign it.'

'Make sure what?'

'That it's what we really want.'

Silence. Outside, I could hear a posh mum walking by with her kids. 'Come on, Euphemia, don't put your rice cakes in your gilet, eat them, please.'

'But…you kicked me out. You said there was no chance.'

He rubbed a hand over his face. 'We both said some things at the time. I was angry, about…'

Don't say it, don't say it.

'…you know, everything, and now I've had time to think about it, it wasn't so bad, was it? I know I was working too much, and everything with Dad really threw me, but before that we were happy, weren't we? Our wedding was lovely. We had some great times together.'

I was still saying nothing. I hadn't seen Dan in so long, after being with him every day, sleeping pressed up to him every night. His presence was a physical shock to me. 'We did, but…'

'We can get it back, can't we? I just can't…' He was groping for my hand, holding it. His was clammy. 'I can't face it, Rachey, going back out there, trying to make it work with someone else, selling our house, the home we made. Can't we just try again, before it's too late? You can get your dog, anything you want. I promise I won't complain about money. We can… We can go overseas if you want. Have adventures. All the things you wanted to do, the dancing and that, going out—we can do it. I promise.'

'We lived in the suburbs,' was all I could think of to say. 'People don't have adventures there.'

'Then we'll move. We'll move back to London.'

'We can't afford it.'

'I'll get a different job.'

'With more stress? Dan, it doesn't work. You must see that.'

'But what can we do?' he said, almost despairing. 'If we're not together, in our house, then where are we supposed to go? What are we supposed to do with our lives?'

'I…' I spread my arms wide. 'Anything. Anywhere. That's the scary thing. All the doors are open again.'

'I don't want them to be. I liked what we had. Our house, and our life, and you and me. Together.'

I was staring at the grain of the table, trying not to cry. It was a lovely table, old and well used, polished to richness. A table for family dinners and late-night chats and maybe even sex on it when the kids were asleep. But not a table I'd chosen. That was an inferior one, but it had been mine, and Dan and I had eaten at it every night for five years. Nothing in this house, lovely as it was, belonged to me.

'I don't know what to say.'

'It's sudden, I know. I said some things when you went…'

'Like how I had no loyalty or concept of marriage?'

He winced. 'Did I say that?'

'Yes.'

'I'm sorry. I was upset.'

'We both were.'

'You said I was a cold-hearted workaholic who was losing my hair.'

'That wasn't nice of me.'

'No.' His hand went to his head.

'It's not true, by the way. Your hair is fine.' I still hadn't said anything to his proposal. Time seemed to slow as I stood there thinking about it, how I could almost close my eyes and get back to where I'd been, get helped up that ladder again, live in our house among my dishes and plants and cookbooks, watch TV with Dan, lie beside him at night, have someone to kiss hello when they came in and hug me as I fell asleep, someone to vent to when my freelancing went badly or I felt fat or fell out with one of the girls, someone to roll my eyes to when Ian made a tasteless joke. Dan. Like the rest of my things, a little battered, maybe not top of the range, tired and sad, but unequivocally mine. At least until I signed the forms.

'Your mum said you were seeing someone,' I heard myself say.

'Did she? She'd no right.'

'Who is it?'

He looked awkward.

'It's someone we know, isn't it? You don't have any new Facebook friends.'

Dan said, very slowly, 'Theresa.'

Of course. God, why didn't I twig? Theresa. His colleague at work. Head of Leisure Services. Divorced, with two Pekineses Dan called Yip and Yap. Thirty-five-ish. I was incredulous. 'Really? Even with the dogs?'

'They're not so bad. She…she was there for me when you went. It was company.'

'Does she know you're here?'

His silence told me she had no idea. 'I just thought I should come to make sure. Before it was too late.' He rubbed his face. 'You know, everything is easy at the start. But, after a while, it gets hard too.'

'I...'

Understanding was dawning on his face. 'I thought I'd give you another chance. Your landlord told me you'd been struggling.'

'Patrick said that?'

'He didn't tell you? He called me. To say you've been living here as some kind of unpaid au pair—' he gestured contemptuously round the kitchen '—and you're off doing all these crazy things, dating and picking up losers, jumping out of planes, for God's sake! You hate all that. You would barely go up the Eiffel Tower when we were in Paris!'

'Maybe I've changed.'

'People don't change. You're just having an interlude. This isn't your life.'

I looked around the kitchen I'd grown to love, the bulging spice rack, Alex's drawings pinned to the cork board, Max's basket with its vague musty smell, the wine rack full of Patrick's reds, his shoes caked in mud by the back door. On the fridge were various pictures of us, me up on stage, and in my skydiving gear, and holding up my plate of sushi, and at Disney World, and walking Max. All things I would never have imagined doing a few months ago.

If you can't go back, you have to go forward.

'I can't,' I heard myself say to Dan. 'Part of me wants to, but I can't.'

'What does that mean? If part of you wants to, then do it!'

'I just can't. We don't work. We don't make each other happy every day.'

'For God's sake, Rachel. No one is happy every day. Life isn't a fairy tale. People work hard, and they're tired, and you have problems and not enough money, but you stick together. Your parents did it. Mine did, until we lost Dad. Mum would give anything for another chance with him, I know it. We've still got that chance.'

'It's not the same! Your parents, I don't know, they were happy, I suppose, or more likely they hadn't any choice. Look at mine—do you think they're happy?'

'Yes,' he said, surprising me. 'I think they're one of the happiest families I've ever seen.'

That silenced me. 'I— What we have isn't what they have.'

'Because we didn't give it long enough. It grows. You grow together.'

'I…I can't explain it. Maybe we could have, if I hadn't done what I did, or if you'd…'

'But I forgave you.'

'You did not, Dan.'

'OK. I was angry. I couldn't believe you'd… But I forgive you now. I forgive you.'

'It doesn't work that way,' I said quietly. 'We broke it, Dan. It's sad, but it's not fixable. Not with all the glue in the world.'

He stood looking at me for a long time. 'I can't believe you. I'm giving you a second chance here, after what you did!'

'That doesn't sound like you forgive me.'

He looked away in annoyance. 'Look, Rachel, you're not in the best situation here. You can't afford to live on your own, can you? I'm willing to support you, pay for you. But you can't have it both ways. If you want my help, you have to give me something in return. Compromise.'

Compromise. The art of neither of you being happy, Patrick had once said. And I wanted to be happy. I was greedy for it. I didn't want to compromise any more.

Mutely, I shook my head. Dan picked the papers up off the table. 'I suppose you better sign these, then. Since you're just giving up on our marriage.'

'I'm not giving up. It was dead long ago. It was just on life support.'

He was raising his voice as he stumbled to the door. 'You'll be sorry, Rachel. When you're alone and struggling and you can't pay the rent, you'll be sorry you turned me down. I loved you. I supported you. For God's sake, I even forgave you when you cheated on me. My own wife. Have you any idea what that felt like?'

'Yes! OK! I know. I messed up. I did a terrible thing. But I can't keep paying for it, over and over.' Tears swallowed my voice. 'That's why we're broken, Dan. Because it was already cracked, and I smashed it into pieces.'

Dan stormed into the hallway, where Patrick was standing on the stairs.

'I…I heard shouting. I was just coming to…'

Dan turned to him. 'I don't know why you rang. Maybe you and her had something going on, I don't know. But you shouldn't just kick her out. She doesn't deserve to be out in the street, no matter what she did.'

Dan was gone in an angry swirl of steps and a bang that rattled the stained-glass panes of the door.

I glared at Patrick. 'You called him? You wanted me gone so badly you'd turf me back to my ex-husband?'

'He's still your husband,' said Patrick brutally. 'And it seems you haven't been honest about what actually happened.'

'You heard?' I didn't really have to ask. I could tell from the fact he couldn't look at me that he'd heard every word. 'Let me explain.'

'No need to explain. It's all very clear. You cheated on Dan.'

'I… Not exactly. It's just…'

His voice sounded strange. 'I trusted you, Rachel. I let you into my house and my family. And all this time you've been lying to me. About the one thing you knew I'd hate most of all.'

'I…' There was nothing I could say. I put up my hands to stop the warm tears that were rolling down my face. And now Patrick knew what I'd been doing my best to hide from him—I was just as bad as Michelle.

'Don't bother,' he said, turning to go up the stairs again. 'I hope you've been looking at flats. Because I'd like you to move out as soon as possible, please.'

Trembling, I took out my phone. The ladders had all fallen to pieces now, and I was deep at the bottom of the pit. Who could I call? Cynthia was leaving soon, and Emma and Ian were embroiled in splitting up, looking at flats, totally broke. I scrolled through the numbers on my phone, pressed one, heard a familiar voice.

'Hello?'

My voice hitched with tears. 'It's me. I'm— I've really messed up this time. Can you come and get me, please? I'm sorry to ask. I just— There's no one else I can call.'

'Of course,' said my sister. 'I'm on my way.'

List of worst moments of the life of Rachel Kenny (ongoing)

1. Oh look, I'm really racking these up, aren't I?

Chapter Thirty-Five

A memory has always stuck with me about the time, the long drawn-out time, when Dan and I were losing each other, like two shipwrecked people gradually letting go of the driftwood they're clinging to. Just after Christmas last year, Dan and I were driving to Cambridgeshire to stay with Jane, stuck in horrendous traffic on the M25. But in this particular memory I was in a service-station toilets somewhere in Surrey, and I was crying. Big, noisy, snot-stained tears that drew looks of alarm from innocent service-station pee-ers. The alarm seemed to be exacerbated by the fact that I was wearing a bright red Christmas jumper with reindeer on it.

The cause of this service-station weeping was yet another of the many conversations we would have over Christmas on the topic of: is our marriage falling apart? Which is a question that, if you have to ask it, the answer can only be 'yes, yes, it is.' (Much like: is it a bad idea to sleep with my ex? And am I an idiot for voting in *The X Factor*?)

Why was the marriage falling apart? What happened?

This is the first question you get asked when you tell people. In truth nothing happened. Or everything happened. It isn't really the best story, but I'll tell it all the same.

List of reasons my marriage fell apart

1. Technology

We all know the fall of man began with an apple. Likewise, the fall of my marriage began with Apple. I could blame it on Steve Jobs, but he's dead and I think he has enough to answer for at the Pearly Gates, what with crushing the music industry, exploiting workers in China and making men think it's OK to wear roll-neck jumpers (it isn't). Dan was into gadgets. We had things that sharpened knives, things that regulated temperature, things that weighed bananas. So what happened was a screen came between us. In the evenings, he began to stare at his BlackBerry or iPad or phone all the time. I would talk to him and he wouldn't answer, because he'd be playing a game or reading emails or have headphones in. He would deal with work at midnight. I'd get undressed for bed and he'd be on some device, not even looking up. Evenings went by in grunts, bad films and four to five hours of computer games.

This led, directly or indirectly, to the problem of...

2. Babies. Or the lack thereof

I thought I'd done it all right. I'd rescued my university run of bad relationships, got married at twenty-eight, bought a house, a car and a set of Le Creuset pans. The scene was set. My womb had a TO LET sign on. It was baby time.

Except it never happened. We weren't bothered at first.

We were young. There was time. It would happen the next month. Or the next.

Two years went by like this. I went for tests and worried and ate fish oil and forced zinc supplements on Dan and put my legs in the air and counted dates and was disappointed over and over, and then one day I woke up and realised, *I'm not pregnant. THANK BLOODY GOD FOR THAT.* It's a funny thing, but not getting pregnant is often the way when you pretty much never have sex. So that was point 2, BABIES, which it turns out, was really about point 2b, SEX. At first I put it down to Dan's father dying—of course it would take a while to get over that. But then a while went on much longer than a while. It turned into a patch. Then a slump. Then, most worryingly, a trend. No one *tells* you. No one gives you any advice at all about marriage, and yet it's the most important and dangerous thing most of us will ever do. I mean, for God's sake, they don't even let you get on planes without explaining how to put on an oxygen mask. I needed an oxygen mask. I needed to fit it on myself before helping others.

There was also the issue of:

3. The suburbs

I can trace many of our problems back to the moment when Dan said, 'Hey, maybe after the wedding, we should look at moving somewhere with more space. Maybe buy a place.'

And I'd laughed and pointed round our two-room flat in Hackney, with hot and cold running mice and downstairs who kept a lively neighbourhood business dealing drugs. 'OK, which trust fund will we cash in to get it? We can't afford anywhere in London, silly.'

And he'd said, 'I was thinking somewhere a bit further out. I've been looking at jobs with Surrey County Council.'

People tried to warn me. It's boring, Rachel, and the shops all close at six, and the last train is at eleven, and people only worry about parking regulations and the frequency of council recycling collections. But it seemed like a good idea at the time. Like shell suits, and the nuclear arms race. With equally disastrous consequences.

Gradually, day by day, I realised that all the things I was supposed to want, the house and the husband and the car, they weren't what I wanted at all. I was in big, big trouble.

I didn't cry much during all this time. If you read *Eat, Pray, Love*—and I have, twice; I know, once is unfortunate, twice looks like carelessness—you may find yourself drawn into competitive grief. If your divorce does not involve near-suicidal weeping, an existential crisis where God talks to you, and a trip round the world where you meet a hottie and write a bestselling book and Julia Roberts plays you in the film, you're not doing it right! No, beyond the racking service-station sobs, I didn't cry much. I was mostly just doleful, and anxious. I didn't sleep much for several years. My ancestors were from Ireland, after all—one thing we were excellent at is sustained, unobtrusive misery. We're the people who managed a whole famine only a hundred and fifty years ago, in a country that was still exporting tons of food every day. What we weren't good at, unlike the English, is denial. Denial is a waste of good misery, frankly. But the English! If someone fell asleep on your arm, you'd chop it off to avoid waking them and having to have a conversation. And so when I asked my husband how we were, he'd say: fine. We're fine. Everything was fine. Even though we were quietly falling apart. It was still fine.

4. The Incident

When someone's parent dies, you're supposed to cut them a fair amount of slack. You're supposed to be OK with doing everything round the house and all the cooking and laundry and going to visit his mother every weekend because she isn't coping on her own. You're supposed to be understanding when your husband starts staying at work until 2 a.m., insisting that it's vital he sorts out the collection of glass jars in the Guildford area. You're supposed to get used to scraping uneaten dinners in the bin, or taking off the lingerie you foolishly put on in the hope that tonight might be the night to rekindle things, as let's face it, six months is quite a long dry spell when you're just married and not even thirty yet. Yes, you're supposed to do all this, because you aren't a terrible person, and he's grieving. And if you ask about the ongoing dry spell and he says it's because you've put on weight, well, you might have a little cry in the bathroom and start sleeping in very baggy pyjamas, but you can tell yourself it's the pain talking, not him. But are there some things you can't forgive?

For as long as Dan had known me I'd wanted to be an artist. On our very first date at the student union bar, he'd come back to my room and I'd shyly shown him my drawings, and seen on his face he was genuinely impressed. In our twenties, we'd lived in London and I'd worked at the design agency while freelancing in my spare time. But, once we got married, he pushed me into the job at the council, and I had no time to draw. But I still kept my artwork in the attic, carefully wrapped up—my best work, my favourite sketches and paintings. It was a way to show myself that I was still an artist, and that maybe one day, I'd pick it up again, do it for a living. Until the summer things started to go really badly wrong for us. I'd gone to stay with Mum and Dad for the weekend, putting in the groundwork in case things didn't work out with Dan and I. As I approached the house on my way back, I could smell burning. Puzzled, I went around the back to the garden, where I saw Dan had a bonfire going. He was chucking handfuls of leaves into it— that was good, I thought at first. He was doing the garden. He was showing an interest in something other than work.

I went a little closer, and that's when I saw what else he'd been stoking the fire with. I may not be the world's best artist, but I have a quite distinctive style.

I stared at him. For a moment I thought I was dreaming, and I'd wake up. I didn't. 'You...you burned my artwork?'

Dan rubbed his face, which was streaked with soot. His eyes looked far away. 'It was just taking up space, Rachel. Anyway, haven't you given up on all that?'

But I suppose the proverbial straw that broke our backs, the final nail in the coffin, the death rattle for our marriage, was that traditional cliché:

5. The Third Party

If you're married, and you're going to fall in love with someone else, there are advantages to picking someone who won't love you back. You won't find them on your doorstep at midnight, mournfully shouting your name. But there are also disadvantages, namely that your heart will get stomped on as if by feet in hobnail boots.

Simon Caulfield had been at university with us back in

the day. I'd never been into him, because he was really good-looking and popular and played varsity hockey, and no one can say I didn't like to set my sights nice and low. He cut a swathe through the pretty, shiny-haired girls who did History with Emma and History of Art with me and Law with Cynthia. Not-so-simple Simon, we called him. He acted in plays, rowed, ran for Student President, then got a first and left for some big banking job in New York. I think in the entire time at university he addressed two sentences to me.

Once, in 2002, at a school disco night: 'Do you know what's in this punch?'

I didn't, but judging by what came back out of me later that night, it was probably tequila and Blue Curacao. By then it was too late to pass on my learning, however, as Simon had gone home with a girl called Molly who had long blonde hair she could sit on.

Then, in late 2005, before we graduated: 'Have you seen Venetia?' This was a girl on my course, with whom he was studying the nude in contemporary art. I hadn't seen Venetia.

And I settled down with Dan and watched some box sets and didn't think of Simon at all for another eight years, when it was time for our university reunion.

I'll admit, I went to this with a degree of smugness. I was married and had a house, and I owned actual furniture that wasn't from Ikea. I, Rachel Kenny, was winning at life. Then I walked into the wine bar near London Bridge and he was the first person I saw, leaning against a wall in a dark blue suit.

'Rachel Kenny,' he said, with a slow smile. 'Where've you been all these years?'

You know this kind of guy. I cleverly managed to fall for someone who viewed emotions as nasty things that happen to other people, which you might catch if you're not careful—a bit like athlete's foot. So he didn't want to be with me. And I didn't want to be with him, except in the darkest bowels of the night when I lay awake wondering what on earth was going on in my life. How could this happen to me? For the past ten years my state of mind could have been summed up as ninety-nine per cent happy, one per cent 'but shouldn't we be having sex more?' Overnight it was thirty per cent guilt, fifty-four per cent crazed lust, two per cent horror, five per cent fear and ten per cent wondering if there was a chance, just a chance, it might work out with him—does that add up to one hundred? Maths, as my father pointed out, was not my strongest skill.

What really clinched it was Simon saying, 'Hey, do you still draw? You used to be really good!' then somehow we arranged that I would show him some of my stuff—that hadn't been burned—because he was 'getting into art in a big way'—yep, he said stuff like this—and somehow this turned into lunch and then dinner and then… Anyway. It went on for a while, seeing each other in a way that I could tell myself was allowable, but I knew wasn't, because I was lying to Dan about it, then before Simon went back to New York there was a tortured incident involving too much vodka and, eventually, a kiss on the freezing-cold platform of Waterloo Station as I missed my last train home. A kiss that shattered me down to my very bones and built me back up again totally different.

And Dan could see it on me when I went home and he asked me that question Patrick had asked Michelle and the answer was the same.

None of that went very well, as you can imagine.

So what happened to my marriage? There was that,

obviously—the Third Party (if only we could take out third-party damage insurance, like on cars, I'd be loaded). But things with Simon really only showed me that all the desire I'd packed away was still there. It was spilling out of my lofts and cupboards. I was in big, big trouble.

As I said, it isn't the best story. It doesn't reflect very well on me. And it doesn't really explain why Dan was there in our house with our pots and pans and plants and DVDs, and I was in the box room of a stranger, or why we couldn't make it work. But it's the only story I have.

Things that suck about divorce, number one: you have to be divorced.

Chapter Thirty-Six

Moving is never as simple as it is on TV. There you just carry a few boxes, with your hair knotted up in a vintage print scarf, and perhaps wearing dungarees with an endearing smear across your nose. It's all as simple as putting a pot plant in a corner. In the real world it's exhausting. Every spoon and poster and book I moved out felt like yet another backwards step, from a place I had, fleetingly, learned to think of as home. There was so much paperwork too—bills to set up, delivery men to wait in for, furniture to buy, more things to buy when I realised I'd never had one of them, lease agreements to sign and vast sums leaving my bank account for a few square metres of mildewed London real estate.

Jess was amazing during this time. She drove up the same day I phoned, having already bookmarked lots of flats in my meagre price range. Then she took me round them, bargaining with the estate agents, pointing out mould spores and walls that needed painting, sorting out my references and deposit, while I stood, barely suppressing tears, looking round each dingy one-bed or studio we found. What was I doing here, with this view of the M3, lorries thundering past, the curtains coming down off the wall in the bedroom? I didn't live here. I lived with Patrick, and with Alex, and Max, in the Hampstead house with the turret.

At the last place we went, Jess was talking to the estate agent about tenancy deposit schemes and deep cleans and lease clauses. Even though she was wearing jeans and Uggs, she was confident and clear-voiced, as if addressing a court-room. I looked at myself, shaking, miserable, my jeans torn and my shoes leaking water. 'I'm just going to look outside,' I muttered, sliding out the door. The rain was pattering apathetically into a puddle filled with rubbish. The flat was in a dingy seventies block with a council estate behind and an arterial road in front.

'I think we should take this one,' said Jess, coming up behind me. 'It's the best of a bad bunch and they're willing to drop the rent because of the mould.'

It was nice of her to say 'we', but it was me who was going to have to live here. She'd be going back to her husband and kids, in her lovely house with its wooden floors and green Aga. 'OK,' I said, staring at the grimy steps.

'I'm sorry,' she said. 'I'm sorry it didn't work out for you. It wasn't fair.'

'No, it was. It was exactly what I deserved.' I blinked. 'How do you do it, Jess? I mean, make your life work? How do you manage to fall in love with someone and have kids, and stay together? I just don't think I know how.'

'You will. When it's the right person.'

I shook my head miserably. 'If I couldn't make it work with Dan, I can't make it work with anyone. He loved me, at least to start with, and I ruined it.' I couldn't even talk about Patrick. It was still too hard to think about. 'I can't do anything. And you...you get it all right.'

Jess burst out laughing. 'Me? What have I ever done? I'm a country solicitor, for God's sake. I wanted to move to London and read for the bar. Instead I do boundary disputes over people's leylandii trees. I don't even do that now. I just change nappies and watch *Rastamouse* all day long.'

'But you've got it all—the house, the husband, the kids.'

'Rach. You followed your dream. You're doing something real—I'm so proud, do you know that? When people ask me about my sister, I say she's an artist, she lives in London.'

'That makes it sounds a bit cooler than it is,' I observed, looking round at the yard, where some suspicious rustling in the bins made me try very hard not to think of rats. 'I just draw cartoons, and only because I can't get a proper job in design.'

'Rachel Kenny. Do you or do you not earn money from something you've created entirely by yourself, out of your own brain?'

'Well, I suppose, but I don't earn much.'

'Oh for God's sake, stop moaning. No one said this kind of career was easy, but you're doing it. And you'll do better as time goes on. You were always much braver than me.'

It was my turn to laugh. 'Jess, I'm not brave at all. I'm scared of everything. I'm scared of sharks, and heights, and needles, and being alone, and being with someone, and particularly deep tube stations, and roller coasters, and oh—*everything*.'

'And have you or have you not experienced most of those things this year, despite that?' She fixed me with her lawyer's stare.

I thought back, about Splash Mountain and the tattoo, the climbing, the skydiving, leaving Dan and being with Dan in the first place. 'I suppose I have.'

'Well, then.' She squeezed my arm briefly. 'It's not brave if you never do anything, just in case it scares you. Only if you're scared, and you do it anyway. I mean it, Rachel—you've got no idea how much you inspire people.'

'Oh, I don't…'

'I'm going back to work next month. Part-time, to start with.'

'That's great!'

'Thanks. I wouldn't have done it unless I saw how brave you were being. So quit being down on yourself, you whinger. I'll tell him we're taking it, OK?'

I stood in the rain and thought about what Patrick had said—that being brave was a habit, like anything else. That you had to practise as much as you could, so that when you needed it, it was there. About what Alex had said about closing your eyes, so your feets didn't know they were somewhere up in the air. And I went back in to see my new home, all mould spores and rickety Argos furniture and fraying carpets.

I wish life was like on TV. I wish the temporary characters in the sitcom of your life could vanish from your thoughts as easily as they do from the screen. I wish out of sight really did mean out of mind. I wish big love existed, not worn down by life, the shopping lists and bathroom cleanings and all the lies we tell each other every day.

I wish this story had a better ending.

Moving out of Patrick's was almost worse than leaving Dan. I realised now how much the blow had been softened by living in his lovely, fully appointed house. Now I found myself in a rented flat in Lewisham, one of the few areas where I wouldn't have to sell a kidney to pay the rent. Mum had lent me the deposit, and I'd scraped together the first month's rent, but if I didn't get a job after that, I'd be in trouble. I'd started registering with temp agencies, who rolled their over-mascaraed eyes at my 'artistic' career and made me do typing tests with a big foot pedal.

The worst bit, aside from the loneliness, and always having an ear out for Max, or Alex, or, God forbid, Patrick singing along to Absolute 80s, were all the gaps I kept finding. I'd grown used to the big gaps—no man, no job, no credit rating and almost no home—now it was the smaller things that crushed me. I'd go to make a cheese sandwich and realise I didn't own a grater. I'd fall into a big spiral of how I was nearly thirty-one and had no cheese grater, let alone a baby, car, dog, husband or pension. Some days it was hard to see the fabric between all those gaps. My friends, who had previously held me together with their bossy lists, were falling apart themselves. Cynthia was gone, her stuff in storage while the palace of white was on the market. Emma and Ian were still struggling to live together while looking for separate places to rent. Even Ros rang me to 'catch up' and ended up crying about how Poppy wasn't fitting in at nursery and Ethan wouldn't feed and Paul was no help at all, falling asleep in front of the Dave channel every night and forgetting to buy nappies. She'd even gone through his phone to see if there was someone else. I despaired. Was there no such thing as a relationship that worked? Would I find out Mum had been having a long-term affair with the milkman (Jess has always been weirdly tall)? I kept thinking about Dan with Theresa, her blowsy laugh and collection of china figurines.

So there I was in my grotty rented flat, the only living thing I had for company the mould spores on the bathroom tiles, kept awake by loud shouting and the smell of frying okra from the flat below. Weren't you supposed to progress through life, earning more at thirty than you had at twenty-three? Go from owning your own house to owning a bigger one, not renting from a landlord who took his decor inspiration from slum tenement Paris? Have a car, then a bigger car, not a bike bought round the back of Lewisham Library and most likely stolen? I'd gone about this all wrong. If life was a ladder, I'd lost my balance horribly and was lying at the bottom with a broken leg. In my darkest times I made lists of 'things I don't have'—dog, car, husband, house, job, cheese grater, Jamie Oliver Flavour Shaker—and 'things I messed up at'—marriage, freelancing, oh, and Patrick, of course.

Patrick. I did my best not to think of him, the smell of his jumper, the sound of him singing badly in the kitchen, but late at night, when it was just me in the flat, I couldn't help it. I'd do that awful thing where you realise part of your heart is always looking for a person who isn't there, and jump out of my skin every time I saw a man in dark-rimmed glasses, or with a leather jacket and sheepskin collar. My heart was very stupid. What would Patrick be doing in the queue at Sainsbury's in Lewisham, shouting into a mobile about the BNP?

The only upside was that, with no TV or internet and no one to talk to (see list), I began to work like never before. Not once did I switch on the news during my lunch, only to find myself still watching *Doctors* at three o'clock. No longer did I follow a link on Facebook and spend the whole afternoon clicking on YouTube videos of cats running into walls. I would wake up as the family downstairs began shouting, and after a period of self-pity—it's important to make time for your hobbies—I'd brew tea, I could still afford that at least, and settle down at my drawing table in the watery sunshine and rush of traffic outside. I would rule out my cartoon strips and get drawing. Different ideas, but I most often found myself coming back to the one Patrick had liked so much, Max the maudlin dog. I enjoyed drawing his little face, the sad eyes and big nose. I even gave him a human sidekick, with dark hair in pigtails and a sardonic approach to life. Somewhere between me and Emma and Cynthia. I called her Anne Hedonia—after anhedonia, the condition of not being able to enjoy life. It made me miss Max though, how I would turn around to find him silently watching me, his pink tongue hanging out with the effort of getting upstairs, or jumping up on the bed, where of course he wasn't allowed, to doze in the sun and watch me. I missed Alex too, clattering in from school, sitting in his vest and wellies while he got his 'medniss', chatting on about trains and biscuits. I even missed the house itself, the smell of old wood and the way that people on the doorstep turned green and purple as you went to let them in. I didn't want to think about what else I missed.

The days went on like this and I started to think about losing, as I huddled inside blankets in my chilly flat, or walked home from the pound shops laden down with cheap laundry baskets and loo brushes and other items from the '50p or less' bin, or lay in bed reading, since I didn't have a TV. You could lose an awful lot and still be happy—when I left Dan I'd lost my house, husband, car, set of Le Creuset pans and chance of having kids—or so my brain aka

mother had told me. But I'd been OK. I had a place to live,
and I had my drawing, and the freedom to come and go as I
pleased, to talk to people, even return the smile of a stranger
on the tube, or go out with friends and not come home to a
darkened house and body stiff with resentment in the bed.
*Have fun, did you? Well, some of us have to get up early,
so maybe you'd keep it down.*

It was a cliché, but that sort of freedom really was beyond
price, even if I now wasn't sure how I would replace my
Converse, which had the soles hanging off and flapped as
I walked. I'd have made a joke about the place being sole-
less, but there was no one to laugh, or even frown and tell
me my jokes were pathetic, as Dan would have done.

But God, I missed them. I kept thinking of the squashy
hug Alex had given me when I left. 'Bye, Rachel. I'll see
you soon?'

'Well, you might not see me for a little while.'

'You mean after school?' It was heartbreaking, his clear
dark eyes, trusting as Max's.

'Longer, I think.'

I watched understanding dawn, and I could hardly bear
it. 'You mean you're going like Mummy.'

'Not really—I mean, I won't be over the seas. I'll be
nearby.'

But would I ever see him again? He was just my ex-
landlord's son. He was nothing to me, or I to him. I didn't
see a way I could stay in his life.

Chapter Thirty-Seven

One day in April, Emma came to see me, bringing a pot plant and some news.

'Are you OK, love?' She settled into my shabby brown sofa.

'Yeah, you know, carrying on.'

'I'm sorry I haven't been around much. It's just...'

'It's OK.' We were now living on opposite sides of London, and I knew she was so busy at school and unpicking things with Ian. She looked tired and drawn after months of falling apart.

'How's work?' she asked.

'Actually, not too bad. I've been offered a job. Sort of.' I'd had a phone call from Louisa at the nice design agency—she loved the Anne Hedonia cartoons I'd sent her and wanted to talk about syndicating them on various blogs. I'd still be freelance, but there'd be a steady stream of income, and, thanks to Patrick's advice about wedding fairs and so on, my other work was coming in strong. It looked as if I might not need to get an office job after all anyway.

But I wasn't going to think about him. 'So what's new with you?'

'Oh, you know. We got some new crayons at work, and I've sold my bike… Oh, and Ian proposed to me.' She smiled awkwardly.

'*What?* But I thought you weren't…'

'No. He's been sleeping on the sofa for ages. It's been horrible. Then the other night I came home—teaching all day, like, Play-Doh in my hair, dog-tired—and he gets down in the hallway, in the middle of all our junk, and says, oh, what was it—"Em, I know you hate me right now, and I know I got a bit silly over your friend for a while there, and I know you can't stand my jokes and my bikes and my beard and my job, but I love you, and I can't imagine ever going to bed with anybody else and not hearing your weird sleep-talk or feeling your cold feet and jaggedy toenails. Will you marry me?"'

I stared at her. 'He didn't.'

'Yep.'

'That's…that's…' I couldn't help it. I burst out laughing. 'It's so Ian.'

Emma was smiling too. 'I know. A dream proposal, eh? Who *wouldn't* want their toenails mentioned as part of a declaration of love?'

A thought occurred to me. 'You didn't say yes, did you?'

'Of course not. Like I want to tell my children that Daddy proposed in a hallway covered in engine oil, and when he got down on one knee, he knocked into the shelf with his tools on, so a spanner fell out and hit him on the head.'

'But…'

'But I said yes to trying again.' She looked at me defiantly. 'I suppose you think I'm daft, giving him another chance.'

'Honestly? I think that if you didn't, it would be the biggest mistake of your life. Even worse than when you went out on the windiest night of the year wearing only two scarves dressed as Xena, Warrior Princess. It wasn't so bad, what he did. He made a mistake, Em. Everyone does.'

'Except me, according to you,' she said drily.

'Well, I'd forgotten about the scarf incident when I said that.'

'Thanks, Rach. You're a true friend.'

'So are you, Gusty.'

After Emma went, I looked around my damp little flat. It wasn't much, but it was mine, and I was paying for it with work I did myself, conjured up with my own head and hand. And that was…something. It really was.

I went into the tiny kitchen and looked in my cupboards. I didn't have much in, but there was flour, and packets of the dried yeast I'd been using in Hampstead that day when Patrick came in to find me singing. I didn't have him any more, but I could still bake. I could look after myself. I could do my best with what did remain.

Fifteen minutes later, I had a tight ball of dough, smooth and stretchy, ready to be left in the bowl to rise up, the yeast performing its magic. You wouldn't be able to see it, but when you went back, it would all be totally changed. The perfect relationship should be like that too—not clingy, not crumbly, but strong and elastic and just like home. I realised I was salting the bread as two tears plopped down into it. I wiped them away with the back of my hand. I'd be OK. I'd been through worse before. And, after all, if you can't go back, you have to go forward.

Soon, another month had gone by. I'd unpacked all my clothes, and I'd amassed a big pile of Maudlin Max and Anne Hedonia drawings and was just wondering what to do with the rest of my life.

That's when he came.

It was a normal day. In a romcom, I'd have just showered and be wrapped in a towel, a pretty rose flush in my cheeks and tendrils of hair falling down, or I'd be sitting on my porch in a floral dress, barefoot, in a pair of glasses that just made me even lovelier. Who does that when they're alone? I wasn't expecting to see anyone, seeing as I lived alone and this was London, where calling round unannounced was a social offence up there with fly-tipping and standing on the wrong side of the tube escalator. I was in my work attire—tracksuit bottoms tucked into white bobble socks, and a T-shirt that said 'I love Robbie Williams'—ah, the late nineties, a desert for music. My hair was unwashed and up in a messy bun, and, speaking of messy buns, I'd been eating lemon cake and it was all down my front. So when the doorbell went, I froze with my hand inside the cereal box—there were perks to living alone—and put down my well-read copy of Jilly Cooper's *Rivals*. Outside, a steady tattoo of rain drummed on the windows.

My first thought was it must be the neighbours to complain about my ultimate show-tunes album again, or perhaps the landlord to measure up for the curtains he'd promised me. I ignored all my father's advice about security chains and peepholes. I wrenched open the door in all my fluffy-socked glory. 'Sorry, but it's *Phantom*, and if you don't like that, you must be dead inside...'

'Hi, Rachel.'

It was Patrick. All six foot two of him, all expensive leather jacket of him, all citrus-scented, grim-faced gorgeousness of him. On the landing that smelled of cat's wee.

Of course I was rude to him. I hadn't seen him in months, had been doing nothing but think of him in that time, so naturally my first reaction was to tell him where to go.

'What are you doing here?' I held the door open a crack, trying to hide my grimy T-shirt. He looked solemn. His hair was plastered to his face with rain, and he held out a large manila envelope.

'This was delivered for you. I thought it looked important.'

'Oh. How did you find me?'

He frowned. 'You left a forwarding address.'

'Of course, of course.' I reached out to take it—I could already see it was the divorce papers. The decree nisi, most like. For a moment we just stared at each other.

'Well, I hope you're OK.' He started to turn.

'Wait! Will you— Do you want tea or something? A towel? At least come in.'

He waited for what seemed like ages. 'OK. Just for a minute.'

I buzzed around, finding him a towel, putting the kettle on, surreptitiously removing my face-mask-encrusted headband. Of course I had to be wearing my ugliest possible clothes. 'Would you like coffee—er, no, I don't have any, sorry. Tea?'

'OK.' He was standing in the middle of the floor, dripping. I wondered if he'd see the threadbare bits in the carpet and the mould on the kitchen tiles. I felt a burst of unwarranted

anger—we couldn't all afford three-storey houses with turrets.
I was poor, but at least I was independent.

'You didn't go back to Surrey, then,' he said.

I shrugged. 'It's over. I knew that. There was no way
back.'

'Hmm.' He was looking all round him. 'So it's just you
here.'

I was startled. 'Of course it is. Who— I mean, I needed
to be on my own. Because of work.'

He remained silent and I realised he was thinking about
Simon. 'It's just me,' I repeated. 'Patrick, what you heard
about me, what Dan said, it was long ago. It was nothing.
It was never going to be anything.'

'It was none of my business,' he said flatly, pretending to
be interested in my collection of Russian dolls. 'I shouldn't
have said what I did.'

'No, no, you were right. It was an awful thing, the worst
thing, but, you know, it happens. Sometimes people are so
unhappy and you don't think you'll do it until it's right in
front of you.'

He nodded. I was embarrassed, thinking of Michelle and
her banker boyfriend, of how he must be feeling, what he
must think of me. 'It happens,' I said again lamely.

'I know it does.'

'Anyway, I'm on my own,' I said. 'No Dan, no anybody
else. That's probably our divorce papers there. That's never
going to be anything either. He's gone.'

'So has Michelle,' he said, still looking at my books, my
posters, my laundry drying embarrassingly on the radia-
tors. Anything but me. 'Gone away, I mean.'

'Hmm?' I stopped stock-still. My hands had begun to
shake, slopping the tea onto my out-of-date T-shirt.

'She left. Just for a while, this time.'

'Alex?'

'No, he's with me. We realised—well, she decided—it wouldn't be right to take him out of school, not when he's been so ill. They put insurance caps on the treatment over there—if his inhibitor came back, it could cost millions. Not to mention Max, he'd never get through quarantine, and it wouldn't be right to take him away from Alex.'

'So you're...'

'I'm staying too. She's going to move back as soon as she can—I guess she and Alan will live next door. It's not going to be easy, but, well, we don't see any way round it.'

'Oh.' I remembered and gave him his tea. It was almost like old times, except we were in my grotty flat and down-stairs I could hear every word the neighbours were scream-ing at each other over Kirstie and Phil trying to find two-bed flats for fussy couples in Manchester.

'My friend got back to me, by the way,' he said, eyes fixed on my poster of the Eiffel Tower being hit by lightning.

'Which friend?'

'The one who works on the paper.'

'But I didn't...'

'You left some drawings behind in the room. Along with four socks, a hairbrush, an old flip-flop, five mugs...'

'I'm sorry.'

'Anyway, I showed him. I hope you don't mind. And I know you said not to tell you if he said no, so the reason I'm telling you is, he's interested. He'd like to see some more of your work.'

'You're kidding me.'

'Of course I'm not.' And it was true, I'd rarely seen him look less jokey. 'I'll put you in touch with him and you can set up a meeting maybe. There could be some nice freelance fees in it, at the very least.'

'That's… Thank you. That's amazing news.'

'That's OK.'

We fell silent again.

'They miss you,' Patrick said suddenly. 'Alex keeps asking where you are. Max sits by the door waiting.'

'I didn't want to go,' I mumbled. 'But I had to. I couldn't rely on you forever. I had to go out in the real world. Even if it's got rising damp and smells of cat pee.'

'Is that what it is?'

'Don't ask.'

'I hate to think of you alone.' He was staring at my washing again.

'We're all alone. When you come down to it, it's more lonely coming home to someone you don't love than coming home to nothing.'

'It wasn't lonely coming home to you.' He was looking at the carpet, his tea abandoned.

'No. I wasn't lonely either.'

'So what does that mean?'

'I've no idea.' What was he doing here? What was this about?

'You don't?'

I didn't know what I was supposed to say. We still weren't looking at each other. 'No.'

For a moment, Patrick's shoulders sagged. He set down his cup. 'Right, then. I just wanted to give you those letters, and say, you know, I'm sorry for what I said. Also, I just miss you. I know that's stupid and it couldn't have lasted and I know I'm older than you and I'm not what anyone would… But I just miss you. That's all there is to it. Bye, Rachel.'

And before I could stop him he was banging out the door and I heard his heavy footsteps going down the stairs.

I stood there in silence, looking at the patch of wet he'd dripped onto the carpet. I had an absurd urge to lie down and put my head on it, then cry a bit. What did it mean? he'd said. What *did* it mean? I was miserable now, and I'd been happy there with him. And he'd been happy too, but now he looked like me—tired, and pale, and glum.

We say all the time that we're looking for love, or we're afraid we'll never find it. The truth is, we're already surrounded by it—from our families, our friends, even our pets. And the answer to any problem is surely to give more back. Be like a love tree. Take in the knocks of life and transmute them into more love. Breathe out that love oxygen. As Karen Carpenter sang, it's the only thing there's just too little of.

Admittedly, that was written before the oil crisis really took hold, but still. I think the point stands.

List of really bad decisions I have made in my life

1. Going anywhere near Simon Caulfield

2. Letting Lucy Coleman wax my eyebrows, aged twelve

3. Getting married, moving to the suburbs, giving up my cool job

4. Neglecting my friends for ages while I wallowed in self-pity

5. Falling out with Patrick and leaving the place I was happiest in my life

6. The one I was just about to make right now. Possibly.

Suddenly, I was out the door, running down the stairs with their smell of wee, and throwing open the front door.

God, it was wet. It soaked right through my socks as I stood there shivering. Which way had he gone? I looked left and right down the busy street. He'd have driven, I thought, so that could mean anywhere. I spotted brake lights reflecting down the street and I began to sprint. Luckily, Patrick was a cautious driver, like with everything else in his life. Slow. The opposite of me, barging about, making a mess of everything. I ran up and banged frantically on the hood of his car.

He stopped, opened the door, got out. 'What are you doing? I could have run you over!'

'I wanted—to tell—you something.' Good God, I needed to get fit. Even that short sprint had made me gasp. 'I'm sorry, OK? I'm an idiot. I make a mess of everything. I always have.'

'So do I,' he said, staring at the puddles. 'It's no surprise women keep leaving me.'

'I didn't—you kicked me out!'

'I didn't mean what I said that day. I was just angry. Then next thing I knew you'd gone. Never mind me, but Alex hasn't a clue what's going on. I find him outside your room most days, just sitting on the stairs. And, as for Max, he's even more maudlin than before.'

'I'm sorry,' I said miserably. 'I really messed up, but it was just so nice. Being there with you all.'

'You were happy?'

'Of course I was.'

He said quietly, 'I think it's the happiest I've ever been.'

I said nothing. I couldn't.

He cleared his throat. 'Oh, I thought of a number ten, by the way. For my list, I mean.'

I tried to hide the fact I was close to tears. 'Making cocktails? I knew it.'

'No.'

'Sharks? I told you, no sharks!'

'It's not sharks.'

'Um, is there vomit involved?'

'No. Well. Possibly.'

'Oh, what is it?'

'It's just…to be happy. With or without diving, or holidays, or being drunk, or going on dates, or any kind of agenda. Just to be as happy as I can, every day, with Alex and Max, and hopefully with you too.'

'Just be happy?'

'Yes.'

'That's all?'

'All? Have you any idea how bloody hard that is? And did you miss the part where I said, "with you"?'

'Um, I'm still trying to take that in.'

'Take it in faster. Please.'

'I think…it's doable.'

'Yes?'

I spoke slowly. 'All we need is a really good list. How about this for an idea?' The rain was leaching up my legs now, soaking my tracksuit bottoms. My hair lay in rat's tails. The perfect look for a romantic declaration, in fact. 'Patrick? Do you ever think about making a joint list? One for both of us?'

He looked at me as if I was mad. 'What do you mean?'

'Well, maybe step one could be, stop standing here in the rain.'

'Is it still raining? I hadn't noticed.' Was that a vague smile?

I pressed on. 'Eh, step two could be, I live here, you live there, but we meet. Somewhere.'

'You mean for a prearranged romantic occasion in a mutually convenient location?'

'Perhaps. As long as it's not in Fulham. Step three, we talk about normal things. Dogs and holiday and reality TV, not divorce and infidelity and life-threatening conditions and so on.'

He looked at me. 'Rachel. I'm old. I have more baggage than a branch of the Luggage Shop. I wear cords. I'm grumpy.'

'Well, I'm really untidy, worse than you realise—me at your house, that was me actually making the effort—and I'm afraid of everything and I don't have a proper job or any money or a cheese grater.'

'But I know all that. Well, except for the cheese grater thing, which is a bit of a shock, to be honest, but I'm absorbing it. I *know* you, Rachel. We'd be starting about ten dates in.'

'Is that a good thing or a bad thing?'

'Based on our experience of first dates, I'd say it's a good thing.'

'Hmm.' I stared at him. My heart was pounding out of my chest, and not just because of my run downstairs.

'So, this new list of yours. What's step four?' He moved a step closer to me. The rain was running off his shoulders, dripping from his hair.

'Well, if we were enjoying it, and we both felt it was going well, maybe you could—'

'Yes?'

'Kiss me?'

Patrick stepped forward, put his hand to my face. With his large thumb, he wiped the rain from my cheek. 'Personally,

I've always liked to mix up the numbers of my lists. Live on the edge.'

His thumb was tracing my mouth. My heart was bursting; I was breathless. 'You are a real…edge-liver.'

'I am since you.' He smiled at me. 'Come here, Rachel. Step four.'

Then his mouth was on mine, hard and warm, our faces cold and wet, and I was stretching up to meet him, feeling his hands move over my back, my own pushing back his sodden hair. Step four. Step four. Step fourrr. And a bit of step five. I broke off, lay my head on his chest, and he stroked my wet hair, and we stayed like that for some time, the rain still pouring down on us.

A while later, I said, 'Hey, Patrick? Do you think you could resurrect the climbing one on your old list? Like, say, right now?'

He blinked, looking a little dazed. 'I suppose so. Why?'

'Well, I've locked myself out.'

Epilogue

I looked at the wedding dress hanging on the door. It was perfect. Lace and silk and little sparkly bits sewn into the skirt, so it would catch the light as you moved down the aisle, dispensing gentle blushing smiles to your groom waiting ahead.

This was everything you were supposed to want. The perfect day, the perfect dress, the perfect man. Happily ever after. This was the moment. Except, as I knew only too well, there was no such thing. After the wedding was just the start of your marriage, trying to get along together day after day in the face of problems and loss and worry.

But the dress. Pristine, shining, perfect as hope. For a moment, staring at it, I could almost forget all about the events of the past year. I could almost believe a fresh start was possible.

'I suppose I better put the bloody thing on,' said Emma, standing there in her rather un-bridal M&S undies and bra. She'd refused to buy a whole new outfit for the wedding, saying no one was going to see her undies but Ian, and he was already well used to them. She'd had her hair done though, and allowed her mother to force her into a tiara-type ornament of pearls and diamanté, so I suspected she wasn't totally opposed to 'all this wedding bollocks', as she put it.

'You're definitely wearing the Converse?' I asked.

'Of course. Cost me a bloody fortune in crystals bejazzling those bad boys. Anyway, it'll be a totally cool *Father of the Bride* reference.'

Emma's mum, who was in the bathroom putting on her lipstick, shouted, 'It won't be so cool when the hem of that lovely dress is dragging in the mud!'

'Can't hear you!' Emma shouted back.

'Nothing wrong with some nice heels, give you a bit of posture.'

'Mum! There is no way I'm submitting to voluntary footbinding on my wedding day! Anyway, you went to your wedding in the back of a van that was delivering copies of the *Socialist Worker*. Don't be such a hypocrite!' Ah, my old Emma hadn't gone anywhere. She had eventually accepted Ian's revised proposal after a month back together— this time it had been more carefully planned and involved her favourite music, candles and a vegetarian meal with 'Marry me?' picked out in carved carrots. Unfortunately, Emma had eaten one of the 'R's before she realised, which led to some momentary confusion of the 'WHO IS MARY? TELL ME, YOU BASTARD' variety.

Ian was still in his regular job, and spending all his evenings and money going to comedy gigs, but he was happy, and Emma was talking about enrolling in a proper craft course, what with all the time she had to spare. Needless to say, she was a regular visitor at Hobbycraft during the wedding preparation, and every name tag, order of service, invitation and favour had been crafted to within an inch of its life. I wasn't sure I would ever get the glitter glue out of my hair.

'I can't believe you're making us wear these,' said Cynthia, coming in from the hallway, where she'd been practising walking in the purple Converse Emma wanted us in, to match our purple prom dresses. I felt pretty cool in mine, like a waitress at a roller drive-in, but Cynthia was not impressed.

'You'll be thanking me by the end of day,' said Emma, dusting her face with powder. 'No blisters, you can dance all night. Anyway, you've been living in flip-flops for ages now.'

Cynthia had been in Jamaica, getting to know her father and his family, up until a month ago. She had returned relaxed and happy, her hair grown out into its natural halo of curls, and about a stone heavier on all the delicious chicken and rice and plantain sandwiches her relatives had forced into her. She had even, finally, learned to cook a little. 'My grandma was horrified I couldn't,' she said. 'She marched me into the kitchen and made me watch her behead a chicken. So, after that, it all seemed easy.'

She planned to go for another visit in a few months. Meanwhile, she and Rich were getting divorced, and she'd moved into a smaller, yet still tastefully minimalist loft apartment in Docklands, and would start looking for a new job when she felt like it, she said. Although she was sad about the divorce, I thought she seemed much more relaxed than she had in years.

Emma's dad came in, fussing. He was in a vintage suit, the same one he'd worn to get married in 1978, though this time he wasn't carrying a copy of the *Socialist Worker* or sporting a large Che Guevara moustache. I was planning to include all this in my cartoon of the entire wedding party, which I was giving Emma and Ian as a present—only I hadn't finished yet as I'd been quite busy with commissions from Louisa and Patrick's newspaper friend Matt, the fees from which were mounting up quite nicely in my bank account and saving me from lying awake at night worrying about my overdraft.

'They're ready,' Emma's dad said gloomily. 'I suppose we better go, and not keep the agents of the capitalist state waiting.'

Emma patted his arm. 'It's OK, Dad. It's a fun wedding. Not a formal wedding.' Cynthia and I exchanged smiles. We'd heard this catchphrase many times, and yet Emma had still gone through exactly the same wobbles over guest lists, seating, music and colours—'I cannot find the right shade of glitter glue to match the bridesmaids' dresses. The wedding is OFF!'—as every other bride.

'I don't see why a fun wedding means we have to wear *training shoes*,' said her mother, coming out with what looked like half of a forest attached to her head.

'I'm with you, Mrs P.,' muttered Cynthia, but quietly. Then we all trooped down the stairs of the hotel and into the room for the civil ceremony.

We spend so long planning our weddings, trying to make them special and individual and true reflections of ourselves, but, in the end, they are all essentially the same. Everyone cranes to see the bride as she comes in, and looks at what other people are wearing, and waves across the church/registry office to friends they know. I always cry a bit when it starts and again when they kiss. There's always chatter, and too-long waiting around for food, and a bit too much wine, and the speeches are always funny—sad—dull—sweet.

This was the first wedding I'd been to since my divorce, and it was too easy to remember my own—the swell of music as I walked in on Dad's arm, the faces turned towards me like flowers in the sun, the blurred shape of a man at the end of the aisle. Smells of lilies and perfume and candle wax. I took a deep breath as I walked beside Cynthia, focusing on putting my feet in the right place. I was looking out for him, worried I wouldn't see him in the crowd, but there he was, near the back, smiling at me. Alex was waving, wearing a little suit that matched Patrick's. I waved back.

That's the thing about weddings—no matter what you've gone through to get there, or however bad your own love life might be, or whatever you've lost, they are pure joy and hope and positivity all in one day. It's a way to say, hey, life is hard and everything sometimes fails and people let each other down, but I love you, and this is a day set aside to say how amazing that is.

Unless, of course, you are a character in *Hollyoaks*, in which case it's a day to confess to your spouse that you've been having an affair with their dad/mum/boss and the baby isn't theirs, after all, oh, and you're taking the proceeds from the tanning salon and leaving to start a new life in Magaluf.

Later on, after the ceremony, which featured personal vows—Emma: 'I promise to always laugh at your jokes, and if I can't do that because I've heard them literally five hundred times before, at least not to roll my eyes and say, "Don't give up the day job, Michael McIntyre."' Ian: 'I promise not to buy Peperami on the way home drunk and hide them in the toothbrush holder, so you wake up to find your toothbrush smelling of reconstituted pig'—and music from the Smashing Pumpkins and Hole, and a reading from Emma's favourite kids' book, *Goodnight Moon*; after we'd milled outside the hotel while the photographer fruitlessly attempted to arrange us into groups, trying to stop our strapless dresses from rolling down round our waists—me anyway—Patrick pulled me aside. 'Shall we throw some confetti?' He opened his hand, revealing a handful of torn-up papers, with scribbled writing on them.

'That better not be another one of your vote-rigging attempts you're trying to cover up.'

'Don't you recognise it?' He held up a scrap that said 'do stand-up comedy'.

'The lists?'

'The lists. I kept them after you went. Sentimental, I suppose.'

I looked down at the bits of paper. 'I don't think we were wrong to do them, you know. It brought us together, and we learned lots of things, like that you're scared of little sweet ponies and have a grubby aura.'

'And that you're afraid of any height above your own shoulder.'

'Maybe. But at least I know now I never want to be the kind of person who skydives, or does a lot of yoga, or dances the tango.'

'It was kind of fun though, wasn't it?' He smiled.

'Yes. Fun in the kind of way that you're mostly just happy it's over.'

'I think they've served their purpose now, don't you?'

I leaned over to kiss him, breathing in his smell of lime and soap. 'I do.' And we hurled them in the sky, a riot of hopes and dreams and plans for the future, and then we got in trouble with the groundskeeper, because that's the kind of thing that always happened to me.

Then, once we were called to our tables, which were named after places Emma and Ian had been together—France, Acton, Antigua, Southend—it was time for the speeches. Ian stood up, tinkling his glass with a fork—not one that cost £70. He was wearing a purple velvet suit and floral shirt, like an Austin Powers impersonator. 'Hi, all! Hope you're having a good day so far. Since this isn't a traditional wedding, and we aren't having any of what this lovely woman here calls that "honour and obey bollocks", this speech is going to be made jointly by me and…my wife!'

Whoops and cheers as Emma got up and took the microphone. 'Hi, everyone. We're really glad you could be here today with us. And anyone who slopes off to bed early will be Facebook-defriended on the morrow as quickly as other brides change their name, OK? Now. This here…husband… and I—' She broke off, smiling, as everyone cheered. 'We've decided to share with you all some things we've learned about love. A little list, if you will. Inspired by the favourite pastime of one our best friends, without whom we might not be here. Rachel!'

Suddenly, everyone was cheering for me and I was blinking. What on earth?

Emma and Ian took turns to read off cue cards. In true Emma style, they had been jazzed up in the wedding colours of purple and silver.

Emma began. 'Number one: the perfect partner is like the perfect pair of shoes—supportive, comfortable, looks good with all your outfits and not too binding.' I smiled to myself, scuffing my comfortable Cons under the table.

Ian: 'Number two: sometimes love means not keeping your inner tubes in the bath. Or so I'm told.' Laughter.

'Number three: people make mistakes. It's not a mistake to forgive them.' I could see Emma look at Cynthia when she said this, and a smile passed between them.

Ian: 'Number four: it's important to take time every day to talk, and laugh, and dance together to the theme tune for *University Challenge*.'

Emma: 'Number five: if your wife thinks she is right about a question on *University Challenge*, and you think she isn't, sometimes it's better to let it go. Love is more important than quizzes.'

Ian leaned over to the mike. 'She wrote that one. I remain unconvinced. Anyway—number six. When you find the right person for you, treat your relationship every day like a really expensive car. Keep it fuelled, protect it, wipe it down—steady, tiger—and never put it away wet.'

I studiously avoided Patrick's eyes at the mention of cars. It was still something of a sore point between us.

Emma: 'Number seven: falling in love doesn't mean losing your friends. Your friends are like your family—if they don't like the person you love, maybe you should rethink it. If they tell you to hang on to them, maybe you should listen.' I couldn't look at Emma during this because I was afraid I might cry.

Ian: 'Number eight: respect each other's weird habits, as this is why you fell in love in the first place. Even if this involves vegetarianism or stand-up comedy.'

Emma: 'Number nine: money doesn't buy love. But it does buy minibreaks, chocolate and a cleaner so you don't fall out over the dishes. Ian, did you change that one?' Emma swatted at him affectionately while everyone laughed.

Ian held up the last card. 'Finally, drum roll, please... Oh, wait, the band aren't here yet... Never forget that love really is the answer, as The Beatles said. Unless the question is, who are you? In which case the answer is, "I am the walrus. I am the eggman".' Ian held up his glass solemnly. 'Do do do do. Cheers, everyone. To love!'

'To love,' we all chorused. I caught Patrick's eye. *Sorry about the car,* I mouthed.

He smiled and whispered in my ear as everyone else drank their toast. I felt his breath on my neck and shivered a little. In a good way. 'I hope you treat me better than a very expensive car. I won't survive being driven in third gear the whole way across London or crashed into a gatepost.'

I stuck my tongue out at him, and he smiled back, and I knew, I almost sort-of knew, in as much as you ever can really know, this was the person I was supposed to take the piss out of, maybe, possibly for the rest of my life.

And then there was champagne, and cake, and dancing, and Alex bossing round the table of children and teaching them to play poker, and Emma and Ian's first dance to 'Stand Inside Your Love', and her dad's speech about how despite marriage being a bourgeois institution designed by the capitalist overlords, if his daughter had to go into it with anyone, he was glad it was Ian, and Patrick taking a turn on bass with the wedding band, and us demonstrating our tango skills, and Cynthia getting chatted up by the swooningly good-looking French waiter, and at the end of it was Patrick's arm around me and his voice in my ear: 'I think this is my number ten, you know. Just being here, with you. I think this is it.'

* * *

Things that don't suck about divorce, number one: it means you can start over, and turn a new page, and have the chance to do it all again, and maybe, just maybe, this time, get it right.

* * * * *

ACKNOWLEDGEMENTS

Hello, I hope you have enjoyed reading *The Thirty List* (and that perhaps you're now making and/or ripping up some lists of your own). I really loved writing this book and I hope that if you're also having something of a trying year (or decade…) you can relate to it and maybe feel that things will pick up for you soon as well.

A huge thank you is due to my wonderful agent, Diana Beaumont, who whipped the book firmly yet gently into shape. It would not be anywhere near as good without her wise words. Thanks also to Anna Baggaley and everyone at Harlequin for their enthusiasm about the book, which is always amazing for a writer to experience. And thanks to the Marsh agency for the fantastic job they're doing with overseas rights.

They say that good writers borrow, but great writers steal. In that case I must be truly great, as I have shamelessly stolen many, many jokes from my amazing friends to put in this book. I'd like to thank so many people for this and for helping me get through my own 'disastropiphany', by making me laugh, offering me house room, listening to me moan, and supplying wine and good cheer. It's no exaggeration to say I just couldn't have done it without you. Thank you all so much. Special thanks to my limers Sarah and Angela—at least partly for the invention of 'spox', but mostly for round-the-clock support, interventions when needed, and too many LOLs to count. Thanks also to Kerry for extensive discussions about the concept of the book and also for making me laugh so much in Vienna that passers-by almost called the police. Thanks also to: Alex, Beth, Kelly, Hannah, Isabelle, Jillian, Gareth, Tom, Sarah, Sara, Jill, Kate, Jo, Margaret, Jake, Edwin, Stav, Imogen, Jamie, Katherine, Ali and everyone else who's been there for me in the past year or so. Secret extra thanks to the friend who's responsible for the pants anecdote and to anyone else whose experiences I may have unwittingly (or wittingly) borrowed.

Thanks to my family, who don't seem to mind my ongoing disastropiphanies, but do need some gentle reminding about Christmas stockings from time to time (I am NOT too old). I should point out my father has never put a ship in a bottle and has no interest in Morris dancing whatsoever, and that I don't think my sister has ever bought anything from Boden.

Thank you to my brother-in-law for co-creating 'Banjo's Ghost'.

If you would like to find out more about haemophilia, you could visit www.haemophilia.org.uk

And lastly thank you to you for reading—without you this would just be a rambling collection of jokes I tell to myself and then laugh about alone on the bus. And no one wants that.

Lots of love,

Eva

x

Don't miss Sarah Morgan's next Puffin Island story

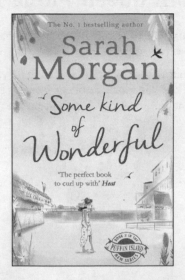

Brittany Forrest has stayed away from Puffin Island since her relationship with Zach Flynn went bad. They were married for ten days and only just managed not to kill each other by the end of the honeymoon.

But, when a broken arm means she must return, Brittany moves back to her Puffin Island home. Only to discover that Zach is there as well.

Will a summer together help two lovers reunite or will their stormy relationship crash on to the rocks of Puffin Island?

Some Kind of Wonderful
COMING JULY 2015
Pre-order your copy today

The fantastic new read from rom-com queen Fiona Harper

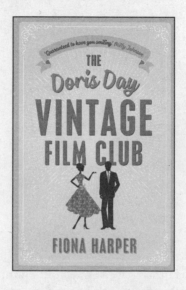

Claire Bixby grew up watching Doris Day films and yearned to live in a world like the one on the screen—sunny, colourful and where happy endings were guaranteed. But recently Claire's opportunities for a little 'pillow talk' have been thin on the ground. That is, until she meets Nic.

Sparks soon start to fly, but Claire's now questioning everything Doris taught her about romance.

Can true love ever really be just like it is in the movies?

Perhaps, perhaps, perhaps…